LUKE IRONTREE & THE LAST VAMPIRE WAR

Book 0 - The Centurion Immortal
Book 1 - Dark Fangs Rising - March 22, 2022
Book 2 - Dark Fangs Raging - April 19, 2022
Book 3 - Dark Fangs Descending - May 17, 2022
Book 4 - Blood Empire Reborn - August 23, 2022
Book 5 - Blood Empire Avenged - September 20, 2022
Book 6 - Blood Empire Infiltrated - October 18, 2022
Book 7 - Blood Empire Burning - November 15, 2022
Book 8 - Ancient Sword Falling - March 21, 2023
Book 9 - Ancient Sword Unyielding - August 22, 2023
Book 10 - Ancient Sword Shattering*

The Luke Irontree Historical Adventures
Rise of the Centurio Immortalis - April 5, 2022
Fall of the Centurio Immortalis - May 31, 2022
The Moonlight Centurion*
The Highway Centurion*

*Forthcoming
Titles and release dates may be subject to change.

BLOOD EMPIRE REBORN

LUKE IRONTREE & THE LAST VAMPIRE WAR
BOOK 4

C. THOMAS LAFOLLETTE

EDITED BY
SUZANNE LAHNA

BLOOD EMPIRE REBORN
C. Thomas Lafollette

A Broken World Publication
13820 NE Airport Way
Suite #K395495
Portland, OR 97251-1158
Blood Empire Reborn
Copyright © 2022 by C. Thomas Lafollette
ISBN 978-1-949410-70-9 (ebook);
ISBN 978-1-949410-71-6 (paperback)

Cover Design: Ravven
Developmental Editing by: Suzanne Lahna
Copy/Line Editing: C.D. Tavenor
Proofreading: Amy Cissell

CONTENTS

CONTENT WARNING

This book contains some gore and body horror. There is also gun and sword violence. There are also scenes of child endangerment and a description of a kidnapping.

For Dan
Thank you for your support and enthusiasm for this series

PRONUNCIATION GUIDE & AUTHOR'S NOTES

Pronunciation: Latin names and words are mentioned throughout the book and are intended to be read with the classical Latin pronunciation. For instance, "c" is always pronounced hard, like a "k." "U" is always a short "oo" sound. "V" typically sounds like a "w." There are plenty of resources on the internet if you wish to learn more about Classical Latin pronunciation.

- Lucius – Loo-kih-oos
- Silvanius – Sihl-wahn-ih-oos
- Ferrata – Fehr-rah-tah
- Jung-sook — Yoong-sook
- Jan - Yeahn
- Ndiaye - En-Dee-eye-ay (French Pronunciation) or Nj-eye (Senegalese Pronunciation)

Latin Words: Latin words are used for effect and to add to the "flavor" of the story, not to reflect Latin grammar/declensions/conjugations.

CHAPTER ONE

Luke raised his hand, signaling for the team to stop. Pulling a short tube with a ninety-degree bend at each end from his belt, he crouch-walked to the end of the immaculately trimmed hedge. He extended the tube, flipped the caps off both sides, and lifted it so the top, with its bend, poked slightly above the flat top of the hedge.

Looking into the other end of the periscope, he swept it back and forth for a minute, then issued a series of hand signals to the team... *—two guards moving counterclockwise. Two guards moving clockwise. Three to the left. Three to the right. Two hold here.*

Collecting agreement from his friends, he nodded and looked back into the periscope. When the two teams of two guards passed in front of the house and walked away from each other on their patrols, he capped the periscope and contracted the tube, putting it away.

He inhaled deeply. Letting his breath out slowly, he settled his nerves. Even after over nineteen-hundred-years of fighting and operations, he still felt the nerves and anxiety before making the plunge into imminent violence. He wrapped his hand around the hilt of his wooden rudis and pulled it from its scabbard.

Delicate lines of silver filigree danced up the wooden blade, ending at the point. A silver-iron alloy cutting edge ran up both sides of the blade. Behind him, people pulled out various implements ranging from classic stakes to knife blades carved from wood and affixed to a bayonet-style handle. Judging his crew ready, he stood and jogged toward the left side of the house, ensuring his footfalls were measured and quiet to avoid alerting their quarry.

He didn't have to look to know Delilah and Pablo were behind him, ready for action. In the year since they'd met, he'd come to trust them more than anyone in at least a few centuries. They'd become his left and right arms. Sam, the fourth member of his inner circle and as dear to him as the sister he'd never had, led her team of Jungsook and Rhonda to the right.

When they reached the corner of the house, Luke halted and looked around the corner. The guards were about halfway down the side. Holding up his hand, he counted down, folding a finger for each number. Three. Two. One.

Pablo hurled a large rock over the guards, where it landed with a thunk. As they bent over to inspect it, Luke dashed around the corner, using all his supernatural speed. The guards approached the back corner then turned, finally realizing someone was behind them. The guards' eyes flew open, wide as saucers, as three armed people sprinted toward them. They brought up the barrels of their submachine guns, but before they could pull back the hammers to rack a bullet, Luke shoved the barrel away and sank the rudis into the vamp's chest. He yanked it out, destroying the vampire and sending it splattering to the ground in a pool of goo. Delilah, following closely behind Luke, kicked the barrel of the other vamp's gun aside and finished with a stake to the heart. The second vampire joined the first to soak into the mossy ground.

Delilah and Pablo quickly scooped the straps of the guns from the ground and slung them around their backs. It'd become standard practice to recover all guns and quality weapons so they could be added to the pack's growing arsenal. Vampires had expensive tastes, and the pack was quickly gaining a top-shelf weapon collection.

He peeked around the corner; Sam poked her head out. They gave each other a thumbs up.

Luke turned to Pablo. "Can you give the signal to the rest of the team?"

Pablo jogged back to the other corner, returning a few moments later. "All good."

Luke nodded and swept around the corner, keeping his shoulder near the wall. Ducking under the rail along the deck, he crept toward the elegant French doors. When Luke reached them, he peered in, but a sheer white curtain trapped between the glass and the plywood blocked his view.

"What's the plan?" Sam whispered, standing on the other side of the door. She pantomimed pumping a shotgun and tilted her head in question.

Luke inspected the top of the door, then the bottom. Next, he checked the edges. Nodding, he handed his rudis to Delilah, then held his hands out to Sam. She tossed the shotgun over. Catching it, Luke slipped the safety on. With the butt toward the door, he busted out the glass, clearing any clinging shards out of the way. Finished, he tossed the shotgun back to Sam.

Everyone prepared to move in case they needed to defend Luke or attack. Cautious of any lingering glass, he reached through and pulled the pin down, unlocking the top of the door from the frame. He pulled the pin at the bottom next, then reached through the middle and unlocked the door.

Delilah handed Luke his rudis, and he stowed it in its scabbard. With her help, he removed the Winchester M12 shotgun from around his back. He checked in to make sure everyone was ready. He hated going in blind, but there were few options, and they needed to clear this house. Laying his shoulder against the plywood, he pulled back and slammed his body into it. The plywood buckled, and Luke tumbled to the floor, tangling in the curtain and pulling it down with him. The sound of shells pumped into shotgun firing chambers followed his calamitous crash.

"Luke, duck!" Sam yelled.

Luke pulled his legs and arms in and made himself as small as possible as his friends leapt over him. The room filled with shotguns discharging and the indistinguishable yells of the combatants.

Fighting the curtain, he shoved it away and scrambled off the busted plywood. He saw Delilah and Pablo disappear into a room while Sam, Jung-sook, and Rhonda swept upstairs, leaving Luke alone in the dining room with broken glass and plywood.

Someone outside rang the doorbell. Luke strode up to the peep hole and peered through, seeing Ahmed and Charlie, the new trans man who'd joined the core team after Archie's death at the battle of Mt. Hood. Lifting the crossbar from the front door, Luke tossed it aside, letting the rest of his team in.

"Welcome," Luke said with a sweeping bow.

"Clear," Pablo called, walking out of the room he and Delilah had just swept through. Delilah followed him out, grabbed the doorknob of the next room, and pulled it open, letting Pablo sweep in before following.

"Sam and the rest of the gang are upstairs." Shotgun blasts punctuated Luke's words. He gestured with his head toward an unopened door under the stairs and grabbed the knob.

Luke pulled it open, revealing a closet. He shoved some coats aside with the barrel of his M12. The closet was probably just a closet based on the architectural cues, but better thorough than dead. He shut the door and opened the door next to it, revealing stairs. Ahmed swept down them; Charlie followed, flipping on the light switch.

About ready to follow, Luke stopped when his phone vibrated in his pocket. Only a handful of people had his number and could override his do not disturb setting, and none of them would call while he was out with his team unless it was an emergency. He pulled out his phone. Pieter. The phone stopped, then started again.

"Hmm." Luke answered the phone. "Hey, Pieter. What's going on?"

"Hello, Luke. Is this a good time to talk? If you're not in the middle of anything…"

Shotgun blasts erupted from the basement, along with shouting.

The commotion pulled his attention away from Pieter. "I'll call you back when we're done here."

"Alright, thank you." Pieter hung up.

Luke stowed his phone, his eyebrows narrowing in curiosity. Calls from Pieter had been sporadic and vague, and now he called when he knew Luke would likely be out hunting. He pushed back his rising anxiety. One worry at a time.

He pumped a shell into the firing chamber and poked his head into the stairwell down to the basement. "Coming down!"

"Understood," Ahmed yelled.

Luke moved cautiously, sweeping his barrel around, looking for fangers. A few more blasts flashed in the basement. A wall of shelves stood to his right; he moved left and followed the sound of more shotgun blasts.

"Clear," Ahmed called. "Coming out."

"All clear," Luke replied.

Ahmed exited the room they'd just swept. "It's messy in there."

Luke looked over the tipped metal shelving, cans of paint and other household supplies scattered around. Ahmed and Charlie must have yanked the shelves out of the way to reveal the room behind it. "It's a mess out here."

Ahmed chuckled. "Didn't feel like stacking it neatly."

"Hey, Ahmed, Luke, come here," Charlie called.

Luke followed Ahmed into the hidden room they'd found. Charlie was pulling back the molding from the far corner of the room.

"You don't usually see molding running from floor to ceiling in a corner that's attached to a hinge," Ahmed said.

"You do not," Luke replied.

Charlie looked back at Luke and Ahmed. "There's a handle here."

Luke nodded and raised his shotgun. Ahmed shoved shells into his magazine, then reloaded. Charlie pushed his hand into a hole hidden by a flap and pulled. The latch clicked. Charlie pulled back, and the wall swung out, folding from the middle. When the door was open, they saw the outline of shelves. Luke pulled a flashlight from a pouch on his belt and shined it in. Next to Luke, Ahmed whistled appreciatively.

"Looks like there's a switch over there." Luke shined the light toward a switch just visible past the secret door.

Charlie turned it on.

Shelf after shelf of high-powered weaponry stood before them.

"Holy shit," Charlie said.

"Ahmed, head upstairs and call in the backup. I want to clear this room out immediately. Take a handful with you," Luke said. He slung his shotgun over his shoulder and grabbed an armful of guns before following Charlie and Ahmed upstairs.

Sam, Jung-sook, Pablo, Delilah, and Rhonda were downstairs.

"All clear upstairs," Sam said. "We snagged a few laptops while we were there."

"Nice. Pablo, Delilah, you're on guard duty up here. Everyone else downstairs. We found an arsenal. I want it." Luke turned to Sam. "Check with our lookouts to see if Portland's finest are headed this way."

"Luke?" Rhonda said.

Luke turned toward her. "Yeah, Rhonda?"

"I saw suitcases upstairs," She replied.

"Nice. Go get them, please." Luke smiled. The vampire arsenal would make a nice addition to the pack's weapons store. He liked the idea of letting the fangers pay for their own destruction.

Rhonda nodded and ran upstairs.

"No cops yet." Sam shoved her phone back into her pocket.

When their backup team arrived, they systematically stripped the arsenal room, checking for any tracking devices or bugs. By the time they were done, the bed of Pablo's pickup was significantly heavier and the pack far better armed. With everyone loaded up, they rolled out.

Luke, sitting in the back of Pablo's truck, leaned forward. "Mind cutting the radio? I need to make a call."

Delilah turned the radio off.

Luke dialed Pieter's number and waited for him to answer. "Hey Pieter, what's going on?"

"My father needs to arrange a time to speak with you. We're sending a secure satphone by courier. They'll be arriving on the usual ride. If you can arrange a pickup, that would be appreciated."

"You OK, Pieter?" Luke asked.

Pieter sighed. "Let's just say it's imperative you take my father's call tomorrow."

Luke's brows furrowed. The tension in Pieter's voice, coupled with the secretive plans, spiked Luke's anxiety. He simultaneously needed to know what was happening in Belgium, yet dreaded the arrival of the courier. "You know I will. How will we recognize your courier? Is it going to be you or your brother?"

"No. I don't want to say more, but when you arrange the pickup, hold up a sign that says 'Rubenson.' Our courier will look for that sign."

"Consider it done," Luke replied.

"Thank you. Until tomorrow?" Pieter asked.

"Until tomorrow," Luke replied.

THE NEXT MORNING, Luke met Maggie for a brunch date while Pablo and Sam set up the pack guest house in case the courier needed a place to stay. With an official message coming in from the pack leader of one of Europe's most wealthy and powerful packs, Holly wanted to show all the proper courtesies as the North Portland packleader, especially since Pieter had done so much to help the pack the previous winter.

"Maggie." Luke let Maggie pull him in for a hug as they kissed each other on the cheek.

"Luke."

They sat down and ordered coffees while they looked over the menu.

"How did it go last night?" Maggie asked.

"Pretty good. No injuries. Very interesting ending though." Luke smirked, thinking about the cache of expensive weapons they'd picked up from the vampires.

Maggie raised an eyebrow. "Oh?"

Luke looked around at the packed tables near them. "I'll fill you in later on that side of the deal."

Maggie nodded, smiling.

Luke loved Maggie's smile—the way the corners of her mouth tipped up, the line of her lips, but most of all the gentle sparkle in her eyes. While they drank too much coffee and enjoyed their brunch, they chatted about unimportant things for the purpose of hearing each other's voice. It had been too long since they'd had quality time together, and Luke, being honest with himself, missed her.

He and his team had been extremely busy hitting nest after nest once the feds pulled out of Portland after their investigation. Luke and the pack spent the months sweeping their tracking teams through Portland, documenting every whiff of vampire smell the werewolves could pick up with their sensitive and now well-trained noses. The vampires, in disarray after Cassius's death and the loss of so many vampires at all power levels, were keeping a low profile. Luke and his teams would strike when the opportunity arose, but kills had been few and far between as both sides avoided the FBI and the DOJ.

Luke checked his watch; he still had a couple hours before the courier would be on site at the pack's guest house.

"Have to get going?" Maggie asked.

"Not for a bit. Would you like to join me for a walk? Assuming you don't have to get back to the clinic. I want some more Maggie time." He smiled warmly, trying to convey his high regard for her through his eyes.

"I'd like that. I'm off today." Maggie stood, offering her hand.

They walked out of the brunch place and took a right, following the sidewalk up to a park. Holding hands, they enjoyed the late summer warmth and strolled through the park filled with roses in bloom until they found a shady bench. The other nice thing about Maggie: they could sit together without the need for talking. Even after living for nearly two-thousand years, Luke had never really developed an appreciation for small talk, although he could do it if he had to. Maggie never asked it of him, not caring for it either.

When it was time to depart, Luke walked Maggie back to her

car, collecting several kisses along the way, then hopped into his Volvo and drove to the pack's guest house. After parking out front, he punched in the door code and let himself in to start coffee for their jet-lagged guest. While he waited, he pulled up a book on his phone's reader app and relaxed in a comfortable armchair in the living room.

When he heard people on the porch followed by a code being punched in, he closed his book and stood up. An umber-skinned Black girl of about ten or eleven years old ran through the door chattering in Dutch. Behind her, a tall, elegant Black woman with onyx skin followed, her hair styled in a series of braids. Delilah and Pablo followed them in.

"Amiata van den Bergh?" Luke said.

"Mr. Irontree, it is a pleasure to see you again." She extended her hand.

Luke nodded and shook her hand. The girl, surprised to see Luke after so long, stood behind her mother, suddenly quiet and shy.

"And you remember my daughter, Olivia Adelisa." Amiata gently moved Olivia Adelisa forward.

"Of course I do." Luke switched to Dutch. "Hello, Olivia Adelisa. Welcome to Portland."

"Hello, Mr. Irontree. I speak English now," Olivia Adelisa said with heavily accented English.

"Yes, you do." Luke smiled at the kid before turning to Amiata. "I'm surprised to see you. Are you my courier?"

"Indeed." She set a briefcase down on the coffee table and rotated the dials next to the latches to unlock it. When the top opened, she pulled out a satellite phone and handed it to Luke. "Pieter is going to call in"—she checked her watch—"forty-seven minutes."

Luke nodded, his heart rate picking up at the imminence of the call. "I have coffee ready in the kitchen. I'm not sure if there's anything here for your daughter. I didn't anticipate needing refreshments for a child."

"We have some flavored sparkling water in the fridge," Pablo said. "We have snacks as well."

"That'll do for now," Amiata said. "Thank you. We'll need to get some food into her after, though. Pieter tells me you own a brewery and restaurant.

"And we would love to host you for lunch," Pablo replied. "I'll run into the kitchen and get something for Olivia."

Amiata smiled and nodded. "Thank you, Mr. Sandoval."

"Please. Call me Pablo."

"Do you mind if I turn the TV on for her?" Luke gestured toward Olivia. "So she has something to do while we talk."

"Not at all, Luke."

Luke turned on the TV and grabbed the remote, finding We Bare Bears. "My niece Gwendolyn is about your age. She is very fond of this show. I enjoy it myself on occasion."

"OK. Thank you," the girl said, shuffling nervously from foot to foot.

Luke handed her the remote as Pablo returned and set a can of water and some cookies down for her. The adults headed into the kitchen.

"Is everyone here?" Amiata asked.

"We're just waiting on Sam. She should be here any minute," Luke replied.

Amiata nodded and turned to Luke, raising an eyebrow. "Did you say you have a niece?"

"She's my ward. We use the uncle-niece relationship for simplification and official paperwork."

"I did not know that." Amiata pushed her lips out, nodding.

"When you and I first became acquainted, Gwen and I hadn't met yet. That was before I got involved with the North Portland Pack. Gwen has been living with me for over six months now—a year in mid-autumn."

Amiata nodded.

He was giving Amiata a brief rundown of what had happened since he freed her from the vampire queen of Wallonia—The Mistress—when Sam walked into the house and joined them in the kitchen.

Luke stood up to introduce everyone. "Amiata van den Bergh, this is Samantha Wakamatsu—member of the pack council of the

North Portland Pack and wife of the packleader. Sam, this is Amiata, the wife of the packleader of Belgium and southern Netherlands. The child in the other room is her daughter, Olivia Adelisa."

"Welcome to Portland!" Sam said, a broad smile on her face as she reached out to shake Amiata's hand.

"Thank you for hosting me. It is much appreciated," Amiata replied, checking her watch. "Our call should come in shortly."

A few moments later, the phone rang.

Holding his breath in anticipation, Luke answered it and set it to speakerphone. "Hello. This is Luke. You're on speakerphone."

"Hello, Luke! This is Pieter. Good to hear from you, my friend. Who all is there?"

"Besides Amiata, Delilah, Pablo, and Sam are all here," Luke replied.

"Good, good," Pieter replied.

Luke leaned closer to the satphone. "Are we waiting on your father?"

"No. He's currently detained elsewhere and asked me to take care of this."

"Hey, Waffleboy!" Pablo grinned broadly.

"Pablo, my friend! It's good to hear from you."

"You too. What can we do for you?" Pablo asked.

"It's, uh…a bit of a sticky situation." Pieter sighed. "I'll just get right to it. I think we're in need of your services again."

Luke rubbed his chin. "Does this have anything to do with you being recalled last spring? And your long silence?"

"Yes. The vampires have been amassing along our southern border and taking chunks of our territory. They are rallying around a vampire known as Le Mousquetaire. I hate to admit it, but we're being out maneuvered. It's like…" He paused. "Damn it. Amiata, you're going to have to fill them in on some of the details."

"Even with a satphone?" Amiata asked.

"I hate this paranoia, but it's too important to let bullheadedness create more problems. Luke, my father is asking you personally for your aid."

Luke made eye contact with Amiata. Her furrowed brow and pursed lips relayed much without her saying it.

"OK, Pieter. Let me talk with Amiata and get the details. I'll call you back."

"Thank you, Luke." Pieter hung up.

Pieter's inability to give any details out of a fear of the information falling on the wrong ears turned up the tension in the room, everyone palpably looking on edge.

"Another round of coffee?" Sam asked.

"Please," Amiata replied. "And a sparkling water would be nice."

Sam topped up everyone's coffees, pulled out several cans of sparkling water, and set them down before fetching glasses in case anyone wanted one for their water.

Amiata cleared her throat. "What Pieter didn't want to say, even over a secure satphone, was that we fear Le Mousquetaire is getting information from within the pack. My husband and Pieter and Jan are having trouble dealing with treachery within what they view as their family. They feel deeply betrayed."

"Do you have any idea how close to the inner circle the leak may be?" Luke asked.

Amiata made a disgusted noise. "Close. Too close. The vampires have been given secret locations of our facilities in the south along the border. They've murdered too many of our packmates."

"And how does your husband think I can help?" Luke asked.

"Well, he and his sons are hoping you will fly to Belgium to help them sniff out the traitor and counter 'Le Mousquetaire,'" Amiata replied.

Pablo whistled. "That's not a small ask."

Amiata leaned on the table. "No, it's not. Especially after the year you've had here."

"What's our timeline looking like?" Luke asked.

"I guess that depends on you. If you're able to come to Belgium, they won't hold you there if you need to return home. They understand you have responsibilities here." Amiata intensified her gaze, silently pleading with Luke.

Luke looked around the room at his friends. "Amiata, can you give us a few minutes to discuss this?"

Amiata nodded and stood. "Of course. I'll go watch some television with Olivia." She shut the door behind her and turned up the TV when she got to the couch to give them a semblance of privacy. Although, if she chose to, she could probably hear them with her enhanced wolf hearing.

"You wanted to reach out to the Belgian pack," Sam said. "This might be an excellent opportunity to forge a more solid alliance."

"It would be a good show of force against the vampires if they see you're not isolated to just one city," Pablo said.

Delilah pulled up a chair and sat. "That's all important, but Portland still has a lot of vampires."

Luke sat back in his chair, hands on top of his head as he looked around the table at his friends, contemplating what they'd just said. "But we're not seeing anything intense or coordinated. I don't think we'd want to take the whole trained crew, just a handful of people, maybe a few more."

Pablo took a drink from his coffee. "Who are you thinking?"

"I want the four of us, of course," Luke replied.

"Who's going to be in charge while we're gone?" Delilah asked.

"I have full faith in Ahmed, Jung-sook, and Rhonda to maintain what we're doing and organize any strikes. They're very competent. And if things go sideways, we're a half-day's flight away."

Sam nodded along with Luke's assessment. "I'd put Jung-sook in charge, with Ahmed and Rhonda as her lieutenants. Her military background will help her lead, and she's earned the respect of everyone on the teams. Do you want to stick to just us four?"

"No, I think we need a few more people, just in case." Luke turned to Sam. "I'd like to take Jamaal for tech support."

Sam nodded. "Jamaal would be an excellent choice. Hersh can handle things here since he's trained up, and it's been quiet. It'll be a good opportunity for him to strike out on his own. Who else do you think would be an asset?"

"I'm not sure. We can figure that out later. We'll want to get more details on the situation so we can make those kinds of decisions. Let's get Amiata back in here." Luke stood up, opened the door, and called her in.

"I think we're decided, Amiata."

"You'll help us?"

Luke nodded.

Amiata visibly relaxed, before tensing again. "I have one more request on behalf of my pack. My husband requests sanctuary for me and my daughter in Portland until things clear up in Belgium."

Luke looked to Sam.

"You're part of the council, too, Luke," Sam said.

"There are three of us here. Do we need to take this to Holly or the full council?" Luke asked.

"You're on the pack council?" Amiata asked. "A human? Very unusual."

"We figured it was best since he's been leading our people against the vampires," Sam replied.

"And he's proven that he cares about the pack and its interests," Pablo added. "I think between the three of us, we can make that decision."

Luke, Pablo, and Sam exchanged looks and nods.

Sam spoke up first. Even though Pablo was officially the number two in the pack, Sam often spoke on behalf of Holly when she wasn't around. "You and your daughter are welcome to stay with us as long as you need to."

"Thank you on behalf of the Flanders Pack and on behalf of myself and my daughter." Amiata once again relaxed.

"For now, this will be your home. It's the pack guest house," Sam added.

"In case the pack needs the house, Amiata and Olivia Adelisa can stay in my house," Luke said. "I'll be sure to leave a key with Holly. Shit. I'm going to need to find a place for Gwen to stay. She's about to start school." The ramifications of his decision hit him. He'd be leaving Gwen behind, and most likely Maggie too.

"I'm sure if you ask Maggie, she and Zel will look after her," Sam said.

"I know, but I hate leaning on her all the time to help with Gwen.

I just feel like I'm not doing a good job as a parent since I'm gone all the time."

"Gwennie understands," Delilah said. "Besides, she's an independent kid."

"I know, but she shouldn't have to be. She's only twelve." Luke frowned.

"I don't think you could get her to go anywhere else. She's pretty attached to you," Sam said.

Luke nodded. "I'd hate for her to go. I just wish…"

Pablo reached over and patted his shoulder. "I know, buddy."

Sam, with a reassuring smile, reached over the table and grasped Luke's forearm. "She's the pack's kid too. When we brought you both into the pack, we took responsibility for you both. We all love Gwen, and we'll make sure she's taken care of while you're out of town."

"Thanks. I really do appreciate all you do for us, even if I'm still unused to having people who I can rely on. I guess we'll all have to make arrangements if we're going out of town." He turned to Amiata. "How much about the situation do you know?"

"I don't get a lot of the details. It's not my area. I'm not a fighter or a leader, not in that way. My primary concern is protecting my daughter. We were targeted once. Her father and I don't want her to experience that again."

"I can understand that," Luke said.

"We'll take good care of you. There are plenty of pack kids about her age, so she can have friends and work on her English too," Sam said. "We'll hold a little welcome dinner for you and introduce you around."

"That's really kind of you," Amiata replied.

"Now we just have to figure out logistics," Luke mused. "It's going to be a real pain to smuggle weapons into Belgium."

"That actually shouldn't be an issue. The pack will send a private plane to take you all over. You'll be able to pack what you need without worrying about airport security in Belgium."

Luke turned toward Sam and Pablo. "Does the pack have

anyone in place at the Portland airport who can help us move our weapons past security?"

Sam shook her head. "No. But, I'll talk with the Beaverton Pack. They have people installed at the Hillsboro Airport. It's probably better to fly a private jet into Hillsboro than PDX. I'm assuming you have security covered on your end, Amiata?"

"Yes. We control the airport you'll be flying into," Amiata replied.

Pablo smiled. "Sweet! Private jet. I could get used to being an international wolf of mystery."

Luke sat quietly in his seat, watching a movie on his laptop. Pablo and Delilah had fallen asleep. Jamaal's nose was in a book. Tanika and Will, the other additions to the team for this mission, were watching movies in the back of the plane. Luke never could sleep on a plane. Even after nearly two-thousand years, he still enjoyed travel. The journey was exciting, even if the actual travel part wasn't that great.

When he checked his phone, they still had several hours left of their flight. Even though he'd spent as much time with Gwen and Maggie before his departure, he missed them both already. Since he had his phone in his hand and a Wi-Fi connection, he sent a text to Gwen to say hello and one to Maggie as well.

"Mind if I join you?" Sam asked, standing in the aisle.

"Not at all," Luke replied, smiling at the message Maggie had sent back.

"Texting with Maggie?"

"How did you know?" Luke asked.

"The look on your face. You always get the same silly look on your face when you're texting her."

"I'm silly?"

"It's very sweet. I like seeing that kind of look on your face. I'm glad everything is working so well for you and Maggie. She seems to make you happy. How are you doing with the polyamorous nature of things?"

Luke tucked his phone back into his pocket. "Good. I like Zel. They seem to like me. I think they gave me their blessing at the big celebration up at the farm."

Eyebrows raised, Sam quirked her head to the side. "Oh?"

"They took me aside and told me they think I'm a good person, and they're choosing to trust me." Luke paused, thinking about the conversation with Zel. "They asked me to be gentle with Maggie's heart."

Sam reached over and took Luke's hand in hers, patting the back of it. "Zel is protective of Maggie. They have a deep relationship. I can always see the hurt in Zel when someone leaves Maggie. All Zel wants is for whoever Maggie dates to love Maggie in the way they feel Maggie deserves to be loved. It's good that Zel is on your team."

Luke nodded. "I think I'm falling in love with her, Sam."

Sam leaned her head on Luke's shoulder. "That's sweet. She's good for you, and I think you're good for her."

They sat there quietly, looking at the movie and captions, but Luke wasn't paying much attention to it, thinking about Maggie and what Sam had said about her. He'd meant what he said—he was falling in love with her.

Sam broke the silence. "Have you thought about dating someone else? I mean besides Maggie, since it's an available option to you."

"I don't think so. I've thought about it, but I don't have the time or emotional energy for it. I feel bad enough not being able to see Maggie as often as we'd like, since most of my duties are at night. I couldn't do that to another person. Besides…" Luke left it hanging there.

"Besides, it would be too hard to find someone understanding of your unique place in the world?"

Luke chuckled. "Yeah. You could say that. There's no way a relationship with a non-supernatural would ever work, not without serious ethical issues on my part. I couldn't maintain the elaborate web of lies to maintain the secrecy of our world, and I won't do that to someone."

"You're a good man, Luke. I can understand your position. It almost means your entire dating pool is restricted to werewolves. I mean, things could be worse. Werewolves are fun, zesty people." Sam winked.

Chuckling, Luke shook his head. "I'm not really interested. I don't have the emotional energy to seek that kind of relationship. One zesty wolf is enough for my happiness for the time being."

"Maggie is a lucky woman to have someone like you in her life. I consider myself lucky to claim you as a friend," Sam said.

"I feel fortunate to have you both in my life. You're a very dear friend, Sayumi."

Sam chuckled. "That's an old name. Only Holly uses it."

"Pablo told me."

"Pablo is a blabbermouth." Seeing Luke's concern, Sam added, "But we've become close enough that you may have my name."

After the private jet landed in New York to refuel, their next destination was Flanders International Airport, a small airport near Kortrijk and Wevelgem in West Flanders. Controlled by the pack, it allowed them to skip the busy airport outside Brussels and all the dangers of inquisitive eyes. When they arrived, Pieter and Jan van den Bergh met them.

"How was the flight?" Pieter said, shaking Luke's hand.

"Good. Much nicer than riding coach all the way," Luke replied.

Pieter chuckled. "You remember my brother?"

"Jan, it's good to see you again."

Jan nodded. "Mr. Irontree. It's a pleasure, although I could wish for better circumstances. I hope you won't find it rude to skip introductions until later. I want to get on the way before anyone knows you're here."

"Yeah. Let's not give away the element of surprise." Luke, tucking in behind Pieter and Jan, motioned for his friends to follow him into a warehouse near the hangar where the Bombardier had been stowed.

Luke only stopped to grab the large plastic travel case he used for his gear. Sliding the handle out, he towed it behind him.

"We'll move the rest of your baggage," Jan said.

"Sorry, this always travels with me. There's no replacing what's in here." Luke patted the case.

"Ah. Of course." Jan turned and led the way.

When they cleared the door of the warehouse, a fleet of identical SUVs and several unmarked box trucks greeted them. Luke, Delilah, Pablo, and Sam loaded into Pieter's SUV, while Jamaal and the rest climbed into Jan's vehicle. When the doors shut, all the SUVs pulled out of the warehouse and made their way to the roadway exiting the airport. Periodically, one by one, an SUV would peel off and disappear down a different road. Eventually, it was just the two SUVs with Luke's crew—until the one driven by Jan disappeared down a side road.

"Um, where'd everyone else go, Waffleboy?" Pablo asked.

Pieter cleared his throat. "Sorry for the overabundance of caution, but part of the reason you're here is because we don't know who we can trust internally. We've done what we can to keep your visit off the books, routing everything through little-used channels only the family knows. We're hoping to give you some time on the ground uninterrupted so you can get a jump on our leak and help us plan a response to Le Mousquetaire."

Luke nodded. "I see. It's probably for the best. Since we're on the ground, where are we headed?"

"Father wants to prepare a proper welcome for you and thought dinner at 't Hommelhof would be an ideal way to welcome a bunch of beer-loving Portlanders to Belgium. He's booked the restaurant for the evening and is having Chef Stefaan prepare a special menu with beer and wine pairings. But first, I'll drop you off at the St. Bernardus Bed and Breakfast. You'll be the only guests. We've already swept the rooms for any bugs."

Luke turned and smiled at Sam, Delilah, and Pablo. "We're in for a treat. It's been a while since I've dined at 't Hommelhof, but it's always exceptional."

"Good beer and food? And on Waffleboy's tab? This

international werewolf of mystery stuff is pretty all right." Pablo put his hands behind his head and relaxed.

Delilah elbowed him in the ribs, knocking the wind from his sails.

As they drove through roads and villages of West Flanders, Luke stared out the window, saying very little.

"Dude, there are a lot of war cemeteries and memorials," Pablo said.

"Yeah. Yeah, there are." Luke's response was curt and clipped.

Pablo grunted as Delilah elbowed him again, this time harder. "Sorry, Luke. I didn't think…"

Luke took a deep breath and held it for a moment before letting it out. "It's OK, Pablo. It always takes me a little time to adjust once I return home."

"Do you still consider Belgium home?" Sam asked.

Luke thought about it for a minute. "I guess so, in part. Portland is also my home, but I was born here. I've spent a lot of time here over the centuries. It's centrally located but still kind of a backwoods, at least in the eyes of the surrounding countries. It's a good place to hide without being out of the way." He stared out the windows, squinting into the distance. "We're getting close to Ieper. I spent the first year of the war here in the muck and blood of the trenches."

He sighed and pulled out his phone, patching it into the SUV's sound system to play Jeff Buckley's cover of "Lost Highway."

Pablo leaned forward and squeezed his shoulder. Sam reached up from her side and patted his other shoulder, and Delilah slid forward and rubbed his arm.

He smiled sadly. His friends were good people, and their simple gestures went a long way in assuaging the rising pain of past traumas. "I love this land. I've watched it grow and change over two thousand years, but it's seen a lot of my pain too. Over the centuries, I've gotten used to being back here. After a long absence, I just need a little time to put everything back into perspective. When we arrive at our rooms, let's freshen up then meet downstairs for some cold beers, and I'll welcome you to the country of my birth. It's too bad it's not spring, or I'd take you all to the Hallerbos and we could find a patch of bluebells to lie in and watch the clouds sweep by over-head." Luke turned his head away from his friend and returned to staring out the window.

"Bluebells?" Delilah asked.

Sam whispered to Delilah, "I'll explain when we get to the B&B. Let's let Luke have some time to himself."

AFTER A SHOWER, Luke dressed in a pair of designer jeans and a black button-down shirt. The shower helped clear away the long day of travel and the encroaching fatigue as well as the melan-choly threatening to settle over him. Normally, he'd seek solitude until he could manage his tempestuous emotions, but his friends were waiting downstairs. That option felt better than being alone.

Pablo had beat Luke downstairs and had already poured himself a beer from the fridge. He sat in a chair scrolling through his phone. Luke pulled open the beer fridge and smiled, taking out a St. Bernardus Wit. He popped the top off the bottle and poured it into the bulbous bowl of a branded stemmed glass. He took the seat next to Pablo. The first sniff of the beer drew a contented smile to Luke's lips. After his first sip, he released a happy sigh.

"Good beer?" Pablo asked, not looking up.

"One of my favorites. It feels good to be back here, especially with my friends. I hope we get some quiet moments so I can show you around."

"I'd like that. Do you really still consider Belgium home?"

"I guess, in some part it always will be. So much of my history is here and my blood, but Portland is also my home, but it's more the people that make it home—you, Sam, Delilah, Gwen."

Pablo looked up, an eyebrow raised slyly. "And Maggie?"

"Yes. Maggie too. I'm glad you all are here with me, it makes being here feel less lonely, but I feel incomplete without Gwen and Maggie here too. I don't know if I thanked you, but I'm glad you helped Maggie cut through my obliviousness." Luke smiled warmly at his best friend.

Pablo laughed, raising his glass. "Here's to me and Maggie!"

Luke tapped his glass against Pablo's and took a drink.

"You boys celebrating already?" Sam asked, entering the room.

Luke set his glass down on the small table next to his chair. Crossing the room to Sam, he pulled her into a hug and kissed her forehead. Sam wore a wrap dress with teal and black diagonal stripes. Her black hair was pulled back in a ponytail.

"How are you feeling, Luke?" Sam asked.

"Better."

"Good," Sam replied, a bright smile dazzling her face.

Nodding, Luke grabbed an empty glass. "Can I get you a beer?"

"Sure. I'll take something light."

Luke poured a Wit for her.

"I'll take one of those too, please," Delilah said, joining them.

Luke grabbed another bottle and opened it for Delilah, then walked over and grabbed his glass. "I'm glad you are all here with me. In the year we've been working together, you've become my trusted comrades and my dear friends. I just wanted to thank you. For everything." He raised his glass.

Everyone clinked their glasses against Luke's.

"You're feeling introspective today," Delilah said.

"I guess so. It's being back in a place so full of memories. It's one of the reasons I moved to Portland; it was a clean place until recently. A memory-free place. I could hide and be no one." Luke turned to Pablo, nodding his head in respect. "Then I met Pablo"— he nodded at Delilah—"and Delilah, and you both refused to leave me alone. Eventually you made me your friend. Then I got to know you, Sam.

"You've all meant so much to me and have become my favorite people. I couldn't imagine being here without you and doing this by myself. It would feel like I was missing important pieces of myself. I feel grateful for your friendship and support. I just wanted to let you know, before we sink too deep into our mission here, or I become overwhelmed by the weight of memory."

Pablo pulled Luke into a one-armed hug. "You know I love you, buddy. I'll always be there with you, if I can."

Delilah hugged him on the other side, not saying anything. She'd been unnaturally quiet since she'd returned from Virginia after visiting her grandmother. Luke wasn't sure if something had happened on her trip east, or if she was still dealing with the emotional aftermath of finally carrying out her revenge against Cassius. Her whole life had been firmly fixed on one goal. Her life in Portland had happened by accident as she become involved with Luke and Pablo, and through him, the North Portland Pack.

Now, she had a job building a martial arts center to teach the pack's children and help Luke and Sam train the patrol teams to deal with Portland's vampire infestation. She had friends, people who cared about her—even someone she'd been dating for a brief time. At the end of her quest for vengeance, she'd decided to start a new life in Portland with her new friends and as a member of the North Portland Pack.

The four friends sat down as the rest of the team gathered in the sitting room of the bed-and-breakfast. Jamaal joined the foursome, joking with Pablo, the two playing off each other's sense of humor. Soon, even Luke was laughing, setting aside his thoughtful mood, giving into the joy of camaraderie, and living in the moment. When Pieter and Jan arrived to take them to dinner, Luke felt content and at peace, at least as much as he ever felt and probably more than he'd known in a long time.

When they arrived at 't Hommelhof, the parking lot was uncharacteristically empty save for a few poorly disguised tourists whose gazes were a bit too sharp and attentive. Some wore Adidas track suits, one or two wore suits, while a few others wore picture tees and ball caps.

"Your security could use some lessons on looking more natural," Pablo said to Pieter.

"Sometimes looking like security is just as useful," Pieter replied. "We're a series of Black SUVs with NATO decals on the door and Americans in the back. To everyone around here, it's just a group of dignitaries making a trip out to the country from Brussels to one of our more renowned restaurants."

"And are they secure? Have you screened them?" Delilah asked, taking the pointed questions.

"These are some of our most trusted and longest-serving pack members. The family has trusted them with our lives on many occasions. Some are cousins or nephews and nieces. Others have married into the family. This is our righteous core. They've swept the restaurant for any bugs, and the restaurant has allowed us to install basic sound proofing in the room we'll be dining in. Short of being in a concrete bunker, we should be fine for basic discussions. Since we're almost there, I have a few instructions. You are the American dignitaries, no names until we're in the room, and let my people open doors for you."

Pieter parked and turned off the engine. He stepped out of the SUV as the other doors were opened from the outside, letting Luke, Delilah, Pablo, and Sam slide out. The other SUV received the same treatment.

Pieter stepped next to Luke and leaned in close, whispering, "Do you sense any vampires?"

Luke's eyes twitched around, inspecting the buildings and looking for hidden nooks. "Nothing since we've arrived."

"Good." Pieter gestured toward the restaurant. A couple of the pack's security personnel opened the door. Pieter led the way in, stopping next to the chef.

"My friends, please allow me to introduce Chef Stefaan who will be our host this evening and has prepared a special menu featuring some of Belgium's finest local products."

"Welcome to 't Hommelhof," the chef said. "I hope you enjoy our menu as much as we enjoyed creating it for you."

Luke stepped up and shook Stefaan's hand and spoke in Flemish Dutch. "Thank you for having us this evening and for preparing a special menu. It has been too long since I've dined here, and I'm glad I have the opportunity to once again taste your fine cuisine."

Pablo leaned over to Jamaal. "Now he's just showing off."

Delilah snorted.

In the same language, Stefaan replied, "You speak excellent Flemish for an American. Do all your party speak it so well?"

"Just me, although they have a host of other talents," Luke said, nodding his thanks.

Pieter led Luke toward the room in the back while everyone shook the chef's hand before following Luke and Pieter. When Pieter's father, also named Pieter, saw Luke, he walked across the room, placing his hands on Luke's shoulders and pulling him into a hug and a greeting kiss on the cheek.

"It is so good to see you again, my friend, although it seems like it can never be under better circumstances," Pieter van den Bergh the elder said.

Luke nodded respectfully. "It's the way of things for people like us. It is good to see you again."

"Would you care to join me for a drink?"

"Of course."

Pieter the elder grabbed a full glass with "Boon" scrawled on the side and handed it to Luke. "The Mariage Parfait Geuze Boon. I believe you're a fan?"

"Your younger son has an excellent memory," Luke replied.

"I requested some be brought in for the dinner."

One by one, Luke's friends joined them in the room as servers handed out glasses of the same beer. Pablo wandered over, looking at his glass thoughtfully, and took another sip.

"I don't think I've ever had a beer quite like this," Pablo mused.

Luke chuckled. "I don't think you have the time, space, or set up to brew lambic."

Pieter the elder looked confused.

Luke put his arm around Pablo's shoulder. "My friend here is a brewer and owns a brewpub back home."

Once everyone had a glass, the servers left the room, Jan shutting the doors behind them. Bolsters at the top, bottom, and sides of the door helped sound proof the room. Jan pressed his ear to the door, his werewolf hearing allowing him to listen easily. After a moment, he looked at his father and nodded.

Pieter the elder, face stern, nodded. "Thank you for coming, Luke, and for putting up with all the subterfuge. If I had my preference, I'd host you in one of the finest restaurants in Antwerp."

Luke smiled. "It's no problem, but I'm not sure you could have done much better than 't Hommelhof. It's one of my favorites."

Pieter leaned over closer to Luke. "Ah, mine too if I'm being truthful. I hope your friends enjoy it as much as you do."

"They're an easy-going bunch. I'm sure they'll be satisfied. Please, let me introduce you." Luke turned to his friends. "This is Pieter van den Bergh the elder, our host and leader of the Flanders Pack. Pieter, these are my friends and comrades." Luke chuckled and smiled at Pablo as he concentrated on the sour beer in his glass. "Pablo is the second of North Portland Pack and is currently figuring out if he can start making spontaneously fermented beers in Portland."

Pieter laughed and nodded.

"Sam is the wife of the packleader and a senior council member. Jamaal is another member of the pack council."

Jamaal nodded politely.

"This is Delilah. She's the other human in the group and a fierce fighter and dear friend. She's also a student of art and aficionado of the Flemish masters."

Pieter's eyebrows moved up as he made an appreciative sound. "If we have time, I'd love to talk art with you."

Delilah blushed and stammered, "I'd...I'd r-r-really like that, sir."

Luke introduced the rest of the crew. When he was finished, Pieter the younger introduced the Flanders Pack members in attendance for the dinner.

While they waited for the first course, Belgians and Portlanders mingled, getting to know the people they'd just been introduced to. Though they were meeting under less-than-ideal circumstances, both sides put it aside to enjoy meeting their new allies. Luke stepped back and watched the room, spying Delilah also standing out of the way. He grabbed a bottle and topped off his beer before strolling over to his friend to lean against the wall next to her.

"Two years ago, did you think you'd be in Belgium about to have dinner with three of the Flemish masters because you're here to help kill some vampires?" Luke asked.

Delilah laughed. "No part of that sentence would've ever crossed my mind in a million years. It's fucking surreal."

"If you like the surrealists, we can try to find time to visit the Magritte Museum in Brussels."

She smirked and shook her head. "I suppose you used to pal around with René Magritte back in the day?"

Luke chuckled. "No. I didn't get in with the Belgian surrealists. I spent the twenties and thirties in Paris, then left for the US a few years after the Second World War ended. How are you doing, Delilah?"

"Tired."

"Yeah. I hope they don't plan on keeping us too late. I can keep going if I have to, but I'd like to tuck in and get a good night's sleep." Luke stifled a yawn.

When a diffident knock on the door drew their attention, the van den Bergh's directed everyone to sit down for the first course. The chef lead them through three immaculate courses featuring late summer and early fall fresh food sourced locally and prepared perfectly. Each course was paired with beer or wine, depending on the diners' preferences. By the time they reached the dessert course, Luke and his friends were decidedly mellow, full of delicious food and drinks, and tired from their travels. After the dishes were cleared, they ordered digestifs and a round of coffees, Luke taking a decaf espresso. They notified the staff that if they needed anything further, they'd open the doors and request their presence.

Pieter the elder stood, holding up a glass of expensive cognac. "I wish to thank you all for being here and raise a glass to our new friends from Oregon."

Everyone hoisted their glasses, touching them against the glasses of those around them.

"I wish this dinner could have taken place during a time when we weren't gathered for urgent business." Pieter sighed. "No one likes to admit this, least of all me, but we have a leak in our pack, one that is betraying vital secrets to our enemies, the enemies of all decent people—human or wolf. This leak"—he said, his lip curled in disgust as if the word stunk—"is feeding our movements and details of our operations in the south to the new leader of the vampires trying to retake Wallonia, the one who calls himself Le Mousquetaire. Whether he was one of the elite soldiers of Louis XIV or Cardinal Richelieu is unknown, although rumor says he wields a period rapier and knows how to use it. We have lost many packmates to the vile hands of the vampires."

He took a swig of his cognac and exhaled loudly. "We've invited you here to help because we've exhausted our internal options short of interrogating every person in the pack one by one. It's hard to investigate what the left hand is doing using the right hand…" Pieter sat down and ran his hand down his face. "We hope you can find what we haven't been able to, but whatever happens, we will be eternally grateful to you and hope this is the start of a deep friendship between our packs."

The early air of conviviality disappeared, replaced by a general wariness as eyes narrowed and shoulders rose. Until then, everything had been basic logistics, easily solved. Now, with their feet on the ground, they'd need to get to the bottom of Pieter's problem, one that could easily beset the North Portland Pack if the vampires got their way. Luke hoped they'd be up to the investigation—hoped he'd be able to help his friend and keep his packmates safe. They'd been successful so far, but after nearly dying and losing Archie, what would be the price this time?

SLEEPY AND WELL FED, Luke and his crew returned to their vehicles. Pieter the younger and Jan jumped in the backs of the SUVs and grabbed two guards who hadn't had anything to drink to function as the team's chauffeurs. Jan and Pieter's father were staying in the nearby town of Poperinge.

They followed the packleader's cars out of the parking lot and took a right while Pieter the elder and his escort proceeded straight down Douvieweg. After a couple hundred feet, Luke's team turned onto Trappistenweg, the road that'd led back to the St. Bernardus Bed and Breakfast. A few minutes later, they were parked and standing around outside enjoying the warm night air.

"Would you care to share a bottle of the Abt 12 with me before heading to bed?" Pablo asked Luke.

"Sure, I think I've got room for a few more ounces of beer," Luke replied.

"Mind if I join you?" Jamaal asked.

Luke stretched. "Not at all."

The sound of Pieter's phone pulled Luke's attention away from his friend.

"Shit!" Pieter paced back and forth, then hung up. "We have to go. Father was ambushed."

Brow furrowing, Luke exhaled aggressively through his nose. "Fuck. So much for that beer. Give us a moment to gear up."

Pieter exchanged a look with Jan, then nodded. "Hurry."

"You heard the man," Luke called, striding toward the entrance.

Everyone jogged into the building and up to their rooms. Luke opened the lid on his travel case and pulled the top protective layer out. In a few moments, he wore his armor along with the tactical utility belt and straps for his weapons—gladius strapped to his left hip and his wooden rudis slung over the shoulder for a left-hand draw. He stared into the case for one moment, then made a decision. He reached in and grabbed a new sword with a black leather scabbard accented with silver. The small hilt guard featured a series of interconnected swirls resembling a stylized cloud.

Luke was the last down the stairs, but only by a few seconds. "Delilah?"

The tall Black woman stepped out from behind one of the SUVs, a Winchester M12 in her left hand. "Yes?"

"I wanted to do this with a bit more ceremony, but you'll have to give it a baptism in blood." Luke held out the jian, laying it horizontal across both hands. "I had it custom made for you. There's a bit of silver in the alloy as well as in the etching of the design."

Delilah reached out and took the hilt in her hand—Luke gripping the scabbard—and pulled the straight, double-edged short sword from its sheath. The light danced down the blade and the intricate engraving featuring a sun motif.

Sam had wandered over and peaked around Delilah. "Oh, that's gorgeous, Delilah."

Delilah, the words stripped from her, could only nod.

"Y'all about ready?" Pablo called, shutting the back of the SUV he was loading.

Delilah grabbed the scabbard and shoved the sword back into it.

The crew piled into their vehicles, and they were soon on their way, speeding down the narrow country roads.

"Right onto Kapellestraat," Pieter called from the front passenger seat. "It'll be the second left. Spaarpotweg."

"Understood," replied their driver.

Pieter turned to speak to the rest of the passengers. "We're only a couple minutes out. Once we arrive, let's sweep out. The drivers will stay with the vehicles to defend them. Father said they'd hold out as long as possible."

Pieter tried to contain his worry, but Luke had come to know him well during their time working together in Portland; he could hear the concern bordering on distress in his friend's voice.

Pablo, looking Luke over with his exposed armor, pointed at Luke's chest. "Going for the shiny look tonight?"

"I was trying to save an extra second or two by not looking for my hoodie. Besides, It's dark out here and you all are going to have shotguns. Shiny seemed like a good idea. Let's give Pieter my M12. I'll sweep up the middle, y'all sweep out on either side."

"Right," Pablo said.

Pieter slid his phone into his pocket. "Jan and his team are going to go around and come at them from the other side." He reached out and tapped the driver's arm. "This will do. We'll go the rest of the way on foot. Let us out and get the car turned around in case we have to move fast."

The SUV stopped, and the team jumped out, meeting at the back hatch to hand out the shotguns and ammo belts. Geared up, they shut the door and jogged up front, Pieter slapping the hood of the SUV to let the driver know they were off. The headlights shifted around as the driver followed his instructions to turn around.

They looked down the road, surveying their surroundings.

"That brush and those trees mask what's further down the road and around those curves," Luke said. He hated blind approaches.

"There's a faint glow down further. Maybe a house light or something," Sam replied. "Pieter, do you know what's up ahead?"

Pieter shrugged. "Not really. There are a lot of farms around here. Maybe a farmhouse?"

"You feeling any vampires, Luke?" Delilah asked.

"Yeah, not sure how many, though. Anyone hear anything?" Luke directed that question toward the werewolves.

"No. Not nearly enough noise, that's for sure. We should be hearing weapon fire." Pieter's face tightened with concern.

Luke squeezed Pieter's shoulder. "Alright, it's likely another ambush. Let your brother know. Let's get moving."

"I guess so. It worked the first time." Pieter nodded and pulled out his phone, sending a text to his brother. "OK. He's prepared."

Pointing toward the distant glow, Luke jogged up the middle of the small road, Pieter and Delilah on his right, and Sam and Pablo on his left. Delilah had shoved the scabbard of her new jian under her belt like Sam wore her wakizashi and katana. Each of them held their shotguns, shells loaded and ready to fire.

They jogged around the left curve. Ahead, they could see a flickering light.

"Fire," Luke muttered, hoping it wasn't.

When they approached the end of the right curve, Luke held his hand up to halt his friends. He reached across his body and pulled his gladius from its scabbard before moving forward.

"By that break of trees, there's a small cluster of buildings. I think I see something on fire ahead," Luke whispered over his shoulders, waving everyone forward.

As they made it around the curve, Luke moved to the left edge of the road and waved to the right. Pieter hopped the fence and fanned out wide. Delilah lined up on the right edge of the road. Pablo and Sam swept out on the left side.

So far, Luke saw no motion except the hulk flaming in the middle of the road near the cluster of buildings. The light on the side of the house combined with the flames of what had been one of Pieter the elder's vehicles. A few lumps lay ahead in the road around the burning hulk. He hoped they weren't what they were likely to be, but with every step closer, that hope become more foolhardy.

When they reached the first one, Luke squatted next to the body of a man. Grabbing the man's shoulder, Luke flipped him over, recognizing one of the guards who had patrolled the parking lot outside 't Hommelhof just thirty minutes ago. His throat had been ripped out, taking most of the neck with it.

"Luke! Incoming!"

Doors banged open on the farmhouse on his left and the scrappy outbuilding to his right. On both sides, the sound of M12s barked to life, spewing death toward the undead. Luke pulled the rudis from its sheath on his back and waited for the first vampire to reach him.

The gleam of the fire flickered over something metallic and dark in the vampire's hand. Luke spun around and darted behind the burning hulk, catching another vamp by surprise. Luke hesitated—surprised as well—but lashed out, stabbing the fanger through the stomach with the gladius. The vamp grasped toward Luke, but he batted her arms aside with his rudis and pulled the gladius out, shoving the vampire back. Without the blade in her guts, she doubled over. He pushed her toward the burning debris of the SUV and followed, stabbing her through the heart with the rudis as she tried to backpedal away.

"You..." The vamp with the gun had cleared the car.

Luke spun, holding up the vampire he'd just stabbed and using it to block the armed vamp. He charged forward and dislodged the cadaver, launching it toward the other vamp. As the body left his rudis, it dissolved into a mass of goo, its momentum carrying it into the vamp with a gun. In the split second of the goo's impact, the vamp cringed away, signing its death warrant as Luke lunged forward, plunging the gladius into its heart and turning it into a cloud of dust.

Luke turned and looked for the next vamp to engage. Finding one, he charged after it. Luke pressed against the wall of the farmhouse. He whipped around at the sound of feet pounding down the narrow road. He was readying for a fight when the familiar face of Jan van den Bergh materialized out of the dark. Luke heaved a sigh of relief.

Seeing Luke, Jan called a halt and directed Jamaal and the rest of the Portland crew, sending two right and two left, before jogging up to Luke.

"You find any of our people?" Jan asked.

"Not alive. You?"

"No." Jan deflated. "What now?"

"Let's clear up these vampires and go from there."

Jan nodded and pulled the hammer back on the submachine gun strapped over his shoulder. With a grim face, he walked along the wall and stepped around the corner, opening fire on the vamps pinned down by Sam and Pablo.

When his gun clicked empty, he called out, "Clear!"

Luke followed Jan around the corner and tidied up, sending the vampires, some still moving feebly, to their final deaths. Jan pulled the empty magazine from his gun and replaced it, racking a bullet into the firing chamber. Sam and Pablo jogged up. Taking the opportunity, they shoved shells into the magazine on their shotguns.

"What next, Luke?" Sam asked.

"You three, come with me. Let's sweep the house."

Just then, Jamaal and one of the Belgians rounded the corner, guns at the ready. The sound of guns firing by the other building rang out.

"Jamaal, you two check if you can help across the way, we're going to sweep through the house."

"Got it, Luke." Jamaal gave a salute and jogged off, the Belgian following behind.

Luke, Jan, Sam, and Pablo readied themselves near the back door into the house. Luke counted down from three, then shoved the door open, stepping out of the way as his comrades swept in. While they checked the rooms, Luke flipped on the lights and checked the room to his left, peeking under the bed and tossing the closet.

"Clear!" Sam called.

"Clear," Pablo added.

"We've only got this last door, looks like a basement." Jan pointed toward a door next to the one Luke walked out of.

Luke reached down but only felt jeans. He hadn't taken the time to grab his sawed-off Stephens 311s from his gear case. They were perfect for situations like this.

"Looking for your sawed-offs?" Pablo asked.

"Yeah. Didn't take time to throw them on."

"Do you sense any vamps? With all the smells, it's hard to tell if there any live ones left over here," Sam said.

"I don't think so, but better safe than sorry," Luke replied.

"I got it." Pablo stepped toward the door.

Luke grabbed the handle and pulled it open. Pablo jumped in, pointing his shotgun down the stairs. With each step down, the stairs creaked eerily.

"Luke, hit the light switch," Pablo called up.

Luke reached into the doorway and flipped the switch on the wall.

"Holy fuck…" Pablo gasped.

"Is it clear?" Luke asked.

"Yeah."

Luke started down the stairs and stopped behind Pablo, bending over to look under the ledge of the ceiling. A pile of bodies was stacked in the far corner, blood splattered around the walls and leaking from the corpses, sending rivulets across the floor where it sloped to the middle.

Pablo took his first step since stopping, his legs wobbling. Luke sheathed his weapons and stabilized Pablo, helping him down the stairs. Once they reached the bottom, Pablo, tears in his eyes, turned and faced the wall so he wouldn't have to look at the sight anymore.

"Luke, what's going on down there?" Sam asked.

"The fucking fangers slaughtered the family that lived here. Stay up there. You don't want this in your head," Luke yelled upstairs.

He placed his arm around Pablo's shoulder and leaned into his best friend. "It's OK. You don't have to be down here. Do you want to go back upstairs?"

Pablo nodded weakly.

Luke turned and yelled upstairs, "Sam, can you kill the lights down here for a minute?"

"Sure."

A moment later, the lights flicked out. Luke turned Pablo toward the stairs and helped him up the first few steps, standing between Pablo and the view his werewolf eyes might still be able to see. Once Pablo's head cleared the ledge so the view was blocked, Luke gave

Pablo's shoulders a final squeeze and let his friend walk the rest of the way up.

"Lights on again, please," Luke called once Pablo was out of the stairwell.

"You sure you don't need some help down there?" Jan called.

"I don't. Stay up there."

Luke had no idea what horrors his friends had seen over their long lives. At around one hundred seventy some years old, Sam was the youngest of the quartet. Luke had been subject to the horrors perpetrated by vampires for over nineteen hundred years. The sight of the brutally murdered family had shaken Pablo to his core.

Luke steeled himself and turned around. Although he was inured to it, largely, those visions still stuck with him, haunting his memory and dreams. His near-perfect memory allowed him to perform his task as Mithras's chosen soldier against the vampire scourge, but it meant everything he saw could be called up whether he wanted that information stored in his brain or not. Maggie, comforting him, had said his humanity, and the fact he still cared so much after surviving and witnessing horrors, was one of the special things about him. He wished he could forget at least some of it. He'd tried numbness, but that hadn't worked in the end, burying him in a world of isolation and depressed loneliness.

He scanned the basement to see if there was anything that should attract his attention. Finding nothing of significance, he moved closer to the bodies. The kills had been brutal. The parents and three children didn't stand a chance when their house became the randomly chosen site of a battle between vampires and werewolves. The vamps had trapped Pieter van den Bergh the elder on this side road and simply taken the house when they wanted to set their ambush for the next round.

As much damage had been done to the bodies, at least their demises would have been fast. He shook his head and stood up, turning around. There was nothing more he could learn from this mess.

When he rejoined his friends upstairs, Sam had her arm around Pablo's shoulder as he rested his head against hers. Jan stood to the side, minding his own business with the people who were virtual strangers to him. Luke didn't hear any gun fire outside.

That mystery was solved a moment later when Pieter jogged up to the door and popped his head in. "Cleaned them out over there. At least as far as I can tell."

"Thanks, Pieter. We should get everyone gathered up. We're bound to get someone officious here soon to check out this mess."

"Did you find father's…" Jan stopped before saying "body."

"No. None of the bodies are him," Pieter replied. "I have the box van we used on its way so we can clear out the bodies."

"That's a good idea," Luke replied. "We don't want to leave any evidence that'll interfere with what we're trying to do."

"What about father?" Jan asked.

Luke put his hand on Jan's shoulder, giving it a reassuring squeeze. "Right now, no news is good news. If we're not finding him here, that means there's still a chance he's alive. He's far more valuable to the fangers breathing than dead."

Luke was nearly as worried about his friend as his sons were, but right now, the best thing he could do was remain strong and in control to ensure things didn't worsen.

Jan nodded.

One of Pieter's werewolves jogged up and said in Flemish, "The van is here."

"Good, get the bodies loaded up and get out of here. Take them back to Antwerp so we can deal with it there," Pieter replied.

Sam cleared her throat. "What do we do about…downstairs?"

Pieter looked confused.

"The bodies of the people who owned this house. The vampires were not kind when they took this house," Luke supplied.

"They'll have to be left for the local authorities. We'll investigate later and intervene if we need to," Pieter said.

Luke nodded. "OK. Let's move—"

"Luke, get out here!"

Just starting to come down from the initial adrenaline dump, a new one surged through his veins at the sound of urgency. Luke ran to the door and through it, Pieter joining him. Jamaal waited for him at the corner of the house and turned and walked back to the road. When Luke cleared the corner of the house, he saw what had drawn the attention of Jamaal. The bright beams of a car illuminated the tiny road.

"What's going on?" Luke asked.

"They pulled up and parked a minute ago," Jamaal replied.

Luke squinted, trying to determine the newest threat. "Did they look like cops or anything?"

Jamaal shrugged. "Don't know. Couldn't see. It's darker than the inside of my boot out here. They stopped and flipped the lights on. They've been sitting there since."

While they waited, someone stepped out of the car and stepped in front of the lights. They held their hands in the air and slowly walked forward.

"Dogs!" the silhouette yelled in Flemish.

"What do you want?" Pieter replied.

"We have the old man!" He waved one of his hands. "We'll call you with instructions. If you want him back alive, you'd better listen." He bent down and set something on the ground. "I'm going to leave now. If you try to stop us, we will kill the old man. If you kill any more vampires, the old man dies. The more transgressions you stack up at his door, the longer we'll take doing it, and it takes a long time for a werewolf to die. Do you understand, dog?"

"I do," Pieter replied.

The silhouette backed away and slid into the passenger side. The door slammed shut, and the car moved in reverse, pulling into the field before turning around and slamming into drive, sending up a cloud of dirt and dust from the field. When their taillights disappeared around a corner, Luke and Pieter walked up to inspect what the vampire had left.

Luke pulled out his cell phone and turned on the flashlight. Together, they squatted over the cheap burner phone, checking to make sure it was as it should be. When Pieter looked at him, Luke shrugged. Pieter picked the phone up and looked over the mobile device, popping off the battery cover and sliding it back into place.

"Looks like a mobile," Pieter replied. He turned the mobile phone on and looked through it. "Nothing here."

"When we get a moment, I'll have Jamaal check it over for any tracking or bugs we don't want giving us away. Do we wait here for a few more minutes, or do we move out?" Luke asked.

"We've been here too long. We need to move," Pieter replied.

"Right." Luke placed his hand on Pieter's shoulder. "We'll get him back."

Pieter nodded. "Get everyone back to the bed-and-breakfast. They've got my father. I don't think they'll make another run at us tonight."

"I'll see you shortly." Luke turned and walked back to the crowd waiting to see what was happening next.

Once his team was in their ride, they took off for the short drive back to their bed-and-breakfast.

"Do you think we'll be safe? Do you think they know where we're staying?" Sam asked.

"Probably. To both. But we should keep a watch tonight. I'll take the first one. Tomorrow, we'll go to ground for a few days and sort things out." Luke turned and stared out the window at the dark farmland rolling by. They weren't covered in trenches like a hundred years ago, but they were just as blood-soaked after tonight.

CHAPTER
FOUR

The following morning, Luke and Pieter met in Luke's room to discuss their next move. Pieter paced back and forth, his anger barely contained under the surface.

Luke tried to keep his turmoil under control, wanting to be a steadying influence for his friend. "Pieter, you'll need to trust me. Give Jamaal time to run through the phone to make sure it's not going to track us. If it's good, I know a place we can hide out for a few days."

"If it's one of your properties, whoever is fucking betraying us might have that information," Pieter replied.

Luke raised an eyebrow at the profanity from his friend. Usually he was more collected and rarely cursed, at least to Luke's recollection. "Not this place. It's not one of the properties I told your father about." Luke stood up and grabbed his shoes, before sitting down again to put them on.

Pieter stopped his pacing and looked at Luke, eyes squinting. "Will it be habitable?"

"It's ready." He paused and looked at Pieter. "Have you called Amiata yet?"

He shook his head. "Not yet. Jan and I discussed it. We'll wait until we hear from the kidnappers."

Luke nodded, unsure waiting longer to tell her would do much good, but it wasn't his decision to make. He stood up and headed to the door. "I'm going to go get some breakfast. You should come join me."

Luke walked out and headed downstairs, leaving the door open behind him. A few moments later, the door shut and the sound of Pieter's feet on the floorboards told him Pieter had followed. The rest of the crew was seated in the covered porch dining area surrounded by glass walls. Pieter took a spot next to his younger brother; Luke pulled out the empty chair next to Delilah, sitting down and filling his cup from the coffee carafe in the middle of the table.

"So what's the move?" Delilah asked.

"Right now, we wait. Jamaal is going to dissect the phone. Once we have the go ahead from him, we'll be moving to one of my properties so we can regroup and plan. I don't think anyone anticipated them hitting that hard this fast."

"Yeah. We've barely been here a day and then that." Pablo picked up a plate of bacon and scooped a few pieces onto his plate.

"Did you sense any vampires at the restaurant last night when we left?" Sam asked, grabbing a roll and some butter.

"I didn't," Delilah said.

Everybody at their table stopped talking, looking up from their plates to stare at their friend. Luke really needed to have that talk with her about her father, but he still hadn't found the opportunity.

"Neither did I," Luke said, breaking the silence. "But they have servants other than vampires. Thralls and others who curry their favor can get the job done without us detecting them."

"Are we OK to talk about this stuff here?" Delilah asked.

"Yeah. Pieter paid the staff to clear out after the food was dropped off. There could be listening equipment hidden, but we haven't said anything critical, although we should avoid anything sensitive." Luke grabbed a pastry and tore off a bite, stuffing it in his mouth.

The team took their time enjoying the breakfast. The staff had prepared plenty of extra coffee before leaving them to their privacy. When Luke finished his food, he grabbed a carafe and adjourned to the sitting room to relax and check messages. He'd planned on texting with Maggie after dinner, but by the time they finished with last night's fucked up adventures, he just sent a check-in message saying he was OK and at his bed-and-breakfast. Now, it was the middle of the night back in Portland.

After he filled his coffee up from the carafe, he opened the message from Maggie and smiled. She's sent a couple pictures. The first was a selfie with her and Gwen. The second was a picture with only Maggie. Her soft closed-mouth smile and sparkling blue eyes lit up her pretty face — a stray strand of blond hair falling over her forehead begged to be lifted out of the way. It had been a long time since he'd had someone to miss while he traveled; now he had two some-ones. It wasn't the worst problem to have.

"Is that your girlfriend?" Jan asked.

Luke hadn't heard him walking up, too absorbed with thinking about Maggie. He handed Jan the phone.

"Sort of. I guess for all practical purposes, yes," Luke replied.

"She's very pretty. Is the kid hers? Yours? Both?" he asked, handing the phone back.

"No. It's a long story, but to make it short — she's my ward." Luke closed the photos and grabbed his cup.

"Like Batman and Robin?"

Luke laughed. "Kind of like that. It's funnier when you find out my pet cat is named Alfred."

Jan chuckled and sat down in the chair next to Luke's. "It seems like you rescuing members of my family is becoming a habit."

"I don't know if twice is a habit, but I'm here to help my friends," Luke said.

"It was fortuitous that our paths crossed. Your friendship is a valuable thing to have." Jan refilled his cup from the carafe.

"Luke?" Jamaal slid into the chair on the other side of Luke.

"What's the word, Jamaal?" He hoped he'd get the answer he wanted from the pack's tech expert.

Jan held up his hand, holding Jamaal from answering. He turned his head and yelled, "Pieter. Come here."

Pieter poked his head into the room and, once he saw Jamaal, stepped in and grabbed the fourth chair, completing their circle.

Once Jan lowered his hand, Jamaal continued, "Phone looks clean as far as I can tell. They activated it late yesterday evening. I don't think they had time to do anything to it."

"I'm starting to suspect this was a hit of opportunity." Luke took a sip of his coffee. "Does your father usually have a bigger escort?"

Pieter steepled his hands in front of his face. "Yeah. We've increased his guard since the vampires have been causing more trouble. He thought it would be better to slip out of town with a minimal escort to keep from alerting whoever's selling our secrets."

"OK. Until we hear anything, I think we go to ground. I don't think any of the vampires saw me last night. It's probably best to act as if they know I'm on the ground, but for now, let's disappear," Luke said.

"Is that possible? I'm sure there are vampires in every city watching for any of us," Jan replied.

"There's a pocket on the border where we'll be virtually invisible, and completely invisible to vampires and any of their pets." Luke pulled his phone out and punched in his destination. "It's about a two and half hour drive from here. We'll be deep in Wallonia on the French border, and within striking distance of Mons, Charleroi, Namur, and Liege."

"Where are we going?" Pieter asked.

Luke shook his head. "I'll keep that one to myself for now. Let's split up. I'll drive one car. The other car will head toward Kortrijk along with the gear van, and then I'll send an update if we look like we're away with no unwanted tails. I have an idea for a lunch meet up, then we'll head to our sanctuary."

Jan and Pieter nodded, appreciative of his caution. Once everyone finished breakfast and drank enough coffee, they packed up and left. Pablo, Delilah, and Sam joined Luke's vehicle. Jan drove Jamaal and the other Portlanders, while Pieter volunteered to drive the gear van. With no need to stay together, Luke took off, since they were packed and ready. Within a few minutes, they'd left Belgium and entered the French countryside of Nord Pas de Calais.

"Welcome to France," Luke said. "Please keep your heads and arms in the car at all times. In a few minutes, we'll be passing by Lille, then traversing a few regional nature preserves before we reach our lunch destination—Chimay."

"Oh, too bad, buddy." Delilah patted Pablo on the head. "I know how you like to stick your head out the window and let your tongue hang out your mouth. Maybe if you're a good boy, Luke will give you a belly rub when we get to our destination."

"Hey." Pablo turned to look at Delilah in the back seat. "Don't underestimate the joy of a good belly rub."

Luke chuckled, the banter of his friends lightening the dark clouds hanging over him. Before they passed Lille, Luke had Pablo relay the next instructions to Jan and Pieter, sending Jan toward Charleroi and Pieter toward Mons. They weren't in a terrible hurry, so Luke picked the more scenic roads through the nature preserves, stopping a few times to stretch their legs and take some pictures, although everyone refrained from posting to social media where the images would be geotagged. They even asked an elderly English couple to snap a few pictures of them so they'd have a group shot.

He enjoyed showing his friends the lovely French countryside. It helped to distract him from the growing worry at what they were facing. His friends, ever sensitive to his mood, kept up their joviality to help assuage his growing anxiety.

After their last stop, Luke directed Pieter in the van to wind along the border to the Auberge at Chimay, relaying the same information to Jan when that vehicle neared Charleroi. Luke and his car were the first to arrive at Chimay's Auberge.

Luke walked up to the host's podium and switched to French. "I have a reservation under Luc Grandbois."

"Ah, yes. Come with me, Monsieur Grandbois, we have your tables ready," the maître d' replied.

"Excellent. The rest of my party should be along shortly," Luke said.

"Very good, sir."

Luke and his friends followed the man to the back of the restaurant into a smaller private section. They started with a round of

Chimay Doree while they waited for everyone else. When the rest of the team arrived, Luke ordered plates of the famed monastery's cheeses to start, then several regional specialties for his friends from Portland as well as a few different Chimays. Luke, Pieter, and Jan kept things reasonable since they had to drive, only having a glass or two of the lower alcohol Doree. It wouldn't be a hardship; Luke planned to buy a few cases of beer on the way out so they'd have stock when they got to their hideout.

After they loaded their beer and a few chunks of cheese, Luke took Jan and Pieter aside and whispered a phrase into their ears, asking them to repeat it to him.

"What does it mean?" Pieter asked.

"What language is that?" Jan looked confused.

"It roughly translates to 'Mithras guide me and watch over me.' It's an ancient Persian dialect. It was a defunct language by the time I learned it in the mountains of Armenia in 117 CE. You'll start to feel foggy the closer we get, along with an urge to turn off and drive in a different direction. Keep that phrase in your mind. Say it out loud if you need to. It'll let you push past those feelings and keep following me. If you end up making a wrong turn, just park and call me. I'll come collect you. Got it?"

They both nodded.

"You'll know you're in the right spot once you work your way down a steep, windy road. At the bottom, you'll see the cottage," Luke said.

They nodded again.

"Alright, let's get out of here." Luke turned and hopped into the SUV he was driving.

"Giving some directions?" Pablo asked from the back seat.

"Something like that. I had to inform them of the pass phrase to keep in their mind when we approach the cottage. Otherwise, they won't be able to find it." Luke backed out of the parking space.

"Wait." Sam turned in the front passenger seat to more fully face Luke. "Do you have a magic house, Luke?"

"No. The house isn't magic," he replied.

"You're going to be cagey about this, aren't you?" Sam asked.

"It'll be my surprise. I'll answer questions to your heart's content…mostly, when we get there. We'll arrive in about an hour." Luke pulled out of the parking lot and pointed their small caravan northeast.

Luke's friends enjoyed the drive down the two-lane road through the winding, rolling hills of Wallonia, fields interspersed with patches of forests mixed between deciduous and evergreen trees. They kept reasonably quiet, taking advantage of the downtime to find some inner peace after the events of the previous night. Seeking solace in song, Luke turned on his playlist, Joshua Radin's "No Envy No Fear" emerging from the speakers. Taking a right, Luke pulled onto a bridge over a winding river.

"What's the name of this river?" Sam asked.

Luke turned his head a little so he could speak to everyone. "The Meuse. We're almost there. So just a warning. You're going to feel weird as we get closer. You'll want to turn around, especially as we make a final turn to the road leading down to the cottage." When they pulled into Heer, Luke took a left onto N989 and continued north. "In a few minutes, we'll be driving along the edge of my property. You may start to feel the beginning of what I'm talking about."

"Yeah, I'm feeling it," Delilah said, looking decidedly uncomfortable.

With a small smirk on his face, Luke kept an eye on his friends as they got squirmier the closer they got to his property. Checking the rearview mirror one last time to ensure Pieter and Jan were behind him, he pulled off N989 and parked. He stepped out of the SUV and opened the gate, waving the other SUV and the box van through before returning to his SUV.

"Dude, dick move making us sit here with this," Pablo complained.

Finally relenting, Luke spoke the ancient Persian phrase and watched as his friends visibly relaxed.

"Will you have to renew your magic words? Or are we OK now that we're here?" Delilah asked.

"They're not magic words, it's just Old Persian." Luke repeated the phrase again. "'Mithras guide me and watch over me' is what it means. While you're staying here, you're under the protection Mithras affords me."

Luke put the SUV back in drive and pulled onto the narrow road leading down the side of the cliff that overlooked the Meuse and his property.

"Whoa…" Pablo gasped as they pulled through the trees that blocked the view.

"Welcome to the cottage," Luke said.

The property was nestled in a bend of the river and featured a large, old building that might be more properly categorized as a small château than a cottage. Three stories high, the cottage featured arches over the first-floor windows and elegant gables along the roof. A large solarium wrapped around the southern side. The landscaping, while sparse, was neatly maintained. Once they made it down the driveway, Luke parked next to Jan and Pieter.

Luke's car joined everyone else in getting out and stretching their legs.

"Did you call this place a 'cottage'?" Jan asked Luke.

"Yeah, I'm not sure he's aware of what a cottage is…" Pablo said. "Luke, this place is swanky."

"Who takes care of it?" Sam asked. "I would have figured it would be overgrown."

"Is it going to be all dusty and dirty inside? Bruh, I didn't fly across the Atlantic to clean your house." Delilah crossed her arms and stared at Luke.

"Don't worry. I employ caretakers."

"You trust random people to take care of your castle?" Pablo's eyebrows arched up. "That doesn't seem in character."

"They're not random. The family who takes care of this place has done so for a very long time. They are completely loyal to me and are compensated extremely well. Let's go inside. I'll show you around my humble abode." Luke climbed the few stairs to the entrance and punched in a security code to open the door. "I'll get you all codes."

"Luke, where's the nearest restroom?" Sam asked.

"Down this center hall, last door on the left." Luke picked up an envelope set on a side table. He walked to the first door on the left. "When you're done, we'll meet here, in the bar."

"Dude, you have your own bar?" Pablo followed Luke in.

The bar wasn't large, but it featured several tables and chairs tucked beneath dark wood walls covered in tin brewery signs from Belgium's past and present.

Luke stepped behind the bar and grabbed a glass. Turning on the sound system, he found Nathaniel Rateliff & The Night Sweat's "Howling at Nothing" to play. He smiled as the easy groove of the music settled into his bones as his head bobbed along. "Now it's my turn to pour you a beer. What can I get for you? Looks like my caretaker put a keg of Caracole Troublette Blanche and their Nostradamus Quad on. They're local. Also, Bavik Super Pils and soda water."

"Well, not sure I'm ready to tuck into a quad yet."

Luke flipped the glass over and pushed it down on the glass rinser, sending a jet of cold water into the upside down glass. Shaking the last drops out, he flipped it over and set it under the faucet and pulled the tap handle, pouring a perfect beer up to the 25cl line with a thick, pillowy head on top.

Pablo picked up the glass and lifted it to salute Luke. "If you ever give up the vampire slaying game, I've got a job for you behind the bar. You know your way around a tap."

Luke winked at him and pulled another glass out to rinse and fill. He set the glass of blanche on the bar when Pieter walked in.

"Pour one of those for me too?" Pieter asked.

Luke slid the glass over and grabbed another. As his friends filtered in after using the restroom, he poured blanches for everyone except Jan, who took a Bavik. When he finally poured his own, he grabbed a chair at the tables clustered together as one large table.

"So how long are we here, Luke?" Jamaal asked.

"As long as we need to be. Once we hear from the vampires, we can plan our next move, but for now, we stay off the grid. We have plenty of beer. There's some wine kicking around as well. The chef is excellent. They'll have dinner prepared for us this evening at seven.

Not so elaborate as 't Hommelhof or today's lunch, but you can only eat that way so often."

Pablo patted his stomach. "Speak for yourself. Being married to Tony, my belly has become accustomed to a certain lifestyle that it's unwilling to give up."

Luke chuckled. "Don't worry. If we're here long enough, I'll have them arrange a proper banquet."

He hoped they'd be there for a little while. Just being on the property felt good, knowing they had more protection here than anywhere else they might choose to stay. The old familiarity of the land sank in, leaching some of the tension from his shoulders, though the addition of his new friends would change the feel of the place. It had been a long time since he hadn't been alone here.

uke shivered. As he squinted, trying to focus his eyes against the glare of the sun and cold wind buffeting his face, he shaded his eyes with his hand, angling it to block some of the wind. He failed. The wind nearly seemed sentient, seeking out his defenses. He couldn't be sure if his eyes were clearing, the surrounding white reflecting the sun. He clamped his eyes shut and took in a deep breath, the cold air biting his lungs, then released it slowly, opening his eyes gradually in time with the exhalation.

His vision sharpened, the tableau before him coming into crisp contrast. He stood on a field of snow on the side of a mountain, a reasonable sized stone shelf providing him a place to stand on the side of the ragged peak. Looking down, he realized why the cold sank into his core. He only wore a pair of pajama bottoms—the new ones Maggie had bought him with vertical black and silver stripes. Why would he be on the side of a mountain in his pajamas in Belgium, a country devoid of real mountains and certainly not these soaring towers of stone and snow?

Once again, he closed his eyes, pulling a more appropriate outfit from his memory to enclose him in the imaginary landscape. When he looked down, he wore a thick black cloak with shaggy bear hair covering his shoulders. Two gold medallions bearing the seal of

Marcus Aurelius linked and closed the cloak with a gold chain. His steel armor caught the sun and reflected the sun and snow's glare. Under his thick tunic, he wore black woolen leggings covered in white stars. They'd been his favorite set of woolens given to him by Marpesia during their mission into the Montes Sarmatici—the Carpathians—seventeen hundred years ago. The harsh wind pulled at the transverse centurions crest on his helmet, flicking the long hairs out behind him wildly.

Seeing the woolens and feeling their familiar texture against his skin nearly floored him, his knees trembling as a deep hollow pit opened in his stomach. The sight of the clothing she'd given him brought the feel of her hand against his cheek with it, the softness of her lips against his, the tickle of her hair against his nose as they snuggled together to conserve body heat in the deep cold of the harsh mountain winter during Constantine's Gothic Campaign. As his breathing shallowed, coming in short bursts, the corners of his vision blurred and darkened. He covered his eyes with his hand and reached up to massage his temples with his thumb and middle finger but was blocked by his helmet.

From deep in his subconscious, the calming voice of Dr. Hamdi reached out to Luke, telling him to breathe and hold it, release it and hold it, then repeat. Working his way through the exercise his therapist had gone through with him, Luke brought himself back from the brink of despair. The feelings for his first wife had long been buried until more recently when he'd started talking about her with Maggie. He'd even mentioned a few snippets of their life together to his other friends.

When he'd returned himself to a state of relative calm, he opened his eyes, letting them readjust to the harsh sun reflecting off the snow. Across the ravine, motion drew his eyes. Squinting, he could make out two men dressed in the attire of the Roman legions, one holding up the other as they limped up a rugged path, one of them wore the crest of a centurion. Both men looked wounded. A young adolescent trailed behind them, a bow in one hand with the other holding the end of an arrow nocked and ready to be drawn and shot.

The wind carried on it shouts as the boy drew back and let his arrow fly, quickly pulling another from his hip quiver to chase the first. Luke blinked. When he returned his gaze to the running battle on the nearby mountain, the two Romans had disappeared. The boy had stopped to fire off several more arrows before running after the two men. Luke narrowed his eyes, keeping them glued to the young man as he darted behind a sharp column of stone to disappear into the cliff side.

Before Luke could decide what was happening, he felt fingers hook into his guts and yank him across the ravine. A scream died in his lungs before escaping past his lips as he cringed, turning his face and covering his head with his arms as the invisible force pulled him toward the side of the mountain. But instead of slamming into its side, he continued flying forward, pulled inescapably through the solid stone wall into a cavern.

Torches flared to life as he stood at the juncture of a natural cave and the carved columns and walls of a temple cave—a Mithraeum. Every element of the temple was carved from the mountain. Tall columns rose from the floor and ended along a barrel vault ceiling that, with the two narrow edge running down the length of the temple, looked like a long Omega extending from the front of the Mithraeum to the rear. In front of each column stood tall braziers flickering and releasing light, but they did so without fuel to burn or smoke to cloud the air. Benches jutted out from the wall diagonally, angled so those who sat could focus on the altar at the far end of the temple.

The altar caught every ray of light and reflected it back into the chamber, magnifying its brightness. The central figure, carved from stone, looked nearly alive save for his larger-than-life size. The man wore a green tunic over blue leggings with a red cape at his back and a Phrygian cap on his head. His face bore the features of a Persian, skin painted light brown with olive-tinged tones to match. Under his red cap, black curly hair cascaded down around his ears and shoulders.

The sculptor captured the intense concentration of the man as he heaved back on the head of a bull, holding it still as his short sword sliced the bull's neck, spilling its lifeblood. Every muscle of the man and animal rippled in their struggle. Two painted and carved figures in chariots flew across the painted sky.

Sol Invictus drove his sun chariot led by a team of four white horses. Opposite him, on the right, hovered his celestial counterpart, Luna—though Luke preferred her Greek name, Selene—and her oxen-pulled moon chariot, one ox dark the other light. Along the walls on either side, murals of more deities of the Greek, Roman, and Persian pantheons looked upon the scene at the end of the temple.

Gasping, Luke's eyes widened as the head of the statue turned, the black infinite pools of his onyx eyes seizing Luke. The statue extricated himself from the bull, leaving the animal mid-struggle, captured in its stony stasis. With each step toward Luke, the statue of Mithras softened into the form of a living being—an infinite, divine soul.

Mithras reached out with an open hand. Luke, not thinking, extended his in return but froze as Mithras quickly closed his fist around Luke's spine. Although the deity stood thirty feet from Luke, Mithras held him firmly in his grasp. With a quick yank, Luke slid toward the god. Unsure if the god swelled in size only because Luke drew closer or if he was indeed becoming taller and broader, Mithras towered over Luke as he ground to a halt a few feet away.

Tremors rocked Luke's body as his knees lost their battle with functioning, and he sank onto them, hanging his head to avoid the disappointed look on the face of his patron. The grip inside Luke lessened.

"You have failed to pay me the honors due to me in far too long, Roman." The sound of Mithras's voice boomed through the temple and inside Luke's head.

"I know…" Luke whispered. "I am so tired, Father of Fathers."

"I care not. The duties you owe me are unpaid. The role you accepted is unfulfilled. Darkness spreads across the world virtually unchecked. I am uninterested in the excuses of a less than diligent son."

Eyes firmly fixed on the floor between himself and his patron god, Luke slumped, the last starch leaving his shoulders. "I have failed."

"Not entirely, not while you still have air in your lungs and blood in your veins. Not while you have my sword and the muscle to wield it. You have not failed yet. Rise, son."

Luke bobbed his head in a nod of obeisance. "Aye, Father of Fathers."

He leaned forward and used a hand to brace himself, bringing one foot flat to the ground so he could push off and up. Standing, he swayed before catching himself. He spread his feet to stabilize his base. Although he stood, the stone floor between the two still held his gaze.

"What would you have of me, Father of Fathers?" Luke asked.

"WITNESS!" Mithras extended his ethereal hand and grasped Luke's spine once again and pulled, flinging Luke at the altar.

Luke's muscles tensed, though he couldn't move his body to react or protect himself from slamming into the stone bull. Instead of shattering against the stone, Luke floated through it, coming to a stop in a chamber behind the altar. Before Luke could see what the room looked like, Mithras turned his body. He faced a different altar that disappeared into a series of translucent shadows and lines, as if he were looking through steam or undulating air of the desert heat. Once again, his body was not his to control as he stood as still as Mithras's statue.

The Roman bearing the crest of a centurion stepped into the room. The journey he'd taken to arrive in this temple had taken a toll on the man in his late twenties or early thirties. A broken-off arrow protruded from his thigh just below the line of his tunic, blood soaking the wool of his trousers. Several slashes were visible on his arms, revealing skin and bloody gashes below the ripped wool of his tunic. The edges of his cloak were stained and ragged. Yet, he stood defiantly, his gladius naked, though it to bore the signs of hard use to get here—nicks littered the cutting edges.

Much like it had unfolded for Luke moments ago, Mithras transformed before the young Roman's eyes, becoming a living, flesh being—a live deity eclipsing the room with his size and presence.

"Who comes before me in my home, my sanctuary?" Mithras's

voice boomed through the temple, practically shaking the mountain to its roots deep in the earth.

The centurion fell to his knees, grunting in pain as he bent over low to pay respects to the god who suddenly confronted him.

"Father of Fathers! Forgive me for intruding upon your sanctuary," the man replied, his voice edging along the line between control and terror.

"Speak thy name," Mithras boomed.

"Lucius, Father of Fathers, Lucius Silvanius Ferrata, a centurio of the Roman Legions. I have been sent on behalf of Roma's Imperator and on the order of the Pater Patrum who serves the Imperator."

"I ordered that the finest warriors of Roma be sent to me, yet you are alone."

Lucius pulled back slightly. "I am not alone. A legionnaire of Roma is with me, though he is nearly unconscious and may soon succumb to his injuries, and an Armenian boy of noble blood."

Mithras looked up and directed his gaze through the walls that separated Lucius from his two companions. **"I have no use for boys or the nearly dead."** He returned his gaze to Lucius. **"Rise to your knees, Centurio of Roma."**

Lucius obeyed, sitting on his knees while directing as much weight to his uninjured leg as possible.

"And what rank amongst my servants do you hold, Centurio?" Mithras asked, his voice slightly less booming and piercing.

"I have achieved the fifth rank of Perses, Father of Fathers."

Mithras stepped forward and bent over. The centurion visibly held himself still—his body vibrating with the effort—not giving into his urge to pull away from the overwhelming presence of the deity. Mithras placed his hands on Lucius's head, a palm on each temple. Lucius's eyes shot open and froze as his entire body went rigid. His mouth slowly opening, Luke winced as Lucius unleashed a deep scream that started low and rose to vibrate off the stone. It reached through to the core of Luke's gut.

Luke felt the phantom pains of his ancient self as he watched the old memory brought to life. His breathing shallowed and quickened, his body taut with tension.

When Mithras released Lucius, the man's body slumped to the floor as his chest heaved to get air into his lungs. Mithras stepped away, caressing the neck of the stone bull before turning around to look down at the soldier. Life stirring in the centurion, he forced himself onto his hands and knees, his lungs still heaving as a line of spittle dripped from his lip until he forced himself back onto his knees, using the back of his hand to wipe away the drool.

Lucius raised his head, his gaze unsteady but with an edge of strength or defiance in it. He didn't quite raise his eyes to Mithras's, but this was the boldest he'd looked since entering. As he kneeled before his deity, his body swayed in a wobbly circle.

Mithras's back straightened as he rose to his full height, fixing his eyes on the centurion. **"Are you willing to serve?"**

"Aye, Father of Fathers." Lucius's voice gasped out, raw and ragged from the soul rending scream he'd let out a few moments earlier.

"Until the task I lay upon you is done?"

Luke closed his eyes and hung his head. He hadn't realized how long "done" would take. After nearly two thousand years, the mission he'd accepted blindly still looked nowhere near completion. Opening his eyes, he snorted. The illusion of choice.

"Aye, Father of Fathers. I will serve you until you release me."

"DONE!" Mithras reached out, his hand disappearing into the centurio's chest.

Lucius's body convulsed, his arms thrown wide, as the god grasped his heart, his face locked in a primal but silent scream. When Mithras withdrew his hand, Lucius collapsed into a heap on the stone floor, unmoving save for the ragged rise and fall of his chest.

As Mithras turned, the altar slowly transformed, melting into a new shape. The bull, now dead, lay on its side, its tongue lolling out of its mouth, a stream of crimson blood extending from the gash across its throat. Sol Invictus dismounted from his chariot and glided forward, growing as he strode forward until he stepped out of the stone and joined Mithras as a being of flesh and enormity. The two gods clasped hands before taking a seat on the dead bull, one on each end of the carcass. A black kylix appeared in Mithras's hands. The wide, shallow bowl had two handles and a base extending from its bottom. In intricate detail, several Mithraic scenes in the red-brown of the clay covered the outside of the kylix around its edge.

After taking a deep drink of wine, Mithras handed the kylix to Sol Invictus, who drank deeply as well. Above, Selene stepped down from her chariot and glided toward Mithras and Sol Invictus until she too joined them, standing tall and lively, a gentle rosy blush tinging her pale cheeks.

Selene nodded to Sol. "My brother."

Sol smiled at the luminous goddess. "Sister."

Turning to Mithras, she smiled. "Mehr, my friend."

The corner of Mithras's lips tipped up slightly as his eyes warmed into genuine affection. "My dearest, Selene."

Sol handed her the kylix. Selene took it in both hands and bent her neck to place her lips on the edge, gently tipping some wine into her mouth. Sighing happily, she handed the kylix back to Mithras and turned around, walking to the lump on the floor.

Selene lowered herself gracefully, reaching out and running her hand along Lucius's jaw until her fingers rested just under his chin. "Rise, my brave soldier."

The centurion's breathing calmed as he pushed himself off the ground, her gentle fingers aiding him until he was once again on his knees. A soft smile on her face, Selene leaned close to Lucius until her lips were barely a hair's breadth from his left ear. She rested her left hand on his right cheek.

Luke felt the warmth of a hand on his cheek, but when he reached up, found only his own hand and face. When Selene whispered into the centurion's ear, the words also fell on Luke's ears.

"The night is your domain now. My gift to you is clear perception and bright vision. No more will the darkness shroud your eyes, nor will the creatures who hunt the night be able to cloud your mind. Now stand, my champion of the night." Selene stood up and offered her hand to the Roman who took it and stood.

The soft words of the goddess coaxed the tension from Luke's body as he watched the scene that had unfolded one thousand nine hundred and two years earlier. For the first time since he'd entered the temple, Luke let his lungs fill to bursting with air before letting it out to carry more rigidity from his muscles.

Lucius's hand still in the goddess's, she led him forward until he stood before the two gods reclining on the slain bull. Sol Invictus stood, extending his hand toward the centurion. Lucius took it, and the man and god shook.

"To you, soldier of Roma, I give you the intensity of the sun — the speed of its light, the strength of its fury, and the clarity of its purpose." Sol Invictus released Lucius's hand and returned to his seat on the bull's hindquarters.

Finally, it was Mithras's turn. He stood, also taking Lucius's hand to shake. **"My gifts to you will protect your body and extend your life. The steel that encases you shall be your sanctuary."**

Mithras snapped his fingers, and Lucius's armor glowed intensely, forcing him to close his eyes. Standing on the other side of the altar, Luke was able to watch without having to squint. Sparks flew from the centurion's armor. When they settled, Lucius's segmented lorica and the manica running down his right arm were covered in engravings in Latin, Greek, and Old Persian. Luke reached down and rubbed his fingers over one of the bands on the armor he wore, feeling the engraved words that had protected him for nearly two millennia.

The centurion's helmet, likewise, had received its own set of engravings, as well as several more brass ornamentations than it had before. The steel greaves, which had been simple steel wrapping around the front of Lucius's legs, were transformed into works of art. On the left knee, the moon of Selene rose from the steel. On the right knee, the sun of Sol Invictus formed its companion. Along the shins, the scene of Mithras quelling the bull stood proudly.

"Your sword, Centurio," Mithras said.

Lucius pulled it from its sheath and laid it across Mithras's outstretched palms. The god's palms flared with light, forcing Lucius to close his eyes. When he opened them, his simple gladius, with its long point and tapered waist, now featured elaborate engravings.

Mithras offered the blade to his soldier. The dark wood of the pommel ball and hilt guard remained the same, as did the bone handle. On one side of the blade, another of Sol's suns extended from the hilt guard out onto the steel, sending its rays of light flickering down to the tip. Lucius flipped the sword over to view the other side. On it, Selene's moon balanced the sun from the inverse side, but instead of rays of light, stars flew from the embrace of the crescent moon's arms.

Luke could see the reluctance in the centurion's eyes when it came time to sheath the sword, not wanting to take his eyes of the beautiful weapon, but he put it away none the less.

"Lucius Silvanius Ferrata, do you know the story of a rudis?" Mithras asked, turning away from the centurion.

"Aye, Father of Fathers. They are given to a gladiator to free them from their slavery."

Mithras turned around. A wooden sword lay across the god's palms. **"And so shall this one free you from servitude."**

Luke took it from the god when he extended his arms toward the centurio. "Free me from servitude to what?"

"Death."

Lucius looked up, his eyes going wide as blood drained from his face.

"Its use shall extend your life and give you the power of your enemies so you may use it against them."

Lucius, trembling, licked his lips. "How?"

Mithras leaned forward and whispered into his ear, **"Place it into the heart of the monster you have defeated, then place your head upon the pommel and whisper the incantation. It will transfer the blood demon's ill-gotten gains to you, giving you speed, strength, and life beyond what even Sol and Selene have granted you."**

Like Selene's words, Mithras's whispered words dripped into Luke's ear as well. The tension he'd released earlier returned in some measure, thinking of the full implication of Mithras's "gift" and the dark side of its practical applications.

"Father of Fathers, I thank you and Sol Invictus and Selene for these gifts, but I'd ask a boon of you..." Lucius bowed his head respectfully.

"What else would you have of us, my brave soldier?" Selene asked, a soft smile spreading across her face.

"My friend, he won't live long, not once we leave this cavern. Can you heal his injuries?"

Seline gracefully bent her long neck, nodding. "It is done."

The sound of a large bird's caw drew everyone's attention toward the wall to Lucius's left as a spectral raven flew through the stone wall to land on Selene's shoulder. Her eyes lost focus as the raven clicked its beak near her ear. When the bird finished, her soft smile was replaced with a frown that furrowed her brow.

Selene addressed Mithras and Sol. "Our enemies await our soldier outside, a great horde."

The cavern trembled slightly, although Luke couldn't feel the ground shaking. No dust flew or rocks fell, the quake a psychic reaction to the gods' anger at having their mountain disturbed by the vampires that waited outside.

Sol stood and extended his hand. "Your sword for a moment, Centurio."

Lucius pulled it out and handed it to him. Sol wrapped one hand around the hilt while covering the pommel with the other. He closed his eyes for a moment, then handed Lucius his sword back. Mithras stood and walked to the wall, rubbing his hand over a seam that appeared. A line of light formed on the stone until an opening appeared, a blast of cold air pumping through the door.

"Go gather your friends and leave through this exit," Mithras instructed.

"Run, but when you have no choice but to fight, put your gladius through the heart of the first demon you can," Sol said.

Lucius bowed deeply. "It shall be as you say. I will carry out your will and fulfill my pledge."

Lucius rose and jogged out to gather the young man and the boy who'd accompanied him. Soon, they reappeared and ran to the exit. The man and boy ran through, ignoring the room. Lucius turned and took one last look, nodding to the three deities as they nodded in return. When the centurion disappeared, they turned to Luke.

Sol Invictus nodded at Luke and faded away.

Mithras's gaze bore down on Luke, causing his knees to tremble, and nearly forced him to the ground. ***"REMEMBER."*** Then he, too, faded away.

Only Selene remained. She walked forward and stood before Luke, the gentle smile returning to her lips. When Luke dared raise his eyes to meet hers, he was nearly overwhelmed by the sadness and empathy pouring from them. She brought her hand up and laid it across his cheek.

"Your journey has been far longer than any have foreseen. I am glad you have joined forces with some of my children. You were never meant to stand alone under this burden. Let those who are willing shoulder it with you. Keep going, my brave soldier. The world needs you, both your arm and your spirit. My blessing is still upon you.

"And one last word, look you to Camaracum, the center of power of your ancestors, and do not tarry long if you wish to save your friend. Time is not on your side." She leaned down, placed a kiss in the middle of his forehead, and disappeared.

The morning after Luke's vision, he sat in the large glass enclosed solarium in a cushy chair, an espresso on a side table and an old book in his hand. Though Mithras's presence and less than subtle reminder were intense, the final renewal of Selene's blessing had brought with it a modicum of serenity he so rarely felt. He flipped the page, then picked up his tiny cup for a sip when Delilah and Sam walked in.

"I don't know if I've ever seen him look so relaxed. He almost looks chillaxed," Sam said to Delilah.

"Not without Maggie around at least," Delilah replied.

Luke slid a bookmark into his book and set it down. "It's been a while since I've been here. Besides, I'm just another duck on the pond. Would you like coffees?"

"You can make espresso too?" Pablo asked as he walked in. "You've been holding out on all your valuable skills."

"Cappuccinos?" Luke asked.

When everyone nodded, he went to the coffee machine and pulled four espressos, one for himself, and foamed some milk, constructing four cappuccinos. Serving them to his friends, he joined them and talked amiably, renewing their friendship for another day.

Taking the last sip of his coffee, Luke set the cup on its saucer, a touch of anxiety seeping into his being. "I would like to show you all something, the reason we're safe here. It's... If you have any religious objections, I'll understand, though."

"Why you so nervous, buddy?" Pablo asked.

"It's my Mithraeum. I haven't been in it in a while. A long while. I've been..." He hesitated, his shoulders tense and his brow furrowed. "I've been avoiding my religious duties for a long time."

"Why?" Sam asked. "Isn't that how you maintain your powers?"

Luke looked around to make sure they were still alone. "I know this sounds petulant, but I've not been terribly grateful to my benefactor for this life. I've said it before, but the twentieth century did a lot of damage to my psyche. I don't know if I've told you this, but I've been in therapy for a while now. I think I'm proving a bit difficult for Dr. Hamdi."

Pablo chuckled and reached over and patted Luke's knee. "I bet. Where do you start with a two-thousand-year-old man with way more than the average amount of trauma per year of life?"

"Something like that. Anyway, I've been more than resentful for something I didn't exactly seek or understand when I initially accepted the responsibility."

"I always just assumed you were some farm boy chosen by whoever, and it involved some prophesies from the Oracle at Delphi or something," Delilah said, placing her empty cup on its saucer.

Luke chuckled. "No prophesy that I'm aware of, anyway. And I'm not sure I qualify as a farm boy; my mother and father weren't farmers." The smile slid off his face. "In reality, I got here because of two things—duty and surviving. I'm sure it was meant for my centurion to be the one. He was from a prominent family closely allied with Trajan. I'm just the only one sent on the mission to survive and make it to Mithras's temple. When I got there, I dutifully accepted the mission that was placed upon me by the gods."

Pablo made an "s" sound, then said, "Gods? As in plural? How many powerful immortals do you have riding your saddle?"

"Three were there that night—Mithras, who I've mentioned before, Sol Invictus, the unconquerable sun, and Luna, the goddess of the moon."

"The goddess who took in the werewolves when they ran away from their creators?" Sam asked.

"Yes, Selene. There are some different aspects between the Roman Luna and the Greek Selene, but she was there." Luke smiled tenderly. "She is a gracious and kind deity, at least with me she was, is…"

"Is?" Delilah's eyebrows rose.

"I think I'd like to save that story for the cave, if you're willing to join me."

"You know I'm down, buddy." Pablo smiled, downing the last of his coffee.

Sam nodded and smiled. "Me too."

"I'm not sure my granny would like me fraternizing with pagan gods, but as long as you don't rat me out, I'll join you," Delilah said.

Luke zipped his lips, locked them, and threw the key away. "Your secret is safe with me." Looking at everyone, he stood. "I've prepared some food for us to take. We can share it inside. It's traditional to share food in the Mithraeum. Pablo, mind helping me with the basket?"

Luke and Pablo grabbed the baskets from the kitchen and met Sam and Delilah out front. Stepping into the lead, Luke headed toward an outbuilding against the rock wall backing the property. It sheltered the spot upriver and downriver, isolating it except for the narrow road leading down the edge of the cliff. After punching a code into a pad next to the door of the outbuilding, Luke ushered his friends in. On another keypad inside, Luke punched in a different code, and the back wall slid down into the earth.

"That's slick as shit, dude." Pablo nodded appreciatively.

"He does like his secret doors," Sam added.

"If I can't have cool secrets and fancy doors, what even is the point of living this long?" Luke set the basket down and pulled a flashlight and a lighter from the basket, shoving the latter into his pocket where he could reach it easily. After picking up the basket, Luke pushed the flashlight's button and stepped into a natural fissure in the stone. "Watch your head here; you'll want to duck."

He slipped under the low hanging rock and straightened up,

turning to the right. After twenty feet, he stopped, waiting for everyone to join him. He shuffled nervously as Sam took her time admiring the cave, strolling with her hands in her pockets.

"Sorry, Luke, I just like caves and this one is pretty neat," Sam said. "Please, lead the way."

"This is it." He handed the flashlight to Delilah. "Mind lighting the way so I can ignite the braziers?"

Delilah nodded and took the flashlight. Luke pulled the lighter from his pocket and stepped into the Mithraeum. The braziers flared to life, spilling a delicate silvery light from their iron bowls. Mid step, Luke stopped and nearly fell over at the unexpected illumination.

"Well, that's cool. Did your caretaker upgrade the lighting?" Pablo asked.

"No." Luke walked over to the nearest brazier and looked over the edge of the rim.

The caretaker had prepared the braziers with oil—it was standard procedure to have the Mithraeum readied for him even if he didn't end up visiting it—but the wick was unlit, nor was the light the color of dancing flames.

"It's beautiful, Luke," Sam said, stepping into the room and looking around.

The caretaker's eldest daughter, a trained artist, had appointed herself the guardian of the Mithraeum and studied the art of Mithraeums as well as ancient art in general. Luke had always kept the walls of the cavern whitewashed, but she'd used the space to paint Mithraic scenes in vibrant colors, trying her best to match the colors and techniques of the ancients.

It had taken his workers months to shape the fissure in the rock into a rectangular room with tall walls and a barrel vault ceiling. As the original paintings faded over time, he'd hired artists to renew them, but none had ever done a finer job so perfectly taking the temple back to its original roots. She'd even applied a fresh paint job to the tauroctony central to the story of Mithras.

"It is beautiful," Luke said, trying to take in everything at once.

"You sound surprised," Delilah said, standing next to him.

"I've not seen her work before. I mean, I've seen her art. She emailed me images when she pitched the idea of renewing the art in here, but I never opened the images she sent when she was finished."

"Who's 'she'?" Sam asked.

"Why not?" Pablo asked at the same time.

Still looking around, a look of awe and wonder on his face, Luke explained, "She is the current caretaker's daughter. Anne-Marie is a trained artist."

"I'll say." Delilah stepped closer to one of the images along the wall.

Sam walked back over to Luke and linked her arm with his. "Why didn't you look at her work?"

"I've been avoiding everything to do with this cave. I've not visited it in years and years. I think maybe thirty years ago? Maybe more? And even that was a quick inspection to see what work I needed done. I've always maintained this temple, even if I've not been an observant and regular devotee."

Delilah stood next to a brazier and inspected it. "Luke, where's the light coming from? The oil isn't burning."

"Do you really want an answer to that question?" Luke stepped into the center of the temple.

"Yeah, I think I do," Delilah replied.

Luke gestured to the stone benches and sat on one facing the front of the room. Sam sat next to him while Delilah and Pablo took the bench opposite them and faced them and the back of the temple. Pulling out four glasses, Luke handed them out, opened a couple bottles of Chimay White, and split them between the four glasses.

"Feeling like a little day drinking?" Pablo asked, taking a sniff of the Trappist Triple.

"It's traditional when you're on vacation in a foreign country. I'm just giving you the full experience," Luke replied with a friendly smile. He raised his glass to offer a toast. "We've come a long way in almost a year. I couldn't have made it here without you, and I'm glad you're all here with me as we're about to embark on a new, dangerous mission."

They leaned in, tapped their chalices, and sipped. While his friends chatted, Luke pulled out cheese, bread, and fresh fruit, divvying it all out so everyone could break their fast.

Sam popped a grape into her mouth and chewed it before washing it down with a sip of beer. "What changed your mind about entering your temple?"

"I had a dream last night..." Luke let the thought hang unfinished.

"A dream or a *dream?*" Delilah asked.

"A *dream*." Luke told them about his summoning and witnessing himself take his initial oath to the cause of ridding the world of vampires.

"Pieter and Jan aren't going to be happy about Selene's warning," Pablo said.

"No. I don't expect so," Luke replied.

Delilah looked through the basket next to her until she found what she wanted, pulling out another bottle of beer. "How do you know that was a real dream? I mean, not a normal dream, but a god dream?"

Luke looked around at the room, his eyes stopping at the braziers. "We're sitting in the light of the moon now. Selene's gift to me was clarity. She came to me in my dream, she gave me direction, and now she's blessing our gathering with her light. I'd be a fool to ignore such clear signs, especially with her being the velvet wrapping the iron fist of Mithras."

Everyone filled their glasses and sat in quiet, contemplating Luke's words while sipping their beers.

"Well, if we're not waiting for demands, what are we doing and where are we going? If we start causing trouble in Belgium, that'll be a disaster for the Flanders Pack," Delilah said.

"Selene gave me a city. Camaracum," Luke replied. "It was the seat of power for my people, the Nervii. Today, it's known as Cambrai.

"Do we want to move bases?" Sam asked.

"No, I think... I have a feeling we're going to need to be more flexible. We'll base here where we have significant protection and invisibility. Maybe a night here or there, but I think we need to be a mobile force attacking hard behind enemy lines."

"We need some decoys," Pablo said.

"What?" Luke said.

"Well, whoever the rat is inside the pack knows or suspects something is up, especially with the pack leadership trying to be secretive and showing up out in the country. They know Pieter went to Portland, and the vampires know where you are." Pablo took a deep drink of the triple and sighed happily. "Damn, this is good. We need a fake Luke. No one knows what you look like. If Pieter and Jan show up alone, that'll look suspicious."

"Where are we going to get decoys?" Delilah asked.

"We brought them with us," Sam interjected. "We wanted to get Jamaal onto their computers to track down the leak if he can. Send him back with Pieter and Jan. Let him dig around. We can send Will and Tanika to give Jamaal a little more added security."

"So Tanika, Will, and Jamaal go north, and Will gets to pretend to be me." Luke raised his glass and took a drink. "Are you sure they're ready to be out on their own?"

"That's why we brought them. They're ready," Sam said.

"Will they buy it? Has anyone else in the pack seen the real you?" Sam asked.

"Pieter, Jan, their father, a couple bodyguards, one of whom died in Watou, and a man who brought my alias documents last year. Amiata and Olivia Adelisa, but they're safe in Portland." Luke counted off everyone who might recognize him as the Centurion Immortal. "Pieter and Jan can handle anyone who's seen me."

Delilah raised her hand a little to get everyone's attention. "You're forgetting one thing though." She looked around at everyone as if to see if they were going to notice what they were missing. "I imagine you're just as known for your equipment. They're your calling card."

"It shouldn't be too hard to source some here, should it?" Pablo asked.

"Except it creates trails." Luke looked at Sam. "Would someone like a free trip to Antwerp? I can have Maggie and Gwen get the decoy gear from the house, and someone can bring it over. Another person from Portland hanging out with the crew in Antwerp wouldn't go amiss for verisimilitude."

"I'm reluctant to thin our street teams out further with eight of us gone," Sam said.

"They don't need to be fighters. Obviously, there is some risk just because of the situation, but they're not required to fight. Will can handle himself, but everyone is supposed to be behaving themselves, so that shouldn't even matter."

"So just the four of us against France?" Pablo asked.

Luke made eye contact with each of his friends and nodded. "Four of us against France."

CHAPTER
SEVEN

P ablo was right; Jan and Pieter weren't happy with the change of plans, but more so because it took them out of the action and put them on the bench so they could play the part demanded of them by the vampires.

"Are we leaving one of the SUVs with you?" Jan asked as they sat around on the patio by the river, enjoying the afternoon warmth.

"No. I have a ride that's not connected to you in any fashion. I think it's best if we go completely off the grid. No contacting us, no support of any kind. I have enough documents and funds to take care of everything we need. Everyone here has spare aliases as well. I think you should head out first thing in the morning. Let the vamps go to bed, take the back roads until you can lose yourself in Brussels traffic then head home," Luke said.

Pieter nervously tapped his foot. "Should we take care of the tickets from Portland? So they're connected to us?"

"Yeah. Keep a receipt, you can bill me later when we get your father out of this and find your mole. Fly them first class. It'll make it more important, plus whoever Sam gets to volunteer isn't going to be one of our trained fighters, so I want to make the risk worth their while." Luke popped a piece of hard cheese into his mouth.

Pieter chuckled. "We'll be sure to show them a good time and make sure we're seen. I'm confident they've got spies everywhere."

Will, his brow furrowed, shifted uncomfortably in his chair. "Do they know your name?" Seeing Luke's confusion, he clarified. "Do I need to have everyone call me Luke?"

Luke shook his head. "I don't think so. Anyone who might have heard my name is probably dead. It's probably more important to be confident and let the rest of the team appear diffident toward you. It's more important to look like the leader than to have a name that could just as easily be an alias." Luke looked down at his phone as it buzzed.

"Maggie?" Sam asked.

Luke nodded. "I need to take this." Luke grabbed his phone and walked downriver to stand under the shade of a willow, a smile spreading on his face as he answered the phone. "Good morning, Maggie."

"Hi, Luke. How are you doing?" Maggie replied.

"Not bad. I'm glad to hear your voice." Luke's heart warmed at the sound of her voice.

"Me too. Sorry to cut to the chase so quickly, but I got your message. Gwen and I are here to gather up your stuff and feed Alfie, but, um… We can't get into the house."

Luke's brows furrowed. "What? Is the lock not working?"

"I don't know. We can't even get that close to the house. If we move off the sidewalk toward the house, both of us feel…repelled." Maggie sounded slightly frustrated.

"Oh, shit. I think I know what's going on. I think my shrine has awoken." Luke shook his head.

"What?" Maggie sounded confused.

Luke ran his free hand through his hair. "I'll explain later, if that's OK. I can call you back this evening. We're in a planning meeting right now."

"OK, understood. But how am I going to get in?"

Luke explained the pass phrase and had her recite it back to him. When she had it, she put Gwen on so Luke could relay it directly to her as well.

"Would it work on a recording?" Maggie asked.

Luke rubbed his bearded jaw, pondering the question for a moment. "I don't know. I've never tried it. As far as I'm aware, it only works if you receive the words directly from me. Maybe from the caretaker's family... I guess we should try it sometime—for science."

"It's worth a try. Anyway, here we go," Maggie was silent for a few seconds. "We're in. I look forward to your explanation later."

"Thank you, Maggie. We'll talk later. Give a hug to Gwen for me, please."

"I will. We're headed into the clinic today. She's studying while I hold hours. I'm free from noon to two."

"Perfect. That'll be after dinner. I'll call, and we can talk," Luke replied.

"Bye, Luke."

"Bye, Maggie." Luke hung up and walked back to the meeting, a smile on his face and a bit of swagger in his step.

Pieter's brow furrowed, confusion spreading on his face. "I'm not sure I've ever seen you so..."

"Happy looking?" Pablo supplied.

"Yeah," Pieter replied.

"He's got a girlfriend," Pablo teased.

"Maggie? Wait. The pretty doctor with the Polish accent?" Pieter asked.

Luke nodded, smiling.

"Good for you, my friend." Pieter smiled and nodded in acknowledgment.

Luke turned to Sam. "Maggie is picking up the gear. She'll take it with her to the clinic, so let whoever our courier is know."

"Okie dokie. If you don't need me, I'm going to go make some calls. I've got a few emails back already on my volunteer email."

Luke nodded. "I think we're pretty much done here, Sam."

Sam stood and departed to find some privacy.

"Can you keep us up-to-date on your progress?" Jan asked.

"No. Let's not risk it," Luke replied.

"We could do burner phones," Delilah suggested. "It wouldn't be the first time. At least for emergencies."

"She's right. We need some way to communicate if something important crops up," Pieter said.

"Alright. I'll have the caretaker pick us up a couple." Luke picked up his phone and sent a text, receiving a response promptly. "He says he'll drop them off by dinner time."

"That's efficient," Pieter said.

"They're used to it when I'm in country. Émile and his ancestors have worked for me for a long time. I'm not here very often, so they live a pretty sedate life. I pay them very well, so they're more than happy to take care of my needs when I'm here. When I'm not here, they take care of the property, which isn't terribly arduous. The rest of the time, they pursue whatever other interests they have."

"Is that why the caretaker's daughter is an artist?" Delilah asked.

Luke nodded. "Yup. She has all the time in the world to paint and study art. I'm guessing she'll take over when her father retires. Her brother doesn't seem that interested—he's a doctor."

With talk of business done, they sipped German Riesling in the sun and enjoyed the sound of the river and nature, soaking in the peace while they had the opportunity. When the chef called them into dinner, Émile met Luke out front and handed him two boxes with burner mobile phones. Luke took them inside and set them up, giving one to Pieter.

Dinner was a big affair, the last they'd share as a full group for a while. Luke had let the caretaker know they wanted to celebrate, so the chef had planned accordingly. As drinks flowed, their laughter grew loud and more carefree. It felt bittersweet. The camaraderie they were developing, beyond Luke's leadership cadre, showed great promise both for friendship and their ability to fight as a unit. Fortunately, those kinds of bonds would carry over for the occasions when times were tough.

When the alarm he'd set for nine went off, he refilled his glass from the bottle of Vieux Telegraphe Chateauneuf du Pape and strolled out to the chair he'd set up by the river.

He texted Maggie. *Are you free to talk?*

In answer, Maggie called him back.

"Hi, Maggie."

"Hi, Luke. How are you?" she asked.

"Good. Just stepped away from dinner. Got a glass of wine, and I'm sitting by the river."

"Your house is by the river?"

"Yup." He clicked a picture and sent it to her. "Don't share that with anyone. Maybe delete it when you're done."

"It's beautiful. Do you have a picture of the house?" Maggie asked.

He turned around and clicked one of the house, light pouring from the glass walled seating area as his friends laughed and shared drinks.

"That's your house?!" Maggie sounded shocked. "It's huge."

"It's not small," he replied. "If we have the opportunity, I'd love to invite you to stay with me here sometime."

"I'd really like that. I hope we get the opportunity soon."

"How's the kiddo?" Luke asked.

"Good. She's taking a break from studying and watching TV. When we're done, I'm taking her out to lunch. So, what's going on with your house?"

Luke leaned back in the chair, stretching his legs in front of him. "There was an incident last night of the religious type. I have a small temple here and being in proximity to it called down a visitation from Mithras. Well, apparently, it activated or strengthened my shrine back home."

"It was weird. When I stepped on the path to the house, I got the urge to be elsewhere. It was fairly subtle. If I didn't know who you were and what you are, I would have shrugged it off."

"Yeah, it'll repel anyone who isn't welcome. It's particularly strong and subtle on vampires. Mostly it just makes you want to keep moving, but not really aggressively so."

Maggie chuckled. "It's probably good to have some extra security while you're gone. Will I need to call you again to get in?"

"You shouldn't. Just think back to the phrase and you'll be fine."

"It's not going to bring any…unwanted attention to me, is it?" Maggie asked, a bit of trepidation slipping into her voice.

"No. You're safe unless you actively pursue an interaction with Mithras."

"Good. I'm happy with my relationship with HaShem and am not looking for other interactions," Maggie replied.

Luke chuckled, taking a sip from his glass and sighing happily. "You'll be fine." He took another sip. "Damn, I'll have to remember to bring a bottle of this wine home to share with you."

"Good?"

"Very. Hey, you mind putting the kid on for a minute? I want to say hi."

"Sure." Maggie called Gwen over.

Luke and Gwen talked for a few minutes, Gwen asking for him to bring her some chocolate and waffles before she said goodbye.

Maggie took the phone back. "She's been studying Belgium's products. She's not interested in sprouts or endive, but very much is into the waffles and chocolate."

Luke laughed. "I'll make you both proper waffles when I get home; it's kind of hard to transport a waffle. But there will be loads of chocolate. You prefer dark, right?"

"You noticed?"

Luke could practically hear her smile through the phone. "Of course. I'll bring you some tasty stuff. I should get back to everyone."

"Yeah. I'm kind of hungry, and I'm sure the kid is starving. I should take her to lunch."

"Maggie… I miss you."

"I miss you too, Luke. Be safe."

"I will. Talk to you soon." Luke hung up and headed back in. Their mission had gotten off to a bad start, but tonight they'd enjoy their camaraderie while they could. Tomorrow would start the next phase in their war against the vampires of Belgium and France.

PIETER AND JAN and the other half of the Portland team left later in the morning than they intended after staying up later than planned, enjoying Luke's fine collection of wine and liquor. They still looked a bit fuzzy when they climbed in their vehicles and drove off with waves and a promise to keep each other informed if anything important popped up.

Shading his eyes from a sun shining outrageously and entirely too bright, Luke waited until they'd made it up the narrow road and disappeared.

"So what's our ride situation while we're here?" Delilah asked.

Luke smiled and gestured for everyone to follow him. He walked toward the rock cliff and the building next to his hidden entrance to his Mithraeum. Punching in his code, he opened the garage doors, revealing a shiny black Volvo 242GT and a red and white VW Van.

"Huh. Another old Volvo and a VW hippie van?" Delilah shook her head. "Bruh. You're killing me here. Can't you own like a new beemer or something? Do these things even run?"

Luke looked shocked. "Of course they do. They are scrupulously maintained."

Pablo walked up behind them and put a hand on Luke's shoulder. "Cherry rides, dude."

Sam stood quietly to the side. "I like the style, Luke, but Delilah might be right. We may need something that can go faster than a VW bus and easier to get into than a two-door 242GT."

Luke sighed. "Y'all are cramping my style, but you're probably right this time. I'll arrange something a little more suitable, but if you're ready, let's at least go get some lunch and take a swing through Cambrai. I'd like to do some surveillance before we just plunge in."

"It's not quite lunch time yet," Sam said.

"I know a place. It's a nice drive there, then we can head south to Cambrai after," Luke replied.

"Alright," Delilah said.

Sam folded her arms across her chest. "Isn't this all a bit casual? It feels like we should have more of a sense of urgency."

Luke shrugged. "Cambrai is tiny. We have plenty of daylight to get there and do a basic look around. We really can't do much against the vampires until after dark—not until we get an idea where their lairs are. Nothing says we can't enjoy our jobs a little along the way."

"I like European Luke. It's refreshing." Pablo patted him on the shoulder.

Luke snorted and smiled at his friend. "Let's meet down here in twenty minutes. Bring your gear with you in case we need it."

Twenty minutes later, they loaded a locked trunk into the back of the van. Pablo had declared it the vehicle he wanted to ride in, especially since it was roomier than the backseat of the Volvo 242GT. Luke fired up the old VW and pulled out of the garage.

The ride to Brasserie Au Baron, out in the countryside on the border between Belgium and France, was a quiet affair. Everyone enjoyed the scenery while feeling the need for solitude after last night's raucous dinner. Wanting something to keep his mind focused, Luke hit play on his music app, opting for the airy sounds of The Shins "Sleeping Lessons." By the time they arrived, they were ready for lunch on the patio by a small creek. Once they got back on the four-lane D649 heading west, Pablo sat forward, resting his elbows on the backs of both the front seats.

"How about another round of versus?" Pablo asked.

"You got a good one?" Sam asked.

"Oh, yeah. I think I do," Pablo replied, a broad grin on his face.

"Go for it, wolfboy," Delilah said.

"OK. Luke versus Dean and Sam Winchester." Pablo sat back into the bench seat next to Sam.

"Wouldn't we be natural allies, though?" Luke asked. "We're all three exceptionally handsome monster hunters."

"You watch Supernatural?" Delilah asked, incredulity staining her tone.

"Yeah. Maggie introduced me to it. We've been working our way through the series, so no spoilers."

Sam laughed. "I wouldn't think of ruining Maggie's fun."

"So how we measuring this one, Pablo?" Delilah asked, turning so she could more comfortably address Pablo and Sam in the middle row.

"Categories," Sam said. "Let's start with easy ones. Hair."

"Sam has to be the winner there," Luke supplied.

Everyone looked at Luke funny.

Luke shrugged. "What? He's got nice hair."

"Round one goes to young Samuel. Fashion next?" Sam asked.

"I'm going to have to give it to my boy Luke on this one," Pablo said.

"You're very welcome," Delilah said, taking rightful credit for helping Luke update his wardrobe. "And please don't mix in a bunch of plaid flannel so you can cosplay for Maggie."

Sam snorted while Pablo laughed loudly.

"Why do I need to cosplay a monster hunter? I'm the real deal. Sam and Dean should cosplay me," Luke said.

That only set Pablo to laughing harder, Sam and Delilah joining in. After merging onto E19 and passing through the southern outskirts of Valenciennes, the road carried them southwest on the last leg to Cambrai.

"I've got the next category," Delilah said, eyeing Luke. "Car."

"Hands down, Baby is the winner there," Sam said.

Pablo patted Luke's shoulder. "No contest. That Impala is a sweet hunk of Detroit steel."

"So three to one?" Delilah asked.

Luke sighed. "Four to none," he admitted begrudgingly.

"I will say, Luke has way better lairs than the Winchesters," Sam said.

"The Men of Letters base is pretty cool," Luke countered.

"Yeah, but it's in the middle of fucking Kansas, which is conveniently a two-hour drive to everywhere in the US." Delilah rolled her eyes. "And you have a manor house on a beautiful river in Belgium. I firmly put the win in Luke's column here."

Sam and Pablo nodded vigorously.

Luke chuckled, a devious smile spreading across his face. "Who's got the best rag-tag group of misfit sidekicks?"

"Oh, we win that one hands down," Sam said.

"I'm not so sure about that…" Luke said. "None of you are angels. Although Pablo is a cooler werewolf sidekick than DJ, but just barely."

"Thanks, buddy," Pablo said sarcastically.

Luke smirked. "Plus, no wise cracking lesbian computer geniuses here."

"Mmm, Charlie," Sam said, a smile spreading across her face.

Luke caught her serene expression in the rearview mirror.

Delilah's eyebrows furrowed as she pursed her lips and looked back at Sam and Pablo. "Wait. Did Luke just get us debating who has the best sidekicks, as if we're sidekicks?"

"Yup," Luke said smugly.

Pablo chuckled. "I guess Luke gets the win on that one."

They paused the spirited debate as Cambrai appeared in the distance, the VW bus slowly eating up the kilometers as faster and more modern cars whizzed by them on the left.

"We've got a plenty of time before it gets dark. There's a small tank museum around here somewhere. One of the bigger tank battles of WWI took place here," Luke said.

"Were you involved in that one, buddy?" Pablo asked.

"No. I was engaged elsewhere." Luke didn't elaborate.

Neither did they ask for any further details, having learned enough about Luke to know he'd suffered terrible trauma in the trenches and still didn't want to talk about in any kind of detail with them.

"I think we can skip that one. The art museum looks neat, though," Sam suggested.

"As much as I hate to rain on the fun parade," Luke said. "We really should take a spin around town and get a feel for the layout while it's still light. If my feelings are correct, we may be here for a while. We can check out the museum later. We do have a war to fight, after all."

"Luke's right," Sam replied. "We have work to do."

Pablo and Delilah nodded somberly.

CHAPTER
EIGHT

L uke collected the check as the sun made its way to the western horizon. He'd enjoyed the quiet dinner with his three best friends, but as the darkness drew its cloak about Cambrai, he grew increasingly pensive.

"Hey, buddy, what's up? You've gotten quiet." Pablo wrapped his arm around Luke's waist.

"I don't know. I've just got a"—he struggled to find the right way to express his feeling—"heavy feeling. It's been getting worse the closer we get to sunset."

Sam looked thoughtful for a moment, before turning to face Luke. "I know we're usually out much later hunting, but when do vampires start to rise?"

"Maybe an hour before sunset?" he replied.

Pablo stuck his nose into the air and sniffed, turning his face into the light evening breeze. "I'm not picking anything up, at least from this direction."

"Yeah, but Luke's vampy sense is much finer tuned and omni-directional, right?" Sam looked at Luke for confirmation.

He nodded.

"Your contact said this was the place to start," Sam said.

"You sound surprised," Luke replied, tilting his head to accompany his inquisitive expression.

Sam slid her arm under Luke's, taking it in hers to walk beside him. "I realize I'm classified as a supernatural being, but that doesn't mean I'm used to fraternizing with divinities. Unlike you or the Winchesters, I don't have gods on speed dial."

"Let's go find a coffee shop. I want to do some reading," Luke said.

Delilah pulled out her phone and found a coffee shop a few blocks away. There, they could sit and fuel up on some caffeine before wandering the small city to investigate the local illicit phlebotomist population. While Luke's friends chatted quietly, sitting in a far corner of the coffee shop so they wouldn't be overheard, Luke scrolled local news sites and neighborhood bulletin boards.

"You finding anything?" Pablo asked.

"Not too much, actually. About the only thing suspicious is people complaining about a general uptick in 'public drunkenness,' mostly about finding young people passed out in alleys and the like," Luke replied.

"Can I see?" Pablo asked.

Luke slid his phone over.

"Dude. This is in French." Pablo pursed his lips.

"Yup."

"I can't read French." Pablo slid the phone back.

Delilah and Sam snickered at Pablo.

Pablo, looking miffed, turned toward the two women. "Can either of you read French?"

"No, but I'm not trying to read Luke's phone either," Delilah replied.

Sam reached over and patted Pablo's shoulder as he pouted. "So no bodies or missing people?"

"Not that I see, but if they've been hanging out here for a while or plan on it, they may be working on catch and release. This isn't a big town; you wouldn't want to attract too much attention. If people are scared to go out because of too many deaths, it becomes harder to get easy food. If the city picks up police patrols, that makes it harder. If a police officer gets hurt, then you get more cops. Waking up in an alley isn't so bad if you were out having a good time. Who knows, a vampire might even be able to implant pleasant memories with their glamour." Luke shrugged.

"Have you ever been glamoured?" Sam asked.

Luke shook his head. "When you have divine gifts to keep your mind clear, I doubt there's a vamp powerful enough to lay its magic on me. I've faked a few times though."

"Haven't we all…" Delilah said.

Sam snickered, Pablo joining a couple seconds later. Luke just shook his head and scooped up his phone.

"So what's the plan?" Sam asked.

"Back to old school. Let's take a stroll around town," Luke replied.

"Should we split up?" Delilah asked.

Shaking his head, Luke tipped the last of his espresso into his mouth. "Nah. It's a small city. We can walk the downtown core pretty easily. I'd rather keep together instead of split up and get lost, though we should head back to the van to grab my hoodie."

Pablo winked at him. "Feeling chilly?"

"You could say that," Luke replied.

They followed Luke out of the shop and back to the van. In a matter of a couple minutes, they'd geared up. Luke, in his armor with swords on his back, everyone else with stakes stuffed in various pockets. They left the heavy firepower in the van.

Luke mapped a clockwise path around the central core of Cambrai, moving from bar to bar. When Luke felt a twitch, they'd try to chase it down. As they wandered around town, Luke's frustration grew. Between his annoyed huffs and clenched jaw, the team gave him a bit of space as they walked the streets.

Pablo, sidling up to Luke, set his hand on Luke's shoulder. "Ratchet back the angst. You're drawing stares from the locals."

Luke nodded and forced his jaw to unclench, settling into a pose that least looked more relaxed—even if he didn't feel it. He knew vampires were in the city somewhere. Selene had implied, more than implied, outright said to look to Camaracum. Cambrai had formed from the ancient Gallo-Roman city.

"Are you feeling anything?" Pablo asked.

Luke chewed his lip for a moment. "Yeah, but I can't pinpoint anything. I know it's there. It's like an annoying itch I can't reach."

"Do you think your radar could be on the fritz after your dream?" Sam asked, stopping in the shadow of an awning in front of a bakery closed for the day.

"It's possible. We're in the right city. This was Camaracum. I know they're here, though. It's like an oppressive weight on me." Luke folded his arms and shook his head.

"Well, maybe we're not in the right part of town. Let's finish our circuit, then we'll grab the van and circle out wider," Sam said, pushing off the wall she'd been leaning against.

Luke nodded and pulled up the next nearest bar on his phone, pointing in the direction they needed to go. After a few blocks, they stepped off the well-lit street and down a side street until they found the little tavern. Off to the side, an alley cut a dark path through the neighborhood.

"Anything?" Delilah asked, sliding her hand insider her jacket to rest on one of the wooden stakes concealed within.

"Maybe…" Luke checked to see if anyone was looking.

A few people stood outside the tavern smoking. Luke gestured toward the wall and leaned up against it. Pablo, Delilah, and Sam sidled up with their backs to the smokers, looking like the four of them were just forming a circle to chat or smoke themselves. With his view blocked, Luke rolled his back along the wall until he was in the alley.

As he walked down the alley, the sense of something familiar descended. A fanger was near, or maybe had been. He stepped around a dumpster, sweeping his eyes down the dark alley, looking for any movement, any sign of life or the undead. He scowled, squinting but seeing nothing.

He planned to follow the entire length of the smelly alley, then loop back around to meet his friends. When he cleared the dumpster, his heel nearly slid out from under him as he windmilled his arms, slamming into another dumpster. Scowling, he turned around and stepped away from the middle of the alley. He reached into his pocket and pulled out a small flashlight he'd started carrying, getting tired of the shallow field available on his cell phone's flashlight app.

The light reflected off the thick liquid next to the dumpster; it had a red luster, definitely not more of the urine the alley reeked of. He squatted down over the pool trickling away from the dumpster toward the center of the alley. Reaching down, he ran his finger through the thick reddish-black goo and rubbed it between his thumb and forefinger. Luke brought it up to his nose and took a quick sniff.

"Yup," Luke said.

Someone had beaten Luke and his friends to the punch—or stake, as the case may be. He turned around and rejoined his friends, sliding back up against the wall he'd started from.

"Well?" Delilah asked.

Luke held his hand out, showing them the vampire goo coating his thumb and forefinger. Sam leaned in and gave a little sniff.

"I didn't hear a scuffle..." Pablo said.

"There wasn't one. At least not one caused by me. I slipped in this and nearly ate shit," Luke said. "Looks like we might have a new player on the field."

Everyone raised their eyebrows.

"I need to wash my hands. Let's step in here and have a beer, then decide what to do next." Luke stepped away from the wall and waved his friends after him.

Luke moved up to the bar with Pablo while Delilah and Sam found an empty table in the corner. "Quatre bières s'il vous plaît... Licorne Elsass."

"Oui, monsieur," the bartender said, turning to grab, rinse, and fill four glasses from the tap.

Setting the four Alsatian lagers in front of Luke, the bartender asked, "Êtes-vous Belge?"

Pablo took two glasses and headed to the table.

"Oui, Bruxelles. Merci," Luke replied, sliding a twenty euro note across the bar.

"Prendre plaisir."

Luke nodded and took the other two glasses, joining his friends. Keeping his voice low, he leaned across the table. "Let's keep our voices down. I don't want word there are Americans about. I can pass; the bartender pegged me as Belgian."

Everyone nodded, taking sips from their lagers.

"So we have one dead vampire, a potential hunter, and no huge cluster as we hoped…" Luke tallied.

"Yet," Delilah. "We haven't found it *yet*."

Luke nodded, conceding the point.

"I don't see that we have much of an option. Let's continue our circuit and see what we find," Sam said.

Pablo nodded. "It's the sensible option."

"Pablo, sensible? Will wonders never cease," Luke teased, lifting his glass toward his friend. "À votre santé."

They enjoyed their small glasses of beer, talking quietly to avoid drawing attention. When they finished, they slid out of the bar and proceeded toward the next likely spot on the map. Each subsequent spot came up a bust. Luke swept the floor of each alley thoroughly looking for any further dead vampire evidence. Only once did he stumble upon some dust, which the werewolf noses in the group guessed was likely from an older vampire slain after a long life of blood sucking debauchery. By the time they'd finished their circuit, Luke brooded. He kept a slight lead on his friends, ostensibly to look for vampires, but more so because he didn't want to snap and grump at them. He needed a little space on the way back to the van to calm before the next stage of their venture.

Still fully armed and armored, Luke slid into the driver's seat and fired up the old VW, putting it into drive as soon as everyone was buckled in. He pulled out onto to Rue Aubenche and took a left on Rang Saint-Jean. He slowed, looking around as his senses burst into life. Next to him, Delilah shivered.

"You feel it, too?" Luke asked.

"Yeah," she replied.

"We should probably talk about that sometime soon…"

"Yeah, but now's not the time," she replied, looking out the window.

Luke found a spot alongside the parking zone on the right side of the street.

"Vampires?" Sam asked from behind Luke.

"Yup."

Pablo turned and leaned toward the window of the van's side doors, squinting as he peered out. "I think I see someone running… being chased."

Luke popped the door open and stepped up, holding the van's frame to look over the top of the van and out into the dark park that extended north and south along Rang Saint-Jean. Pablo was right, someone was running at a dead sprint, a large group of people chasing after them. The closer they got, the more Luke's vampy senses vibrated.

"Luke, what's going on?" Pablo asked.

Luke ducked down and spoke into the van. "Vampires chasing someone, can't tell if the chasee is human or vamp though."

"How many?"

"Too many. Dozen…maybe more."

The person sprinting ahead of the vampires noticed Luke standing up, watching, and changed directions toward Luke and his van. Squinting, he focused on the person being chased. They were close enough that he was pretty sure they weren't a vampire now that they'd focused on him.

"You!" they yelled in French. "Start the engine! Hurry!" They waved their hand at Luke. "Hurry you, fool!"

Luke ducked back into the van, shutting the door. "We're going to have company. Pablo, get that side door open."

"Is that a good idea?" Delilah asked.

"Sam, grab a shotgun from the case and duck down behind the seat." Luke turned the key and put the van in reverse as Sam crawled over the bench seat into the back.

Luke pulled forward so the nose of the van was ready to pull out onto the street. Delilah rolled down the window, poking her head out to watch as the person drew nearer.

"Luke, the fangers are gaining… If they don't get here soon, we're going to have a horde of vampires on our ass," Delilah said.

Luke revved the engine of the van. "Pablo, you're on the door. Help them in and get it closed."

"You got it, dude!"

The runner leapt from the concrete wall down to the sidewalk running along the park. Luke could hear the pounding of their feet and their breath whistling in and out of their lungs.

"Luke, go!" yelled Pablo.

Luke let up on the clutch too quickly, stalling the van. "Fuck!"

He shoved the clutch down and restarted the van as the runner jumped into the van, Pablo aiding them by pulling them in by the arm and tossing them across the bench seat in the middle of the van, then slamming the door shut. This time, Luke timed the clutch correctly and pushed the gas pedal down, slowly pulling away from the curb.

Behind Luke, he heard the slide drawn back on a semi-automatic pistol, then felt cold steel pressed into the side of his neck.

"Faster!" their new passenger yelled in French, then mumbled, "Who still drives a piece of shit like this?"

Luke put the pedal to the floor, coaxing what little speed he could get from the 1.8L air-cooled engine.

"Parlez vous anglais, asshole?" Sam said, popping up from behind the bench seat as she shoved the barrel of the shotgun into the passenger's back. She emphasized her question by pumping a shell into the firing chamber of the Winchester M12.

The passenger removed the gun from the back of Luke's neck and held it in the air. Delilah reached back and carefully took the pistol from their hand, then trained it on the passenger.

"If you can't find more speed, am I going to have to get out and push?" Pablo yelled.

"Americans? Ugh." The passenger grumbled, folding their arms over their chest.

To emphasize Pablo's point, the sound of vampire claws scraped along the side of the van.

"Look out!" the passenger yelled in English, pointing toward the front.

Delilah whipped around as Luke swerved into the other lane. A group of vampires had split off and were trying to cut off the van on its escape. One, faster than its friends, scrabbled at the side of the van, finally finding purchase on the open passenger window Delilah had been looking out of moments ago. Leaning back, she took aim and fired, shooting the vamp in the face and sending it tumbling, tripping up the small group of fanged chasers.

"We got one on the bumper, dude," Pablo said, working his way to the back to look out the rear window. Pablo leaned his forehead against the rear window. "Ah, that takes me back."

Luke yanked the steering wheel right, then left again, back and forth, swerving over the narrow two-lane street that was thankfully empty at that time of night in the small city.

"Any luck?" Luke yelled.

"One of them is still dragging along. I bet his jeans are all fucked up now," Pablo called back.

"You're running out of road, Luke," Delilah said, her voice nervous.

"I know. We're going to have to turn. What's pursuit like?" Luke took a quick look in the side mirrors and the rear view.

"Too close. Vamps can run fast!" Pablo called.

"Delilah, left or right?" Luke asked.

"I don't know. Right I guess?"

"No! No, not right." The passenger waved their hands to emphasize their point.

Luke slammed on the brakes, the tires screeching. Thump.

Pablo laughed. "He wasn't expecting that."

"Go, go, left! Allons-y!" cried the passenger.

Before Luke came to a complete stop, he mashed the gas down again and turned left.

"Ahhh! Luke, go!" Delilah yelled. "Lots more vamps, on the right. Go!"

The VW bus puttered along, gradually picking up speed.

"I swear to whatever god will listen, if we get out of this, I'm going to push this piece of shit into the river and then shoot you in the foot, Luke." Delilah aimed the pistol out the window in case any of the new group of vampires got too close.

When the bus straightened out onto Rue de General de Gaulle, Luke pulled into the left lane.

"Luke…" Delilah pushed back in her seat, staring forward.

"I see it."

"What?" Pablo asked.

"Car coming straight at us," Delilah squealed.

Their passenger cursed profusely in French, afraid to move with Sam still holding the shotgun steady at their back. Luke laid on the horn. The car, after what appeared to be a moment of panic, yanked their car into the other lane, jamming on their brakes and coming to a stop as Luke cruised by.

"Get on your phone and pull up a map," Luke ordered.

Delilah, prying her fingers from the dash, pulled her phone out of her pocket.

"Next right?" Luke asked, slowing slightly.

"No! One way. Split road. Right after. No! Keep going. OK. Now this right…"

"Pablo? Anyone behind us?" Luke asked.

"Not that I see, dude. I think we outran them, although that was close. This hunk of junk is never going to make the Kessel run in twelve parsecs."

Luke turned right, finally getting off the one way they'd been driving the wrong way down and onto Rue des Bouchers, heading the correct way. Once he calmed his breathing after their little adventure, he asked Delilah to navigate them out of town to the north.

"Wait. What about me?" their passenger asked. "My stuff is back there."

"I'm not interested in checking back in with the welcoming committee," Luke replied. "Were you the one killing vampires tonight?"

"I do not know what you're talking about," the passenger replied.

"What are we going to do with her, Luke? We can't take her with us…" Delilah said, looking back and forth between Luke and the passenger in the back.

Luke's eyebrows shot up in surprise. He hadn't been looking for the details of their new passenger as she ran up to the van or after when he was too busy trying to drive away. Now that he had a moment, he flicked his eyes up to the mirror, checking her out. A beautiful, if sweaty, Black woman stared back at him.

"Whether she's interested in telling us about the vampires she's killed or not, we can't release her back into Cambrai, not after the hornet's nest she kicked over, not with that many fangers looking for her. Pablo, if we're clear back there, would you mind disarming our guest completely? I'm sure she's got more than a handgun stashed away if she's serious about her business. Sam, keep your M12 on her," Luke called from the driver's seat.

Pablo worked his way from the back up to the seat next to their passenger. The passenger eyed them, sighed, then started pulling weapons from the recesses of her bulky clothes. Luke, taking peeks in the rearview mirror, watched her pull stakes and large knives out of her pockets and off her person, including a long, thin blade strapped to her calf. It appeared the only gun was the one she'd pulled on Luke.

He gestured for Delilah to move closer. "Find us a place north of town we can pull over and have a little chat with our friend."

Delilah nodded and sat back in her chair, looking over her phone. Luke took several series of turns, working his way toward one of the roads leading out of town to the north.

"I think I have a spot. Pull onto the D630…Rue du Pont D'Iwuy."

Luke nodded and pulled onto the D630, then pulled off onto a narrow road moving through some open fields. Once Luke decided they'd gone far enough, he stopped and killed the engine before turning around to face their guest.

"Now that we have a little privacy, let's talk. I'm fluent in French if you prefer," Luke said.

"No. English is fine," she replied. She reached up slowly and pushed back the deep hood she'd had covering her head.

The young woman looked in her mid-twenties and had ebony skin approaching ebony, her soft round lips matching the tone. Her dark brown eyes looked nearly black in the dimness of the overhead dome light. Her black hair was pulled into a tight ponytail puff.

"Sam, I think we can lower the shotgun. We're going to keep this friendly and polite." Luke held the young woman's gaze.

"Okie dokie," Sam said, sitting back.

"At this point, you know our names. I'm Luke."

"Sylvie." The woman's eyes darted back and forth between Luke and Delilah.

"Good. Now we're all friends," Luke replied.

Sylvie's nose flared. "I'm not sure it's safe to be friends with a bunch of gun-crazy Americans."

"You're the one who pointed a gun first," Delilah said.

"Besides. There's only one American here." Luke tipped his head toward Delilah. "I'm Belgian, I guess."

"You guess?" Sylvie said, crossing her arms.

"It's a long story. Sam?"

"I'm from Japan."

"Pablo?"

"Mexico."

"See. Only one crazy gun-toting American here." Luke smirked at Delilah.

Delilah shook her head. "Bruh, not cool."

Luke turned back to Sylvie. "So now, back to the vampires."

She looked to her left, out the window of the bus. "No such thing."

"What's that stain on your jeans?" Luke asked as he pointed his face toward the dark reddish patch.

The spot looked like an oil slick and would be mistaken for one if he hadn't spent a lifetime laundering similar stains.

"Delilah?" Luke pantomimed opening a jacket lapel.

Delilah opened her jacket and pulled out a stake, making sure Sylvie saw it before dropping it back into the deep pocket to clack against the other stakes contained within.

Pablo cleared his throat. Once he was sure he had Luke's attention, he put his hands on top of his head, mimicking ears. He also simulated a howl. Sylvie turned her head just enough to catch the end of Pablo's little performance, tightening her arms across her chest and slumping into the seat further.

"Ah, I see," Luke said, nodding in understanding. "Does your pack know you're antagonizing vampires?"

Sylvie mumbled something.

"What?" Luke tipped his ear a little closer toward her.

"I don't have a pack," she grumbled.

Behind her, Sam's expression shifted from neutral to sympathetic.

"I'm sure you can tell Sam and Pablo are also both werewolves. We're all members of an American pack." Luke didn't say which one, preferring to keep the information vague while they still knew so little about her.

"Humans? Are you married to pack members?" Sylvie asked.

"No. We are members in our own right. I'm a member of the pack's council, as are Sam and Pablo." Luke pursed his lips looking over the woman who eyed him warily.

"So what are you going to do with me?" Sylvie asked.

Luke shrugged. "Nothing, really. We just helped someone being chased by vampires. We were in town for the same reason when we found some of your earlier handwork. Your chase scene there put a halt to our search halfway through."

"Although, she saved us the effort of finding the vampires," Pablo said. "Lots of them."

"I guess so," Luke replied, chuckling and shaking his head

"What are we doing about the rest of tonight, Luke?" Sam asked. "Find a hotel or head back to base?"

"I'm reluctant to stop anywhere. They got a good look at the van, and I'm afraid to see what they did to the exterior," Luke replied.

"They got a good look at the license plate too," Pablo supplied, "dangling from the bumper."

"Base it is," Luke replied.

Sylvie looked on the verge of panic. "No! I can't go wherever you want to take me. I don't know you all. What…what about my things?"

"Sylvie," Luke said, trying to convey his sincerity to her. "I promise we'll drive back tomorrow in the light of day and get your stuff. Spend the night with us where you'll be safe. Let us put a good meal in you in the morning. We have to return to Cambrai to finish what we started."

"You have our word as werewolves, no harm will come to you," Sam added.

Sylvie, not taking her eyes off Luke, took a deep breath, narrowed her eyes, then nodded. "OK. Tonight. Then tomorrow, return me to Cambrai."

CHAPTER
NINE

Pablo helped Luke remove his armor while everyone stowed their weapons in the chests, adding Sylvie's gun, knives, and stakes to the lockers. Luke walked around the old VW bus and inspected the damage. The vampire's claws had dented the panels and scratched the paint. With a sigh, he shook his head and climbed back into the driver's seat. A few minutes later, they were back on the road winding their way northeast toward his manor.

Sam took the middle seat of the bench next to Sylvie while Pablo took the end. Luke had removed the rear bench to make room for their equipment. When he looked in the rearview mirror, Sylvie had dozed off, her head against the window. Pablo's and Sam's heads bobbed as they joined her in sleep.

"It's all sleepy time back there," Luke said, turning his head toward Delilah.

She too was asleep, her head propped against the window. He chuckled to himself and shook his head. His friends were still struggling with jet lag. And while he was feeling its effects too, he was used to it after so many trips, although he would have liked some company for the drive back.

Sylvie only stirred slightly when they reached Luke's manor, her deep sleep letting her avoid most of the property's clocking effects.

When he parked in front of his house, everyone finally awoke, save for Sylvie.

"She must be exhausted," Sam said, rubbing her eyes. Sam placed her hand on Sylvie's shoulder and gently shook her awake. "Sylvie, we're here."

The young Black woman stirred and looked out the window. "Merde! Is this your house?"

"It's Luke's house," Sam said.

"Sam, will you find a room for Sylvie? The caretaker should have changed the linens from the rooms everyone else was using. Pablo and I need to pull the trunks," Luke said, fighting back a yawn of his own.

"Sure. Follow me and Delilah, Sylvie. You can borrow a shirt and some shorts. We're about the same height." She gave Sylvie a friendly smile.

The tired woman nodded and followed Sam into the house. Luke folded the bench seat and yanked the trunk out, Pablo grabbing the other end.

"Where do you want to put this?" Pablo asked.

"Just inside the main entrance will do."

"So looks like we picked up another vagabond…" Pablo smirked. "You seem to attract them."

"I guess so. Hopefully she'll give us time to talk her out of rushing back into Cambrai on her own. There's no way she can take out that many vampires." Luke set his end of the trunk down and opened the door, picking the trunk up again. "Hopefully, a good night's sleep and a full meal in her belly will help."

Pablo grunted, setting the chest down out of the way. "I could use a good night's sleep myself. I'm kind of glad we knocked off early. I'm dragging ass."

Luke patted Pablo on the shoulder. "Goodnight."

"Goodnight, Luke."

EVERYONE SLEPT LATE the next morning, waking close to noon after their late bedtime. Sam met Luke in the kitchen, helping him with the coffees.

"Is Sylvie up yet?" Luke asked.

"Yeah, she woke up when she heard me and Delilah moving around. She's having breakfast out in the solarium. Well, more like eating all the breakfast. She's ravenous. She must have been running on thin rations for a while."

"If we need to get her more food, there's plenty in the fridges. I can fry some bacon or sausages," Luke replied.

"Bacon sounds tasty. Mind frying some up anyway?" Sam asked.

"No problem." Luke pulled out a pan and set it on a burner to warm up.

When the bacon finished, Luke took it out, along with more coffee. Sylvie, sitting quietly in between Delilah and Sam, nibbled on a pastry while everyone else chatted, looking uncomfortable surrounded by odd strangers. Luke set down the bacon and pulled out a seat between Sam and Pablo. As soon as the bacon hit the table, Sylvie eyed it greedily.

Luke nodded to her and gestured for her to dig in. She speared several pieces and set them on her plate before picking up a piece and folding it into her mouth. Unable to contain herself, she made happy sounds as she chewed on the bacon. Sam, unable to suppress a smile as, grabbed a couple pieces for herself.

When they finished breakfast, Luke and his friends sat sipping coffee. Sylvie, keeping quiet, pushed her chair away from the table but perched herself on the edge of it, fidgeting, eyes darting from face to face.

Luke set his cup down and brought his attention to Sylvie. "Now, I believe we have a promise to fulfill to our new friend here. Although, we'll have to wait until we have new wheels since ours is a little battle scarred, and they've probably nosed around a description and the license plate number."

"What about the Volvo?" Sam asked.

"We could use it, but it'll be a tight squeeze in the back with an extra body, and it's not a short drive back to Cambrai."

"Wait, how far did we come last night?" Sylvie asked.

"We're in Belgium, south of Charleroi." Luke kept his reply vague, not wanting to give away too much information to the unknown young woman.

"You are Belgian. Your English doesn't have an accent though," she replied, sounding unsure of herself and the strangers she'd gotten mixed up with.

"I'm good at blending in. I've lived in the United States for a while," Luke replied.

"How long?" Sylvie asked.

"The 1950s." Luke spun the espresso cup on its saucer, fidgeting.

Sylvie narrowed her eyes, staring at Luke and likely trying to determine if he was lying. "You're a human, but you only look like you're in your forties…"

Pablo snickered.

Luke pursed his lips and shook his head at Pablo. "Sunscreen hadn't been invented yet, and they were hard years. I think I look excellent for my age."

"That's true. Most people your age are in pyramids or museums." Pablo's lips wiggled as he worked to keep them clamped shut, as if trying to avoid laughing.

"I'm not pyramid old, buddy." Luke rolled his eyes.

Sam leaned toward Sylvie. "Don't mind them. This is an ongoing joke."

"He's not a werewolf. How old can he be?" Sylvie asked, confusion written on her face.

Sam smiled, an open gesture intended to put at Sylvie ease. "Older than any werewolf I know or have ever heard of."

Sylvie's brows furrowed. "He's not a vampire.

Delilah snorted. "He is decidedly not a vampire."

"What is he?" Sylvie seemed annoyed by everyone avoiding her questions.

"That's his story to tell, but we can assure you there's no greater enemy to vampires than Luke," Sam said.

Luke's phone, sitting on the table, vibrated. He checked the message and stood. "Our new wheels are here."

"I hope it's something other than an old Volvo," Pablo commented to the table. "Wait. How'd you get it here so quickly?"

"I put in the request with the caretaker a couple days ago." Luke winked at Pablo.

They stood and followed Luke out the side door that led directly off the solarium. When Luke turned the corner around the house, the caretaker's Peugeot was parked next to a black BMW X5 M.

"Damn! I hope it's not the Peugeot," Pablo said, stopping next to Luke.

Seeing Luke, an elderly white man stepped out of the Peugeot. A white woman with brown hair got out of the BMW. Luke walked up and shook the man's hand, exchanging a kiss on the cheek.

"Monsieur, I have the car I believe will satisfy your requirements," the elderly man said in French.

"Excellent. Now my friends will stop complaining about my poor VW. If they find something to complain about with the Beemer, I might need you to source me some new friends," Luke replied.

The woman handed Luke the keys to the BMW.

"This is my daughter, Anne-Marie." The old man gestured toward the woman standing next to him. "She will take over for me when I retire."

Luke and Anne-Marie exchanged cheek kisses.

"Your work in the Mithraeum is exceptional. It's better than you described it," Luke said, beaming.

"Thank you, that means so much, sir," Anne-Marie replied, giving a slight bow.

Luke gave them a formal looking nod. "Again, I must thank you both for all you do to maintain this place and keep it stocked while I'm here."

"We are proud to serve as our family always has." Émile bowed deeply, holding his fist over his heart.

Anne-Marie bowed as well, replicating her father's gesture. After they straightened, they got into the Peugeot and left.

"Is he some kind of nobleman?" Sylvie asked.

Sam shrugged. "Maybe? We don't know. It's possible he's collected a few titles over the years, but his current title is friend.

He's a good man and a loyal friend. If you need someone to trust, you could do far worse than Luke."

When Luke turned around, Sylvie fixed a speculative and confused gaze on him. He gave her what he hoped was a kind smile.

"Well, we now have a ride that even Pablo can't complain about. Y'all ready to go?" Luke asked.

Fifteen minutes later, they pulled away.

Pablo wiggled in the front passenger, settling himself in. "Now this is what I'm talking about. You're going to have to buy one of these when you get home."

"You could always buy one, Pablo," Luke replied.

"Are you kidding? There's no way I could afford one of these, and there's no way Holly would approve one out of the pack's funds."

"No. She would not." Sam reached up and patted Pablo on the shoulder. "Tough luck there, pal. Looks like it's more butt time in the Volvo for you."

Pablo sighed dramatically. "Suffering is my lot in life."

Sylvie, sitting in the middle between Sam and Delilah, leaned toward Delilah. "Is he always like that?"

"Pablo?" Delilah asked. "Yeah, although he's on his good behavior because we have a guest with us."

Sylvie's eyebrows raised part way up her forehead. "He's normally worse?"

"You have no idea, Sylvie." Sam patted her knee.

Luke chuckled. "Now there's a third person; you're way outnumbered, my friend."

Pablo shook his head. "And the suffering continues…"

Luke turned on some music—Pulp's "Common People"—and set their course for Cambrai, while Pablo basked in the comfort of the leather seats. Sylvie, Sam, and Delilah conversed in the back. Sylvie seemed to be relaxing around them, though Luke could still detect an air of caution and a body tightly coiled to spring into action if necessary. The closer they got to their destination, the more her calm slipped away as she spoke less, the fidgeting becoming more obvious.

Once they pulled into Cambrai, Sylvie directed them toward a sketchy hostel.

"Do want us to come in with you?" Sam asked, opening the door to get out.

"No. I'm fine." Sylvie scooted toward the open door but stopped. "Thank you for helping me last night and for letting my stay with you after. It was nice to meet you all."

Once she stepped out, Sam gave her a brief hug and wished her good luck, watching her walk into the building. Sam pulled the door closed behind her, still looking toward the door of the hostel with furrowed brows and pursed lips.

"Luke. Let's hang out for a minute. I want to make sure everything goes OK," Sam said.

Luke nodded. "Sure. Let me go park up ahead. I see an open spot."

Checking over his shoulder, Luke pulled out of the unloading section and on to the street where he parallel parked into an open spot about fifty meters from where they'd just been. Sam popped out to stand under the shade of the tree they'd parked under; Delilah joined her.

Pablo sighed, looking around the cabin of the BMW X5. "I'm going to get too used to this luxury. You're going to ruin me for my poor Toyota, dude."

"Yeah. This is way nicer than I'm used to. I like my silly old cars, but this is way more comfortable. However, we won't have any problem getting up to speed with this thing if vamps are chasing us," Luke replied.

"That's for sure. This baby has some muscle if we —" Sam's knocking on the window interrupted Pablo, so he rolled the window down. "What's up, buttercup?"

"I'm not sure what happened, but Sylvie came out looking unhappy. She's sitting on a bench near the hostel; I think she's crying. Dee and I are going to go see if she needs help." Sam turned her head to look toward Sylvie.

"OK. Let us know if you need us," Luke said.

Sam patted the door's window frame and walked away.

"Pablo, you mind going with them? I'll stay here in case we need to move in a hurry." Luke patted the gear shifter absentmindedly.

Pablo nodded. "Sure thing."

Pablo stepped out of the car and followed Sam, coming back a couple minutes later.

"What's going on?" Luke asked.

Pablo rested his arms on the car's window frame. "The hostel is being shitty. Since she didn't check out this morning, they cleaned out her bunk and won't give her back her stuff unless she pays for an extra night, and she doesn't have the money. Sam is taking care of it."

Luke shook his head.

"Yeah. If she doesn't have money for that shitty hostel, you know Sam isn't going to let her wander off without at least giving her money, although if I know Sam and Delilah, we'll have a new friend, at least for a while." Pablo shrugged.

"They're good people. Honestly, I'd feel pretty terrible cutting her loose with nothing but a fare thee well. She's killed at least a few vamps, and she doesn't have a pack to go back to…" Luke trailed off, not sure what he was thinking, although it felt weird to not automatically look for reasons to push her away from himself and now his close-knit group.

Picking up on Luke's tone, Pablo chuckled. "You've come a long way, buddy. Time was, we'd have had to pull teeth to talk you into going along with something like this."

Luke snorted. "I guess I've just gotten used to adopting wayward werewolves."

Pablo heard something and looked away from Luke. "Looks like they got her stuff back. They're all headed this way."

Luke got out and joined Pablo on the sidewalk. Sylvie and Delilah stopped, Sylvie rubbing her palm over a cheek, while Sam walked briskly toward Luke and Pablo.

Before Sam even stopped, she opened her mouth. "Luke, look—"

Luke held up his hand to stall her. "Of course, we can look out for her until she can get things figured out."

Sam narrowed her eyes at Pablo. "Did you talk him into it?"

Pablo raised both his hands in innocence. "He came to the conclusion on his own."

"Well, hmph," Sam said. "That takes the fun out of arguing with Luke."

"If it makes you feel better, I can pretend to say 'no,' and then you can argue your case, defeating me with your passion and eloquence," Luke said, smirking.

Sam looked like she was considering it for a moment, then shook her head and sighed. "Maybe next time." She waved Sylvie and Delilah over. When they joined the rest of the gang, Delilah looked over Luke's face, squinting as she moved her eyes around.

"I don't see any bulging veins or hear any annoyed huffs," Delilah said.

"He'd already decided before I even got here," Sam replied.

Delilah nodded appreciatively. "Wow, Luke, glad to see you coming around."

Pablo walked up to Sylvie and offered to take her bags, then stowed them in the back with the rest of their gear.

"Welcome aboard, Sylvie. You're welcome to stay with us as long as you need to," Luke said, trying to make his words and expression welcoming to the young woman, who was still clearly distraught about her situation.

"Sam and Delilah said you're here to kill vampires. Let me kill vampires with you. I can help." Sylvie spoke rapidly, her shoulders tense and brow furrowed as she fidgeted, wringing her hands.

"We can do that. There are definitely too many for you to handle on your own and an extra hunter would help us. Just listen to me when the time comes, and it'll work out. I've been doing this for a very long time." Luke extended a hand to seal the deal.

She looked at Luke skeptically, then nodded, taking Luke's hand and shaking it. "OK."

CHAPTER
TEN

L uke took everyone out to a late lunch, pouring more food into the young woman who'd clearly been going light on meals based on her lack of funds. She looked like she was in her mid-twenties, but she could be quite a bit older as a werewolf. Looks were deceiving when one could live far beyond the age of a normal human.

While they enjoyed coffees and desserts, Luke decided it was a good time to find out what she knew. He looked around to make sure the restaurant was still mostly empty. "Sylvie, what can you tell me about the vampires that were chasing you last night? Do you know where their nest is?"

"Nest? I don't know this word," she replied.

"Where they sleep during the day, their home?" Luke elaborated.

"Ah. Yes. They have several of the old buildings on Boulevard Vauban." She scraped her spoon around the inside of the glass chocolate mousse dish to get the last bit. "It's near the park they were chasing me through."

"Can you show us which ones?" Luke pushed his empty plate away and picked up his espresso.

Sylvie nodded, setting the spoon down after determining she

couldn't get any more from the empty bowl. Luke waved the server over to get the check. Once they finished, they returned to the SUV, Sylvie taking shotgun next to Luke so she could guide him. When they drove by the park where they'd met her, Luke chuckled to himself. The park looked far less sinister in the light of day without a horde of angry fangers chasing the woman who now sat to his right.

"OK. These three on the left, I know for sure. Maybe one or two next to it." Sylvie leaned toward Luke, pointing toward a series of large three-story brick buildings.

Although they were a little worse for wear, the buildings had all the signs of their former glory worked in stone flourishes, arched windows, and beautiful and ornate old wooden doors.

Pablo whistled appreciatively. "Those are some big houses. I bet they can stuff a lot of toothy bastards in there."

Sam leaned forward between the front seats. "Luke, take a left up here. Avenue Michelet."

Luke did as requested, following several more directions from Sam until they were on a narrow street headed toward the train station.

"What are we doing back here, Sam?" Luke asked.

"This field on the left. It backs to the vampires' houses. Those trees are probably screening the property," Sam replied.

"Hmm. We could park at the train station and walk on back and take a look." Luke looked back and forth between the empty lot and the road ahead of him.

"Won't there be thralls watching?" Delilah asked.

"Maybe, but thralls are easy to fool. Besides, they know someone is moving about Cambrai looking for them." Luke rubbed his chin, mulling the idea over.

"It's not the worst idea," Pablo mused.

"What is a thrall?" Sylvie stared at the line of trees.

"A human who serves the vampires. They usually take care of tasks while the vampires sleep for the day," Sam answered.

Luke decided. "I'm going to find a place to turn so we can park and take a look."

"No!" Sylvie said, growing agitated. "Not thralls. Not humans. You can't go."

Luke pulled into the parking lot on the other side of the train station and the bus depot, picking a spot as far away from activity as possible. Turning the car off, he shifted in his seat so he could face her more easily.

"I think we're going to need some more details here," Luke said. He tried to keep the sternness from his voice and face, but they didn't quite manage it as Sylvie lowered her head and hunched her shoulders.

"It wasn't just vampires chasing me last night. It was… It was werewolves too." Sylvie fidgeted with her hands, looking down and avoiding eye contact with Luke.

Sam inhaled sharply. "Are the werewolves aiding the vampires? Are they allies?"

Sylvie pulled her legs up and under her as she turned so she faced the middle of the car. Sylvie looked at Sam in the backseat behind Luke. "They are allies, though lesser."

"The vampires are in charge?" Luke asked.

"Oui."

Luke bit back a curse. "How many werewolves?"

"A whole pack," Sylvie replied. "Maybe more."

"Well, fuck. That's going to complicate things." Luke looked at Sylvie's face as she avoided eye contact with him. He recognized the profound look of sadness, the grief of loss contained in the dark pools of her eyes. Her clenched jaw spoke to the anger accompanying the look of loss.

"You know this pack, don't you?" Luke tried to lessen the intensity of his gaze to keep from intimidating her any more than she already was.

"It…" She paused, unbuckling her seatbelt before restarting. "They were my pack."

"Oh, honey," Sam whispered from the back.

Delilah reached up and patted her knee, resting her hand there sympathetically. Sylvie snatched it up, clutching it in her hand.

Sylvie's shoulder shook lightly as her breath trembled. Sniffling, she wiped the tears from her cheeks with her other hand. Luke reached across the center console and squeezed her shoulder. She took the squeeze as an invitation and leaned into Luke, resting her head on his shoulder as she cried, her sobs growing heavier. Shocked at the sudden change, Luke hesitated for a few moments before wrapping an arm around her, rubbing her back soothingly.

When Sylvie's sobbing slowed to a trickle, she sat back. Sam had fished out a pack of travel tissues from somewhere and handed them to the young Black woman who took them gladly, blowing her nose and dabbing at her cheeks. While Sylvie did her best to clean up her face, Sam whispered into Delilah's ear.

Delilah squeezed Sylvie's knee. "Sylvie, let's step outside and take a little walk. The fresh air will do you good."

Sylvie's answering nod was wobbly, but she opened the car and stepped out. Pablo let Delilah exit, then rejoined Luke and Sam. Delilah took Sylvie's hand and led her away from the car, walking slowly.

When Sam determined they were far enough away, she turned to Luke. "Poor dear. Losing your pack is a profound loss. Losing the pack connection is like losing a piece of yourself."

Luke nodded, brow furrowed. "What does that mean for her family?"

Pablo sighed. "Either willingly or unwillingly, they turned against her and condoned the expulsion or…"

"Or they're dead," Sam finished.

Luke clenched his jaw, biting off some of the curses he wanted to spew. "Shit. This throws a wrench into the works. We can't go up against a werewolf pack and a large nest of vampires with just the five of us."

"Especially not knowing what her skills are, or if she'll be able to fight against a former pack mate if it should come to that." Sam leaned to the side to stare out the window. "They're coming back. I need to give you a heads up. She's young and without a pack. I don't know what kind of pack she was in before, but my guess is it wasn't the best. Sylvie is already starting to treat you like the pack alpha."

Luke's eyebrows shot up at the use of the word "alpha." It was a word they never used for Holly or for their pack situation.

Pablo nodded. "She sees us treating you like the leader, and you exude leadership when you want to. You're paying for things, and you have a big house and a very fancy car."

"Pablo's right. All the markers point to you as the alpha of this group." Seeing the look of shock on Luke's face, she added. "I can see it in her body language. All those subtle cues wolves give off. She's been steadily decreasing eye contact with you for fear of angering you. It's a bullshit thing bully alphas demand. We'll do our best to help her out, but she's going to look to you for leadership and guidance. You're a kind man, but sometimes you can be a little intense."

"You're a good dude, Luke. I think between us, we can coax her out of her shell." Pablo smiled reassuringly at his friend.

Sam nodded, agreeing with Pablo. "It'll be delicate until she becomes more comfortable with us all, but if we can keep her around, we can help her find a new pack. I'm sure Pieter's pack would welcome her, or if she's willing to make the move, we can bring her into our pack."

Luke took a deep breath and let it out slowly. "OK. We'll see if we can do right by her. If I mess something up, let me know. I'm good at leading people, but the intricacies of werewolf hierarchies are a mystery to me."

Pablo reached up and patted Luke's shoulder. "We got your back, dude!"

"Pablo, why don't you ride up front with Luke? Dee and I will work on Sylvie," Sam said.

Pablo hopped out and held the door for Sylvie and Delilah. Sylvie took the middle, letting Delilah have more leg room on the right side.

"OK. Now that we've done recon for the day, I think it's back to base. There's nothing we can safely do today. Plus, I want to check in with Jamaal and see how he and the others are settling in. I'll let Émile know we'll need dinner." Luke turned the ignition on and pointed their ride back to Belgium and their temporary home.

LUKE AND PABLO fetched another round of beers from the bar and brought them back to the private sitting room. They'd retired to it after dinner so they could be cozy. As they drove back, the day had turned cool and drizzly and then the night became cold and rainy. Luke built a fire in the stone fireplace.

"Have you called Waffleboy and let him know the skinny?" Pablo asked as Luke walked through the door.

"No." Luke handed Sam a glass of the Belgian strong dark ale. "With Sylvie's news, I'm worried the leak he's having might be related and I don't want the news that we know getting into the wrong ears. For now, let's keep this close to our vest."

Sam nodded. "That's probably smart."

She sat in a cushy armchair with a blanket wrapped around her legs. Luke handed a couple glasses of the blanche to Delilah and Sylvie who sat on a small couch. Sylvie, her own clothes in need of laundering, wore a t-shirt borrowed from Sam. Sylvie looked tired and sad, her head leaning against Delilah's shoulder, her legs drawn up under her as they shared a blanket.

Luke took his favorite wingback armchair near the fireplace, setting his glass of Nostradamus on the small, round, antique side table. Once Pablo settled down with his beer in another cushy chair, Luke looked around the room and made eye contact with everyone to make sure they were ready, finishing with Sylvie. She hesitated but eventually gave him a slight nod.

Luke licked his lips and inhaled. "Sylvie, first I want to thank you for stopping us before we got in over our head. It is much appreciated. I'm fluent in French, if you can ignore my Belgian accent."

Sylvie smiled at the joke.

Luke continued, "If it would be easier to continue in French, I can translate what needs to be translated to my friends. Although we all are multilingual, I'm the only one who speaks French."

"No. I can do it in English," she replied.

Luke nodded. "I don't know what your goals are, but if you wish to continue hunting vampires, we can help you. My friends here have been doing it for around a year now, very effectively might I add. I've been doing it for a while longer."

Delilah snorted. Pablo chuckled.

Sylvie looked up at Delilah, a quizzical look on her face, but directed her questions to Luke. "Why do your friends always laugh when you're vague about your age?"

"They like to make jokes about my extreme senior citizen status," Luke replied

"Senior citizen? I do not know this phrase," Sylvie said.

"It means he's a really old guy. A gray hair," Pablo replied, chuckling some more.

"Pablo finds it amusing to make fun of my age, although he's the second oldest here by about twice Sam's age. As you know, Sam and Pablo are werewolves. Pablo is the second of the pack we're in. Sam is the wife of the packleader. The three of us are on the pack's council. Delilah is also a member of the pack. She teaches unarmed combat."

Sylvie looked at Delilah again, seeming impressed, before returning her head to Delilah's shoulder.

"Who are you? Humans aren't asked to be on pack councils." Sylvie took a sip from her beer.

"I'm going to extend you the trust of my identity, or at least part of it. I hope you will trust us so we can all work together. My name, currently, is Luke Irontree, although you won't find that name on any official paperwork. I was born about an hour northwest of here, a very long time ago."

"How long ago?"

"A little over nineteen hundred years ago," Luke replied, picking up his beer.

Sylvie eyes grew wide as her jaw slowly dropped. "That's..." She stopped before finishing it with what Luke guessed was the word "impossible."

Luke shrugged. "It's not. Vampires can live that long or longer. I just get my immortality from a different source than vampires.

They're my enemy. I've been fighting them for nearly all my life. If you are an enemy of the vampire, you're a friend of mine, as long as you don't do something else to make an adversary of me. The people you see here are my closest friends—my family. I would trust each of them with my life and have done so frequently. You will find no finer people, werewolf or human, than the people you see here."

Sylvie looked toward Sam who nodded at her, then up at Delilah who gave her a smile and a nod.

"He speaks the truth. He is what he says he is," Delilah added.

Sylvie nodded, returning her gaze to Luke.

"We've built that camaraderie over time and a lot of hard events. Now, if we're going to include you, we might have to skip over the time part, but the hard events… Well, you stepped right in the middle of them, and I'm guessing you're in the middle of some of your own. My intuition tells me you're not a threat to us, that we can place our trust in you. My friends agree. I know you're wary, but I'm hoping—we're hoping—you'll take a leap of faith and give us your trust in kind."

Sylvie sat quietly, her eyes drifting away from Luke's only to dart back into contact again. Chewing on her lips, she came to a decision and nodded. "OK."

"Tell us who you are, please." Luke smiled, but knew authority had crept into his eyes.

"My name is Simone Sylvie Kiara Ndiaye. I'm twenty-five. I'm from Libourne, near Bordeaux." She stopped to take a drink of her beer.

"Can you tell us about what happened with your pack, dear?" Sam asked.

Sylvie nodded. "Yes. I was born in it, but my parents were new members when they joined. They'd migrated from Senegal when they were young and were assigned to the Bordeaux pack."

"How were they? Were they accepting? Welcoming? The pack, I mean." Sam took a sniff of her dark beer, then took a drink and looked to Luke. "Oh, this is lovely, Luke."

"I guess the pack was alright. Some people were nicer than others. I'm not sure what happened, but when I returned home from university, the pack leadership had changed. People started agitating for a 'pure French pack.' Besides us, there were a Moroccan family and a family from Cameroon, so we were greatly outnumbered. I'm not sure what happened to the family from Cameroon, but I think they fled. Then one night…" Sylvie's hands started to tremble.

Delilah gently took the beer from her hand and set it on the table next to her, then wrapped her arm around Sylvie's shoulder, whispering, "It's OK. You can trust us."

Shaking, tears fell from Sylvie's eyes. "They killed them. Maman et papa. Their bodies…"

Sylvie gave into the sobbing. Delilah held her close, rubbing her back and shoulders. Sam stood up, closing the distance quickly, and squatted in front of the small couch, taking Sylvie's hand. When Luke looked to Pablo, his best friend's eyes held profound compassion for the young woman. In a room full of people whose lives were filled with pain and loss, Sylvie was one more wounded soul, and everyone there empathized, wanting to help shoulder her grief.

When her crying subsided, Sam stood and gave her a kiss on the forehead. Neither Delilah nor Sylvie seemed interested in changing their positions, Delilah's arm wrapped around the pretty young woman.

Luke gave Sylvie a kind smile. "I'm sorry for bringing this up for you. You don't have to go into details. I'm sorry for your loss. If you're ready to continue, and it's OK if you're not, but how is the Bordeaux pack involved with vampires?"

Sniffling, Sylvie cleared her throat. "We all knew about the Bordeaux nest. It was a scary rumor, but none of the pack would work anywhere near it nor would they move through the area near dark. It was rumored a powerful vampire lord lived in a château there, and we avoided it…until the new pack leadership took power. We weren't a wealthy pack, but the new pack leaders were dripping with gaudy bobbles and rumors of a powerful new ally who'd reward loyalty. I think the vampires helped them seize control of the pack and now they serve the vampires as their thugs."

"What are they doing so far from Bordeaux?" Pablo wondered.

"I don't know. I've tried to pick up what information I could. I think they're planning to go to war with a powerful werewolf pack."

Luke exchanged looks with his friends. Leaning forward in his chair, he fixed his intense gaze on Sylvie. "Do you know who this vampire lord is?"

"I don't know his name, but I've heard him called Le Mousquetaire."

Once Luke recovered from the news, his mind whirled into action. He'd gotten enough information from Sylvie for the evening; he didn't need to squeeze more from her. Sam and Delilah escorted her upstairs to her room, staying with her for a while and leaving Pablo and Luke in the sitting room.

"I think it's time to send Pieter an update," Pablo said.

"Maybe. I'm thinking we might have confirmation on where his father is being held, although I'm not sure what we can do about it right now. We don't have enough power to go after a nest of vampires that large and concentrated, especially not with werewolves as muscle." Luke reached for his glass, finding it empty.

"I'll go refill us," Pablo said, picking up his glass. Pablo returned with two fresh glasses a couple minutes later.

Luke's eyebrows furrowed in speculative concentration as he held his glass. "Pablo. How hard is it to kill a werewolf?"

"I'm glad you waited until we were good friends to ask that question. It's pretty hard, especially the more powerful werewolves. Old guys like me who can do the bipedal form are tough as old nails. We can take a lot of damage and heal our way out of it, eventually. You can blow up a werewolf, but you've got to get them right in the blast. If you do enough damage that the body can't keep up, you can overwhelm a werewolf's healing ability. The sure way to do it, though, is silver to the heart. In lieu of that, taking out both the heart and brain usually works."

"We're running a bit short on silver weapons right now," Luke said.

"Yeah. As far as I know, your swords are the only things guaranteed to work. I'm not sure if there's enough silver in the one you had made for Delilah."

"Is there a way to test it? Short of stabbing a volunteer in the heart?" Luke leaned forward.

"I don't know. I guess I could touch myself with the blades and see how bad they burn." Pablo looked like the idea was unappealing.

"I think we can forgo that for now." Luke, lips pursed, tried to come up with ways to acquire weapons that might help when he remembered something from earlier in the year. "Shit! I know where we can get a couple more silver weapons."

"Will there be quests and maidens fair?" Pablo asked, sitting back in his chair and stretching out his legs.

"There definitely will be a maiden fair. I'll have to ask Maggie to find them in my basement."

"Wait. You have spare powerful magic weapons, and you didn't bring them with you?" Pablo shook his head. "You're slipping, old man."

Luke snorted. "To be fair, they're new to my collection. Do you remember that bar we raided in Northeast earlier this year? The one where I had the sword fight with that vampire?"

Pablo stretched out his legs before taking a sniff of his beer. "The famous artist vampire?"

"Yeah. Guillaume Geefs. I took the rapier home. It was the same one The Mistress had used to attack Amiata last year when I rescued her for the Flanders Pack," Luke replied.

"Yeah. I remember you telling us about that when we picked up Pieter from the airport."

Luke took a sip of his beer, then a second. "It's got silver in it. I also picked up a dagger from The Mistress. I'm not sure if it's killing levels of silver, but it'll sure give a werewolf a hell of a bad day."

"Yeah, especially if you put it in their heart. If it doesn't kill them outright, it'll take them out of commission for a long time, which will serve just as well in a fight." Pablo got serious for a moment, moving his jaw back and forth as if he were chewing over an idea. "Another thought, and you can tell me if this is stupid or not, but have you thought about asking your…benefactor? Mithras? If he can make some more, or maybe supercharge Delilah's or even Sam's swords?"

"I don't know…" Luke replied, looking away from Pablo. "I don't know what kind of contract would be asked for in exchange for that kind of favor. It might put you guys on the hook to a god you don't understand and don't want to stand in the path of. It's a dangerous business crossing paths with a deity. I'll have to think about it."

"Fair enough." Pablo took a deep drink of his beer, sighing happily. "You know how to treat your friends. The beer choices are tops. Four stars—manager is a bit grumpy though…"

"Hush you. I'm going to call Maggie. There's still time to get the weapons to a courier." Luke stood up, went into the small office, and grabbed the caretaker's address from the desk. Looking at the door, he shut it and sank into the chair behind the desk. A smile on his face, he called Maggie.

"Hi, Luke!"

"Hey, Maggie."

"You just can't get enough of my voice, can you?" Maggie teased.

"It's such a lovely voice." Luke's smile broadened into a grin.

"Oh, you're such a nice man."

"It is good to talk to you, but I need to ask a big favor, or more accurately, one that I need done right now, if it's possible. We've got a bit of an emergency here, and we need some special weapons I have in my collection."

"Of course. I can call in one of the other doctors to handle this afternoon's appointments. Everyone knows I'm your contact, so they're on call to help me if needed."

Luke gave her the description of the weapons and where to find them along with a shipping address. "Gwen can help you find them. Take them to a courier. The pack accountants will reimburse you; they know the accounts."

"OK. That's an easy favor to execute. I'll call my replacement and gather up the little one." Maggie had picked up Luke's habit of calling Gwen "little one."

"Oh, be careful with the weapons, the blades contain silver," Luke warned.

Maggie chuckled. "I'd guessed as much since you're doing what you're doing."

"Thank you, Maggie."

"Of course, Luke. Take care."

"You too. Give Gwen a hug for me." Luke sighed as he hung up then rejoined Pablo.

"Why so forlorn, buddy?" Pablo asked.

"I miss Maggie."

Pablo chuckled. "You really like her, don't you?"

Luke nodded.

"Good. She really likes you too. She's good for you." Pablo stood up. "I think I want another beer. You good for another?"

"Sure. I'll take a blanche," Luke replied.

"Me too," Sam said, reentering the room.

"Delilah coming down too?" Pablo asked.

Sam shook her head, returning to her chair. "Delilah is staying with Sylvie for a little longer. I think she needs the company of someone closer to her own age. I think her pack was very hierarchical and even though I think she likes me, I'm still an 'elder,' especially since we all hold rank in our pack."

Luke nodded. "That's understandable, for sure."

Pablo returned with their beers. Together, they chatted, sipping their drinks. When Sam finished hers, she took herself to bed, leaving Pablo and Luke. Enjoying the quiet time with his friend, Luke stayed up late talking.

LUKE SLEPT LATE. When he woke, he dressed in workout clothes, figuring he'd get in some exercise. He found Sam with a book and a cup of coffee.

"Where's everyone else this morning?" Luke asked.

"Delilah and Sylvie are outside doing some training. I think Pablo went with them," Sam replied without looking up.

"So the old dog is still wanting to learn new tricks?"

She laughed. "Yeah. He wants to be a kung fu werewolf. Last I saw him, he was singing that ridiculous theme song he's been creating for the anime-style cartoon someone's going to make about him and he's going to star in."

Shaking his head and smiling, Luke laughed with Sam. "He's a goofball, that's for sure. I think I'll go join them. I could use a bit of a sweat." He set down the burner phone. "Mind monitoring this in case we get a message from Pieter?

"Not at all. Have fun. I could use another coffee."

Luke waved to Sam as he left out the side door then followed the sound of voices. When he found them, he hung back watching. Delilah, a natural teacher, walked around Pablo and Sylvie as she guided them through some basic drills. Pablo was quite a ways ahead of Sylvie, but to Luke's surprise, Sylvie wasn't entirely unskilled. As Luke watched them, Sylvie had trouble keeping to the forms Delilah was teaching, often falling back on something else.

After a few minutes, he stepped forward and greeted everyone. "Delilah, I'm curious about something." He gestured toward Sylvie and Pablo. "Do you mind?"

Delilah shook her head and stepped back.

"Sylvie, I want you to forget, just for now, about the moves Delilah is teaching you and use what you already know."

Sylvie nodded.

"Pablo, attack with any sequence you want. Let's not go full speed, though. Keep it under control," Luke instructed.

"Got it," Pablo replied.

When Pablo checked with Sylvie to see if she was ready, he got a nod, then launched a punch at her. Sylvie knocked it aside and easily moved out of the way of the slow jab. Pablo paid for his ill-conceived punch. As she moved out of the way, she planted and spun a round-house kick, catching Pablo in the ass, and knocked him off balance. As he lumbered toward her trying to reorient, she shot into grappling range and used Pablo's momentum to take him to the ground, wrapping him up.

With a grunt, Pablo tapped out. Sylvie let him go, her eyes wary as she backed away, probably worried he might lose his temper. Delilah laughed as Pablo picked himself off the ground, grumbling.

"That'll teach you to be patronizing, Pablo," Delilah said.

Luke chuckled. "Very good, Sylvie. That was an interesting combination of moves. What were you doing?"

"It's…uh…it's a combination of savate and laamb ji." She avoided making eye contact with Luke.

"I'm familiar with savate, a bit, but what's laamb ji?" Luke asked.

"It's Senegalese wrestling." Her back stiffened as she held her head high.

"It was an effective combination, very impressive. How much training do you have in each?" Luke stepped forward into the circle the three had formed.

"My father taught me and… We started when I was young, seven or eight, maybe? I learned savate at university. Me and a girl from Senegal taught ourselves how to combine them. I've been doing savate since I was eighteen." Sylvie shuffled nervously while standing next to Luke.

"What's savate?" Pablo asked.

"French kick boxing," Luke replied.

As he moved next to Sylvie, she stood a half foot shorter than his and Delilah's six feet. She was closer to Pablo's height. She also lacked Delilah's broad shoulders and hips, having a slighter frame. She'd used her werewolf speed and strength to make up for her size.

"Sylvie, how confident do you feel with your savate?" Luke asked.

Before Sylvie could answer, Delilah held up her hand to interrupt. "Luke, she prefers Simone. Sylvie was just the name she gave us at first."

"Ah," Luke said.

Simone slouched. "I'm sorry—"

"Don't worry about it. We've all used aliases before. Do you think my name is Luke? It's one I've used over the centuries, and it's close to my original name, but it's not. Pablo?"

"Nope. Not even close to my original name. Not even the same language," he replied. "Nice take down, by the way. Sorry for not taking you more seriously."

Simone nodded.

"I think Delilah is the only one still using her original name," Luke said.

"That's not true," Delilah interjected. "Johnson is my mom's last name. Oyelakin is my last name."

"You're African?" Simone asked.

Delilah smiled warmly at Simone. "American. My father immigrated from Nigeria. My mom was American."

Luke and Pablo exchanged a look, learning something new about their often reticent friend.

"Delilah, I'm feeling like a little sparring. You feeling up for it? I'm thinking some pure kung fu might be fun instead of going more free form fighting." Luke locked eyes with Delilah as she thought about it, her eyes briefly flicking to Simone before returning to Luke.

"Let's do it. I could let off some steam." Delilah turned and walked a few steps away from Luke before turning around, her feet set shoulder width apart.

"Sylv... Simone, let's get out of their way. This will be fun to watch. It'll be one of the few times you'll see Luke evenly matched or maybe even outmatched." Pablo gestured toward the nearby patio with its chairs.

"Is Delilah good at kung fu?" Simone asked, looking Delilah over.

"Just wait and see." Pablo's grin made him look eager.

"Mind if we start slow? I need to warm up these muscles before we go full tilt." Luke rotated his shoulders, loosening up.

"Same." Delilah bowed, then stepped into her starting position.

Luke bowed in return and readied himself. Together, they sparred lightly, more executing moves and blocks to get the blood flowing and to get in sync with each other. After a few minutes, they picked up the speed slightly until Delilah decided it was time and unleashed a blindingly fast flurry of kicks and punches that put Luke back on his heel. He barely kept up with her until she stumbled a bit on the uneven ground.

Luke responded immediately, setting up his own intense series of moves, including some more elaborate and showy ones he rarely got to break out in combat. A small smile pulled the corner of Delilah's lips upward as she dipped into her vault to bring out some of her favorite combinations. While both of them were still trying to land blows, the main objective became to use more elaborate and beautiful moves to achieve their strikes.

Lost to the world around them, their violent dance ranged around the grounds while keeping in view of their audience until Luke overextended a kick a fraction too much and Delilah pounced, using his mistake to toss him to the ground. Air whooshed from his lungs as he landed on his back. He lay there for a minute, catching his breath. Delilah flopped down next to him, breathing hard.

"You OK, Luke?" Delilah asked.

"Yeah. That was spectacular, Dee. A truly amazing display of skill." Luke rolled over and stood, helping Delilah to rise.

They bowed to each other, bookending their sparring match. When they turned to Simone and Pablo, Sam had joined them, and the three of them clapped. Luke pulled his shirt up and wiped his face off before pulling it back down. He followed Delilah over to their friends.

"That was… That was magnifique!" Simone declared.

Luke smiled, seeing Delilah's awkward response to the young woman's praise. Sam pulled a chair out from the table and set it out for Luke, then moved one toward Delilah. Luke sank into it, wiping more sweat from his brow. Once Delilah finished accepting her praise from everyone, she took the chair, slumping into it.

"Since we're all here, let's figure out our next moves," Luke said.

"Actually, that's why I popped out. I mean, besides wanting to watch Delilah beat you." Sam pulled the phone out of her pocket and handed it to Luke. "We received a message from Pieter."

"He's got news. I'm going to call him." Luke dialed and waited for Pieter to pick up.

"Hello, Luke. How are you?"

"Good, Pieter. You?"

"Eh. You know," Pieter replied. "I got news."

"Me too."

"You go first," Pieter said.

"Well, I'm pretty sure we've found where they might be holding your father," Luke said.

Pieter exhaled explosively. "Really? Already? Where?"

"We think he's in Cambrai. I even think we've got it narrowed down to a few buildings near the train station." Luke stretched out his legs. "But keep that strictly between you and me. No one else."

"Not even Jan?" Pieter replied.

"No. Let's keep it just to you for now," Luke replied.

"OK. I'll tell no one. Can you get him out?" Pieter sounded eager.

"Well, there's a problem. It's three to five buildings, and a lot of vampires. Not sure how many. But here's the kicker. They've got a whole pack of werewolves providing muscle."

Pieter let off a string of curses in Flemish. "A whole pack? Are you sure?"

"Yeah. We ran into a former pack member who filled us in on the details," Luke replied.

"Which pack?"

"She says the Bordeaux pack..." He looked over at Simone, checking in on her. Seeing the look on her face, he nodded toward her. Delilah nodded and whispered into Simone's ear. Together they walked away. "Sorry about that. I'm not sure if you're familiar with them. But she says they went through a leadership change recently and the new pack leaders purged anyone who wasn't 'pure French' and probably anyone who disagreed with them. She thinks the local vampires were involved—Le Mousquetaire."

"Son of a..." Pieter let out another string of Flemish curses. "Are you sure this information is accurate?"

"Yeah. We're pretty confident about her news. Her parents were one of the families purged..." He looked around to make sure

Simone wasn't near. "She didn't get into details, but it sounds like they were murdered pretty brutally."

Pieter sighed. "You always seem to pick up the orphans, my friend. Well, if you vouch for her, she'll have a home with us if she wants it—assuming we still have one when this all done."

"What's your half of the equation?" Luke asked.

"We received our first round of demands. They want Liege back, specifically The Mistress's mansion, but the rest of the city as well."

"What are they offering in exchange?"

"Nothing. They want to call it a gesture of good faith on our part," Pieter spat out.

Luke groaned, hearing the disgust in Pieter's voice. "That's a shit offer. Have they given you any proof he's alive?

"Just a video with no sound with them holding up a newspaper next to them like some fucking movie they saw once." The anger was plain in his voice.

"Tell them you want to video chat with your father first. If you can, record the conversation. Mind sending me the video they sent you? I want to see it. Any word from Jamaal on who your leak might be?"

"Not yet. He's splitting time between that and helping track down my father," Pieter replied.

Luke nodded. "OK. How are the decoys doing?"

"Good. I'm sure we're being watched, so Will pretends to be you most of the time."

"Alright. Here's what I want to do. Agree to cede Liege. Set the time and date and make them send witnesses so they can't say you're double-crossing them. Once you've got your date, we'll set up surveillance on our suspected houses and monitor the flow in and out. If this is their main force, we'll be able to watch the force flow out. If it looks like we can use their assault on Liege to our advantage, we'll go in and see if we can rescue your father."

"OK. I think that's workable. Is there anything we can do to aid you?" Pieter sounded mildly optimistic.

"No. I can handle it on this end. I don't want your leak getting wind of anything. My caretaker can source the bit of equipment we might need." Luke made a mental list so he could let Émile know.

"Keep me apprised of your situation. I'll let you know if anything changes," Pieter said.

"We'll get your father back, my friend."

"I know. Good luck."

"And to you." Luke hung up.

When he looked up, Sam was sitting next to him with her phone and a smile on her face. "I took pictures when we drove by yesterday. Looks like this building next door is either for sale or rent. Not sure what the French sign in the window is."

Luke took her phone, looking over the images. "Nice." He punched the phone number from the sign into his phone. As the plan formed in his head, he looked around the circle of his friends, old and new, before settling on Simone. "I'm not sure if you'll like this plan, but I think it's the right one for now." He turned to Delilah. "Delilah, I'd like you to stay here with Simone and keep training with her."

"But—" Simone sat forward, a pleading look in her eyes.

Luke held his hand up to stall her. "You won't be staying here long. I'm going to take Sam and Pablo, and we're going to secure us a place to set up our little operation. I'm guessing you'd be recognized by any of your pack members?"

Simone nodded.

"Once we have a place set up, we'll fetch you two and get you secured so you don't accidentally give our operation away, that way you can be on hand to help us." Luke gave her a soft smile.

Delilah reached over and took her hand, squeezing it. "Simone, this is the best plan. Luke's right, if they saw you while they're trying to secure a place, it would give us away. Once they get an apartment, we'll be on site and ready to go in."

Simone locked eyes with Delilah. As understanding passed between them, Simone finally nodded.

Delilah, still holding Simone's hand, turned to Luke. "You got a place to pop off some guns? I'm guessing Simone has never handled any firearms, beyond her handgun."

Simone shook her head. "No. I haven't."

Luke nodded, liking his friend's thinking. "Yeah. I have a range in the cliff. You can run her through some shotgun training. Use the standard shot since we don't have an easy way to get reload right now for the special shot."

"Right." Delilah turned back to Simone and gave her a smile. "We'll use the time before they come collect us."

Luke, finger tapping the table, picked up the bottle of water he'd brought out earlier. "Actually, I'll just give you the keys to the Volvo. It'll probably be good to have a second car on hand if we need to split up for any reason. Plus with only three of us in Cambrai to make arrangements and keep watch, this seems like the best solution. I'll ask Émile to keep you fed until it's time to rejoin us. Enjoy anything in the wine cellar. You know how to pour a draft beer."

"When do you want to move bases?" Pablo asked.

"Let's get everything ready today. I have to show Delilah the shooting range, and we need to make sure we have all the equipment we need sorted out. Showers, then lunch, then let's get organized. Tomorrow morning, we move to Cambrai for a while."

CHAPTER
TWELVE

It took Luke a few days, but even real estate deals can be sped up with the right amount of incentive in the form of a fat stack of euros. When Luke finished wheeling and dealing, he bought the house next to the first of the vampire nests and rented one on the opposite side of the street a block down on the corner with its perfectly placed windows.

The house next to the nests was too close for them to stay in, but it made a perfect place to set up several unobtrusive cameras covering the street and the park across from the nests, as well as the doors of the nearest couple of vampire houses. They set up cameras in the rental as well, ensuring they had maximum coverage no matter the circumstance.

"I wish Jamaal was here," Pablo said for about the dozenth time.

"You're doing a good job, Pablo. You're plenty handy," Sam reassured him.

Pablo sighed. "I know, but he'd have it done by now and it would be way better."

Luke, sitting on the floor in a pile of particle board panels and lock bolts, flexed his hand. "I'll trade you. I'll set up the security system and you put together the IKEA furniture." He returned to his project, tightening the connectors until he slipped and barked his knuckles. "Ugh. I fucking hate Allen wrenches."

"Wow, you guys are awfully whiny today." Sam kicked back in a comfy chair bought from a local store, a glass of wine in her hand, her eyes fixed out the window at the vampire nests.

Luke and Pablo made eye contact, shaking their heads at each other.

"How are the kids getting along?" Pablo asked, changing the subject.

Sam, who'd just finished talking with Delilah a few minutes previous, took a sip of wine. "Good. Delilah says Simone is coming along nicely. She's still uncomfortable with the shotgun, but she's doing well with it."

"How's Simone doing? She was feeling pretty down." Luke grabbed another shelf to attach.

"Delilah says she's doing alright. Still having some bouts of deep sadness, but seems happy to be part of something even if it's not her pack. Oh. Dee said the caretaker dropped off the package Maggie shipped to him."

"Good. Although I'm not sure who can use the rapier. It's not exactly an ideal weapon for fighting in houses, but at least it's got some silver in the alloy. The dagger will be more useful."

"Do you think the vampire shells will work on wolves?" Sam asked.

Luke thought about it for a moment. "Should work fine on them as long as they're in human form. Also probably in regular wolf form as well. I'm just concerned it won't penetrate deep enough on a hulked-out wolf in biped mode. That looks like a lot of flesh to go through. It'll piss them off and hurt like hell, but we won't know its effectiveness until we can give it a run, and that's a dangerous prospect if it doesn't even give us much stopping power. Also, I'm concerned about popping off guns in town. I think French cops are going to be a bit more uptight about gun fire than Portland's donut chasers."

"OK. I think I got it." Pablo stood up and turned on the monitor, an image of the street below and the vampire houses popping on the screen. "And we have snooping power!"

"Now I'll have to set up the unit down the street," Luke said.

"Don't want me to do it?" Pablo asked.

"Probably best not to put strange werewolf smells next door to their nests," Luke replied.

Pablo looked offended. "Dude. I'm house trained. I shower regularly. I'm not going to pee on their mailbox to mark my territory."

Sam laughed. "He's probably right though, Pablo."

Crossing his arms, Pablo stuck his tongue out. "Fine. When we moving the kids up?"

Sam chuckled. "If you call Delilah a kid to her face, she'll thump you. Simone'll probably help her. On second thought, do it. I could use a good laugh."

Luke reached for a shelf and set it into place. "Not until we have the place set up. We need more beds, but I'll probably have them make the move in a couple days, unless things change from Pieter."

"They still stalling him?" Pablo asked.

Luke nodded. "I think they're getting the pieces in place and aren't ready."

"At least they're giving Pieter solid proof he's alive," Sam said.

Luke grabbed another bolt. "Yeah. At least we're getting that. I hate to leave Pieter's father in captivity, but as long as he's alive, this gives us time to get ready."

WITH THEIR FURNITURE assembled and in place, Luke made the call for Delilah and Simone to move bases. Using the cloudy, rainy day, they slid into the apartment with their hoods up to help hide Simone from anyone watching who might recognize the young woman.

Once they got settled, Luke and Sam went to fetch takeout while Pablo stayed behind to keep an eye on their monitors.

It was good to see Delilah again. Not having her with him had left an empty spot Luke was used to her filling. They'd been a team for a while now, relying on each other to protect each other's backs, and while many other people had moved through their teams or worked alongside them, she filled out the quartet that had been his constant for months.

After nearly a week together with no one else around, Delilah and Simone had grown much closer. The budding friendship with Delilah seemed to be working wonders on the woman who had been so nervous and diffident. He could tell she was still uncomfortable around him, but she wasn't as obviously displaying subservience markers in his presence. He'd hoped time with just Delilah, who was only a few years older than Simone, would help her settle in with the team and learn that their little group wasn't the pack she'd come from. When he had a moment, he'd check in with Delilah about Simone's development.

What he wasn't expecting was for the moment to arrive so soon. After their dinner, Delilah pulled him aside, asking to speak with him alone. They grabbed Delilah's jian and tucked it into Luke's backpack with his gladius and rudis.

"We'll be back in a bit; we're going down to the wine bar to talk." Luke waved, holding the door open for Delilah.

They walked to the little bar he and Sam had gone to a couple times while Pablo had been on watch. It was nearly empty on the weeknight, so Luke requested a corner table away from the few other patrons. Once they got settled and Luke paid attention to Delilah, he noticed her nervousness as she fidgeted, looking near him but not at him. Luke ordered a bottle of Weinbach Riesling for them to share.

"So what's got you so anxious, Delilah?" Luke asked by way of an opener. "Something about Simone?"

"Simone? No, she's wonderf— No, it's nothing to do with her." Delilah closed her eyes and took a deep breath, straightening up in her chair. Once she felt ready, she opened her eyes and brought her gaze level with Luke's. "It's about my father."

She reached inside her jacket and pulled out an envelope, holding it for a moment before setting it on the table and sliding it toward Luke. On it, Delilah's name was scrawled in a bold and slightly messy script. He set his hand on the edge closest to him, waiting for Delilah to release her end.

Delilah licked her lips nervously, looking Luke in the eyes. "When I visited my granny this summer, she gave me this letter from my father. He sent it to her a few months before he was killed with instructions to give it to me when I turned thirty."

"I didn't think you were quite thirty yet," Luke interrupted.

"In a few weeks, but granny gave it to me since I was there, and it's not as easy to visit now that I'm no longer living on the east coast." Delilah lifted her hand off the letter and sat back, picking her glass up for a sip.

Luke didn't pick it up, leaving his hand on it. "I don't need to read your private letter. You can give me the important parts."

"I know. But I want you to, maybe need you to." She took another drink, watching his face, her eyebrows furrowed lightly.

Delilah's mysteriousness piqued his curiosity. He'd long suspected there was a lot more going on with her father than she suspected, only to get confirmation of it from Cassius's lips directly that Delilah's single dad had been a vampire hunter. He'd put the information away until he could find the right moment to tell Delilah, but it had receded to the back of his mind after the chaos of the battle to take out Cassius. Luke picked up the envelope, opened it, and withdrew the letter.

My dearest Delilah,

How does one start a letter like this, my daughter? It's important you know the truth about me and my works from my own hand. I suspect I am not long for this world. I have crossed dangerous powers and believe I've been marked for death.

I came to New York City not to seek the American dream as so many other immigrants do, but to hunt down the ancient enemy of humanity, the vampire. I assure you I am of sound mind and possess all my faculties. The creatures who drink blood are indeed real, although the tales told in popular entertainment get most of the details wrong. They are real, and they are profoundly evil.

I have dedicated my life to their eradication, as did my father before me and his before him, in service to the most ancient and noble Òsóòsi, the wise hunter. This may sound farfetched to you, but it is all truth. When I arrived on the shores of America, I was pursuing a vampire nest that had fled Nigeria as I was hunting them down. When I arrived, I took a job as a custodian at a university. It allowed me the time to continue my hunt. What I hadn't counted on was meeting and falling in love with your mother.

I had hoped to shield you from this lifestyle, allowing you to seek your own destiny. When I first held you after you were born, I could not allow such a precious child to be brought into this dark task. If the line ended with me, Òsóòsi would find a new hunter to take my place as he did when our ancestor became Òsóòsi's chosen.

With this letter, I have included the diaries of my life as a servant of Òsóòsi. The oldest I have translated from Yoruba to English for you. Making my story available for you has been the most important work of the last few months. I want you to know me, and if my enemies succeed, I want you to know why I died. Even if my life is taken by one of these monsters, my life will have been dedicated to saving those who can't defend themselves from these soulless creatures.

I have sent this letter, my diaries, and a few other personal effects to your mother's mother. She doesn't know about my life nor what is contained within, but she has promised to pass them to you when you reach your thirtieth birthday.

Being your father has been the greatest honor and privilege of my life. You have far exceeded any hopes and expectations I had for you. Know that I'm so proud of the woman you have become.

With my eternal love,

Bamidele Oyelakin

Luke folded the letter and returned it to its envelope, giving it back to Delilah. "That is a beautiful letter."

Delilah nodded. "I read all the diaries after my granny gave them to me. My mom knew about his hunting. They never told me or let on at all."

"Do you feel betrayed?" Luke asked.

Sipping her wine, she thought about this question. "At first, but I've seen too much, done too much to hold that feeling. He didn't want this life for me, and I can see why. But..." She stopped.

Luke let the silence hang until his curiosity got the better of him. "But?"

"But he left instructions on how to seek out Òsóòsi should I wish to take up his mantle as a hunter."

"You're already a hunter," Luke said.

Delilah nodded, then shrugged. They paused while the server stopped by their table to refill their glasses from the bottle sitting in a chiller on their table.

When she returned to the bar, Luke leaned across the table toward Delilah. "Are their benefits?"

Delilah nodded. "Speed, strength, endurance, and certain increases in clarity. I think I already inherited some of those from my father…"

"And going through it would make it even more intense? I've always thought you were merely an exceptional human. You were such a good fighter. So fast and strong. But you can feel vampires, although not as well as me, and you're immune to glamour. Not all humans can be glamoured. The truly strong of will can overcome most vampire's attempts to glamour them. Now I know part of where your exceptionalness comes from, besides your amazing father."

"Thank you. My mother was pretty talented in her own right. She was a PhD." She sighed sadly. "I've been thinking about my dad's diaries since I read them this summer, debating about what's contained in them. Whether I wanted to keep hunting. It wasn't until I returned home to Portland—and it's my home now—that I realized, for better or worse, I am a hunter. You and Sam and Pablo and little Gwennie are my family now. I know it's only been a year since we met, but we've all become so close. I think my dad would have loved you all."

Luke smiled at Delilah. "I feel the same. I missed not having you around when we left you with Simone." He sighed. "Are you thinking of going through with it? Becoming an official hunter of Òsóòsi?"

"I may need to. We may need the extra boost. Even if they send most of the vampires and wolves from the houses north, we're going to be outnumbered and out muscled, even with Simone." Delilah looked nervous and unsure, two things the confident woman rarely was.

"What are the downsides? I don't know very much about the Orishas." Luke picked up his glass and swirled it before taking a sniff and a drink.

Delilah shrugged. "As far as I can tell from my father's diaries, nothing. I mean, except for the violence of being a hunter and potentially getting murdered by a vampire."

"What about your religious convictions?" Luke had never asked her what she believed, assuming like most modern people in the US she was probably Christian, at least nominally. It had always been safest to not ask when needing to blend in during times less tolerant of pagans.

"I guess I'm agnostic. Mom was raised a Baptist. Granny still attends church regularly. But mom and dad raised me to make my own choices. I guess 'I don't know' was the place I ended up, but now I've seen too much shit. Stuff I can't explain. You—evidence of the power you were granted by a god. It's softened the edges of my thinking on the subject."

"Are you willing to dedicate your life to a deity you're not really familiar with, that you weren't raised with?" Luke asked. At the thought of a deal with a god, his shoulders tensed slightly as his chest tightened a bit from the added anxiety.

Delilah shrugged. "I don't know. I can't tell how much worship is required or if any is at all. From what my dad said in his diaries, his task was to seek justice for the vampire slain and to hunt and eliminate them to spare future people from feeling the injustice of a death at the hand of an abomination to life."

Luke nodded, thinking. "OK. I guess you have to weigh your knowledge about your father and his desire to keep you out of the life and the information telling you how to get into the life. It doesn't sound like he's trying to soft sell it, but you'd know better."

"I don't think he would. He was always very open with me, unless I was too young to know about something," Delilah shook her head. "I just don't know what I should do." Wrinkles formed over her forehead as she stared at Luke, seeking guidance.

Luke reached across the table and squeezed her hand. "It's a big decision. If you decide to do it, what all do you need? Do you need a priest of Òsóòsi? Or will any follower of the Orishas work?"

"I think I have everything already. He left me all the things I'd need, and as a powerful hunter with your connections, you'd be able to perform the ceremony for me." She looked pensive, putting her confusion and indecisiveness on the table for Luke to help and guide her through the thorny path available to her.

"That's very ecumenical. Well, I'll support you no matter what, and if you decide to go through with it, I'll perform the ceremony for you." He smiled, trying to relay his support for his friend as best as he could.

Delilah nodded and smiled. "Thank you, Luke. Should I talk to the others about it? I mean, it affects us all."

"You can if you want to, but it has to be your decision. They won't try to talk you into or out of it. They're your friends and love you; they'll support your decision. None of us are Christians, so you won't be offending anyone's sensibilities with a pagan deity. This is one hundred percent up to you, and we'll be here to support it either way. Don't make a decision because you think it'll help us out. Make this decision because it's right for you." He leaned forward, holding her gaze to emphasize what he'd just said.

Delilah nodded, looking thoughtful. She sat back in her chair and picked up her wine glass. Luke relaxed some and pulled his phone from his pocket, checking to see if he had any messages from Pablo or Sam while allowing Delilah some space to mull over their conversation. He couldn't lie, having Delilah tap into the full abilities she'd displayed the very edges of would help them. And protect her.

As the only unaugmented human on the team, she'd always been the most vulnerable to vampires who were vastly faster and stronger. They'd developed their team's fighting style to allow Delilah to perform to the best of her ability, but gaining the powers of a true hunter would allow them to increase their collective power. He'd never say any of those things to her though. He couldn't influence her, not after the life he'd led as someone who made the mistake of crossing paths with a god and accepting his mission.

Allowing her the time to think, they quietly finished the last of their wine and walked back to the apartment. Delilah remained silent, holding her hands behind her back as they walked. He checked on her out of the corner of his eye, wondering what was going on behind the pensive expression on her face. Delilah's news was one more calculation he needed to figure into everything else.

L uke and Delilah didn't speak any more about Òsóòsi or
taking the next step in her life as a hunter. She still had the
option to leave behind hunting and find a normal life. Once
she took the next step, that avenue would likely close or at least
narrow significantly. He wanted a life for her beyond the kill or be
killed world of vampire hunting. His own brief glimpses of a life
outside of Mithras's mission always made him long for something he
could only have for small pieces of time.

Right now, he had a child to care for and a woman he was
growing increasingly fond of—more than fond of, if he let himself
think about it. He'd pulled the North Portland Pack, and Maggie
along with it, into his world, although they'd been in it without realizing it until a few vampires started trouble in Pablo's brewpub.
Gwen, he'd saved when he and the pack broke up the vamp blood
farm and breeding center set up in Wapato Jail.

It was possible to have a meaningful life while fighting against
the soulless vampires, but it increased the risks of loss or having
loved ones becoming pawns in a game bigger than they knew.
Maggie had lived through horrible times, suffering violence first-
hand. She knew the stakes of what Luke was doing. So did Gwen.

He hoped Delilah would be able to find someone who could understand what she was doing with her life and be supportive. She deserved that if she chose to keep doing this. After getting revenge for her father's murder, she'd had her first off-ramp but skipped it in favor of supporting her friends and the mission they all believed in.

They spent their days and nights in the apartment they'd rented, watching the video feeds and cataloging suspected werewolves in the day and vampires at night. Simone and Delilah took the day shifts since Simone could identify by sight most of her former pack members while the rest split up the other shifts, with everyone pitching in so people got proper breaks.

They'd discovered that five full houses were indeed being used, thanks to Simone identifying werewolves going in and out. In total, they'd counted thirty werewolves and about sixty vampires or thralls, although there could be more inside that just hadn't exited their houses.

On the third morning since he and Delilah had their talk, he woke to the sound of giggles and the smell of coffee. Rubbing sleep from his eyes, he dressed and slipped out of his room. When he looked out into the main room where the monitors were set up, he saw Delilah and Simone sitting next to each other on the floor, their hands close with Simone's pinky rubbing over the edge of Delilah's hand. He backed up and feigned a cough to let them know he was up, then gave them a second before walking into the hall on his way to the restroom. He smiled; they'd moved their hands a few inches apart.

After a grabbing a cup of coffee, he sank into one of the cushy chairs they'd acquired for the apartment and pulled his phone out to check for any news.

"Where are Pablo and Sam?" Luke asked once he realized he hadn't seen or heard them yet.

"They went out for some breakfast and to stretch their legs." Delilah stood and went into the kitchen to get coffee for her and Simone.

"How are you this morning, Simone?" Luke asked, trying to keep the knowing smile off his lips.

"I'm OK, and you?" Simone replied.

"I'll let you know when I get to the bottom of this coffee cup." He held up the cup and smiled.

Simone chuckled politely.

Handing a cup to Simone, Delilah sat down in the chair opposite Luke. "So what's the plan for today, besides more binge watching of the world's most boring TV show?"

Luke snorted. "We need to make sure the gear is ready to go; I want to be fully prepared if the alarm goes off. Then we need to refine our plan and make sure we have contingencies in place. Why don't you two slip out after dark when it's clear and get some dinner and a glass of wine?"

After he threw out his plan, he tucked his nose back into his phone but looked up as Simone and Delilah exchanged an excited and slightly flirtatious look. He was eager to read the email Maggie had sent and reply to the text from Gwen. Finishing his coffee, he looked out the window at the sunny mid-morning sky.

"You know what, I'm going to go grab a croissant and sit in the sun for a bit. You two can handle yourselves and your binge unworthy TV. If Sam and Pablo get back before I do, let them know where I am. I'll have my phone on me if something happens." Luke rinsed his cup in the kitchen, grabbed his wallet, and took off.

THE NEXT MORNING, when Luke woke, he dressed and slipped into the restroom. It wasn't until he emerged that he noticed the activity in the main room. It could wait until after he had a cup of coffee in his hands, but Pablo had thought of that and handed a full cup of piping hot coffee to him as soon as he left the hallway.

"What's the word?" Luke asked, letting the rich scent rise to his nose on wisps of steam.

"Pieter called a little before sunup," Pablo said. "Tonight's the night."

Luke nodded, blowing over his coffee before taking a sip. "OK.

You should get to bed and grab a few hours of sleep. We can handle final prep."

"Right." Pablo patted Luke on the shoulder as he headed toward the back of the apartment and the room he shared with Luke. "Call Pieter when you're done with your coffee."

Luke sat down to enjoy his coffee while everyone waited expectantly. "Come on, people. We know the plan. Me finishing my cup faster won't change anything."

Delilah rolled her eyes and returned to loading practice with Simone and the M12. He didn't want to resort to guns. It was a fast ticket to French cops getting involved. Although there weren't many here in Cambrai, it would complicate things vastly. All the same, they were all going in carrying in case they needed to fall back on their firepower. The tight confines of a house were an ideal killing ground for the twelve-gauge shotguns. If things went sideways, they'd use the lethal efficiency of their special anti-vamp shells. Assuming they didn't run into the entire Bordeaux Pack—they still had doubts about the shells' efficacy against werewolves.

Finished with his cup, he pulled out the burner phone. "Hey, Pieter. Pablo told me it's tonight."

"Ja, finally." Pieter sounded tired and annoyed. "I was beginning to think they'd keep us waiting forever."

"Do you have a time for the exchange?" Luke asked.

"Zero thirty in the morning." Pieter yawned.

"OK. That timing works. It's nearly a three-hour drive from Cambrai to Liege. Looks like they're waiting to move out when it's fully dark. We'll tally up the numbers coming at you if we can. We'll be on full alert this evening." Luke handed the empty cup to Sam who was walking to the kitchen for a refill.

"Are you still thinking it's Cambrai they're coming from?" Pieter asked.

"There's too many vamps packed into this small of a town. That and the werewolf muscle points to this being their temporary base. I could be wrong, but it's the best lead we have." Luke carefully slid his finger through the loop on the offered cup. "How goes the other project?"

"Still no updates. Jamaal is getting frustrated. He's beginning to think our problem may be more low tech than high tech." Pieter yawned again.

"You sound tired, my friend. You should get some sleep before tonight," Luke said.

Pieter laughed. "Are you going to be my mother now besides my friend?"

"Not today, but the advice is sound." Luke chuckled. "After tonight settles out, I think I have an idea."

"Anything is better than sitting around on my ass doing nothing because I don't know who will betray me." Pieter's frustration resurfaced.

"I can understand. I'm not much for sitting around myself, but right now, it has been the best plan."

"You ready for your part?" Pieter asked.

"I think so. You?"

"As we'll ever be. Luke, good luck tonight. I hope my father's there, and you can free him."

"Me too," Luke replied. "Good Luck."

Luke hung up the phone and looked around the room at Sam, Delilah, and Simone. "We go at eleven tonight, twenty-three-hundred hours."

Sam nodded. "Good, I'm ready to get moving again."

"Me too," Luke said.

He stood up and went to the kitchen to fix himself some breakfast. When he finished, he joined the women to do a final check over the gear. Looking over their assembled weapons, Luke saw a piece missing. He dug through his baggage until he found it—a long backpack similar to his. "Delilah, I have a little something for you. To go with your jian."

She opened it and smiled, then turned to Simone. "Have I shown you my jian?"

Simon shook her head and a slow smile spread across her face as her eyebrows raised.

Delilah fetched the sword from their shared room and showed it to her. "Careful, there's silver in the blade."

Simone took the handle and examined the sword, turning it to different angles as the light reflected from the steel and silver of the blade. "It's beautiful," she said, handing it back.

Delilah, with backpack in hand, slid the sword home into the sheath within. "Fits like a glove. Thanks, Luke."

Lude nodded. "You're welcome."

When the jian was stowed, he retrieved the dagger from the packaging Maggie had sent. "Simone, I'd like you to have this dagger. I took it from a vampire who ruled Wallonia—after I killed her. Careful of the blade. It also has silver in it."

She pulled it free from its leather sheath. "Thank you! I promise to use it well."

"I know. I wish we had more time so we could give you some proper blade training. When we get through this, I'll run you through some dagger exercises," Luke said.

Sam dug around the box Maggie had sent and pulled the rapier out by the hilt. She turned around and posed with it, affecting a Spanish accent. "Hello, my name is Sam Wakamatsu. You kidnapped my friend's father, prepare to get poked!"

Luke and Delilah laughed; Simone looked confused.

Sam returned the rapier to the box. "Have you not seen 'The Princess Bride,' Simone?"

"No. Is it a television show?" Simone asked.

"It's a movie." She turned to Luke. "When we get some time, I'm declaring a movie night. We can't let Simone go any longer without seeing 'The Princess Bride.'" She took Simone's hand. "It's a classic. There's a wonderful sword fighting scene where two of the characters use rapiers."

Delilah smiled at Simone. "It's a fun movie. I think you'll like it. Besides, after sitting around staring at monitors and the tension of waiting, I could use a fun night to blow off some steam."

"I look forward to it." Simone held Delilah's eyes in her gaze.

Sam, not facing them since she was inspecting the basket hilt of the rapier, missed the warmth exchanged between the two women. Allowing them some privacy in the moment, he turned around to join Sam in admiring the weapon.

"Do you feel comfortable enough with the rapier to use it? I'd like to have as many silver weapons as possible," Luke said.

"I've taken a few fencing classes; I think I can handle it. I've spent all my life with swords and can put it to good use," Sam replied.

He pulled the scabbard and baldric from the box and handed them to Sam. "I hope our enemies are prepared to die."

Sam laughed. "I hope they're not prepared for us, otherwise we're up shit creek."

"And a rapier makes a poor paddle," he said.

LUKE ARRANGED for Moroccan food to be delivered so they could feast while keeping all eyes on the monitors and record the comings and goings of the vampires and werewolves down the street. While the sun neared the western horizon, the werewolves and possibly a few thralls buzzed about busily, preparing crates and loading box vans. When the sun tucked behind the western horizon, several vampires emerged to direct the next stage of their plans.

"There's definitely something going on. We haven't seen this level of activity since we've been here," Sam said.

Pablo scooped up some hummus with a pita and popped it into his mouth, "Defunlee somefing."

"Don't talk with your mouth full, Pablo," Delilah scolded.

Pablo swallowed. "At least we know all the sitting hasn't been for nothing."

"Look." Simone pointed west. "There's a string of cars coming."

Luke joined Simone at the window. "The box vans are leaving." He looked at the clock on his phone. "Timing is about right. Everyone on counting duty!"

They kept a running tally, with Simone pointing out the werewolves. Luke, with nearly two-thousand years of experience, picked out those he suspected were vampires. Anyone neither of them could safely categorize got put in an "other" column. All told, over half of the werewolves and vampires loaded up in the cars and followed the box vans out. Luke relayed the information to Pieter, then helped everyone prepare.

They all started with a dark-colored base layer—a mix of yoga pants, running tights, and dark jeans. Over his clothes, Luke slid into his armor, then situated his tactical straps with their attachment points where he could affix his gladius and rudis. As Pablo helped him, Simone stared, wide-eyed, having never seen the process or the equipment. Other than knowing he was the leader of the group, no one had gone into detail about who he really was other than a very old vampire hunter. France, as part of the Roman Empire, was littered with ruins and the skeletons of the empire that had dominated Gaul until they were ultimately replaced by the Franks.

Simone turned to Delilah and asked quietly, "Is he for real?

Delilah nodded. "Yup. Weird, isn't it?"

"So when he says he's from near Brussels, he means...?" Simone trailed off.

Luke, shrugging and wiggling everything into position, said, "He means from a small village in Roman Belgica and this was mine from when I was in the Roman legions."

Pablo strapped the rudis onto Luke's back for a right-hand draw. The gladius Luke attached to the front, planning to move it to his hip once they penetrated into their enemy's lair. Pablo, staying true to form, disappeared into the bedroom to slip into his snap on warm up gear so he could easily shed his clothes and go full wolf. He still felt more comfortable fighting that way if it came down to hand-to-hand combat. The shotguns, they loaded into duffel bags.

"Everyone ready?" Luke asked, looking around at friends.

Sam handed out light-weight, knee-length jackets that hung low enough to conceal anything they might have hanging from their belts save for swords. She pulled her own jacket on and tied the waist belt, pulling it shut. Picking up the bag concealing her katana, wakizashi, and the rapier, she opened the door and locked up after everyone else marched through. They tossed their bags into the cargo area behind the rear seat of the BMW, then piled in, Sam in the driver's seat.

She dropped them around back at the parking lot of the train station, each person taking a bag and disappearing into the shadows in their dark clothing. Once Luke, Pablo, Delilah, and Simone made it through the small lot and into the tree line backing the properties, they halted, backs to the tall brick wall separating the row houses' backyards from the weedy lot and the train station.

Luke waved Delilah over, then stuck his finger up, twirling it. Delilah turned around so Luke could access her backpack, pulling out her jian and handing it to her so she could put it on her belt. Next, he pulled out a thick black coil and a small portable monitor. Uncoiling the bundle, he stuck it into the air to see if he'd extended it enough, then uncoiled it a couple more times until it was taller than the wall. He pulled it back down and bent the flexible top so it was bent at a forty-five degree angle. He plugged the other end into the monitor and turned it on.

The low light camera transmitted a grainy black-and-white image to the monitor's screen. He poked the camera up and propped the top on the edge of the fence, then angled the lens toward the back of the vampires' houses, sweeping for balconies and open windows along with anyone keeping watch from them. Satisfied, he pulled the camera down and bent the flexible end so it would point more downward. He poked it back into the air and checked the yard of the first two houses next to where they stood. To be on the cautious side, he checked the house on the other side as well. Everything looked clear.

Luke squeezed Pablo's shoulder. Pablo patted Luke's butt, then sprang up, grabbing the top of the wall, and pulled himself up, dropping to the other side. Luke took a quick look through the camera again—nothing and no one stirred. After handing the camera to Simone, Luke squatted by the wall, cupping his hands for Delilah. As she balanced herself, Luke hoisted her up; she jumped and grabbed the edge of the wall. Luke tucked under her as she pulled her legs up. He grabbed her ankles and guided her feet to his shoulder so she could stand up and crawl over the top of the wall.

He took the camera back from Simone and checked again. Behind him, Simone breathed shallowly and quickly, on the border of hyperventilation. He set the camera and monitor down and sidled up to her, placing his hand on her shoulder and squeezing reassuringly.

Listening for a moment, he leaned forward until his lips were next to her ear. "You'll do fine. You're tough and smart. Listen to us and stick to the plan. We'll get you through this. OK?"

Simone nodded nervously and whispered, "OK."

Luke checked the camera again, then gave Simone the thumbs up. She squatted and jumped, catching the ledge of the wall, and pulled herself up. She lay flat on the top of the brick wall and lowered a short rope with a hook on the end. Luke hooked the first duffel bag to it and let her haul it up to be dropped onto the other side for Pablo and Delilah. After the hook dropped again, Luke attached the second bag and Simone hauled it up, repeating the process. She had the third bag half way up the wall when the sound of an opening door dumped adrenaline into Luke's veins. He heard a small gasp from the top of the wall.

With the open door, two male voices argued in French.

"We're not supposed to be going outside," the first voice said.

"Fuck off, I just want a cigarette," the second replied.

"Do you want to get us in trouble?"

"If you shut your mouth, no one will get in trouble. If you can't, I'll rinse your corpse down the drain of the bathtub."

"Asshole," mumbled the first voice.

The door shut. A few second later, the sound of a lighter flicking was followed by the scent of tobacco smoke. Luke looked up; Simone's face hung over the edge of the wall, her eyes as big as saucers as she tried to control her breathing. Every second of the cigarette felt like an eternity. Simone licked her lips and squeezed her eyes shut. He listened hard, praying not a sound would escape his companions. After what seemed an hour, the smoker finished his cigarette and returned inside, slamming the door behind him. They waited for a few moments longer to make sure he was gone. When Luke made eye contact with Simone, he nodded, and she brought the last duffel bag up.

Luke poked the camera up for one last check, then handed it to

Simone to drop to Pablo and Delilah. Simone slid off the wall and fell to the other side. Luke took a deep breath and leapt up, catching the wall, and pulled himself over. He dropped to the other side, landing nimbly in the weedy back area of an abandoned convenience store that stood at the end of the row of vampire houses.

Simone, her body shaking, leaned into Delilah as the taller woman enfolded Simone in her strong arms, holding the back of her neck. Luke took the camera for one last check of the side yards and found nothing. He disconnected the handheld monitor, coiled up the spy camera, and tucked it away in Delilah's pack.

Luke looked up at the flat room of the store. Sam, standing on the roof, leaned up against the wall of the first vampire house on this side, her arms crossed as she watched from on high. She'd jumped up from the front of the one-story building after stashing the car. Luke smirked and shook his head, giving her a quick wave.

While Delilah soothed Simone, Luke tossed the rope up to Sam so she could bring the bags up to the market's roof. By the time they finished, Simone had calmed somewhat. Luke was impressed she'd held it together stranded on the wall top, holding a bag halfway up. She was scared, and her confidence wasn't strong at the moment.

Luke fixed his eyes on her, holding her gaze. "Simone, you did really great on the wall," he whispered.

She nodded, taking a calming breath.

"Ready for the next part?" he asked.

She nodded, getting lined up just under the edge of the abandoned shop's roof. She leapt, grabbing the edge. Sam helped her up. Next, Luke and Pablo formed cups for Delilah to stand in. She climbed up, steadying herself on the bottom of the roof's overhang. Luke and Pablo squatted with Delilah then lurched upward, tossing her at the same time she jumped. She caught the edge of the roof, Sam and Simone helping her up and onto it. Pablo bent down and cupped his hand for Luke and launched him up like they'd just done for Delilah. Luke scrabbled up and over the roof's ledge. Moving out of the way, he helped Pablo when he latched onto the ledge.

They took a moment to move their weapons, so they'd be easy to draw and strapped shotguns over their backs, stowing the duffel bags in Delilah's backpack. Looking down the line, Luke collected a nod from each of his friends. They'd successfully snuck into their first objective without detection. Now he had to hope the rest of their plan went as smoothly.

L uke peeked around the corner of the first vampire house, finding the second-floor balcony empty. He couldn't tell if anyone was in the room off the balcony; no light spilled out. Readying himself, he edged forward until he only had one foot on the roof while gripping the wall with one hand. He swung himself over, grabbing the balcony railing and landing one foot on the floor. After he climbed over the rail, he drew his gladius.

Out of the corner of his eye, he saw Pablo poke his head around. Luke reached out and grabbed the door handle. He was about to push the lever down when it was yanked out of his hand, pulling him into the threshold.

"What the fuck?" a vampire gasped in French.

Luke slammed his shoulder into the vampire, knocking him to the ground. Dropping to his knee, he plunged the gladius into the chest of the vampire, sending up a cloud of dust. Luke, coughing, stood up and tucked in next to the door, feet pounding on stairs coming from the other side. A feminine grunt drew Luke's attention briefly back to the balcony. Sam poked her head into the room then darted in, pulling the rapier from its scabbard. She hid behind the open door into the bedroom.

"What's going on up here?" someone called.

Luke, trying to sound like the vamp he'd just killed, replied in French, "Nothing. Just tripped."

The foot falls stopped but were replaced by sniffing. As soon as Luke heard a floorboard squeak, he stuck his foot out, catching the vampire in the ankle and sending it tumbling into the bed. Sam sprang from behind the door and ran him through with the rapier, covering the bed in a thick puddle of reddish-black goo. As the next vampire came in, their momentum too much to stop after the rapid death of their compatriot, Luke shoved them in the back as they flew by, sending them tumbling into the goo that had been their friend. Sam struck a second time, finishing them off.

Luke didn't want to get bogged down in their first room and get stuck fighting their way out. He needed to make more room for his friends to enter so they could all get to work. The third vampire in line was more cautious after the first two were so easily dispatched, so Luke grabbed their arm and yanked them into the room, blocking the doorway with his body so no one else could get in. He shoved backwards, tripping another vampire and going down with them.

As he landed on his back in a pile of vampires, he rolled off and into a crouch. With a quick lunge forward, he stabbed a female vampire in the gut, then pulled his blade and finished her in the heart. Sam had followed him out, albeit more gracefully. She quickly tidied up the last couple vampires tangled in each other and struggling to get up.

As the bodies dissipated into goo or dust, Luke stood and backed against the wall next to a door on the opposite side of the hall. Sam stepped out to block the door as Pablo, Delilah, and Simone joined them in the hallway. Pablo had taken a minute to strip off his clothes and make the shift to his bipedal werewolf form. He hoped his pal remembered to duck when going through doors. Delilah drew her jian, standing next to Sam to block the hallway. Simone stood behind them.

Luke waved Pablo over, then grabbed the doorknob he stood beside and pushed, storming in. The room looked empty. When

Pablo ducked into the room, Luke pointed toward the bed with his gladius. Pablo solved the problem by picking up the bed. Luke bent over and looked under it. Nothing.

Signaling Pablo to set it down, Luke turned to the closet. He eased the door open. The closet had a door at the back end. A rattle behind him followed by a thump and feet scrabbling on the hard wood drew his attention. He spun around.

A vampire had attempted to hide in a wardrobe. Thinking Luke was in the closet, he'd tumbled out and tried to run away. Pablo handled the situation, wrenching the vampire's head off before it could make so much as a peep. Luke finished the body with a stab to the heart.

Luke returned to the closet, poking aside some clothes to inspect the back of the space. He saw nothing unusual, so he waved Pablo in behind him. Twisting the knob and pulling it back, he slipped into the room. As far as he could tell, it was empty except for a bed. There was nothing under it, thanks to a helping paw—two of them, from Pablo. But what was unusual about the room was the lack of a second exit into the hallway. The only entrance was through the closet. The window was even boarded up, no light peeking in from outside.

He waved Pablo closer. "Do you smell any recent habitation in this room?

Pablo gave him a thumbs up.

"Same vampire as one you just killed?" Luke asked.

Pablo shook his head.

"Many?"

Pablo nodded.

Luke nodded toward the closet. "Let's go, wolfboy."

Pablo stuck his wolfy tongue out between his long, canine fangs. Luke chuckled and followed Pablo from the room. When they rejoined Sam, Delilah, and Simone, they found more bodies on the floor, including a couple human-looking bodies. Luke wasn't getting "vamp" from them. Simone looked a bit shook up but held her blood-coated dagger steady.

"We had some company." Sam pointed to the mess on the ground where the goo and dust of young and old vampires mingled, trickling down the stairs.

"I didn't hear a thing while we were in there. What about those two?" Luke pointed to the two bodies.

"Werewolves," Delilah said.

"Simone's pack?"

"Yeah." Delilah rubbed her hand up the back of Simone's arm.

Luke and Pablo swept the last room on the floor, finding nothing. The few vampires on the floor must have responded to the incursion on the balcony.

"Clear up here. We're going to need to check for hidden rooms," Luke said. "Ready? Delilah with us."

When Delilah slid up next to him and Pablo, they ascended the stairs and headed left, leaving Sam and Simone to watch the stairs coming from the ground floor. When they swept through the upstairs rooms and found nothing, they rejoined Sam and Simone, then made their way downstairs, creeping slowly while avoiding the trickle of vampire goo.

They found the ground floor empty while checking for any doors, obvious or secret, that might lead to a basement or hidden subfloor. Again, they came up with nothing. Even the back yard was vacant. As they worked their way toward the stairs, his friends looked nervous, darting their heads around, their eyes moving over every inch, looking for something they were missing—more vampires and werewolves.

The lack of resistance felt wrong, especially after the fangers so boldly kidnapped a powerful pack alpha in their effort to reclaim the southern half of Belgium. Back on the second floor, Luke and his team stepped back out on the balcony once they determined the balcony next door was clear. He led, leaping across the narrow gap. This time, the door was locked. The doors and windows had been upgraded in the last few years and were thick, double pane numbers.

Shrugging, he knocked on the door loudly, then stepped behind the brick segment separating the door from the window. He knocked again, this time louder. The light inside flicked on.

"If you locked yourself… Oh my God…" The woman who'd opened the door backpedaled, her eyes opening wide.

Luke didn't get "vampire" off her, but he had no idea if she was a werewolf or some human thrall. Thus far, she hadn't been aggressive toward him, so he merely followed her into the room, keeping his gladius in front of him. She looked like she was about to scream, so Luke lifted his finger to his lips and shushed her, raising the gladius slightly to emphasize the point.

As Luke's friends joined him in the small room, the woman trembled as her back ran up against the wall, her hands raising above her shoulders to look non-threatening. When Simone, who was second to last, entered the room, the woman's face flashed from disbelief to fear into a moment of cunning, then relief.

"Oh, Simone!" she said in French. "I'm so glad to see you."

Luke flicked his eyes toward Simone. Everyone else was watching the woman, so Luke was the only one who saw Simone's eyes change from a moment of terror to pure hatred. She yanked her dagger from the scabbard on her belt and advanced.

"No! Simone… Please, I didn't mean… It wasn't me… They forced me…" the woman pleaded.

"Liar!" Simone yelled.

Luke cringed at the noise. They were going to have company soon.

"Do you think I didn't hear the racist words you called me and my family? The other non-white pack members? That you weren't one of the ringleaders to 'purify' our pack?" Simone's hands shook, her breathing shallow and quick between clenched teeth.

The woman's shocked face, clearly feigned, changed to disgust as she started to grow. Hair sprouted from her arms and face, claws extending from her fingertips.

Simone reacted instantly, diving forward and plunging the dagger into the woman's chest. Simone's tormentor gasped, air wheezing from her lungs as she shrunk back to her previous proportions, the hair and claws disappearing. As the woman sagged against the wall, Simone pulled the dagger out and plunged it into her heart again and then a third time. She looked about ready to keep going when she pulled her arm back, ready to strike again, but instead, she stepped back, loathing on her face. When the woman sagged to the floor dead, Simone spat on her body.

Luke whipped his head around when he heard a deep, grumbling growl. Pablo, his lips drawn back, snarled.

"We've got company, Luke," Sam said as she set her rapier down and stripped.

Finally hearing the heavy footfalls and the occasional low yip or growl coming from outside the door, Luke locked it and shoved his shoulder against it, planting his feet and legs to stabilize the door leading to the hallway. Simone, her face a mask of determination, handed her dagger to Delilah and stripped down as well. In a matter of moments, three werewolves filled the room. Simone's werewolf form was a bit shorter than Sam's and several inches shorter than Pablo's. Unlike Pablo's brown fur and Sam's more creamy tan, Simone's fur was a lustrous black. Delilah gathered everyone's clothing and shoved it into her backpack before slinging it over her shoulder.

Pablo stepped to the front while Simone and Sam reclaimed their blades. Sam, with one paw, moved Delilah behind her. Pablo looked at Luke and tapped his chest, then raised his paw to count to three using his claw-capped wolf fingers. When Pablo curled the last digit into his palm, Luke unlocked the door and hauled back on it hard. As soon as there was enough space, Pablo surged out, Sam and Simone following. The wolves released a cacophony of growls and snarls, the war cries of their kind.

"Delilah, we got to be really careful out there. Dart in, dart out. Be precise. You and me, let's watch each other's backs and help our friends." Luke said, half pep talking himself. He'd only seen a few werewolf-on-werewolf fights in his nearly two-thousand-year life, and they were terrifying memories.

Delilah, her eyes wide in shock, nodded, gulping down air. Counting down in his head, Luke plunged out the door, tackling the first wolf he came in contact with, one who'd slipped behind Luke's friends. The wolf was not expecting the power of Luke's body slam and was taken completely by surprise, letting up a piteous yelp as Luke plunged his gladius through the werewolf's chest. The wolf's body collapsed, robbed of fight, and began shifting back to its human form.

With the threat to his friends neutralized, he saw they'd effectively blocked the hallway and prevented the rest of the enemy wolves from getting behind them. The hallway and the stairs helped Pablo, Sam, and Simone nullify the enemy's superior numbers.

"Luke!" Delilah cried, shoving past him in the opposite direction from their werewolf friends.

She lunged forward, catching the first vampire in the chest. The blade Luke had commissioned for her received its first blooding, destroying the vampire, albeit slower than one of Luke's enchanted blades. As soon as the vampire sloughed off her jian, she kicked out in front of her, catching another one. She followed the kick with a slash and brought the blade around for another strike.

Checking back on the wolves, it appeared they had the situation under control. Sam's and Simone's martial arts training served them well as they mixed the brute strength and speed of a werewolf with their deadly arts. Simone had integrated the dagger into her savate to good effect, although it looked a bit awkward. Pablo just waded in, ripping and biting with his muscular power, mixing in the fighting he'd been learning in the year they'd been working together.

Delilah was no longer visible. Luke sprinted forward and slid into the room where she'd disappeared. He found her just inside the room, holding off several vampires using some cool kung fu sword techniques designed for just such occasions. He backed up a few steps to ensure he didn't foul her movements.

"Dee, I'm right behind you. Break left on my signal." Luke kept his voice low so it wouldn't distract her or potentially alert their fanged foes. "Go!"

Delilah lunged forward, skewering a vampire, then fell back to the left, clearing the entrance for Luke to come all the way through. He ran forward, springing on the bed, and launched himself off the mattress feet first, delivering a brutal two-footed drop kick to the vampire nearest the wall to Luke's right. Like a cat, Luke rolled in the air and landed on his hands and knees, popping back up to stab the nearest vampire. He caught it in the neck. The vampire fell away, clutching its throat as the thick reddish-black sludge coated its fingers. Turning, Luke dropped and took out the fanger he'd drop kicked. Delilah had dispatched another two, leaving one along with the vamp Luke had stabbed in the neck. Before it could start healing, Luke finished it off while Delilah took out the final foe.

"That was a pretty slick trick with the drop kick," Delilah said, breathing heavily.

"Thanks, nice rhymes. Mind checking on the rest of the gang?" Luke headed toward the closet door, yanking it open but only finding a closet devoid of anything that might be secretly something else.

Delilah poked her head back in. "Luke!"

Luke dashed out of the room. Their friends were being pushed back under the weight of too many werewolves, although Sam, Simone, and Pablo had thinned out a lot of the enemies with bipedal forms. The full wolves were fast and nimble, harrying his friends in teams. Their friends leaked blood from cuts and bites to their limbs.

Delilah, falling back on her favorite tactic, darted in and out from behind her bigger werewolf friends, using attacks of opportunity to keep from getting in trouble with faster and stronger enemies, although this was the first time she'd had to use it against werewolves.

Luke felt awkward about it. Werewolves had been his friends and allies for the last year. He was dating one. Now he had to fight them.

Taking a cue from Delilah, he worked the perimeter. With the added assistance from Luke and Delilah, Pablo, Sam, and Simone took down the remaining bipedal werewolves. Once their muscle fell, the four-legged werewolves tucked tail and ran.

As soon as they made it down the stairs, Luke guessed they had transformed back to their human shapes and ran out the door. Paws and teeth weren't ideal for doorknobs. He had no idea if they would run away naked or shift back to their full wolf form.

"You OK, Delilah?" Luke asked between pants.

"Yeah, think so." She stood bent over with her hands on her knees, chest heaving.

Luke waved his hands toward the werewolves. "Check on them. I'm going to make sure we're clear here."

Luke ran down the stairs, quickly pulling the front door closed and turning the lock. He didn't want some random passerby checking on why the door was open. He efficiently moved through the ground floor, making sure there weren't any more werewolves or vampires hiding about. He didn't see anyone.

When he rejoined the rest of the team on the next floor up, Delilah and Simone were missing. Pablo and Sam sat on the floor and leaned up against the wall.

"Where'd they go?" Luke asked.

Sam pointed up.

Nodding, Luke ran upstairs, calling out, "It's just me."

"It's clear up here," Delilah replied.

Luke slowed, taking the stairs at a reasonable rate. He checked out the rooms, looking for any hidden doors, rooms, or passages. So far, the first row house was the only one with any interesting architecture. When Delilah popped out of the last bedroom, she had her arm around werewolf Simone, helping her limp out.

"She insisted on escorting me in case someone was up here," Delilah said, seeing Luke's eyes drift toward Simone.

"Need any help?"

"No, I got her. How are Sam and Pablo?"

"Looking pretty tired. They're still in wolf form, so I wasn't able to find out how they're actually doing. I'll go check on them since we're clear up here." He turned around.

He'd hoped they wouldn't get bogged down on their way through the houses, but it seemed like most of the remaining werewolves had been holed up in this house. There was nothing he could do about it now. His friends' health would always be his priority.

He shook his head, huffing in annoyance. Every moment's delay meant their rescue was less likely to be a success, but if he rushed out the door, he'd likely be outnumbered and fail, anyway. Better to be smart and cautious.

When he rounded the stairs to the middle floor, he only saw Pablo sitting against the wall, still in wolf form.

"Where's Sam?" Luke asked.

"In here!" she called. "Can you have Delilah bring me my clothes please? I forget I didn't have them."

Delilah had just cleared the stairs.

"Dee, Sam needs her clothes. She's in that bedroom." He indicated which room with his thumb.

Delilah nodded and helped Simone into the room where a nude Sam waited for clothing.

Luke squatted in front of Pablo. "How are you doing, pal?"

Pablo shrugged and gave a huff.

It was hard to tell what blood was his and what blood came from the werewolves he'd fought. Luke couldn't see anything serious— Pablo's superior werewolf healing was taking effect. Pablo placed his paws on the ground and looked like he was going to get up so Luke stood and extended his hand, offering to help his best friend off the floor.

Sam popped out the door, dressed. She shoved the rapier back into its scabbard. She only looked slightly stiff.

"Feeling OK, Sam?"

"Yeah. A little beat up, but better after washing off the blood. Delilah's getting Simone cleaned up now," Sam replied.

Luke nodded.

"When they're done. It's your turn, Pablo." Sam reached out and squeezed the elbow of her dear friend.

Pablo nodded and limped to the door, leaning up against the door frame.

"Let's wait downstairs, I don't want anyone coming back in and catching us unawares," Luke said.

Sam nodded and followed him downstairs.

"Pablo going to be OK?" Luke asked. "He seemed kind of down."

"Yeah. He doesn't like having to kill werewolves. Neither do I, to be honest, but I'm a bit more ruthless. They allied with the forces of evil; I'm not going to shed a tear for them for bringing their own retribution down upon their heads. Pablo is, ultimately, a very sweet man. It's a little harder on him. It's what makes him such a good second for the pack and for Holly. She's a naturally more reserved and formal person. Pablo is the softy who loves nearly everyone."

Luke nodded. "It's one of the reasons I like him so much."

Sam turned her head and sniffed. "What is that stench?"

Luke lifted his nose into the air and sniffed. "I'm not getting any — Wait, I'm getting something. A faint hint of sewage?"

"It's not quite right for sewage, seems…fresher." Sam moved her heard around, sniffing, and walked around the room until she stopped by a couch. "Luke, come here."

Luke stepped up beside her and looked toward where she was pointing. There were scuff marks where the couch had been repeatedly moved back and forth over the hardwood floor. Luke shoved the couch out of the way, revealing a trap door. It was a rectangle about two and a half feet wide and about six feet long. In the center of the nearest side was a black iron ring. Along the same edge, there were several latches keeping it shut.

As soon as Luke started sliding the latch bars, Sam gasped. "Babies…"

"What?" Luke stopped.

"I hear children crying." She jogged over to the stairs and yelled, "We need Simone down here!"

When Sam returned, she looked worried with a bit of scared around the edge. Luke felt much the same as a frown tugged at his lips. Simone had transformed back to her human self and dressed, but she still needed Delilah's help to navigate the stairs.

"A wolf got her on the back of the leg. She's lucky it didn't sever her hamstring." Sam crossed her arms.

Luke nodded. "Sam, I want you to have a shotgun ready and aimed down, just in case."

Pulling a flashlight from his belt pouch, he reached down and moved the last couple of bars, then grabbed the ring. Sam pumped a shell into the firing chamber and pointed the barrel at the floor, nodding at Luke. He held up a hand and counted down three on his fingers, yanking the ring and pulling the door open. High-pitched screams, feet scrabbling, and chains dragging attacked their ears as the stench of full latrine buckets assaulted their noses. Luke turned on the flashlight, shining it in. Tiny, emaciated faces started at him, squinting or hiding their eyes behind skinny arms.

"Fuck," Luke whispered. He hated vampires.

CHAPTER
FIFTEEN

L uke stared down into the pit under the floor. Moving the flashlight around, he only saw children. Sam engaged the safety on her Winchester M12, removed the shell from the firing chamber, and pushed it back into the magazine. Luke waved Delilah and Simone over.

"Simone, do you recognize any of these children?" Luke pointed down into the pit.

She looked down, moving from face to face. "Yes. A few of them are from the pack, the families that were purified."

"Kiara?" said a tiny voice.

"Idrissa?" Simone cried, tears streaming down her face.

Luke panned the flashlight toward the voice. A skinny Black boy of maybe twelve stared back, trying to shade his eyes from the flashlight.

"Idrissa!" Simone tried to pull away from Delilah, but her leg wouldn't properly support her.

Delilah held her up while she whispered soothing things to her.

"We'll get them out of here," Luke said. "Shit. Shit. Shit." Hearing the squeak of stairs, Luke watched Pablo work his way down gingerly. "Pablo? Can you keep an eye out front?"

"You got it," Pablo replied.

Luke set his gladius down on the ground and worked his way down the rickety steps into the subfloor pit, nearly gagging from the stench.

Fury burning under his skin, he tried to school his face into some semblance of kindness, not wanting to frighten the children. He spoke in French. "We are going to get you out of here and get you help. Simone Ndiaye is with us."

"Kiara!" yelled the little boy who Luke guessed might be Simone's brother.

"They're friends, Idrissa. We're going to rescue you," Simone called in French from upstairs.

Moving the flashlight around the room and floor, the children were locked together at the ankles with manacles attached to a chain run through a ring on the wall to reach the next kid.

Luke turned his head toward the opening above. "See if you can find some keys! We need to unlock them."

"OK, Luke," Sam replied. A few minutes later, Sam poked her head down. "Luke, found them."

Luke went up a couple stairs and grabbed a ring of keys from Sam. "OK, kids. I'm going to get you unlocked. When I get you freed, go upstairs. If you need the bathroom or a drink of water, please do."

A few of the children nodded. Luke started with the first child and worked through the keys until he found the right one. As soon as he lifted the manacle from the kid's ankle, the child scrambled up the stairs before anyone could return the manacle to his ankle. One by one, Luke freed the children. When all was said and done, he'd released eleven kids.

Luke moved the flashlight around the room, trying to find anything that might indicate another room. He pounded on the walls, but only got a solid dull thud in response. Without burning all their time, he'd done as well as he could. He started up the stairs.

"Luke!" Pablo yelled.

Sighing, Luke dashed up the stairs to the window where Pablo stood. A car had pulled up onto the sidewalk in front of one of the vampire houses they hadn't cleared yet. A moment later, a van screeched to a halt behind the car. Vampires scrambled out onto the street, dragging someone covered in a blanket, and piled into the vehicles, shoving the blanket-covered lump into the van.

Luke's stomach tightened into a knot, bile burning in the back of his throat. He didn't know who or what was in that blanket, but he guessed he'd just witnessed their objective being whisked away in the back of a van.

"I hate vampires," Pablo said. "Like really hate them. At least we saved some children. I don't feel so bad about killing those were-wolves now."

Luke wrapped his arm around Pablo's shoulder and gave him a one-armed hug. "We haven't saved them yet, but it does look like we might have missed saving Pieter."

Pablo sighed, shaking his head. "Yeah. Looks like our mission just changed."

"Luke, what are we going to do?" Sam asked, locking her arm in his.

He shook his head, failing to clear the uneasy feeling about what he'd just witnessed on the street. He turned around and surveyed the frightened kids, Simone and Idrissa were hugging on a couch.

"We've got to get them out of here, far away from any vampire that's been feeding on them." He counted everyone in the room. "We can't stay in here either."

"We don't have enough car space to get them out," Sam said.

"I know. I wish we had my VeeDub."

"Do we have time to go get it and come back?" Pablo asked.

"It's not a short round trip, and I have no idea if the fangers are coming back or what other hell they might send our way." Luke paced back and forth. "Shit, I hate to do this."

Luke pulled his phone out and called the caretaker, speaking in French. "Yes. I'm sorry to wake you. We're in a bit of an emergency."

The caretaker yawned. "What can I do for you?"

"I need you to put the rear bench seat into the van and drive it up to Cambrai. We're going to need a doctor too. At the house."

"Are you or any of your friends injured? Will you need me to bring the doctor there?"

"No. None of us are injured. We found some…children, orphans."

"Vampires? Have they bitten the children?" The caretaker sounded disgusted.

"Yeah. They've been fed on," Luke replied.

"I'll arrange food and beverages for them. They'll need both. I'll send my daughter. She'll bring the family van. It'll be more comfortable for the young ones. She has a couple children's seats as well."

"Thank you. I'll text the address I want you to go to. We're going to move them now, get them to a spot that's a little safer."

"I'll have her along shortly," the caretaker said.

"Thanks again." Luke hung up his phone. Luke waved everyone over to him. "Simone, can you join us, please?

Simone whispered something to Idrissa, then walked, still limping some, over to join the circle with the adults.

"Your brother?" Luke asked.

"Yes. I thought… I thought he was dead," she replied, wiping the tears from her cheeks.

"Is that why you didn't mention him?" Sam asked.

Simone nodded. "It was too painful to think about or even say out loud."

Delilah wrapped an arm around her shoulder and gave her a one-armed hug.

"That's understandable." Luke looked over at the kids, who were all staring at the adults. "Do any of the kids speak English?"

"Idrissa does a little. I'm not sure about any of the others. I don't know them well."

Luke took a step toward the kids. "Parlez vous anglais?"

Most of the kids shook their heads.

"Francais?" Luke raised his hand.

All but two kids raised their hands.

He pointed to the two Black children. "Deutsch?"

They shook their heads. "Vlaams."

Flemish. *Fuck,* Luke thought. He turned back to his friends. "I want to take them over in small groups so we don't look quite so conspicuous taking a train of kids outside this late at night. Simone, you and Delilah take the first group. Sam—"

Pablo sniffed the air. "Sorry to interrupt, but do you smell that?"

Luke stuck his nose in the air, pulling in some breaths. "Not sure. All I can pick up is the waste buckets."

Pablo sniffed his way toward the center of the room. "It smells like…gas…"

As he looked down into the pit where the kids had been kept, flames erupted from the pit's depths. Pablo, still not feeling steady after his various wounds, tried to leap backwards but ended up tripping. Kids screamed and ran away.

"Get the kids gathered. Delilah, you stand by the door and count them up," Luke yelled before running to gather up kids. In French, he yelled, "Children. To the front door, now!"

A few heard him and ran to Delilah. Simone, Pablo, and Sam ran into the mass of kids and just started picking them up and carrying them to Delilah. Luke, seeking the two kids who spoke Flemish, snatched them under his arms and lugged them back toward Delilah.

"Delilah, how many?" Luke tried counting as well.

"Ten."

Pablo ran back into the center of the room rapidly filling with smoke.

"Get them outside and back to our place, fast. Before the fire department comes." Luke ran back into the spreading flames, unzipping his hoodie and pulling the cloth over his mouth. "Pablo?"

"Got him!" Pablo called, coughing.

Luke ran to Pablo and grabbed the kid. The sudden movement wasn't helping Pablo's limp. Together, they ran out of the house and kept running until they were safely away from the spreading flames. Luke set the kid down and all three of them bent over and coughed, trying to get clean air into their lungs. As soon as Luke's coughing calmed down, he squatted.

"Get on my back," he instructed the kid.

The boy wrapped his arms around Luke's neck. Luke scooped the kid's legs in his arms and started toward their base, still coughing occasionally. When they heard sirens in the distance, they picked up their speed into a loping jog, Pablo hobbling along as best as he could. Checking both ways, they darted across the street and hid inside the entryway to their apartment building just as a firetruck flew by.

Luke took a minute to huff and puff after carrying the kid for a block and a half. Once he caught his breath, he asked in French, "Can you walk from here?"

"Oui," the boy replied.

Luke waved everyone forward as they made their way to the stairs up to the fourth-floor apartment. By the time they reached their floor, Pablo was struggling, using the banister to aid his ascent.

"I need serious rest and some protein," Pablo said, grimacing.

"That bad?" Luke asked.

"I've had worse, but wolf wounds always react a little funny. The three of us will need to take it light for a few days."

Luke scowled. "It looks like we have a few days to spare since this fell apart spectacularly."

"Yeah. It could have gone better, but at least we managed to help some kids. No one deserves to be treated like that. The fucking vamps had no intention of freeing them. That hell hole we pulled them out of was rigged with gas. It's too convenient to be a coincidence. If we'd been a few minutes slower finding them, things would have been really bad for them." Pablo wiped sweat from his brow with the back of his hand.

Luke slipped his arm around Pablo's waist to help him down the hall to their flat. "Yeah. I'm thankful for that. Let's see how everyone is doing."

Sam opened the door for them, ushering them in. Simone and Delilah were pulling drinks and food from their cabinets, handing them out to the kids.

"Go slow, kids, or you'll make yourselves sick," Simone said, although it seemed to do little good as the ravenous kids shoveled the snacks into their mouths. Fortunately, she'd kept the portions small.

Once Luke settled Pablo into the comfy armchair, he checked in with Simone and Delilah. "How are the kids? Any serious injuries we need to prioritize?"

Delilah shook her head. "Not that I can see. Simone says no one is reporting anything. They've got some suspect bruises I don't like and signs of regular feeding on their necks."

"Yeah. They look pretty beat up and chewed on. Plus we have a long car trip ahead of us. We should probably get packed up as well. We need to get far away from here while we have the kids. When the fire department clears out, we'll have fangers checking out the damage, and I don't want them to feel the kids this close to their old lair."

"What about the cameras and equipment in the other place?" Delilah asked.

"I'm guessing they'll go up with the rest of houses. We have all the data here, so it's not a huge loss." Luke headed to his room to pack his and Pablo's stuff.

"I had the same thought. I'll help you get everything ready to go," Delilah said.

Pablo tried to pull himself out of the chair. As Luke walked by, he pushed Pablo back into it.

"I got it, buddy. Give your legs a rest. We'll have some work to get everything down to the vehicles. Sam, Simone, you too. Delilah and I will get everything packed so you can rest. Save your legs for the evacuation."

Before Luke started, he pulled out his phone and sent a text to Pieter, letting him know they needed to talk as soon as possible. Luke hoped everything was going smoothly with the trade. After waiting for a moment, hoping to see receipt of the message, he turned the volume up and tucked the phone back into his pocket when there was no sign of life.

He pulled out their suitcases and efficiently disassembled their room in a few minutes, then took care of Sam's room. Nineteen hundred years of moving around and traveling smart made him an exceptional packer. Finished, he piled their luggage by the door, Delilah adding hers and Simone's to the stack. Together, they disassembled their camera system and stuffed it into a spare duffel bag, combining the shotgun bags into one heavy bag.

The kids, exhausted from their ordeal and terrifying rescue, lounged about the room, their eyes drifting closed. Luke stepped into the window to watch the fire department try to contain the inferno the vampires set on their exit. They'd only cleared two of the houses. Who knew what else the vamps had stashed in the other three houses. He shook his head, crossing his arms. He checked the time. The caretaker's daughter should be there anytime. Twenty minutes later, he saw a van park and Anne-Marie step out. She pulled out her phone and called Luke.

Luke and Delilah grabbed the heavy equipment while Simone, Sam, and Pablo grabbed the suitcases. They left the kids upstairs while they packed the gear. Returning to the flat, Delilah and Luke organized the kids to go down in waves. Delilah took Idrissa and one other kid down to join her and Simone in Luke's Volvo 242GT, while Luke organized the next batch. Anne-Marie came up and escorted six French-speaking children to join her and Sam in her van, leaving Luke with the two Flemish speaking kids and one other kid. He got them buckled into the back of his BMW then joined Pablo in the front.

"Here we go," Luke said, starting the motor.

Delilah and Anne-Marie had taken off as soon as they were ready. They knew the way home, and Luke didn't want them bunched together. Off in the distance, he felt the twinge of a few vampires. He wasn't sure if they were watching, but it didn't matter. They were leaving Cambrai and wouldn't be back.

By the time they pulled into Luke's manor, the eastern horizon faintly threatened morning with the first hints of the sun's light peeking over. The kids in the back of his SUV had all zonked out somewhere before Valenciennes, occasionally startling awake only to drift off again. After the long day and intense night, Luke longed for his bed and the sweet release of sleep but knew he still had too much to do to get the kids settled in.

Fortunately, the mystery presented by the two Flemish children kept his mind awake on the drive across northern France into southern Belgium. How they came to be in a vampire's pit in northern France when most of the other children—or maybe all, he'd have to check with Simone to get confirmation—were from the families purged from the Bordeaux Pack would be one of the first mysteries he'd track down. If their parents were still alive, they must be worried sick about their children. If they were part of Pieter's pack, Luke could help them reunite with their family.

Émile met them out front as soon as Luke parked. "Did you have any trouble getting out of Cambrai?"

"No. Seems like we got away without incident. Do we have rooms ready for the kids?" Luke rubbed his tired eyes.

"Yes. I've made up several rooms and split the beds into doubles.

I've got some easy snacks and drinks set up for the kids. My son said he'd be out later this afternoon to look anyone over unless someone needs medical attention sooner."

"No. So far everyone is holding up OK. Some more sleep would do them good. It'll be good to see Alexandre again," Luke replied.

"I'm sure he'll be happy to not have to stitch you up." He looked toward the poor kids. "Though this might not be better. How long will you be staying so I can lay in supplies?"

"I'm not sure. I'll know more by this evening or tomorrow."

"Is there anything more you need at the moment?" Émile yawned.

Luke yawned in response. "No. I think we're set for now. Go get some rest."

The caretaker nodded and walked to his car while his daughter, with Simone's help, organized the kids and moved them toward the snacks. After the long night, Luke needed food as well and followed them in. Once the kids fell on the simple snacks, the caretaker's daughter disappeared, returning with a notepad. She went around the room, asking the kids what size clothes they needed until she got to the two Flemish kids. Luke translated for her so she could finish the list.

"That's good thinking. They'll need some clean clothes so we can launder these. Or maybe just burn them." Luke looked around the room. Under the light of day, the clothes were filthy and ragged.

"I'll get what I can for them. No one wants to put on dirty clothes after bathing. If there's nothing else, I'd like to go home and get some sleep."

"Of course. Thanks again," Luke said.

She patted Luke's arm and left. Luke found himself a plate and grabbed some food. He smelled coffee somewhere, but as much as he wanted it, he needed to crash and get a few hours' sleep. He sat at an empty table, not wanting to crowd the kids who'd mostly picked a couple tables of their own to spread out over. They were quiet, periodically sneaking looks at the adults, save for Simone, who several knew from their former pack.

Sam pulled out a chair next to Luke's. "What are we going to do with all these kids? We can't just leave them here to fend for themselves while we keep hunting."

"No. This has definitely put a crimp on things." Luke picked up a croissant and spread jam on a section before popping it in his mouth.

"Can we get Pieter's help?" Sam asked.

Luke's eyes drifted toward to two Flemish children. "I'm not sure how safe they'll be with an unplugged leak in the Flanders Pack. Plus the vampires are keeping a tight watch on the pack to ensure they don't violate the agreement. We can't risk that."

Sam frowned and nodded. "Are we going to need to organize a rescue crew from Portland?"

"I hate to drag more people into the epicenter of a growing war zone, even if this is the eye of the hurricane." Luke shook his head, smearing more jam on his croissant.

"It seems like rescuing vulnerable people is becoming a habit. I'll reach out to Holly as soon as I finish my breakfast. We may not be able to bring in more fighters, but we definitely have people who can help with the kids. I'll be sure we pick at least a few people who speak French." Sam turned her head and yawned, covering her mouth. "Then mama needs to get her some beauty sleep."

With food in the kids' bellies, Sam found a quiet spot to make her call while Luke helped organize the kids into rooms and showed them the bathrooms for quick showers. The adults broke out spare shorts and T-shirts for the kids to augment the few children's clothes Anne-Marie had brought from her house. It would do until the kids could take more thorough baths. When the last door was shut, Luke retired to his room and took a quick shower to clean off the last of the stench of the pit and smoke before sinking into his bed, finding deep sleep.

AFTER ONLY A HANDFUL of hours of sleep, Luke was foggy-headed and sandy-eyed when he stumbled downstairs to make an espresso. He leaned up against the wall in the kitchen and sipped the coffee, savoring the dark, bitter flavors while letting the aromas tease his senses awake. Feeling a little more ready for the world, he pulled another shot of espresso and headed to find out what everyone was up to.

Before he emerged into the solarium, he pulled out his phone and dialed Pieter, but the call went straight to voicemail. "Hey Pieter, it's Luke. I need to talk to you as soon as possible. A bit worried since I haven't heard from you yet. Call me." He shoved his phone into his pocket.

Once he stepped out of the bowels of the house into the solarium, he heard the sounds of kids playing. Several of the children ran around on the grounds playing some sort of tag-like game. Sam, Delilah, and Simone sat around one of the patio tables drinking coffee. Luke joined them.

"They seem to be feeling more lively," Luke said.

"Mhm." Sam took a sip of her coffee, watching the kids run about yelling. "I imagine they're feeling good to be free and in the sun. I have no idea how long they were there. We haven't pressed them on anything yet except to find out what they want to eat."

Simone, her eyes on her brother as he played with the others, smiled contentedly. "Luke, thank you for returning my family to me. I thought I'd lost all of them."

"What do you plan to do now?" Delilah asked, speculation in her eyes.

Simone turned to Luke. "I'd like to stay with you and help, if you'll let me."

"What about your brother?" Luke asked.

"I can take care of him, and he's old enough to manage on his own as well." She tried to keep her voice steady, but her eyes pleaded with Luke.

He saw a lot of Delilah in her—the angry woman who needed to strike back at those who'd harmed her family and killed her parents. When he'd denied Delilah, she'd resorted to her own devices, pulling Pablo in deeper with her. Luke had been wrong to push her away then, afraid of bringing people into his life, risking their lives and the emotional pain of befriending and losing them. He wouldn't deny Simone. She was far less prepared to strike out on her own than

Delilah had been. Besides, he had a feeling Delilah would be very upset if Luke sent Simone away.

"I can't speak for the rest of the team, but I'd welcome your help. We can figure out how to keep your brother out of trouble." Luke smiled warmly at the young woman.

She smiled broadly. It was the biggest smile he'd seen on her since they'd met. She had her brother back and a place in the world, at least for a while. Delilah grinned, sliding her hand under the table to rub her hand over Simone's knee and thigh. Sam, paying more attention to the kids, didn't notice, chuckling as some of the laughing kids went tumbling into a pile.

"Where's Pablo?" Luke asked.

"Still in bed, as far as I know. I think he was injured more than he let on," Sam replied.

"Will he be OK?" Delilah pulled her attention away from Simone and back to Luke and Sam.

"He should be. If everything's closed up, it'll just be a manner of rest and plenty of protein. Also, I think he's a little homesick for Tony. I don't think they've been apart this long since they met." Sam leaned back in her chair, stretching her legs out in front.

"Who is Tony?" Simone asked.

Sam turned to Simone, a thoughtful expression on her face. "Tony is Pablo's husband."

Simone leaned forward, her eyes intent. "Pablo is gay?"

Sam nodded. "Yup. Our pack is an LGBTQ pack. My wife is the packleader. Luke is dating one of the pack doctors who has a long-term live-in partner. His adopted kid is trans."

"And everyone is welcome and gets to be themselves?" Simone asked, leaning further forward, her eyes growing even more intense as her they narrowed.

Sam nodded. "Holly and I formed the pack as a sanctuary for werewolves who weren't welcome in their own packs. We've grown strong and large. Everyone contributes to the best of their ability, and the pack takes care of everyone. We all work together and share in the pack's successes."

Simone's eyes widened with notes of hope. "Truly?"

"Truly," Sam said. "If that sounds like the kind of pack you want to be a part of, we would be happy to have you."

Simone's face sank. "I don't have any money to move…"

"I can cover whatever expenses you and your brother need to move and get established," Luke offered.

"As can the pack," Sam added.

Simone looked at Delilah, her eyebrow lifted.

"Sam, mind helping me get set up for the doctor?" Luke asked.

"Sure. I could use another coffee, anyway. Too much going on and not enough sleep." Sam stood and took Luke's arm in hers.

Together, they walked back in silence, enjoying the sound of the kids playing, the breeze rustling through the leaves, and the gentle rolling of the river. Luke led Sam to a small bedroom tucked away on the main floor that wasn't being used. Seeing the dust, Luke turned around and grabbed some cleaning supplies from a closet and set about getting the room in order.

"This is an odd location for a bedroom," Sam observed, watching Luke clean.

"It's a 'servant's room.' The architect said it was good to have a place for a servant in case I ever needed something when the full staff wasn't around. It wasn't worth explaining to him I rarely kept much staff on hand, so here it is."

"Why do you have a big house like this if you weren't going to fill it with servants?" Sam ran her finger along a cabinet, showing the dusty digit to Luke.

He sprayed the cabinet down and dusted it. "It was easier at the time to have a sizable manor house here. I have various titles if I want to trot them out. I've kept this land for nearly two millennia. When I built this, it amounted to a sign saying, 'go away.' You don't approach landed nobility to buy their land. I just don't want people around. There's too much sensitive stuff here."

Sam leaned against the wall and crossed her arms. "And you can trust your caretaker's family?"

"They've always done right by me. The work is rarely arduous since I'm gone for long stretches, so they're allowed to pursue whatever hobbies or careers they want. Émile's daughter is a wonderful artist. You've seen Anne-Marie's work. Her brother Alexandre is a doctor. It's handy to have a discrete, trusted physician on hand at times."

"Like today."

"Yup." Luke left Sam in the room and returned with a sheet to put on the small mattress. "Maybe I should have the doctor convert this to a small clinic room. It would be good to have something like that on hand for the random times it's needed. Better than leaving it virtually unused." With the bed made, he surveyed his work. "It'll have to do for now. At least the doctor will have some privacy to examine the kids.

Sam pushed herself off the wall. "Have you had time to think about what's next for us? We're kind of at a standstill."

Luke led Sam back to the kitchen so he could make her another coffee. "That depends a lot on if Holly can get us some support and when. I don't know who we can trust in the Flanders Pack. It could just be a coincidence, or it could be the start of what happened with Simone's pack."

"I hope it's the former and not the later." Sam looked worried.

"Me too." Luke handed Sam her latte and pulled his phone out, checking the time. "I'm worried about why we haven't heard from Pieter yet."

Seeing Luke fixate over the clock, Sam patted his arm. "I'm sure Pieter is fine, and Holly will call as soon as she has any information for us. It won't take her long to come up with a plan and potential roster. She's an amazing organizer and has refined things even further since you've become involved with the pack."

"I wasn't worried about Holly…much. I just promised Maggie and Gwen I'd check in after the operation. Still a bit early for the west coast."

"Lover boy wants to make some smoochie calls." Pablo shuffled in and yawned, rubbing his eyes. His hair looked disheveled as if he'd packed a week's worth of bedhead into a single short sleep.

Luke started a coffee for him. He didn't refute the comment, even if he'd never refer to it in those terms. He missed Maggie and Gwen. They'd worked their way into his heart and without them around, he felt incomplete and slightly off balance. He'd often felt like he moved through life with pieces missing, leaving them scattered throughout history. Some he knew intimately and would never be able to fill — the three wives he'd spent their lifetimes with and some of the amazing friends he'd made over the centuries, all who he'd outlived and buried.

He didn't like being away from the people who'd chosen to inject themselves into his life, like Gwen and Maggie, but he appreciated having people worth missing. He felt less hollow and more connected with the world of the living. Pablo, Sam, and Delilah were part of that connection, but he didn't have to miss them since he'd brought them with him.

"Thinking about Maggie?" Sam asked, drawing Luke out of his silence.

"And Gwen, and how it's weird I have people in my life to miss. I'd consigned my life to having no one in it, and now I have a lot of people in it. Multiple packs of werewolves, including some very special wolves, like you and Maggie and Gwen."

"And Pablo?" Sam asked, a smirk on her face as she eyed Pablo out of the corner of her eye.

"Nah. Not Pablo."

Pablo took a sip of his coffee, pinky up, and gave Luke a haughty look. "Hmph. I'll go where I'm appreciated."

Luke laughed. "You know I love you, Pablo. I just don't often get an opportunity to return the teasing you always give me."

Pablo smiled. "I know you do. I love you too."

Luke's phone buzzed. Picking it up, he was disappointed to see it wasn't Maggie. "The doctor is here. He speaks English. Sam, if you could escort him to the room we set up, that would be appreciated. I'll gather the kids."

Luke headed outside to find Simone. Since she had history with several of the kids, it'd be easier to enlist her help. Delilah and Simone, holding hands under the table, didn't hear Luke walking up behind them until he scuffed his feet and cleared his throat to alert them. They dropped each other's hands.

Luke did his best to hide the smile tugging at his lips. "Simone, would you help me get the children? The doctor is here."

Simone nodded and called her brother over to help. Together, they convinced the kids playing outside to follow them inside. Simone stayed with them while the doctor examined them. Luke went upstairs to gather the children who still hadn't emerged from their rooms yet.

While the doctor examined them, Anne-Marie brought in clothes and sorted them by size so the kids could pick what would work for them. The house was a hub of activity as children milled about and the caretaker's people set about making food for everyone.

This was not how Luke thought this trip would go. So far, he'd seen very little action. Even though Belgium was the place of his birth, it wasn't quite his home anymore and hadn't been for a long time, except for brief stays. Now he had to find a proverbial needle in a haystack in two countries. Multiple needles in multiple haystacks as he fought Le Mousquetaire and tried to find the leak in Pieter's pack.

Waiting on the two Flemish kids, Luke mulled over the questions he planned to ask. He had no idea how much they knew about the larger machinations that resulted in them being held hostage by vampires in a pit with a bunch of French kids. When the brothers emerged from the exam room, Luke took them to get beverages and a snack, then out to the patio where they could sit in the open and enjoy the sun and the sound of nature.

"I don't think we've had a chance to be formally introduced," Luke said in Flemish Dutch. "My name is Luke."

"Hugo," replied the oldest, nudging his brother lightly after he sat silent for a while.

"Noah."

"I'm guessing you're both Belgian. Where are you from?"

"Ghent," replied the older brother.

"How did you end up in that house in France?" Luke asked.

The younger brother, getting fidgety, looked away from Luke and tugged his brother's sleeve. "I want to go play."

"Can he go play? I'll answer your questions. You don't need him," Hugo said.

"Of course he can go." Luke turned to the little boy. "Go have fun, OK?"

Noah nodded and took off at a run toward a few kids who'd found a soccer ball that Anne-Marie had brought with the clothes.

"What was your question?" the boy asked.

"How did you end up in that house?" Luke asked again.

"People came into our house at night and took us." Hugo focused his attention in the middle of the table, not making eye contact with Luke.

"Did you see them?"

"No. They put bags on our heads," the boy said.

"How long were you in there?" Luke leaned forward a little, trying to look relaxed.

"What day is it now?" When Luke provided the current date, the boy replied, "About six weeks."

"Do you know what happened to your parents?"

The boy shook his head.

"Did you hear them shouting when you were taken?"

"No. I just heard the men taking us," Hugo said.

"Did they speak French?"

"No. Flemish," the boy replied.

Luke exhaled heavily. "Do you know which dialect they used?"

Hugo nodded. "I think Antwerp."

Luke switched to an Antwerp dialect instead of the more neutral one he was using and rattled off a few sentences before going back. "Like that?"

Hugo nodded nervously. "Yes."

"Do you remember what they were saying?" Luke asked.

The boy nodded, resting his elbows on the table while looking between his hands. "The one giving the orders told someone to take us to Lille. He said his friend there would put us to good use."

"Anything else?"

"Just some more orders or questions. Was the house under

control? Was the car ready for us? Check for an attic. That kind of stuff."

Luke leaned forward, trying not to look too intense. "Ok. I need you to think about this. Do you think if you heard the voice again, you'd recognize it?"

The boy looked up at Luke finally, nodding his head. "Yes, I think so."

CHAPTER
SEVENTEEN

L uke and the team sat in the sitting room claimed as their evening sanctuary, a fire crackling. Pablo'd just returned with a tray full of beers. The kids were all in their rooms with TVs or sleep to occupy them.

Sam took a drink of the Chimay Red Pablo had brought for her. "Dang, Luke. You're going to turn me into a beer drinker."

Pablo, the owner of the pack's brewpub, looked shocked. "You cut me deep, Sam. Real deep."

Luke, smiling, could tell his friend wanted to dramatically flounce away from Sam, but he couldn't with the rest of the beers still to distribute. As was becoming usual, Delilah and Simone snuggled under a blanket on the love seat. Luke slightly narrowed his eyes at Delilah, a twinkle in them drawing the corner of one side of his mouth up in a quirk. Delilah, noticing his gaze, raised an eyebrow in challenge. Luke smiled and looked to his beer when Pablo dropped it off.

"So he can probably recognize who was speaking?" Sam asked, picking up where they'd left off their conversation when Pablo went for refills.

"He says so," Luke replied.

"Now the trick is to get him in the right place with the right voice without endangering him," Delilah said.

"That is the trick, thought that's probably only a last resort. I'm going to need to talk to Pieter, but beyond him, I'm trusting no one from the Flanders Pack until we can cross them off the list as a suspect." Luke sniffed his beer, then took a drink.

"Still haven't heard from Pieter yet?" Delilah asked.

Luke shook his head. "No. And that's worrying. I've tried calling a few times. I'd have thought he would have wanted to talk after we missed the opportunity to free his father. I hope he's OK."

"Do you suspect someone on the pack's leadership council?" Pablo asked.

"I don't know, but the kids and the leaks have to be related. There's some kind of alliance between the vamp called Le Mousquetaire and a rogue element in Pieter's pack," Luke said, taking a drink of his beer, then letting out a satisfied sigh.

"Do you know if you can trust this Pieter?" Simone asked.

The young woman was usually fairly quiet during discussions as a probationary member of the team and as the least experienced. Also, she still hadn't fully shed the pack subservience forced on her from her former pack.

"That's a fair question," Luke replied. "We've worked with him in dangerous circumstances. He's earned my trust for now, but I'll be cautious."

Simone seemed grateful to have her opinion heard and taken seriously. If they could get her trained on weapons, she'd make a fine addition to their squad. She'd held her own against vampires and werewolves in their raid in Cambrai.

"I think I have an idea how to maybe smoke out our traitor, but I want to go over it with Pieter first, so I can get the information I need. We'll have a few days to iron out any kinks in the plan, unless something new crops up. We can't do anything really until we get our folks here to help with the kids." Luke's phone vibrated. "Speaking of which."

Luke picked up his phone and saw Maggie's name on the screen.

He answered. "Hey Maggie. Can I call you back in a bit? We're expecting a call from Holly regarding the situation here."

"I'm the call, Luke," Maggie replied.

"OK. So what's the plan?"

"I have a small team ready to go as soon as you give us our destination," Maggie said.

Happy to hear Maggie's voice, he smiled. "I've been thinking about that. I don't want anyone near Paris or Brussels. Frankfurt is the best option. Everyone can take the train to Cologne; I'll pick the team up there. You can give them my description if they've not met me before."

"I don't think the team will have a problem picking you out. I'll be leading them," Maggie replied.

"You're coming to Belgium?" Luke asked.

"I lived in France for twenty years after the war. I'm fluent in French, and Holly wanted, and I agree, for you to have medical staff on hand since you're isolated. Don't worry about Gwen, Zel is going to watch her while I'm gone. She's sad she can't come, though."

Luke chuckled, excited to see Maggie sooner than he'd expected. "I bet she is. Let her know I'll bring her for a vacation when we can."

"I will. Is there anything else we need to know?"

"Not that I can think of," Luke replied. "If I think of anything, I'll message you."

"I'd like to finalize plans so I can get our tickets. Once I have them, I'll give you our ETA."

"Sounds good, Maggie. I'm looking forward to seeing you."

"Me too. Take care, Luke."

"See you soon." Luke hung up. "Maggie is leading the team over. Should probably know when they're arriving by tomorrow when we wake up."

Simone looked at Delilah. "Who is Maggie?"

"Luke's girlfriend," Delilah replied.

"I'm going to need a volunteer to come with me to Cologne. I'm guessing we'll have more people and luggage than is probably convenient for just the BMW." Luke looked around the room.

"I should stay with the kids," Simone said.

Delilah's eyes flicked to Simone. "I'll stay and help with the kids as well."

Luke looked to Sam. "Sam, you in?"

"No. I think I'll stay and relax."

"Looks like it's just you and me, buddy. But I ain't driving that bus," Pablo said.

Luke nodded. "You can have the beemer. Want to go a day early? I'll show you around one of the great beer cities of the world."

"I've always wanted to do a beer city tour of Europe. The city of Kölsch is a great place to start. Plus, it's not that far if we have to hustle back for any reason.

"Good. I'll get us a hotel," Luke replied. "But before that…"

He tried Pieter one more time. When the call went directly to voicemail one more time, the knot in his stomach tightened. "Damn it."

"Still not picking up?" Sam asked.

Luke exhaled sharply and pursed his lips. "No."

IT HAD BEEN a few years since Luke had been to Cologne, but between his memory, his map app, and taxis, he was able to take Pablo to several major bars operated by the various breweries of Cologne. They ended the evening at a cool little bar operated by Früh. Luke rarely got to spend non-vampire time with Pablo, but showing him around Cologne and getting to talk beer with his brewery-owning friend had been a rare joy.

As they chatted about the different Kölsch beers they'd tried, Pablo pulled out a notebook to take some notes on ideas he had for a Kölsch-style beer to brew when he got home. The server dropped off another round of .25cl stanges of Früh and marked two more hash marks on the coaster on the table.

Pablo picked up the cylindrical glass and admired it in the candlelight glowing in the center of the table. "I need to find someone who can make these glasses. Don't you think they'd look good with the Howling Moon logo on them?"

"It'd look pretty great." Luke knew Pablo wanted to do more beer activities in Belgium, but he'd been a good sport. Fortunately, they'd started their foray into southern Belgium with a visit to the Chimay monastery, and Pablo seemed happy with the beer selection Luke had provided at the cottage. Luke, letting Pablo admire the glass and beer, sent a message to the caretaker to pick up a few different beers from the local market or distributor.

Luke sipped his beer, relaxing and letting his mind wander.

The server cleared his throat to get Luke's attention. "Excuse me, sir. There's a lady who says she's a friend and would like to join you for a round of beers, on her."

Luke and Pablo exchanged a look. Luke turned to the server. "Certainly. We'd be more than glad to share our table."

The server nodded and disappeared, returning a minute later with a tall, blonde woman in a gray business suit. The server gestured toward the table then disappeared. Pablo stood.

"I don't recall having a friend in Cologne," Luke said, rising to join Pablo.

"You always have friends among those who aren't friendly to the vampir," the tall woman replied.

Luke gestured toward the table. "Please. Join us."

They sat down. The server returned with three stanges of Kölsch, then disappeared again.

"How should we call you?" Luke asked.

"I'm Heidi Sauerwein, the beta of the Rhein Pack, and you are the Centurion Immortal," Heidi said.

"I see you're well informed," Luke replied. "I'm known as Luke in this time and place. This is my friend Pablo."

Pablo nodded. "Pablo Sandoval, second of the North Portland Pack."

Luke looked at his friend, raising an eyebrow.

Pablo shrugged. "Werewolf pack protocol. She gave me her name and position. It's considered poor manners to withhold the same information."

"Ah. I see. When we get a moment, you'll have to update me on werewolf protocol, since I'm on the council now." Luke lifted his glass. "It's nice to meet you, Heidi. I'm Luke Irontree. The Centurion Immortal and recent addition to the North Portland Pack council. I guess I'm their war leader."

Heidi tapped the bottom of her glass against Luke's and Pablo's. "It's a pleasure." She took a hearty drink. "So what brings you to Köln?"

"We're simply enjoying your city's beers, and then in the morning, picking up some packmates from the train station. We'll be out of your territory before the end of day tomorrow," Pablo said.

Heidi waved off Pablo's concerns. "There's no need to worry about that. We assume most American wolves moving through our territory are tourists. I wouldn't be here if you hadn't brought a myth into my city."

"How did you know who I was?" Luke asked.

"We've been paying attention to what's going on in the United States and in Belgium. Some of our pack were at the EDM festival in Liège. We've also got contacts within the Flanders Pack. We keep well informed. Until recently, we believed you to be a legend from the past, but you've been shaking the vampire world pretty hard. And the werewolf world as well."

"Luke does get around." Pablo chuckled.

Heidi fixed an intense gaze on Luke. "Are you intending to bring your war to the vampires in our territory?"

Luke shook his head. "No. We're currently engaged elsewhere and not available to expand this far east."

"That's too bad. The vampir are growing thick in the city, more than I've ever seen. More are filtering in by the night. They're going to great lengths to keep themselves concealed and out of trouble." She picked up her glass and took a drink.

"Are they feeding here?" Luke asked, leaning on the table and peering at Heidi.

Heidi nodded. "They have been very careful to cause no lasting harm, only feeding a little then releasing their victims largely unharmed."

"Catch and release," Pablo murmured.

"Hmm?" Heidi, eyes curious, turned to Pablo.

"It's a term commonly used by fishers who catch a fish, then release it—it's mostly for the sport of it," Luke explained.

"Ah, that makes sense." Heidi smiled at Luke, looking him up and down.

"Have your people had any run-ins with the uninvited guests?" Luke asked.

Heidi thought about it for a moment. "No. We've had a few close encounters reported. A vampir stalking one of our people but probably discovering they were a wolf and not a human."

"It makes sense," Pablo said.

Heidi tilted her head, raising an eyebrow.

"I'm guessing they don't want to risk turning your pack into firm enemies." Luke exchanged a look with Pablo who shrugged. Turning back to Heidi, Luke rubbed his chin, thinking. "Do you pay much attention to the packs in Belgium and France?"

"They're our neighbors," Heidi's responded vaguely.

"We've discovered that the Bordeaux Pack has come under the control of a powerful vampire lord known as Le Mousquetaire." Luke waited to see what her reaction would be.

Heidi sat, her face a calm mask. After a while, she tapped her finger on the table and shook her head. "Scheisse. I'd heard rumors that something was happening in western France. The vampir's name isn't unfamiliar to me."

"Well, neither the Bordeaux Pack nor Le Mousquetaire and his vampires are in Bordeaux anymore. We left them a few days ago in Cambrai, and some of them are now in Liege, reclaiming that city and the mansion where I killed The Mistress after the EDM festival you mentioned."

"They've moved back to Belgium?" Heidi narrowed her eyes, leaning closer to Luke.

"I believe so." Luke pushed his glass around on its coaster, fidgeting.

"I will need to consult with my alpha." She sat back, pursing her lips. "I wondered why I haven't heard from Pieter in a while." Seeing the look on Pablo and Luke's face, she clarified, "The pack alpha's son. He's a...a friend."

"We're familiar with Pieter. He's our friend as well," Luke replied.

"Yes. He mentioned you a time or two. That's one of the other ways I know about you." Heidi scowled, looking Luke in the eyes. "I was excited to meet you—a real life myth in the flesh." She turned to Pablo. "Does he always bring dark tidings?"

"That's my pal—Gandalf Stormcrow."

"Nerd," Luke murmured.

Keeping her eye on Pablo, she smirked. "He's not nearly as dignified and stodgy as I thought he would be."

Luke hitched his thumb toward Pablo. "You can blame my friend here for that. He's worked hard in the short time we've known each other to knock off some of my stodgy edges." Luke paused, then shifted to a more serious face and tone. "I lost my dignity a long time ago."

Heidi raised an eyebrow at Pablo. He shrugged in response.

"You get that from him too," Pablo said. "Along with random historical snippets."

"I bet." She returned her gaze to Luke, appraising him. "Is there anything else you can tell me about what's happening in France and Belgium?"

"We've just met," Luke said. "A lot of what's happening isn't mine to relay to an unknown third party. I'm here to fight vampires and help a friend who's helped me fight them. As long as you don't align your pack with the forces of evil, you'll have no problems from me."

Any humor she'd kept in her expression was wiped from her face at the tone of Luke's words. "What happens to those you do have problems with?"

"I'm still alive, and almost none of them are." Luke kept his face neutral.

"That's plain enough." Heidi sat back and waved the server back for another round of beers. "Can I tempt you two into something a bit stronger? They have a fine schnapps list here."

Luke nodded, smiling. "If they have a good kirschwasser, I'd take a snifter of that."

Seeing Luke and Heidi relax, Pablo let the tension drop from his shoulders and leaned back. "I'm not terribly familiar with real schnapps. Just the garbage they make in the US and call schnapps. I'll take whatever you think is a good choice to start with."

Heidi picked three schnapps. The server nodded, dropped off three more stanges of Kölsch, and disappeared to retrieve their schnapps.

Picking up her glass of Früh, Heidi took a deep drink, sighing happily after. "I can give you my word that our pack has nothing to do with the undead, certainly no alliances."

Luke nodded. "Then we shouldn't have a problem and can be friends."

"It's that easy?" Heidi asked.

"I don't have time to make more enemies," Luke said. "I have too much to do already, and too many vampires to deal with. I can't afford to pick fights with people who I can just as easily leave alone or befriend."

The server returned, setting three snifters on the table, then disappearing again.

Heidi lifted her glass and tipped it toward Luke. "I think I'd like to be your friend."

Luke lifted his glass toward her. "I think I'd like that as well." He took a sip of his kirschwasser. "Excellent choice. Thanks."

Next to Luke, Pablo was smacking his lips, making nummy noises over the glass Heidi had selected for him.

"I think my friend likes schnapps." Luke chuckled.

They chatted amiably for a few more minutes while Heidi finished her beer and schnapps. When she tossed back the last sip, she stood. Luke and Pablo rose to join her.

Extending her hand, she shook Luke's hand, then Pablo's. "Gentlemen, it was nice to meet you both, but I need to report in to my packleader. Don't worry about your tab. It's taken care of." She reached into the pocket of her suit jacket and pulled out a card, handing it over to Luke and locking eyes with him. "This is my number. Call if I can be of service."

After Heidi disappeared around the corner, Luke and Pablo took their seats to finish their drinks.

"I think she was flirting with you, buddy," Pablo said, a grin spreading across his face.

Luke waved him off. "She was just being polite."

"Dude. She was checking you out." Pablo smiled broadly.

Luke blushed, picking up his beer and taking a sip to cover. "Well, if she was, it's nice to be flirted with."

Pablo chuckled, shaking his head. "I'm amazed and impressed Maggie landed you. You're impossible."

Luke laughed. "You're not wrong."

They finished their drinks and ordered another round of the tiny glasses of low alcohol beers and talked about anything but vampires until they decided to head back to their hotel and retire. Otherwise, they'd face the consequences the following day. Luke couldn't remember the last time he'd had a friend like Pablo who he could be himself with and not have to hide behind a façade of an imagined Luke.

Today had been a good day, but despite the fun with Pablo, the growing undercurrent of tension caused by the lack of contact with Pieter couldn't be pushed aside. He hoped his friend was OK.

CHAPTER
EIGHTEEN

After a hearty breakfast to erase the lingering effects of a few too many stanges of Kölsch, Luke and Pablo met Maggie and the team outside of the train station they'd designated. They took everyone out to lunch before the trip back through Belgium to Luke's cottage. Maggie volunteered to ride shotgun with Luke in the old VW bus while the rest of the team opted for the luxury of the BMW.

"How was your flight?" Luke asked.

"Not bad. I got a little sleep. Watched a bad movie. The train ride along the Rhine was beautiful. Old castles and vineyards." Maggie reached across and squeezed Luke's thigh. "How have you been? We've not had much opportunity to really talk."

"OK. I guess." Luke sighed, shaking his head. He couldn't hide things from Maggie and pretend he was OK. She never demanded he be falsely strong for her. "I'm feeling a bit scared, Maggie. There's something bigger going on I can't get my mind around, and I'm afraid I'm missing something important. Something that could blow up in all our faces."

Maggie scooped Luke's hand off his leg and squeezed it, working her fingers between his. "I know it must be weighing on you heavily. Don't forget to share the burden. We're here to help you."

Luke gave Maggie a closed-lip smile, squeezing her hand. He felt better with her here. Her calming presence and kindness helped fill some of the hollow spots inside that still persisted.

"I know, Maggie. There's just so much on my shoulders, countries waiting on my actions. It's been a long time since I've had that level of responsibility to bear. I used to command armies and move the wheels of power, but I've spent a long time running from myself. Hiding from the world. Hiding who I was until that person nearly died, leaving a shell in his place." Luke let the silence hang, enjoying the feel of Maggie's soft hand in his rougher palm. After a while, he turned to Maggie. "Do you feel like taking a more scenic route? The hills and forests of southern Belgium are quite nice."

"That sounds lovely. I'll text Sam and let her know we'll be a bit late," Maggie replied, taking out her phone. "Do mind if I put some music on?"

"Not at all," he replied. A moment later, "Pale Blue Eyes" by The Velvet Underground filled the VW. It was followed by LCD Soundsystem's "Oh Baby."

Luke pulled onto N68 after they crossed the border from Germany into Belgium. They drove in silence as Maggie admired the countryside, skirting by the edge of Hautes Fagnes-Eifel.

"Oh, there's a pullout ahead. Do you mind if we park and take a break to stretch our legs?" Maggie asked.

Luke turned on the turn signal, pulling over and parking in the empty lot. Luke locked the old bus as soon as they got out. Maggie stepped up next to Luke and kissed his cheek. She took his hand and led him toward a path. Together, they strolled under the trees, enjoying the gentle breeze and the birds flitting about, chirping their songs. When they found a bench, Maggie sat down, patting the spot next to her. Luke slid onto the bench, scooping her hand up.

"What's eating at you, Luke?" Maggie asked.

"I don't know if there's enough of that man left to get us through this successfully, Maggie."

Maggie sighed. "Oh, Luke." She reached over and patted his hand. "I never met that man. I have no idea what he was capable of. But I'm getting a good idea of who the man sitting next to me is."

She adjusted her position so she could easily look into his eyes. "I'm learning what kind of man I'm falling for." Reaching up, she laid her hand across his cheek and turned his head. Maggie leaned forward and brushed a soft kiss over his lips.

"Maggie..."

Maggie placed her middle and forefinger over Luke's lips. "I don't know who you were, but I like the man I've come to know. He's strong and kind. He's intelligent and thoughtful. And he has friends who care about him deeply, who can help him shoulder this burden. I don't know if you'll ever be able to find the old pieces of yourself, but I do know the man you are now is strong and capable."

Luke took Maggie's fingers from his lips. Leaning forward, he kissed her. "I feel so brittle, like if more is poured on, I'll break."

"Luke, you're not in this alone. You're a member of a strong pack, who cares about you and supports you. You have friends who would go to the ends of the world and back for you." Maggie looked down at their entwined hands. "I'd go to the ends of the world and back for you."

Luke lifted his hand, resting his finger under Maggie's chin and tipped her head up so they looked each other in the eyes. Since he'd met her and grown to know her, she'd always been so calm and quietly confident, even as she pursued him. This was the first time he'd seen real, deep vulnerability in her eyes. Zel had told him Maggie was falling hard for him. He guessed Maggie wasn't sure the feeling was mutual or as intense, but when she wasn't present by his side, she resided in his thoughts and occasionally his dreams.

"I'd go to the ends of the world for you, too." He caressed her cheek. "I think I'm falling in love with you, Magdalena."

Maggie leaned forward and kissed Luke gently, pulling back she said, "I'm falling for you too, Luke."

They kissed in the solitude of their bench under the shady trees as the warm late summer breeze rustled the leaves above them, then sat holding hands, sitting close. Maggie leaning her head on Luke's strong shoulder.

"I could sit her like this forever," Luke said, "but if we're going to get back to my house in time for dinner, we should get going."

They walked back to the bus and continued their scenic tour of the Ardennes and southeastern Belgium. Luke entertained Maggie with tales from history when landmarks jogged memories to the forefront as they wound their way over the windy roads to Luke's manor. When they neared the turnoff down to his property, he reminded her of the phrase to keep in mind so the property wouldn't repel her, creating discomfort she couldn't turn from since she was the passenger.

Once they pulled out of the trees and Luke's manor came into view, Maggie gasped. "Luke… Is this yours?"

"Mhm," he replied.

"It looks so much bigger than in the picture. It's beautiful."

"I'll give you the grand tour when we have a moment. We'll have just enough time to get you settled. You can freshen up, then go downstairs for a pre-dinner drink. If you prefer, I can have a separate room prepared for you, but I'd like it if you stayed with me in my room."

Maggie placed her hand on his thigh and rubbed his leg. "Unless you're going to come visit me in my room, it would be a lot more convenient to stay with you, you know, for snuggles and such."

Luke parked then pulled the luggage out of the back of the van. Someone must have been keeping watch because everyone came out to help with the team's baggage. Grabbing Maggie's bags, Luke led her up to the top floor and his multi-room main suite.

"The floors are a little creaky, but it's almost two-hundred years old," Luke said, waiting for Maggie's approval.

"It's wonderful, Luke. Do you mind if I take a shower quickly? I need to wash the travel away." Maggie started unpacking, making herself at home.

"Not at all, the bathroom is through that door. There's a shower or a jacuzzi tub."

Maggie looked thoughtful. "Jacuzzi tub? I'd better stick with the shower. Otherwise, you'll never get me out of there."

Once Maggie showered, dressed, and twisted her wet hair into a bun, Luke took her downstairs, showed her his little bar, and poured a couple beers. They joined the noisy crowd in the solarium. The kids ran around making noise as they waited for dinner to be served. Pablo and Sam sat with the three other packmates who had come with Maggie while Simone and Delilah sat nearby with a table to themselves.

"Mind if we join you?" Luke asked, standing next to the empty chairs at Delilah's table.

"Not at all." Delilah stood up and walked over to hug Maggie. "Glad you could join us, Maggie."

"It's good to see you too, Delilah."

"Maggie, I'd like you to meet Simone. She's been helping us out," Delilah said, gesturing toward the Black woman standing next to her.

Simone extended her hand. Maggie took it, smiling at the young woman.

"It's nice to meet you, Simone." Maggie sat in the chair Luke pulled out for her.

"Maggie is on the pack council and is one of the pack's doctors," Delilah said.

"How are the children doing?" Maggie asked, watching as the kids ran around.

"They're better after a couple days of food and hydration, though they get tired easily," Delilah said.

"What's going to happen to them all?" Maggie picked up her beer for a drink.

"If we can find any family members," Luke said, "we'll get them reunited. For those who don't have anyone left, we'll see about getting them adopted into other packs. Simone and her brother are thinking about coming to Portland. We've offered to sponsor them."

Simone smiled nervously, probably feeling awkward as the center of attention at the moment. "Your pack sounds accepting and welcoming. It sounds like a good place for Idrissa to grow up. I have to get him away from this"—she gestured around—"conflict if there's any hope for him to grow up safely. I don't know if we'll ever be safe in France."

"Well, Portland is a lovely city, and our pack is a warm, friendly group of wolves. If you decide to join us, you'd be a welcome addition," Maggie said.

"Excuse me, sir." The caretaker tapped Luke's shoulder to alert him to his presence. "We're ready to bring out the food."

"Please. Let's get started," Luke replied.

Émile signaled the catering crew. They'd set up chafing dishes to hold the pans, serving dinner buffet-style since there was a large crowd. When the food arrived, the kids all settled down at their tables, staring hungrily at the food.

"Why aren't the children lining up?" Maggie asked.

"They won't go until the adults go first," Simone said.

Luke stood and waited for Maggie to join. "Most of them are from packs that are more…rigidly hierarchical than Portland. It's going to take them a while to get used to not being required to be so subservient. We should get our plates so everyone else can serve themselves."

"Is there a reason we're going first?" Maggie asked quietly once they stepped up to the chaffing dishes.

"According to Simone, I'm in charge, which makes me the alpha of this little pack. It's easier to just do it to make the kids comfortable for now. Simone says it's what they're used to." Luke felt uncomfortable, even if he understood Simone's logic.

"I see." Maggie said, scooping Brussels sprouts onto her plate.

Once they'd loaded their plates, they returned to their seats. Pablo, Sam, Delilah, and Simone were currently filling their plates. Setting hers down, Maggie went over to the other three Portland wolves and filled them in on the situation so they could get their plates and allow the kids to go. She sat next to Luke and removed her silverware from the rolled napkin.

"They've had a tough go of it lately. Whatever sense of stability we can provide for them will have to do until we can find a more permanent option for them." Luke cut into a piece of roast chicken.

Maggie nodded.

Once Simone and Delilah rejoined the table, the four ate, Maggie and Simone getting to know each other, Maggie often shifting into French for Simone and to practice. They were nearly finished when the caretaker waved Luke away from the table to a quiet corner.

"Sir, there's someone coming down the driveway. I don't recognize the vehicle."

"I'll go see who it is. Thanks, Émile," Luke replied.

The caretaker nodded and led Luke outside. Luke stood on the top step of the stairs leading down to the parking area, watching the beat up old Citroen 2CV work its way down the ramp along the side of the cliff.

"That car is going to fall apart at any moment," the caretaker said. "They'll never get back up the road in that thing."

Luke nodded, squinting and trying to see who was driving the classic two-horsepower French car. He guessed the driver gave up on the engine and just put the car in neutral. The car drifted down the ramp, picking up speed as gravity did the work the motor seemed incapable of.

Once the car made it off the ramp, the driver hauled the wheel over, trying to coast all the way into the parking area but coming up short. As the car entered the shadow of the house, the reflection on the windshield disappeared, revealing Pieter's face. Shaking his head, Luke stepped out to greet his friend. Pieter climbed out of the car, cursing.

"Stupid piece of shit..." Pieter drew back his foot as if he were about to kick the tire, then thought better of it.

Luke, about to draw Pieter into a hug, stepped back, taking in the state of Pieter and his clothing. They were dirty and stained, with dark patches looking like dried blood. Pieter had a sizable scratch across his cheek, crusted with blood.

"Gods below, Pieter, what happened to you?" Luke asked.

"It's a long story." Pieter shook his head, pursing his lips. He took a deep breath and let it out explosively. "Everything is going to shit, Luke."

"I've been trying to get a hold of you for days," Luke said.

"I know, I saw, but it's been non-stop, then my phone died, then I couldn't get a charger. I only just got away." Pieter paced pack and forth, bordering on frantic.

"Pieter. You're not making any sense."

Pieter stopped, turning to Luke, huffing. "I know."

"Come inside, take a shower, and get some food. We can sit down and sort it out."

Pieter nodded, letting Luke take his elbow.

"Is there a room made up?" Luke asked the caretaker.

Émile nodded. "Yes, sir. We made up four rooms for the newcomers. We didn't know one of them would be staying in your room. Second floor, third room on the right."

Luke smiled. "Excellent. I'll take my friend upstairs. If you can let my associates know Pieter is here and that I'll be down shortly, that would be appreciated. We're also going to need a rental car so he can leave when he's ready to."

"Yes, sir. I'll get something down here tomorrow." The caretaker walked off toward the dining room.

"Someone's staying in your room?" Pieter, despite his exhaustion, quirked an eyebrow up, looking curious.

"Yes. Maggie just arrived with a few others from the North Portland Pack to help us with the children," Luke replied.

"Children?" Pieter sighed. "I have a feeling your story is going to be as lengthy as mine."

Luke escorted Pieter up to the unused room and left him to take a shower. Running up to his room, Luke grabbed a t-shirt and a pair of workout pants, leaving them on Pieter's bed. He returned downstairs and refilled his beer before joining Maggie at their table.

"Pieter's here?" Delilah asked.

"Yeah, he's upstairs cleaning up," Luke replied.

Luke finished his dinner while they waited for Pieter to come down. As soon as he emerged, he filled a plate to heaping levels, sat at Luke's table, and dug in. He was about half through before he noticed everyone staring at him.

"Sorry. It's been a couple days since I've had anything to eat." He looked between Simone and Maggie. "I'm sorry for my terrible manners. I'm Pieter van den Bergh."

Simone reached across the table and shook Pieter's hand. "I'm Simone Ndiaye."

"We've met before, in Portland. Maggie Rabinowitz."

"Ah, yes. Luke said you'd joined him. It's good to see you again," Pieter said.

"Take your time, Pieter. Eat as much as you need to. We'll meet in the sitting room and go over everything there." Luke turned to Maggie. "Can the others get the kids handled for the evening? I'd like you there so you're up-to-date on everything. You'll be in charge here if we need to move out for whatever reason."

"Of course. Let me talk to Fatima." Maggie patted his leg and found Fatima, who'd picked a spot at a table with some of the children. She already had them laughing.

Pieter dove back into his food while everyone else talked idly, keeping the topics light and inconsequential since young, impressionable ears surrounded them. Luke didn't join the conversation, though he tried to pay attention to it. His eyes kept flicking over to Pieter to see if he was done eating. The tension in his gut, growing steadily since he'd lost communication with Pieter days ago, had fully tied itself in a knot. Whatever news Pieter brought, it would not be good.

CHAPTER
NINETEEN

With the kids making their way to their rooms for the evening, Luke joined Sam, Pablo, Simone, Delilah, Pieter, and Maggie in the sitting room, now their communal lounge. Luke, with Pablo's help, switched out his cushy wingback arm chair for an antique love seat so he could sit with Maggie while they had their war council. While the rest got comfortable, Luke and Pablo fetched drinks. Once everyone was situated, Luke shut the door and settled in next to Maggie. She pulled her legs up under her and leaned into Luke, resting her head against his shoulder. Making eye contact with Luke, Pieter raised his eyebrow and smiled.

"Now that we're all here, where should we start?" Pieter asked.

"That's up to you," Luke replied.

Pieter opened his mouth, closed it again, then sighed. "You go first. Get me up to date on what you've been up to."

"OK. Simone, I'm going to summarize what you told us about your pack. If you need to jump in to correct something or add details, please do." Luke filled Pieter in on what happened with Simone's pack and how they found them out of their territory in Cambrai with the Bordeaux nest of vampires.

Then, he broke down their raid on the Cambrai houses and

finding the children, including their failure to sweep the other houses and find Pieter's father. Luke suspected the person dragged out with their head covered was likely him. The closer Luke got to finishing his update, the antsier Pieter became. His fidgeting and discomfort worried Luke. His friend was usually so confident and self-assured. The change in Pieter made Luke want to keep talking, so he didn't have to hear the news Pieter didn't want to talk about.

When he eventually finished, Luke bought more time for his friend by getting another round of drinks for everyone. Maggie offered to help carry drinks back.

"Your friend seems pretty nervous," Maggie said.

"Yeah. I'm a little scared to hear what he has to say. It's not going to be good." Luke poured another beer and set it on the tray.

Maggie, smiling, stepped behind the bar and behind Luke, wrapping her arms around his waist. "You look very sexy behind the bar, pouring drinks."

Luke chuckled, rinsing another glass before putting it under the faucet. "Well, if the vampire slaying thing goes south on me, I can always see if Pablo will give me a job slinging drinks."

Squeezing Luke, Maggie stepped back, resting her hands on the top of Luke's hips. "I have to warn you, I'm not going to carry these beers for free. I expect payment."

Luke turned around, resting his hands on her waist. "Can I pay you in kisses?"

"Acceptable." Maggie tipped up her lips and pulled Luke in for a kiss. When they parted, she walked around the bar and grabbed one of the trays laden with drinks. "That'll hold me for a down payment."

Luke admired her form as she walked out of the bar, the tray balanced on her hand like a pro. When she was out of eyeshot, he grabbed the second tray and followed. Together, they distributed the drinks then returned to their love seat.

"You're pretty good with a drink tray, Maggie," Pablo said. "If you get tired of the doctor gig, I could hire you down at the pub."

"My service industry CV might be a bit out of date. I mean, the last time I waited tables was in Paris in the 1950s," Maggie replied.

Pieter took a deep drink of the strong, boozy beer Luke had

given him. "I guess it's my turn to go." He made eye contact with Luke, focusing on him. "I've lost the entire south of Belgium."

Luke sat up, nearly spilling his beer and unsettling Maggie. "What?"

"When we turned over the mansion in Liege, they hit every one of our strongholds in Tournai, Mons, Charleroi, Namur, and Liege. By the time we realized what was happening, they'd barricaded themselves in the mansion. We rushed to help our other house in Liege, but it was too late. All we found were bodies. After that, I had to call an evacuation of all the families living in the south."

Pieter hung his head, his breathing trembling as he tried to control his emotions. Setting his drink down, Pablo stood up and stepped over to Pieter, squeezing his shoulder. Pieter set down his glass, and stood up, surprising everyone, and pulled Pablo into a tight hug. It took a second for Pablo to respond to the sudden hug from his onetime rival, but when he did, he wrapped his arms around the man, patting his back soothingly.

Once Pieter felt ready to resume, he sat down and took another deep drink. "I've spent the last several days evading vampires and rogue wolves, trying to find any surviving pack members."

"Did you? Find any?" Luke asked.

"A few, and I've been in contact with a few others. Jan tells me several have turned up in Antwerp." He shook his head. "I don't know where they got all the muscle—so many vampires and werewolves."

"Well, I think I know where they got some of the werewolves. Some were from the Bordeaux Pack, but not all the kids we rescued from that house were from the Bordeaux Pack. There were a couple from the Lille Pack. Pieter." Luke waited until Pieter looked up. "There were two from your pack as well."

"What?" Pieter's eyes shot wide open.

"Two boys. Brothers. They said wolves broke into their house and bagged them. They don't know what happened to their parents. They overheard one of the wolves with an Antwerp accent ordering the others to take them to Lille for the vampires."

The blood drained from Pieter's face. "And the boys don't know who kidnapped them?"

Luke shook his head. "No. The one is too young, but his older brother didn't recognize the voices, just the Antwerp dialect."

"What are their names?" Pieter leaned forward, sitting on the edge of the chair.

"Hugo and Noah Maes."

Pieter sighed and shook his head. "I'm afraid I don't have any good news. Their parents were found floating in the canals six or seven weeks ago."

"You don't sound surprised." Sam said, her eyes narrowing.

Pieter, his elbows resting on his knees, stared down at his clasped hands. "I'm not. Since I've returned home from Portland, members of our pack have gone missing or been found dead."

"What kind of members?" Sam asked, peering intensely at Pieter.

"Non-white members." Pieter rubbed his temples. "At first, it seemed random. Sometimes families just disappeared. It's happened that people have moved on without really giving notice. It looked like that. Then a few bodies showed up in local morgues. That's when my father recalled me."

"Who would do this?" Delilah asked.

"I don't know. Father integrated the pack a long time ago; he wanted to make all werewolves in Belgium part of one united pack, where all had an opportunity to prosper. Of course, there were objections at the time, but father and I insisted it was necessary for the pack to survive and grow, and we have. I thought we'd put that behind us." He put his head in his hands. "That's why father sent Amiata and Olivia to Portland. He didn't tell me. I should have seen it, but I was too deluded and ignored the warts. I only wanted to see the good we'd been doing."

"Pieter, I hate to ask, but with the vampires taking your territory, who have they been killing?" Luke asked.

"People loyal to my father."

"Does that include more non-white Belgian wolves?" Maggie asked, her fingers rubbing over the back of Luke's hand absent-mindedly.

Pieter nodded, still looking down. "They've been the most loyal supporters of my father, the most willing to help fight for the pack. They wanted to protect their stake in the pack. Now we've let them down."

They sat quietly. Luke felt for his friend. Pieter was having a crisis of confidence at his inability to protect his packmates. Their deaths sat heavy on his conscience, and if he let it, they could destroy his ability to take the needed steps to move beyond this situation and protect those who still lived.

"You look exhausted, Pieter. You should get some sleep," Sam suggested. "We can't do anything tonight. Let's start fresh in the morning."

Pieter nodded and stood up. "You're right. My brain is dead. I can't think."

Luke kissed Maggie on top of her head. "I'm going to walk Pieter up to his room."

Maggie patted Luke's knee and shifted so Luke could stand. He followed Pieter out and led him to the room originally planned for Maggie. Opening the door, Pieter waved Luke in.

"Everything is going to shit, Luke." Pieter's eyes were filled with pain as his shoulders slumped.

"I know. Get a good night's sleep, and we'll see what we can do to salvage the situation," Luke said.

"You're a good friend." Pieter took a deep breath and rotated his shoulders before looking up at Luke. "So, how long have you been seeing Maggie?"

"Just after the freighter."

"Good for you, my friend." Pieter ran his hands through his hair. "I'll see you in the morning."

"Sleep well, Pieter."

"You too."

THE FOLLOWING MORNING, they met in the sitting room after breakfast to continue their discussions. Pieter, who'd disappeared for a few minutes during breakfast, had new information to present. Once Luke fixed another round of coffees for the gang, they shut and locked the doors to prevent any accidental interruptions.

"I spoke with my brother this morning," Pieter said. "He's heard from Le Mousquetaire. They want to exchange my father."

"In exchange for what?" Luke asked.

"Brussels." Pieter slumped into a chair, his head falling into his hands. "What choice do we have? I don't think we have the wolves in place to defend it or retake it, and we have to get my father back alive."

"Do we have proof he's still alive?" Luke asked.

Pieter nodded. "Jan says he spoke directly with him for a couple seconds."

"Do you have an exchange location yet?" Luke asked.

Pieter sighed. "Not yet. Jan's trying to get it set up. He's organizing our people from Antwerp."

"Do you want us to escort you to the meeting?" Luke slid to the edge of his chair, leaning toward Pieter.

"I don't know. Let me think about it." Pieter stood. "I'm going to take a walk and clear my head."

Luke rose and unlocked the door for Pieter, shutting it after he left.

"Now what?" Pablo asked.

Luke shrugged. "I don't know. I'm getting concerned our decoys in Antwerp might be vulnerable. Whoever is betraying Pieter and his family is not just some lone rogue element. After what he told us last night, I can't help but think it's a sizable force within the Flanders Pack."

Luke paced about the room, holding his hands behind his back while everyone else sat quietly, nervously watching Luke prowl. Finally, he stopped, resting his hands on the back of the chair Pieter recently abandoned. He made eye contact with each person as he looked around the room.

"Sam, recall our people from Antwerp. Tell them to slip out of town quietly if they can," Luke said.

Sam nodded. "Where do you want them to go?"

"Tell them to take the train to Dinant. If they need to, take a circuitous route to make sure they're not followed." Luke looked toward Pablo, Delilah, and Simone. "I want to have all the weapons loaded and all the ammo we have ready to go."

They all nodded.

"What about me?" Maggie asked.

"I'd like to say just relax and keep an eye on everyone here, but that would be foolhardy. Nothing has been going right. Each move we make is countered, and we keep spiraling downward. Work with your team to get the kids ready for evacuation. Let's be ready to go on short notice."

Sam raised her hand, grabbing Luke's attention. "We'll need more vehicles. Even with all three of yours, that's not enough for all the kids and the wolves coming down from Antwerp."

Luke nodded, pursing his lips in thought. "I'll get us two more vans. That should cover it with my vehicles. I can probably ask Anne-Marie if she'd drive her van as well."

"I'll check the rental sites." Sam pulled out her laptop.

"We'll probably have to pick it up in Charleroi or Brussels," Luke said.

"That's OK. If you drop me off at the nearest train station, I can make it from there. I enjoy riding trains. What's your project?"

Luke, his lips drawing into thin lines, took a deep breath. "I think I need to visit the Mithraeum."

Maggie, watching his face, must have noticed the slightly haunted look in his eyes at the mention of his Mithraeum and gave him a comforting smile. Everyone else in the room, save for Simone, nodded lightly at Luke.

Pablo stood and clapped his hands together once to draw attention to himself. "Well, kids, let's go play with guns."

Luke unlocked the door, letting Pablo, Delilah, and Simone out. He was only a few steps down the hall when Maggie caught up. Saying nothing, she wound their arms together and walked out the front door with him, arm-in-arm.

"I've been feeling the pull harder since I returned here, especially after visiting the Mithraeum a few weeks ago. After Mithras invaded my dreams," Luke said when they'd made it halfway across the yard toward the entrance to his Mithraeum.

"Will he be there? Mithras?" Maggie asked.

"I don't think so. The pull toward it is gentler. Kinder. It feels like Selene, the moon goddess."

"The one who accepted the werewolves after they fled their creator?" Maggie asked.

"Yeah, along with Artemis."

"Have you ever met Artemis?" Maggie sounded genuinely curious.

"No. Selene is the overlap. She's also associated with Mithras and his rites, along with her brother Sol Invictus, the unconquerable sun." Luke punched the code into the first door to open it. He turned to Maggie before opening the second door. "Through this door and down a stone corridor is my Mithraeum. This is the last stop if you're uncomfortable with the presence of a divine being."

"Thank you for being so considerate, but I'll go a little further. I'm curious." She tipped her lips up and kissed Luke.

Punching in the code, he extended his hand for Maggie. He led her into the dark stone corridor, letting her know when to duck halfway through.

"Why don't you get that section cut out so you don't have to duck?" Maggie asked.

Luke shrugged. "It's part of the natural corridor. Plus, it makes for a little bit of security if someone comes running in here who isn't in the know."

When they turned the corner, the soft silver glow trickled from the cave's entrance, illuminating the approach to the temple's door. Maggie gripped his hand tighter as they neared it, her nervousness translating through her hand. As they stepped through the door into the rectangular room, Maggie gasped, dropping Luke's hand. He turned toward her to reassure her she'd be fine in his presence, but she'd frozen in place.

Selene materialized from the silvery light emanating from her place above Mithras on the altar. "Have you brought another of my half-lupine children for me to bless, my brave soldier?"

Luke bowed his head respectfully. "No. Her faith belongs to another, though she wished to learn a bit more about the powerful beings who loom so large in my life."

Selene walked toward Maggie, then walked around, stopping behind her. "She's a fine example of the best of her kind—strong, gentle, loyal, protective, wise. She's seen much in her days, a lot of it not good, yet she has come through it with love in her heart." Selene's gaze bore down on Luke. "She loves you. She has faith in you."

Luke nodded. "My feelings for her are strong as well; I just wish I had the faith in myself she seems to have." He couldn't hide his fears from the goddess. The feelings churning under the surface, those he'd been working on with his therapist, felt too potent to conceal. "I'm afraid I'm not enough anymore. Not enough to rise and meet the challenges in front of me. I'm not sure if there's enough of the old me, the old power I had, to get us all through this alive, let alone achieve ultimate victory."

"Who you were—and who you are—are not so terribly far apart, even if the wall you've erected between your two selves is high and thick. I think the friends you have brought before me see more clearly than you do, see less of the wall than you imagine. This one" —Selene rested her hand on Maggie's shoulder—"sees who you are, and she has given you two precious gifts—her love and her faith in you. Your friends have done no less. You merely have to take up their faith and love and let it bolster you."

Luke sighed and sat down. Selene, leaving Maggie, sat next to Luke.

"I sometimes think I was the wrong tool for this task you and the Father of Fathers laid upon me all those years ago, My Mistress." Luke looked down at his hands clasped in front of him.

"You may not be the exact tool the wanderer may have desired. He might have wished for a more martial man, a more ambitious man, but I think you are the person who was needed. I did not wish to raise a monster who would complete his task then set himself up as a bigger terror than those vanquished. This task may have taken far longer than we could have anticipated, but even gods are not all-knowing and all-seeing. I cannot see to the end of this, but I think the compassionate man who showed up for this duty, not seeking it, might be the right person for this task, even if it has taken so many lifetimes to get here."

Luke, still looking down, nodded.

"Now, let us proceed to why you are here. I sense you have a question for me."

"My friends wish to know if their weapons can be enchanted similarly to my gladius so they can face more fully the enemies before us. The vampire lord challenging us has enlisted several werewolf packs, and standard weapons are not always effective. We need the help, but I don't want them crossing Mithras's path and drawing his eye."

Selene nodded. "His aren't the only powers that can achieve this." She sighed, shaking her head. "I did not bring the pleas of the children of Tutyr to Artemis and help her save them from Saubarag and the Lord of Chaos for them only to betray that trust and join the enemies of life. Bring the weapons to me here an hour before moonrise tonight. Now, let me meet this fine credit to the children of Tutyr."

Luke rose and stood next to Maggie, taking her hand and bracing his body against hers in case she fell when Selene removed her from stasis. Luke was glad he had. Maggie slumped into him, her knees going soft as Selene released her.

"What happened?" Maggie asked, discombobulated.

Luke guided her to one of the stone benches and helped her sit.

"My apologies, my child. I wished to have a private word with my brave soldier." Selene nodded her head graciously.

"Maggie, this is Selene, also known as Luna, goddess of the moon. Selene, this is Magdalena Rabinowitz, council member and head doctor of her pack, and my friend and companion."

He could tell Maggie wasn't sure what to do; no one had probably ever taught her the proper etiquette for meeting a goddess. Still unsure of her legs, she opted for a seated bow.

Selene smiled and favored her with a nod. "It is a pleasure to meet you, my child. Though, it is time that I depart on other errands. Don't forget, my soldier, bring the blades an hour before moonrise and know that I am pleased with you. I will leave you both with this blessing—love can be as strong a beacon in the dark of the night as the beams of my moonlight." Selene stood and ran her hand along Maggie's cheek and jaw, tipping her chin up. "She is most lovely."

Luke stood, his hands clasped in front of him.

Selene placed her hands on Luke's cheeks and tipped his head down, kissing his forehead before dissolving in a gentle pulse of silvery moonlight.

Maggie let out an explosive exhalation, drawing in a ragged breath to replace it. Returning to his spot next to her, he reached out and took her hand, winding their fingers together while she calmed her breathing. After Maggie relaxed, she leaned into Luke, resting her head against his shoulder.

"She's...not what I expected," Maggie said finally.

Luke nodded, kissing the top of her head. "She's not. What were you expecting? Out of curiosity."

"I guess...cold, intimidating. I thought her presence would be overwhelming. I mean, it was intense, but not oppressive."

"The ancients described Selene as lovely haired, pale-armed, and benevolent."

"She seems quite fond of you," Maggie said.

"She's always been most gracious." Luke spoke softly, affection in his words.

They sat quietly, the warmth of Maggie tucked into his side soothing his nervousness and fears about the unknown dangers of their upcoming tasks. When Maggie finally stirred, she stood, pulling Luke up with her.

"Take me back out into the sunlight. You can show me around your temple when we have the space to ourselves and you can explain the artwork to me," Maggie requested.

Luke, still holding her hand, led her out through the rock corridor and through the gatehouse back into the late morning sun. Maggie took a deep breath, letting the fresh, early autumn air expand her chest and purge the air of the cavern.

"Thank you for being willing to join me," Luke said, breaking the silence.

"Thank you for sharing this with me, sharing so much of yourself with me." She stopped and pulled him around for a kiss.

"We should go find everyone else," Luke said. "I need to collect their weapons."

"I'll go prepare my people and the children in case we need to evacuate fast." Maggie turned and walked way, holding Luke's hand until the distance pulled them apart, their fingertips brushing over each other.

CHAPTER
TWENTY

The team was excited to hear Selene was willing to upgrade their weapons. In addition to Sam's katana and wakizashi, Delilah's jian, the rapier, and dagger, Luke pulled out a bunch of daggers and bayonet daggers from his armory, along with several swords he gathered. He hoped Selene wouldn't think he was being greedy, but then again, he wasn't asking for presents but the tools he needed to accomplish his vital mission. With the help of his friends, he laid out the weapons on the benches.

When it was an hour and fifteen minutes before moonrise, they gathered in the Mithraeum to witness Selene work. At the appointed time, they gasped when she appeared, surveyed the array of weapons, then nodded to Luke. Raising her arms, the silver glow brightened until it forced everyone to close their eyes. They only opened their eyes again when the light pouring through their eyelids faded. The goddess had disappeared.

Spots still danced about Luke's vision for a few moments as he blinked back to clarity. Several people exhaled breaths they'd been holding in while the goddess worked. Luke, slightly more accustomed to the presence and works of divine beings, was the first to stand. He grabbed the nearest dagger and inspected it.

The weapon gleamed as if new, the blade bright and sharp. The side that had been facing up now contained engravings of Selene's crescent moon and stars with elegant, flowing lines winding their way down the blade to culminate at the tip. Each blade contained the same crescent moon and stars, but the lines were unique to each weapon. When he flipped the blade over, the other side was as blank as it had been before, though cleaned and sharpened. Luke had even thrown in some old beat-up blades, more scrap or artifacts than functional weapons, and they too were returned to like new condition — probably better than new.

Pablo hissed, letting out a curse. "Don't touch the blades. Not sure if she added silver or if it's an anti-wolf enchantment, but that hurt." He shook his hand trying to shake the pain away.

"So don't touch the magic weapons, got it," Sam said.

"Handles are fine, though." Pablo picked up a dagger by the hilt.

"It wouldn't be much good if y'all couldn't hold them, now would it?" Luke shook his head. "She knows what she's about. We're going to need to get scabbards for all these. Not sure what I have in the armory, though. I guess we won't be using them all right now. I just wanted some spares for the future. Let's get these moved up to the house and stashed away. Pick what you want for yourselves."

Luke, running his eyes over the cache of newly enchanted weapons, stopped on a shorter dagger with a twisted hilt. He picked it up and set it with a basket of gathered weapons. When all the benches were cleared, Luke led the way out into the dark and across to the house. They took the weapons to an empty supply closet where they could be locked away from curious hands.

With his friends in tow, Luke's next stop was the armory to find as many functional scabbards as possible. Luke scrounged through it until he found an unopened cardboard box. Popping the top, he found a box full of basic scabbards in various sizes made from simple, modern materials. They weren't ornamental, but they were functional, which was all they needed. Checking the shipping label, the caretaker must have ordered a bunch at some point. They took the box back to the supply closet and found homes for the blades everyone wanted.

When Luke found the appropriate size for the dagger he'd picked out, he went in search of Maggie. She sat on the patio by the river with her team from Portland; together, they appeared to be relaxing after settling the kids for the night.

"Hey, Maggie. I have a little present for you," Luke said.

"Oooh, I like presents." Maggie stood and joined Luke.

He gave the blade in its scabbard to her. "Be careful. The blade is anti-wolf and anti-vamp. I wanted you to have one just in case you need to defend yourself. We have plenty in case everyone would like one. They can turn them in when they get back to Portland. They'll just need to pack it in their checked luggage before returning home."

"Do you need me to turn this one in too?" Maggie asked.

"No. This is a gift from me to you. It's from my armory. It's blessed by Selene."

"I'll treasure it, Luke, though I hope to never use it." Maggie slid the blade back into the sheath.

Luke nodded. "Me too."

NOT LONG AFTER they stowed the blades, Pieter called the team together to fill them in on the details his brother had finally relayed. Luke and Maggie were the first in the room and took the love seat. As the team filed in, the tension in the room thickened as people fidgeted, anxious about going into action after several days of relative quiet.

Luke knew his team was used to more regular movement, patrolling Portland and rooting out the nests left over after Cassius's death. Their trip to Belgium had been spent in the time-honored tradition of all soldiers on campaign—hurrying up and waiting. Their first fight in Belgium had been a spur-of-the-moment occasion as the vampires took advantage of some luck and kidnapped Pieter's father. Their raid in Cambrai had been swift, but familiar, even if it had involved a lot of observation before going in. Now, they were going into a situation lacking both control and intelligence.

He knew he'd felt a constant undercurrent of anxiety and apprehension throughout the quiet times, waiting for the next shoe to drop

—and it always did, ratcheting up the stress for the next period of inactivity. Looking around the room, he knew his friends were in the same boat.

He was confident in his team's ability to improvise and adapt, but it made them nervous, adding to Luke's anxiety. Maggie, sensing his growing unease, grasped his hand and squeezed it. When the last person arrived and shut the door behind them, Pieter stood up and found a spot where everyone could see him.

"Thank you all for being here and offering to help. I've just finished discussing things with my brother Jan." He took a deep breath, his shoulders rising. "The exchange is taking place tonight at midnight at Waterloo."

Luke snorted loudly. When everyone turned to look at him, he elaborated, "It could all be just a big coincidence, but Le Mousquetaire appears to like symbolism. Waterloo is where Napoleon was finally defeated. Now a French vampire is going to essentially conquer half of Belgium, achieving victory, at the site his countryman lost the last of his empire."

Luke sat back, thinking for a moment. "It also works strategically. It's fairly central to all the major cities in southern Belgium and just south of Brussels."

"Hey, Luke," Pablo interrupted. "Just thinking of something Heidi mentioned when we were in Cologne. She said vampires were filtering into the city in large numbers."

Pieter whipped his head around to Pablo. "What?"

"Shit, that kind of slipped my mind after settling our packmates then your arrival," Luke said. "Pablo and I were there to pick up Maggie and the rest of our people when Heidi tracked us down in a little pub to find out what I was doing in the city. She said there were a lot of non-resident vampires moving into their territory."

"Are they making a play for the Rhein Pack, too?" Pieter sounded shocked.

Luke sat forward, resting his elbows on his knees. "She didn't think they were a threat to their territory, although she was worried I might be there to start something. She assured me they had nothing to do with their pack, but you might be a better judge. She said you were a friend."

"We have been for a while. I consider her trustworthy," Pieter replied.

"Do you think the vampires were there to reinforce Le Mousquetaire?" Sam asked.

"It's hard to tell, but they've been acting internationally. We saw that last spring with their whole shipping scheme. I wouldn't be surprised if German vampires are aiding the French and whatever's left of the Belgian nests to retake the French-speaking portion of the country."

Pieter shook his head. "Now there are even more vampires to worry about. Shit. I guess we can't do anything about that now. We're running short on time tonight. I was told I can't bring an escort. Jan has our people ready to take us in. We're being allowed a reasonable bodyguard as a show of faith, though it's more an insult that they don't think we can challenge them even with a sizable escort. You were mentioned by name though. They know the 'Centurion Immortal' is moving about, even if they're not sure where. They know you and I are close, Luke. So I have to go alone when I meet Jan and our people. They'll kill father if we bring anyone that isn't on the list Jan submitted."

Luke pulled out his phone and mapped the route to Waterloo. "Says here it's about an hour and fifteen. If we leave now, I think we can get there before the sun is entirely down. We'll get in and hunker down. Did they say where exactly the exchange would take place?"

"In front of the restaurant and visitor center below the Butte du Lion," Pieter said.

Luke narrowed his eyes and looked down at the map on his phone. "OK, we need to get on the road now. Do you think they'll search you?"

"I don't think so. There are at least some courtesies."

"I'll give you a radio, toss it in your pocket and lock press to talk." Luke stood up, the rest of the room followed Luke's example. "We're moving out in five minutes. Be sure you're ready. Last chance for a bathroom break. Pieter, come with me. I've got a rental for you, and I'll snag a radio, too."

Pieter nodded. "I'll depart in twenty or thirty minutes to meet up with Jan. That should give you plenty of time to get set up."

Luke led the way out with Pieter in tow. Maggie followed them out. After Pieter got his radio, Luke took Maggie aside. "You're in charge here. You've got all the numbers. It's your call if you think the safety here has been compromised. When the rest of the team gets to the train station, they know to call you for pick up. I'll keep you updated whenever I can."

Maggie slid her arms around Luke's waist, pulling him in tightly. "Good luck tonight, Luke. I'll take care of everything here."

"I know. I'm glad you're here. This is one thing I don't have to worry about." He bent down to kiss her, intending a soft kiss, but she slid her hand to the back of his neck and pulled in him in for a deeper, more intense kiss. In it, she poured her fear, anxiety, and love, unleashing matching feelings in his heart.

When she finally stepped back, she pulled Luke's head in and their foreheads touched. "Be strong, be fast, come back to me."

"I will." Luke kissed the tip of her nose. "I'll see you soon."

Maggie turned and walked away. Luke watched until she disappeared into his house. He sighed and walked over to the BMW where Sam, Pablo, Delilah, and Simone waited. He pulled the driver's door open and hopped in, buckling the seat belt. He fired up the engine as everyone else settled in their seats. Once they were buckled, Luke hit play on his music app—"Going Gets Tough" by The Growlers—and sped up the ramp and onto the road.

Luke, using the power and handling of the X5, zipped over the roads, ignoring the posted speed limits. Fifty-five minutes later, Luke pulled off the N5 onto a narrow dirt road with intermittent traces of past cobblestones rumbling underneath.

"That's it to the right," Luke said, not looking. Off in the near distance, the dark silhouette of a perfectly conical hill jutted out from the landscape. The faint outline of a stone plinth sitting on top, the lion at its pinnacle invisible in the post-sunset darkness. "Over these fields is where Napoleon met his defeat. That's the Lion memorializing the victory of the coalition against Old Boney. This all used to be part of the Netherlands then. I led a squadron of Dutch and Belgian Hussars under Luitenant-Kolonel Ignance Louis, Baron Duvivier in the Eighth Hussars."

Simone whispered in the back. Luke wasn't sure to whom, but he guessed Delilah since they were nearly inseparable companions at this point.

"What name were you using then?" Delilah asked.

"Major Luyc de Jaehger. It's one I've used in the past in the lowlands. Most of the men they gave me were a few steps above raw recruits, but at least Wellington and Von Blucher—"

Pablo neighed like a horse.

Luke furrowed his brows, confused. "What? Von Blucher—"

Pablo neighed again.

Shaking his head, Luke rolled his eyes. "Pablo. It's Frau Blucher—"

Pablo neighed again.

Sam giggled in the back seat.

"I know, dude, how often do you get to do that in casual conversation? I'm going to take advantage of it." Pablo sighed. "And I see our young people are not laughing at my perfectly timed jokes. I guess we need to add 'Young Frankenstein' to the movie night list."

"What's a hussar?" Delilah asked.

"It was a cavalry unit armed with carbines and sabers. Light and fast for scouting or flanking attacks. We had fancy uniforms. Being a hussar was a fairly fashionable unit to be in. I might have my old uniform kicking around the house somewhere," Luke replied.

"Oh my god, if you do, there'd better be a fashion show. You know Maggie would love to see that."

"Are you trying to use my willingness to do things for Maggie for your own entertainment?" Luke asked.

"I think that was fairly obvious." Delilah laughed.

"We'll see if there's time…" Luke stopped the SUV in the middle of the dirt and cobble farm road. "Pablo, mind popping out and seeing if there's a ditch hiding under those weeds to our right?"

"Sure thing." Pablo jumped out of the BMW and stomped

around in the weeds at the edge of the cornfield full of its tall, unharvested stalks. A minute later, he stuck his head back in the car. "All good, no ditch."

"OK. Shut the door. I'm going to back in. When I'm parked, we'll want to lift the broken stalks to conceal the car."

Pablo shut the door, then stepped away so Luke could reverse into the field. Once he was far enough back, they piled out of the car and geared up, not bothering with much in the way of overcoats to conceal their weapons, save for Luke, who pulled on a hoodie to hide the shine of his steel armor.

He pulled the zipper up. "Delilah, do you have your machete still?"

"Yeah. I never took it out of the gear box," she replied.

"Good. Can I borrow it?" Luke asked.

Delilah found it and handed it over. He attached it to his belt and secured it with straps around his thigh. Once they were finished, Luke locked the car and handed the fob to Pablo, who put it on a lanyard around his neck. Together, they lifted the bent corn stocks and propped them up to conceal the car as best they could.

"Watch your faces. Corn leaves are sharp and can be pretty rough on your skin." Luke pulled his hood up and tightened the drawstring. "It's about three kilometers. Let's keep the talk down. There's another road before we get to the field with the butte in it."

Luke took the lead, directing his friends down a row. Every twenty paces or so, he'd stop and chop down several stalks in multiple rows. As they got used to moving through the field, Luke picked up the pace to a slow jog, only halting once he heard something ahead. Holding up his fist, they stopped. Taking a moment, he let his senses open. Vamp. Luke held one finger up and pointed two down to indicate one vampire ahead. He pointed to Pablo.

Pablo nodded, peeling his warm-up jacket over his head before bending over to rip his tearaway pants off. Luke cringed as the snaps sounded like firecrackers in the still night. Embarrassed, Pablo blushed as he shifted to his bipedal werewolf.

"Who's there?" shouted a voice in French. "Identify yourself!"

Pablo walked forward, acting as casually as he could. Sam

quickly gathered Pablo's clothes and stashed them in the backpack Delilah always wore. They gave Pablo a few paces, then followed him, keeping back. Once Pablo breached the line of corn, they stopped. Pablo raised his massive, clawed paw and waved, sauntering toward the vamp leaning against a car as if they were the oldest of friends.

"Oh. It's one of you," the vamp said in French. "Find anything?"

Luke held his breath. Pablo didn't speak a lick of French. When Pablo shook his head, he let the breath out quietly, relieved Pablo had guessed the right option. The sound of the car shifting as Pablo leaned on it drifted through the corn. Luke waved for everyone to follow him. He pulled his gladius from the scabbard on his left hip and walked out of the line of trees.

"What the fuck? Who are you?" called the vamp, pushing off the car and stepping toward Luke.

As soon as the fanger turned his back on Pablo, his life ended. The giant werewolf stepped forward, placing one paw on the vamp's chin and the other on the back of his head, and twisted, ripping the vamp's head off. The headless vamp dropped to the ground like a sack of grain.

"Blech," Simone said, covering up a retching sound as she turned away.

Everyone else was used to Pablo's favorite way to neutralize vampires. Luke pulled his rudis and stabbed it through the heart before kneeling over the wooden sword to take the vampire's energy and send it onto a permanent death. The vampire puffed out into a pile of dust. Luke stood and sheathed the rudis.

"Hold up a second," Sam whispered, squatting over the pile of clothes the vampire left behind. After a few seconds, she lifted the vamp's wallet, a set of keys, and a radio with an ear wire. She handed the radio to Luke. He was the best person to pick up whatever languages were being used by those on the other end of the radio.

Luke clipped the radio to his belt and had Sam help him run the long wire up and under the back of his hoodie, clipping it to the edge of his hood before he took it and popped in the ear bud.

"South point, check in? I repeat, south point, check in," said a voice in the ear bud in French.

"South point, clear," Luke replied.

"Why were you late with your check in?"

"I thought I heard something in the cornfield and was checking it out. All clear though."

"Understood. Out."

Luke relaxed, wiping his hand over his brow as if to wipe away sweat that wasn't there. He waved everyone forward. Sam, shaking her head, walked over to Luke and stood on her tiptoes.

"Give us a second to go full wolf. That hill looks gnarly," Sam whispered. She pointed to Simone, then peeled off her clothes.

Simone nodded and began undressing. Luke and Delilah helped with everyone's weapons, then stashed the clothes in Delilah's backpack, sorting the weapons out between the two of them. Once the two women were naked, they blurred into full wolves. They shook out their fur and sniffed the night air. It was the first time Luke had seen Simone in her full wolf form. A moment later, Pablo blurred down from his bipedal shape to his full wolf.

"Don't go up the hill too fast. Scout ahead, but if you find someone, report back to me. Let's not get separated or get too much distance between us. Delilah and I can't move as fast as you can," Luke said.

The three wolves nodded, then disappeared into the cornfield separating them from the Butte du Lion.

Luke and Delilah followed their lupine friends into the cornfield, letting them range ahead, using their superior wolfy senses to take the lead in scouting, although Luke paid firm attention to his vamp senses. A cornfield was a good place to hide and sneak, but it was a double-edged sword. Using the machete, he continued knocking down periodic patches along the line they traversed.

Moving at a quick and steady pace, Luke and Delilah kept their faces down and their hoods up to prevent the stiff corn leaves from slapping their faces. When they reached the end of their row, the wolves were waiting for him, sitting neatly side by side, two facing out toward the hill, one looking back down the row to keep an eye on their humans.

Luke popped his head out of the corn to investigate the situation. A gentle breeze blew into his face. Delilah, moving up next to him, bumped him with her elbow and pointed over her shoulder to her backpack. Nodding, Luke unzipped the front pocket quietly and pulled out a set of night vision binoculars. He slowly scanned along the edge of the cornfield looking for any movement then down the other edge, sweeping out over the clearing between them and the hill. When he turned the binoculars toward the top of the hill, he saw movement and the heat signature of a vampire—lower than a human but slightly warmer than the ambient air. He watched for several seconds as the vampire patrolled around the lion statue on its plinth. He counted off several rotations of the vampire walking the circuit.

"Wolves, when I say go, sprint into that little grove of trees. The wind is in our favor, so we just have to avoid being seen. Once you're across, we'll follow," Luke whispered.

The wolves nodded. Luke, looking back at the top of the hill, found his patrol, and waited until he turned so his back was toward them.

"Go!"

The wolves took off, bunching their muscles and stretching out, their paws eating up the open ground between the edge of the cornfield and the grove. Luke, holding his breath, let the air hiss between his clenched teeth as soon as the last tail disappeared into the shadows of the leafy trees.

He made eye contact with Delilah. "Alright, Dee, you ready?"

"Yeah." She reached down and cinched the straps on the backpack so they were tighter.

"Go!"

Together, they darted out of the cover of the corn and dashed across the grassy strip, their arms pumping as they poured as much speed into their legs as they could without risking tripping. As soon as Luke drew near the tree line, he slowed so he wouldn't slam into an unseen tree trunk hidden in the darkness, coming to a stop just inside the tree line. His lungs heaved in and out for air, as he turned and watched Delilah close the last few yards into the grove.

Once he caught his breath, he worked his way toward the bottom of the hill. Peeking out from behind a tree trunk, he watched the top, making sure they'd made it in unnoticed. So far, the vampire showed no signs of noticing the intruders as he maintained his steady circuit around the top of the hill. The next part, however, was going to be tricky.

The hill had no bushes, just grass. It might be tall enough to conceal a wolf crawling on their belly. He stepped back into the trees a few yards to provide some additional wood between him and the outside world. He gathered the wolves, then squatted down in front of them, going nose to snoot.

"Can you sneak up the backside of this hill without getting caught? Once you get to the top, you'll need to take the patrol down on the backside of the plinth out of sight of the museum and restaurant below."

The three wolves looked at each other. Pablo gave a quick nod, then led his wolves to the edge of the grove. Forming a line, they worked their way through the trees until they reached the end of the grove. Then, one by one, they crawled on their bellies up the hill. They kept their timing tight, flattening themselves when the patrol walked around the back of the plinth.

Luke's eyes grew dry trying to keep them open so he wouldn't miss a thing, eventually blinking to wet them and start over. He listened for any sound that might indicate someone was approaching or that one of the wolves had laid a paw in the wrong spot. The only sound was the beating of his own heart and the soft inhale and exhale of him and Delilah breathing.

He startled when Delilah's hand slipped into his, gripping tight as they watched their friends approach the crown of the hill. Delilah squeezed even tighter when the wolves stopped just below the platform and its surrounding guardrails. Pablo, still in the lead, flattened out. As soon as the vampire at the top made his turn to head back around the front, Pablo transformed into his bipedal form. Grabbing the top of the handrail, he vaulted over and pushed his back against the side of the plinth just around the corner.

"Almost," Luke whispered, squeezing Delilah's hand.

They held their breath when the vampire came into sight around the back. Once the vamp turned the corner, Pablo reached out and covered the fanger's mouth with his massive paw, secured the vampire's head, and wrenched it off. Both he and Delilah twitched, their brains filling in the sound they'd heard so many times while hunting with Pablo. The body slumped to the ground.

"Let's go." Luke tugged Delilah's hand, leading her to the end of the grove. "Slow and steady. You don't want to slide back down."

Luke let go of Delilah's hand, then started up the hill, leaning forward and using his hands to keep his balance. As his feet slipped and he caught himself, he wished he had four legs and claws to aid his climbing. When he looked up, taking a moment to catch his breath, he saw Pablo in his human form patrolling around the plinth. He'd stripped the body of its jacket and pants, but was still barefoot and shirtless. He carried some sort of assault rifle; Luke couldn't quite tell what it was.

When they reached the crown, Sam and Simone were still in wolf form, laying on their bellies in the grass. Luke crawled over the rails and hid in the back shadow of the plinth. He pulled out his phone and checked the time—eleven thirty. When Pablo made his next circuit, he smiled and handed the gun off to Luke. It was another Steyr SSG 69 sniper rifle like the one taken from the vampires during the freighter campaign. It made sense; the top of the hill was a prime sniper nest commanding the territory all around.

On the front side of the hill, Luke could see the roof of the restaurant and museum as well as the stairs and path leading down. Most of the parking area was blocked off in the shadow of the buildings. The large parking lot to his right buzzed with activity. Several cars were parked with their headlights shining toward the center of the lot. In the middle, surrounded by people who could be vampires or werewolves in human form, was a man tied to a chair, his legs and ankles bound with heavy chains. They'd wound ropes around his body and legs to keep him immobile. He had a bag over his head. It had to be Pieter van den Bergh, Pieter and Jan's father and the packleader of Belgium and southern Netherlands.

When Luke circled back around, he stopped briefly. "If you want to come around front, you can watch, just stay low. There's a lip that should cover you, but they won't be able to see you with what's going on." He then continued around.

When he marched back around again, Delilah, sitting on the ledge on the back, raised her hand to stop Luke. "Hand me the binoculars next time you come around and I'll keep watch. I don't feel like crawling around front."

Luke nodded and continued around, handing her the binoculars on his next circuit. When the calls went around asking for check ins, he made the check in for the south check point then changed his voice somewhat for the butte check in when it was called. So far, no one seemed to notice that two of the check ins were one person who wasn't either of their vampires.

"Everything is under control. Situation normal," Delilah mumbled.

Pablo chuffed quietly.

At five minutes to midnight, several cars pulled onto the Route du Lion. When Luke made his next trip around back, he let Delilah know the Flanders Pack had arrived.

The earpiece crackled, "Sniper, into position," then went silent.

Luke walked around front and propped the rifle against the railing. The scope was already dialed in. Reaching into his pocket, he pulled out the radio connected to Pieter and set it down on the ground next to him. A moment later, it crackled to life.

"Luke. I'm here. I'll be going silent in a moment," Pieter said.

Luke picked up the radio. "We're in place on top of the hill."

"Understood, out," Pieter replied.

Luke turned the radio down to a level he could still listen to but wouldn't interfere with anything he might need to hear over the vampire's earpiece. The Flanders Pack parked. A wolf Luke recognized as Jan stepped out along with four others Luke assumed were werewolves and had the bearing of bodyguards. Two of them flanked Jan, while the other two stood to the side. When Pieter stepped out of the rental, he walked between the other two, taking up position next to Jan.

Three men stepped out from the line of people opposite Jan and Pieter. They took up a position leaving the bound packleader in between the two groups.

"We're here, vampire, as we agreed," Jan said, his voice slightly muffled from the inside of Pieter's pocket.

"Welcome, Jan, Pieter." One of the men nodded at the two werewolves, stepping forward.

"Before we go any further, we need to make sure he's alive," Jan said.

The vampire's spokesman stepped forward and pulled the bag

from the prisoner's head. With the light blaring around, the man rocked his head around. When he rolled his head to the side facing Luke, he was able to see who it was. Luke had hoped it was a fake, but it wasn't; it was Pieter van den Bergh—the man who in his first life had been Pieter Bruegel the Elder.

"It's him," Luke whispered.

"Father!" Pieter called, taking a step forward.

"No, stay back." Jan held his arm out, catching Pieter's arm.

"Are you satisfied?" the spokesvamp said.

"I am." Jan shifted his feet, moving his weight back and forth.

"Make the call," the vamp's representative said.

Jan turned toward their line of cars and yelled, "Send the evacuation order!"

"Yes, sir," a voice yelled back.

"The evacuation order has been issued. Our armed forces will be out of Brussels before sunrise. We'll have all families moved out by the end of the week," Jan said.

"And the rest of the Walloon cities?" the spokesvamp asked.

"You've killed most all of them," Pieter spat out. "The rest are out. You've got what you want. Now let my father go."

"I'm sorry; this deal was not brokered with you." The fanger turned to Jan. "Shut him up, or we will."

Jan gestured with his head toward Pieter, while keeping his eyes on the vampire. The musclebound guys behind Pieter stepped forward and seized his arms, pulling him back.

"What? Jan? What's going on here?" Pieter struggled against them, pulling forward. "What have you done, Jan?!"

"Shut him up," Jan said.

One of bodyguards behind Pieter pulled out a pistol from his jacket and flipped it around so he held the barrel. He stepped behind the two men straining to hold Pieter back and brought the butt of the pistol down on the back of Pieter's head. Luke winced at the sound of metal on skull translated through the radio in Pieter's pocket. It didn't knock him all the way out, but it got him to stop talking and struggling as he went limp in the two men's arms.

"Fuck…" Luke whispered. "Pablo, get me all the magazines from that vampire. We're going to need them."

Pablo, in wolf form, crawled around behind the plinth. A moment later, he crawled back in his human form, pulling the jacket with him, in it, he'd laid out five more five round magazines. Luke had thirty rounds to work with. He was by no stretch of the imagination a sniper, but he could shoot. He wished they'd brought Jung-sook to Belgium, she was a crack shot.

"I need to lie down here," he whispered. "Hurry."

Simone and Sam scurried out of his way. Once he settled, he opened the gun's bipod and set it on the concrete ledge running around the observation platform. He pulled the bolt lever up and back then pushed it forward and down to chamber the first round.

"Well, Jan van den Bergh. Are you going to fulfill your end of the agreement?" the vampire asked.

Jan pulled a semiautomatic pistol from inside his suit jacket and pulled back the slide. He took a deep breath then stepped toward his father.

"No, Jan. Papa…" Pieter said weakly, still unable to regain control of his body.

Their father looked Jan in the eyes and straightened his back. Jan placed the barrel of the gun in the middle of his father's forehead and pulled back the hammer.

"Oh no…" Luke couldn't believe what he was seeing.

The man who'd sent him on a mission to help find his father's wife and child had just placed a loaded gun to his own father's forehead. Luke moved the cross hairs of the scope onto Jan, but before he could bring his finger to the trigger, Jan lowered the gun, and Luke let out a small sigh of relief. Crack. Jan put a round into his father's heart. Crack. A spray of red mist shot out from the back of Pieter Bruegel the Elder's head as Jan put a second round through his forehead. Luke's body trembled as he took aim at Jan's chest and squeezed the trigger, sending Jan's body sprawling to the ground.

The vampires scrambled back into the shadow of the visitor's center. Luke took advantage of the confusion, took aim at the bodyguard still restraining Pieter, and put one through his head. Luke pulled back the bolt and chambered another round, placing it into the center of the second bodyguard's torso. No longer restrained, Pieter slumped to the ground. While Luke looked for another target, Pieter crawled toward his father.

Luke returned the scope to Jan and his bodyguards as they leaned over their boss, shielding his body and pulling him away from the carnage. Luke fired, missing, then pulled the bolt back, loading the last round of the magazine. The sudden sound of a rumbling growl next to Luke caused him to twitch, missing his target but putting the round into the thigh of one of the bodyguards. During the chaos, the chair containing the slain packleader of the Flanders Pack had been knocked over. Pieter lay on the ground, cradling his father's head in his lap.

Luke shoved a new magazine into the Steyr and loaded a round into the chamber. Sweeping the area below him, werewolves, who'd been waiting in the cars, scrambled out, shifting into bipedal forms. Luke took aim and put the first round in a wolf's chest. He pulled the bolt back and took aim at another, missing but shattering a wind-shield. Luke's random firing pattern caused the wolves to scramble for cover.

"Luke, coming up on your side," Delilah said. "I'll spot."

"'K," he replied.

"Our wolves are heading down the stairs to get Pieter. Vampires on the left, coming out from the building."

Luke swept the rifle left, pulling the trigger at the first movement he saw, but he missed. He found another target as a fanger darted out and ran across the open space toward the parking lot. Leading his target, Luke pulled the trigger, dropping the vampire. A werewolf ventured out from behind his car. Luke took aim, shooting the hood of the car, causing the wolf to drop for cover.

Someone on the vampire's side must have been counting shots, knowing their sniper rifle only had five round magazines. Several sprinted out from behind the visitor's center with all the vampiric speed they could muster. By the time Luke had the next magazine in place, several fangers had made it to the safety of some trees near the parking lot. A few moments later, a car fired up and sped out of the lot like a bat out of hell. Luke swung the rifle after it, shattering the rear window as the car sped away.

Bringing the scope back around to the center of the open space, Pieter still hadn't moved as he cradled his dead father. As anger shoved aside shock, Luke went looking for Jan, figuring he owed the patricidal bastard another bullet. When he found the bodyguards, now joined by a couple more, he took aim and opened fire, operating the bolt action sniper rifle as fast as he could. He didn't care what he shot, as long as it hit flesh. In quick succession, he emptied the magazine, putting four of the five bullets into one of the werewolves who'd betrayed his friend and murdered his other friend. He wasn't sure if any of the bullets hit Jan or not. He hoped so.

"Luke." Delilah shouted into Luke's ear. "The vampires are trying to get Pieter. Pablo, Sam, and Simone are outnumbered! Forget Jan."

Luke pulled the magazine and replaced it with a full one. He quickly marked the three wolves who were his friends, then took aim at anything that moved near them. He closed his eyes, took a deep breath, then opened them, focusing in on a vampire who wasn't pulling all the way back after darting in to swat at the wolves.

Squeezing the trigger, Luke smiled as the vampire collapsed, a gaping hole in its head. Luke took aim at the next vampire, missing the chest shot he was aiming for but at least hitting it in the thigh, knocking the vamp to the ground. One of the wolves darted in and ripped out the fallen vampire's throat before it could move away.

"Fuck, missed," Luke mumbled on the third shot.

At least it had the effect of driving back the vampires. One wolf, it looked like Sam, was trying to pull Pieter away from his father. All Pieter did was swat lazily at the wolf tugging at his sleeve. Lost in his grief, Pieter ignored the danger around him. Blinking back tears, Luke swiped at his cheeks and placed the crosshairs on the dead body in Pieter's arms. When Sam made another attempt to drag Pieter away, pulling him back, Luke pulled the trigger. The body shook as the bullet plowed into it. Pieter jerked his head around, finally focusing on what was happening around him. Pieter shoved his way backwards, looking around.

"Luke, someone's coming up the stairs! We got to move before we're trapped up here." Delilah sounded slightly frantic.

Luke took aim at another vampire and fired, missing as the vampire scrambled out of the way. Luke pulled the magazine and shoved another in. Then he scooped the magazines lying in a pile next to him, empty and full, and shoved them into his hoodie pockets. Standing up, he folded in the bipod and extended the strap so it would go over his armor.

"Delilah, hold this for a second." Luke handed her the Steyr and unslung the Winchester M12 from his back, then unzipped his hoodie so he could access the shotgun shells on the bandolier ammo belt. He took the Steyr and slung it around his chest. "Let's go. I'll lead."

Maybe thinking they'd got the jump on Delilah and Luke, the vampire sprinted up the last half of the steps, a pistol in his hand. Luke stepped down onto the top step and chambered a shotgun shell. As soon as the vampire saw, he stood up, attempting to pull back. Luke unloaded the shell on the vampire, splattering it all over the stairs into a mess of reddish-black goo.

"Careful down the stairs, it's a fucking young one." Luke moved down the stairs swiftly, only slowing to find some dry patches until he passed the slick vampire remains, then he took off down the stairs.

As soon as he reached the bottom of the staircase, Luke sprinted over to a large tree and hid behind it, sweeping the barrel of his shotgun in front of him while he waited for Delilah. When a head poked out from behind the corner of the building to his left, Luke fired off a round, sending stone chips flying. Delilah finally made it down the stairs and sprinted over to the large round wall of the Panorama building.

Luke waved her forward as he kept an eye on his friends. Pieter, still moving slowly, had finally started shifting. Sprinting forward, Luke fired off the remaining shots in his shotgun, clearing the space around his friends.

"Dee, cover us while I reload," Luke yelled.

"Got it," she replied, stepping up to the fence separating them from their friends. She picked her shots, careful to not waste ammo.

Luke ducked down and grabbed shells out of the bandolier running across his chest, shoving them into the port at the bottom of the gun. When he'd put in six, he stood back up. Pieter had shifted to a full wolf, but he still looked unsteady on his feet; he'd never clear the fence.

"Get back!" he yelled and took aim at the lock on the gate. Luke pulled the trigger, then kicked out hard. The lock busted, and the gate swung open. "Dee, let's clear a path."

Delilah fired off her last round then slung the shotgun over her shoulder, pulling around another one. Between the two of them, they fired off shots left, right, and center, driving the vampires back. Jan's werewolves were more concerned with getting their wounded leader out of there than engaging with Luke. Luke's four werewolves ran through the gate, Pieter wobbling as he went by; Pablo brought up the rear. Taking a leaf from Delilah's book, Luke grabbed Pablo's shotgun from around his back and replaced it with the empty one. He backed up while Delilah fed shells into her empty shotgun. Once reloaded, she started backing up, gun pointed to cover their retreat.

"Delilah, Cover me for one second." Luke grabbed the empty shotgun from his back and quickly reloaded it. Making sure the shotguns were ready to grab and fire, he pumped a shell into the firing chamber of the one he held. "Follow them. Around the base of the hill to that little grove, then make for the path we marked. I'll catch up."

"On it," Delilah turned and ran after the wolves.

Luke backed up, keeping his eyes open. Anytime he saw movement, he fired off a round. Sometimes he'd hear a scream as the sliver burned into vampire flesh. Once he thought he saw a puff of dust. After the sixth round, he slung the gun over his shoulder, untangled one of the other loaded shotguns, and fired a shot to remind the vamps he was still there.

Taking one last look around, he turned and dashed after his friends, too many guns slapping on his back. He disappeared into the small grove of trees and ran as hard as he safely could. When he popped out the other side of the grove into the grassy space between the hill and the cornfield to the south. He looked around, but didn't see anyone.

Sprinting across the open space, he aimed for the row where he'd cut down the stalks to guide their way. He turned quickly to check behind himself, thinking he heard shouting coming from the base of the butte. He ran as fast as he could, the stiff corn leaves slapping him in the face. He hissed as a leaf cut his cheek. Skidding to a halt, he pulled his hood up and drew the drawstrings tight to protect his face, then sprinted off again.

"Shit!" screamed a vampire in French, followed by the sound of bodies tumbling and corn stalks shaking.

The sound was too close for comfort. If Luke ran any faster, he was in serious danger of eating shit like the fangers. He kept going, wishing he didn't have four guns dangling on his back. The weight and movement made running that much harder. Soon, a new noise broke the sound of his whistling breath already accompanied by the rustling and thwapping of leaves against his shoulders as he pelted down the row—footfalls and the occasional knock of a cornstalk.

When Luke thought his tail was nearly upon him, he spun around and fired blindly behind him, the momentum carrying Luke back. As he landed on his ass, he drew a quick aim and fired again. The vampire exploded into a mass of mist and goo, showering Luke on the ground. He spat and wiped his sleeve over his face to get as much of the sludge off his face as possible. Rolling over, he wiped his face with his hands then grabbed handfuls of dirt and rubbed them to get the goo off his palms and fingers. As the sound of feet and corn rustling reached his ears, he launched back onto his feet and took off, leaping over a section of cut stalks.

Finding a small gap he jumped over several rows and into one where he hadn't cut the stalks and turned up the speed. Off to his side and a little behind, his pursuers went down, tripped up on the stalks. Luke would have chuckled, but he had no breath to spare as he pumped his arms. He had to be getting close to the end of the field.

Up ahead, he heard a car start up followed by tires spinning in dirt and gravel as it drove off, the sound heading toward the east. He broke through the last line of corn onto the farm road, a cloud of dust settling over the road. Along the other side, Pablo sat on his haunches, his tongue lolling out of his mouth as he panted. Everyone else was gone.

"They take that vamp's car?" Luke asked, gasping for air as he stopped for a second.

Pablo nodded.

"OK. Good. Take off. Get to the Beamer. I'll be right behind." Luke walked across the road, picking a row near the patches he'd cut down.

Pablo tore off down a row, his fluffy tail disappearing into the darkness. Luke started with a jog, his heart slowing after the short break. As his tired legs adjusted to the terrain, he dug deep into his reserves and accelerated. One foot in front of the other. Don't trip. He hoped the vampires thought all of them had taken off in the car. Whoever was driving hadn't been quiet about it.

He couldn't hear any noise behind him, but that didn't mean anything with the intensity of the blood pumping through his ears. Even after draining two vampires earlier, Luke felt his legs turning to lead, his muscles burning as he asked more from them. When he saw something ahead, shiny and black, he smiled.

He yanked the rear passenger door open. Pulling the guns off his back, he flipped the safeties on and set them on the floor. With one loaded shotgun in his hands, he shut the door and climbed into the passenger seat. Pablo, nude, turned on the car and pulled onto the road, gunning it.

"We're going to have to get the cabin detailed, buddy," Pablo said, breaking the silence.

"I know. Bare ass on my leather seats..." Luke shook his head, untying the drawstrings of his hood and pulling it back.

"Bro, you're covered in dirt and what looks and smells like dead vamp goo. My bare ass is the least of your car's concerns."

"Yeah. We still have to get out of here without being followed," Luke said. He pulled out his cell phone and dialed Delilah.

"Hey Luke. You away?" Delilah asked.

"Yeah. Just about to pull onto the N5. How are you doing?" Luke looked left and right as Pablo stopped and pulled onto N5, heading south.

"Everyone's pretty scraped up from the corn. Pieter's probably got a pretty bad concussion. Shit. Looks like cops are headed that way."

"We'll keep an eye out. Let's go quiet unless something comes up. See you back at base," Luke replied.

"Good luck."

"You too," Luke said.

L uke and Pablo traveled for about an hour from the battlefield at Waterloo and the Butte du Lion, taking random turns while working their way vaguely south and east. Luke had checked in a couple times with Delilah to ensure they were still free and moving. They'd only seen police lights and heard their sirens a couple times and those not far from Waterloo.

"Hey, Buddy," Pablo said, breaking the silence.

"Yeah, Pablo?"

"Mind if I turn the heat on? It's a little chilly in here for some reason."

Luke ran his eyes over his naked friend in the driver's seat and chuckled. "I can't think of a reason why…"

Pablo stuck out his right hand and extended his middle finger at Luke, then used it to turn on the heat. Luke laughed, letting a little of the evening's tension siphon out of his shoulders. He couldn't wait to get back to his house and take a shower. His hoodie stank with the muck of vampire remains and dirt, and his face and the back of his hands itched from the corn, despite all his precautions. Tired of the silence, he turned on some music—Aldous Harding's sweet and haunting voice filled the cabin with "Titus Groan."

He didn't know how Pablo felt after running through the field as a wolf. Did the dirt and grime and corn dust translate through to his human skin? Or did the magic of the werewolf slough off the dirt at the transition? Pablo yawned. He'd ask about it some other time, if he remembered, when Pablo was less tired and less occupied.

As Luke stared over the dark road, one image filled his thoughts—Jan staring his father in the eyes as he lowered the gun and pulled the trigger, shooting his father through the heart before finishing him with a bullet to the brain. Luke didn't know werewolf healing mechanics well, but putting a bullet through his father's heart and brain was enough to end the illustrious life of the great artist Pieter Bruegel the Elder. Betrayed by his own son at the behest of a vampire.

Checking around them, Luke saw no other cars anywhere as they drove down the narrow windy road. "Let's make for the house, Pablo. I think we've thrown our pursuit, if there was any."

"Aye, aye, captain. Mind punching the directions into the GPS?" Pablo adjusted the aim of one of the vents, wanting as much heat as possible.

Luke input in the nearest crossroads and picked the fastest route from their current location. The GPS said they only had about thirty minutes until their destination's end. A sigh on his lips, Luke let his head rest against the inside of the window as he stared off into the darkness, the death of his friend replaying on repeat through his mind.

AS THEY DESCENDED the ramp leading down to the river and Luke's manor, Luke brought his eyes into focus to make sure his friends had made it back safely with their stolen car. Someone must have been keeping watch for them, stepping out of the house to wait by the parking area. He recognized the short, chubby form of Sam. As soon as they parked, Sam walked around to Pablo and handed him his track suit along with a pair of slip-on sandals.

"Thanks, Sam. It's a little chilly without clothes or fur." He pulled Sam in with one arm and kissed her forehead.

After Pablo released Sam, Luke pulled her in for a hug of his own. "How's Pieter?"

"It's hard to tell. He hasn't said a word since he shifted back to his human form. We've had to basically tell him to move and guide him along. It's like his brain shut off. Maggie says he's got a pretty bad concussion, but it should mend up quickly enough." She ran her eyes up and down Luke. "Is that your blood?"

"No. Vampire remains. One got a little closer than I was comfortable with in the cornfields," Luke replied.

Together, they headed up the steps into the entry hall of the cottage. Down at the other end of the hall, Pieter stood in the doorway, Maggie just behind him.

"Looks like Pieter's up and about," Pablo said.

Once Pieter's eyes focused on Luke, he stormed down the hall, his steps still wobbly and unsure.

"Hey Pieter, it's good—"

Pieter's eyes, though unfocused, burned at Luke, his rage over boiling. Before Luke could react, Pieter unleashed a wild haymaker at Luke's face, catching him in the cheek and knocking Luke to ground. Sam and Pablo quickly grabbed Pieter's arms, holding him back.

"You desecrated my father's body!" Pieter yelled. "You should have saved him in Cambrai. It's your fault he's dead." He tried to yank his arms free, but the raging punch had taken a lot out of him. "Let me go."

"No more punches," Sam said sternly.

Pieter nodded once, hard, wincing from the effort. They let him go as he tugged his arms free. Storming by Luke, he disappeared out the front door.

"I'll go keep an eye on him," Pablo said, following Pieter out the door.

Even though Pieter's punch was off target and underpowered, thanks to the concussion, the hit was still nothing to laugh at. He shook his head, trying to clear the stars. When his vision cleared, he looked up into Maggie's concerned eyes as she knelt beside him.

"Are you OK?" Maggie asked, laying a couple fingers alongside Luke's jaw, tipping his cheek toward her.

"I think so. He really rung my bell there. The whole left side of my face is throbbing."

"Can you sit up some? Is this your blood?" She looked him over, her eyes lingering on the dark stains.

"No. Vampire." Luke pushed himself into a sitting position.

"Good." Maggie pulled out a small flashlight and checked Luke's eyes, running him through a few tests. "Well, looks like you may have gotten lucky. I don't think you have a concussion. I'm going to need to feel around to see if he broke any bones."

Luke nodded, wincing. He hissed as Maggie pressed her fingers to his cheek and moved them around, feeling his bones.

Maggie exhaled, her shoulders relaxing. "I think you may have gotten off relatively unscathed. I don't think anything's broken. I'd like to get it imaged, if we can."

"If we have time, I'll speak to the caretaker's son. He's a doctor; he'll have access to whatever you need."

Maggie nodded. "We should get some ice on your cheek."

"It'll have to wait. I need to shower and change. I'll meet you in the sitting room when I'm done. I could use a beer while I ice my face."

Maggie and Sam helped Luke up. Smiling at them, he headed toward the staircase. Maggie followed him. When Luke stepped into his room, Maggie shut the door behind him, silently stepping up behind him. She helped him take off his hoodie, then the ammo bandolier and his tactical vest before they could remove his armor. Maggie set it on the armor stand in the corner. Luke peeled off the armor padding then the sweaty t-shirt under it.

Sitting down, he untied his boots and took them off along with his socks. "I should have taken these off downstairs," he mumbled. He shucked his jeans and underwear and disappeared into the bathroom, turning on the shower. Ten minutes later, he emerged from the bathroom, toweling his hair dry. Maggie sat quietly in the corner, relaxing in a cushy wingback armchair. After Luke tossed the towel aside and pulled on clean boxer briefs, Maggie pulled him into a fierce hug.

"I'm sorry your friend hit you, but I'm glad you're not hurt." She kissed his uninjured cheek then stepped back so he could finish dressing. "I'll meet you in the sitting room with some ice and a beer. What would you like?"

"That would be magnificent. There should be some bottles of Chimay Blue down there. There's a small ice maker in the kitchen next to the fridge." Luke smiled then grimaced at the pain the gesture caused in his cheek.

"Silly man, it'll hurt if you smile," Maggie said, her voice soft.

"I can't help smiling when I'm with you." Luke caressed her cheek.

"I can always go away…" Maggie teased, a small, mischievous smile on her face.

"I thought you didn't want to cause me pain. A punch to the cheek will heal soon enough."

She stepped up and gave Luke a gentle kiss. "You're such a nice man. I'll see you downstairs."

Luke pulled on some pajama pants and threw on a robe before sliding his feet into some slippers. He collapsed onto the love seat he'd moved by the fire the day Maggie had arrived. Someone must have turned it around, so it faced the fire burning merrily in the stone hearth. He let the random pops and crackles of the dancing flames sooth his mind into blankness. He wasn't sure how long he sat there.

"Luke, dear, I have your ice and beer." Maggie set the beer down on the antique round end table to his left.

Luke looked up at the beautiful woman, smiled, then winced, shaking his head at himself. "Sit with me, Maggie."

Handing Luke the ice pack, she sat next to him, pulling her legs up underneath herself as she leaned into Luke's right side. Luke hissed as he pressed the icepack to his cheek, then sighed happily as it started numbing the left side of his face.

"Oh, Maggie…" Luke murmured. "I…"

Maggie gave him some time, but when he didn't say anything

more, she reached across him and gave a squeeze. "Luke, I'm here if you need to talk or if you just want to sit and be. I'm here for you."

Luke, removing the icepack from his cheek, looked down into Maggie's startling blue eyes, the kindness and love he saw in them nearly undoing him. "I need to say something. With everything going on… I don't want to leave this unsaid."

Staring into Luke's eyes, Maggie caressed his good cheek with the back of her fingers. Her eyes were encouraging but also vulnerable.

"I love you, Maggie."

Maggie smiled softly, "I love you, too." She tipped her lips for him to kiss.

Luke leaned his head onto Maggie's. "I just needed you to know how I felt, in case—"

Reaching up, Maggie placed her forefinger and middle finger across his lips. "We can never know what's going to happen, but it's always good to tell people how you feel, often, so they know."

Luke sighed, his body folding in on itself a bit. "I think I've known it for a while, I just… I didn't know how to say it, and then I was waiting for the perfect time."

"And this felt like the perfect time?"

Luke could tell by the tone of her voice that she was teasing. "No, but I couldn't let it go unsaid anymore. You're a very special woman, Magdalena, and I'm happy to know you and to be with you."

"Ah, you say such nice things. I didn't expect to develop feelings for you when we met, but life is full of wonderful surprises. I'm glad you're in my life and that you love me." She ran her hand over his thigh.

They sat quietly, staring into the flames. Behind them, the door opened and shut. When a hand was set on his shoulder, he looked up at Pablo.

"Hey. I got Pieter up to his room. I think he's sleeping. I'm going to clean up and turn in myself." Pablo squeezed Luke's shoulder.

"Good night, Pablo."

"Sleep well, Luke, Maggie." He left, shutting the door quietly behind him.

Luke picked up his beer and took a drink. Maggie held her hand up, so Luke gave her the glass. Taking a few sips, she handed it back to Luke. Together, they shared the beer until it was empty. Luke left the glass on the end table, but he picked up the icepack as they headed upstairs to bed.

The team slept late after the intense night. Despite having Maggie next to him, Luke was plagued by. While the affections of Maggie had gone a long way toward easing his mind, it was still a dark and troubled place. He and his therapist had just started poking its edges.

He woke alone, sandy-eyed and fuzzy-brained. Rubbing the sleep from his eyes, he rolled to the edge of the bed. When his feet hit the floor, he noticed the folded note on his nightstand.

L

Text me when you wake, and I'll have a coffee waiting for you when you come down. Émile brought fresh pastries, and they're divine.

Love, M

Luke smiled and set the note back on the nightstand, sending a quick text to Maggie. Finding a t-shirt and a pair of shorts, he slipped on his house sandals and headed out to greet the day and his friends. He headed straight to the glass solarium, figuring that would be where everyone gathered, trying to enjoy the last days of sun as summer drew near its end in Belgium—and back home in Oregon. Soon, both places would turn gray and rainy.

He gave a Sam a one-armed hug and kissed the crown of her head. "Good morning, Sam."

"Mornin', Luke. You're awfully affectionate this morning," Sam replied.

He pulled out a chair and sat next to her. "Maggie and I were talking last night about telling those we care about how we feel. You've become a very dear friend in the last year, and I'm glad you're in my life."

"That's sweet, Luke. Even if the times are dark, your friendship has been a welcome light in my life." Sam leaned over and gave Luke a kiss on the cheek.

"Good morning, handsome," Maggie said, kissing the other cheek and setting a tray of coffees down on the table. She handed a latte to Sam, then set down one with darker foam for Luke. The last latte was for her. "I made you a mocha. I thought you could use a treat after last night. Émile stocks good chocolate."

Luke chuckled. "Since I'm never here long enough to use everything he purchases for me, he takes the leftovers home and splits it with his family so it doesn't go to waste. He buys good quality stuff. Of course, I request quality ingredients. It works out for everyone."

"That's convenient," Sam said. She slid the silver tray toward Luke.

"Oh, he's gone over the top this morning." Luke smiled giddily. "These look like waffles from Une Gaufrette Saperlipopette." The caretaker had thoughtfully noted what was what with little folded note cards so Luke picked a Brussels-style waffle filled with sour cherries. Grabbing a fork, he dug in.

Sam laughed. "You might have some serious competition for Luke's affections, Maggie. I don't know if I've ever seen Luke make eyes like that at anyone."

"Maggie and I are polyamorous, Sam. I can be in a relationship with her and this waffle," Luke said in between bites.

Maggie snorted, then broke into a laughter. "You're a ridiculous man, Luke, and I love you." Maggie leaned in and kissed Luke's forehead.

After swallowing his bite, Luke smiled. "I love you, Maggie." Then he looked down at the bite of waffle he'd speared on his fork. "Don't worry. I love you, too, waffle."

Pablo pulled out a chair and sat down across from Luke. "Is Luke's heart wandering already?"

"Try one of these rectangular waffles. They're filled with fruit preserves," Luke instructed, pointing to one of them.

Looking over the notes, Pablo transferred an apricot waffle to his plate and dug in. "Oh, wow. You weren't kidding. These are something else."

Maggie looked the tray of waffles over. "I'm not sure I've got a whole waffle's worth of space, but would you split one with me, Sam? As much as these two are raving about them, I want to try them."

"Sure, cherry sound good?" Sam replied.

Maggie grabbed a cherry waffle and cut it in half, passing it from Luke to Sam.

"I'm surprised he let my half get past him." Sam grabbed a fork.

"I gave serious thought to snagging it," Luke said.

"Where did you find this place?" Maggie asked. "They're amazing."

The smile fell from Luke's face, the bite turning to ashes in his mouth. "Pieter's brother told me about it."

Luke couldn't tell if a cloud actually passed in front of the sun or if it was just the mood of his friends clouding over. A soft hand slid into his, Maggie winding her fingers through his and squeezing. He leaned over and kissed her.

Luke sighed and shook his head. "No more dark thoughts for now. There'll be plenty of time for them later. Right now, the sun is shining, and I'm sitting at a table with three of my favorite people in the world. I'm going to have a second waffle because I can, and it'll make me happy."

Around the table, Maggie, Pablo, and Sam nodded and cut into their waffles, letting the tasty confection and the companionship restore their good mood. At first it felt brittle and forced, but as the clouds cleared, their hearts lightened, even if it wasn't as jubilant as it had been a few minutes ago. When they were full, they sipped their coffees and enjoyed idle conversation. Luke, coffee cup empty, made another round for everyone.

Facing away from the door leading into the solarium, Luke didn't see why everyone went silent until Pieter stood in the open space next to Pablo, his hands clasped in front of him, fidgeting. He looked nervous, his eyes still a little unfocused.

"How's your head feeling?" Luke asked, tentatively opening the dialogue.

"It's feels like I got pistol whipped last night," he replied, looking down at the center of the table. "Look, Luke, I'm sorry I hit you. I… I wasn't thinking clearly after everything."

"It's understandable. Last night…wasn't good. I'm sorry I—"

Pieter interrupted, holding up his hand. "It worked. I don't like it, but it got me to snap out of it."

"Why don't you sit down so we don't have to keep craning our necks up at you?" Sam said. "Have some breakfast. Some food will do you good."

"Can I get you a coffee?" Luke asked.

"I wouldn't recommend caffeine after a concussion," Maggie said. "It can have funny effects. Unless you consume a lot of caffeine, then some coffee to ease you down might be in order. Cold turkey can be pretty rough during a concussion."

"A shot of espresso would be nice," Pieter said. "I guess the improvement in Belgium's coffee culture has some negative side effects."

Nodding, Luke went into the kitchen to pull a shot of espresso for Pieter. Since he usually made doubles, he split the other into a cup for himself. When Luke returned to the table, he set Pieter's cup in front of him, then sat quietly as Pieter sipped his espresso, staring into the distance with a troubled brow. Finished, he placed the cup on the saucer and pushed it away, bringing his eyes to Luke's.

"What am I going to do, Luke?" Pieter asked, pleading filling his eyes.

"I don't know, Pieter. What can we do? Jan now has control of the Flanders Pack, having traded Wallonia and your father to secure it. He has at least the approval, if not the backing, of Le Mousquetaire, who has at least three packs of werewolves to call on, plus who knows how many fangers—"

"Luke," Sam interrupted. "Jan was here. Do we need to evacuate?"

"Shit," Luke cursed, dipping into a few languages to add spice to the initial salvo. "Have we heard from the team in Antwerp? They should have been here last night."

"They decided to split up and stay in a couple different cities, then work their way here today," Sam replied.

"We need to tell them to get out of the country. We need to get out of the country." Luke stood up and started pacing.

"Luke, sit down, buddy. You're making everyone anxious," Pablo said, turning to address Luke.

Taking a deep breath and holding it before releasing it, Luke nodded and sat back down. "You're right. Maggie, it's time to move the kids out as soon as we can. Pablo, can you find Delilah and Simone? We'll need them here so we can work through this together. Pieter, when I met with Heidi, she said she was a friend of yours. Is she a friend friend or a political friend?"

"What do you mean?" Pieter asked, confusion spreading across his face.

"Is she a personal acquaintance you'd call a friend? Or is it a friend as in you're both high-ranking officials in your packs and talk about pack issues?" Luke leaned forward, resting his elbows on the table.

"Friends. My father thought we might get engaged at one point. He would have liked to add that connection, but we didn't have those feelings. I trust Heidi, if that's what you're asking."

Nodding, Luke leaned further. "Will she offer our people sanctuary if they can get to Cologne? It's the closest bet to get out of Belgium to a neutral country since France and at least the south of the Netherlands are off the table."

"I think so. After being betrayed by my own brother, I'm not exactly confident of anything anymore. I'll call her."

"Pieter," Maggie said. "Can they make passports for the children? We need to get them to safety. We can find homes for all of them in Portland."

"Oh no...Portland." Pieter's eyes went wide in a mix of horror and abject sadness. "Amiata and Olivia… I'm going to have to call them and break the news."

"Do you think your brother would go after them?" Sam asked.

"I don't know anymore." Pieter leaned forward and rested his elbows on the table, cradling his head in his hands.

"I'll call Holly and have her move them to a safe location." Sam turned to Luke. "If you don't need me for a few minutes, I'm going to make that call, get a hold of our wayward wolves, and get them moving toward Cologne. If nothing else, they can just go to Frankfurt and fly out. It's the kids we'll need protection for. If push comes to shove, we can get pictures back to Portland and have someone courier passports over, although it would be easier if your contact in Cologne can help us there."

"What are you going to do, Luke?" Pablo asked.

"I'm going to go have a talk with the security." Luke stood up and headed toward the door out of the solarium.

"The security?" Pablo asked for clarification.

"Mithras," Luke said over his shoulder as he walked out the door.

THIRTY MINUTES LATER, Luke returned to the Solarium amid a hub of activity as Maggie's people wrangled the kids to get some lunch into them in case they had to bug out in a hurry. Delilah and Simone had joined the table. Once they saw Luke walk in, they went silent as they waited for their stern-faced friend to update them.

"What's the word from your mythological friend?" Pablo asked.

Luke held up his hand and wobbled it side to side. "He can't physically bar anyone if they get through the mental barrier, but he's going to intensify the barrier, including removing Jan's ability to remember exactly where we are, but if they stumble on us, we're in trouble."

"What does 'intensify the mental barrier' mean?" Sam asked.

"I think this property will become extra invisible. They'll drive by the gate and just ignore it. They could float down the river and not pay attention to the house in our little nook in the hillside. It's at least something. Speed and stealth are our best allies right now." Luke pointed to Sam.

She nodded and cleared her throat. "I let Holly know about the situation. She's making plans for Amiata and Olivia as soon as she gets the go ahead they've been informed. I got a hold of everyone who's not here and directed them to Cologne."

"Pieter?" Luke pointed to his friend.

"Heidi has promised sanctuary once we cross the border into Germany, but she can't come in to aid us. Her packleader has forbidden it. They can't make a stand at this point without knowing the true extent of what's going on, but we have their assurances we'll be safe once we get into their territory. They'll make their documents person available to us. She also said she can offer homes for the children if need be."

Luke shook his head. "No. Not after her admission there are too many vampires in town. If the wrong vampire wanders through and picks up the bond with their former food sources, it'll put the kids right back where they started. Portland is the best bet."

"Luke's right," Sam said. "We have a diverse pack and can place them with families they'll be comfortable with." She made eye contact with Simone. "Simone, you're welcome to join our pack with your brother if you're still interested."

She nodded, uncertainty suffusing her face.

"Don't worry about money. I'll take care of getting you to Portland," Luke said.

"And the pack will take care of you once you hit the ground. We take care of our own so no one is wanting. You and your brother will be taken care of while you get established," Sam added.

Simone turned and looked at Delilah. Smiling gently, Delilah nodded. Luke was at the right angle to see under the table and catch Delilah slide her hand over to squeeze Simone's hand. With the reassurances given, relief swept over Simone.

"Portland it is." Simone smiled weakly, accepting the offer to turn her entire life upside down on a new continent.

Sam smiled warmly. "I know it's short notice, but you should probably think of an alias to use for your passports. It's probably best we cover your tracks now, so they can't hunt you down as easily."

Nodding at Simone, Luke turned. "Maggie?"

"The kids don't really need to pack. They don't have much of anything, so we can get them moving as soon as you give the word. We'll start working on names for the kids so we can get their passports ready." She tilted her head to the side and looked toward Pieter. "Pieter, do you know if your friend in Cologne has US passports?"

Pieter shrugged. "I don't know, maybe. They're pretty savvy."

"If not, we'll have them make some passports for a few of us as well, so we can move the kids as their family members. We'll probably have to divvy them up among the few people that can speak French." Maggie, holding Luke's hand, rubbed her thumb idly over the back of it.

"Good thinking, Maggie," Sam said.

"Have you talked to Amiata, yet, Pieter?" Luke asked.

"No. I'll call in a couple hours. She'll still…" Pieter trailed off as his phone started ringing. Furrowing his brow, he answered. "Amiata?"

"Pieter? What's going on? Jan has been calling, telling me to fly home. That Pieter wants us home, but I can't get a hold of him." Amiata spoke in Flemish. Between the volume on Pieter's phone, the urgency in Amiata's voice, and Luke's supernaturally enhanced senses, he could hear her side of the conversation clearly.

"Amiata, do not speak to Jan and do not get on a plane. When we're done with this call, you need to get in touch with Holly," Pieter replied.

"Pieter, where's my husband?" Amiata's voice trembled.

"Father's… Jan killed him, Amiata, shot him in the heart and then in the head."

"What?"

"He's dead. Jan betrayed us and murdered him."

"No… Jan did it?"

"He's been the one secretly purging the pack of our allies. Jan has been manipulating us the whole time. You can't come home." Pieter pleaded with her, filling his voice with urgency.

Luke could hear sobbing coming from the phone.

"Oh, my Pieter..." Amiata sobbed.

Pieter moved the phone from his ear and looked at the screen. "Shit. Jan is trying to call me. Listen Amiata, I have to go. Call Holly as soon as you can. She's got a safety plan for you and Olivia. Don't speak to anyone from the Flanders Pack and definitely not Jan. We have to protect you and little Olivia."

"OK. Holly. Right."

"I love you, Amiata. Take care of little Olivia. Only trust Holly and her people," Pieter said frantically. "We don't know who our friends are anymore. The Portland leadership is it for now. I'll call you as soon as I can."

"I understand. Bye, Pieter."

Pieter switched the call to Jan and set it on speakerphone, laying it on the table.

"Hello, brother," Jan said in English, sounding smug. "I'm assuming Luke and your little friends are listening in."

"Jan... What... Why... You killed papa. Why, Jan?" Pieter asked, raw pain filling his voice.

"Come back to the pack, Pieter," Jan said, ignoring Pieter's question. "I need a lieutenant I can trust. We can return the pack to its glory. With the money from the ports, we can make our pack a force to be reckoned with. I'll forget your past indiscretions. You can marry Heidi from the Rhein Pack. Maybe Belgium can take control of Germany for a change. We have powerful allies now."

"You don't have powerful allies; you have evil masters. You've betrayed our family for the table scraps of vampires. Sold out the people you were supposed to protect. Murdered your packmates."

"They weren't packmates. Our pack will be stronger with only true Belgians. Pieter. I'm going to ask one more time. Come back to Antwerp and swear fealty to me. If you do, I'll let your friends leave unharmed." Jan wrapped his anger with honeyed words, trying to woo his brother back into the fold.

"Just like that? You'll let everyone go?"

"Well, not the Centurion Immortal. My allies want him as a sign of our loyalty. Bring him with you, and all the people from Portland and the children they picked up in Cambrai can go free. If not, we'll destroy them all."

"No," Pieter said. "You murdered our father. You betrayed him. You betrayed me. I won't sell out my friends."

"Luke," Jan said. "I know you're listening. Talk sense to my brother. Turn yourself in to me, and everyone can go free. I'll even let Pieter slink off to Portland. Make the easy choice."

Everyone at the table looked to Luke. Pablo shook his head.

Not letting the silence go longer, Jan upped the ante. "I know where your house is. It's… I'll…" For the first time since he called, his confidence slipped away. "We'll surround Dinant. Every road will be monitored day and night. Wolves are already en route from our pack and our allies. When the night comes, our other allies will hunt you down and feast on you. Take. The. Offer."

"No one here will betray Luke. Nor will we let him sacrifice himself," Sam said. "Certainly not for the promise of a fool and a patricide. I speak for the North Portland Pack, the Coast Pack, as well as the other Portland area packs. Do you wish to declare war on us?"

Jan laughed harshly. "What is a war declaration from packs such as yours? Pieter, Luke. Do the right thing. If you refuse, you'll watch the children die first before your eyes, then you will die with their screams still ringing in your ears."

"Your words are worthless, Jan." Pieter scowled at the phone.

"You can't trust your own brother? You've always been able to trust me before." Jan shifted to smarmy seduction.

"So did Papa until you murdered him. As far as you and I are concerned, I have no brother. I see you, and I'll kill you without hesitation or mercy," Pieter ground out.

"Pieter—"

No one heard what Jan was going to say next. Pieter picked up the phone and hurled it against the wall, the phone exploding into plastic shrapnel. Pieter walked out of the solarium and onto the grounds, stalking into the distance.

L uke, Pieter, Simone, and a boy from the Nord Pas de Calais Pack who'd volunteered to go with them headed toward the parking area and Luke's BMW. It was likely the safest vehicle since the three wolves could sit in the back behind the darkly tinted windows where they'd be less likely to be noticed. It also had the most power of the available vehicles in case they needed to make a speedy getaway, and if things got truly desperate, it's all-wheel drive would allow some limited off-road opportunities to escape.

Luke was just about to get in when Maggie strode purposefully from the front door, wearing a silk scarf over her hair and a pair of sunglasses.

"I thought I'd go with you to further the disguise," Maggie said. "We can be a happy couple out for a drive."

Luke chuckled. "Good thing we won't need to pretend."

Maggie smiled and kissed Luke. "It feels weird to kiss you without your beard." She ran a hand over the left side of his face.

Luke rubbed his other cheek. "Yeah. I feel naked without it. It's been ages since I've been beardless."

Maggie looked closely at his face, checking out both sides of it. "Good thing most of your activity is nocturnal. You don't have much of a tan line where you shaved."

Since Jan had probably nosed around a reasonable approximation of Luke's description, Maggie had helped trim his beard to a length short enough to shave. His skin felt raw.

"You have a nice face, bearded or shaved." Maggie patted his cheek and headed around to the passenger side.

Luke pulled his sunglasses from the breast pocket of the sport coat he wore as part of his disguise. They had weapons stashed everywhere in the SUV, but they needed to look like a couple of wealthy people out and about. Once they buckled in, Luke reversed, then drove up the ramp, stopping in the shadows before pulling onto N989. He wanted to make sure there were absolutely no cars coming before pulling out. Seeing nothing, he hit the gas and sprayed gravel behind him as he lurched onto the road, flying down the curves. Once he felt safely far enough away, he slowed down.

"Can we take some of these little roads through the back country?" Maggie asked.

"Most of them dead end in the hills or at a stream or river or just circle back around to one of the main roads. This isn't a densely populated part of the country," Luke replied.

Luke pulled on to N915 and headed north. He wanted to check the less obvious routes out of the area first. Everyone else had wanted to leave immediately, but Luke didn't trust Jan to not already have his blockade in place before calling. Luke couldn't think of a reason for Jan to wait so late in the day to make the call to Pieter, who remained quiet while Luke and his friends debated their course of action. Once Luke laid out his logic, Pieter had agreed that it was unlikely Jan would have called without having deployed his forces first. If Luke found a hole in Jan's defenses, everyone else was ready to move at a moment's notice.

As they approached a bridge crossing the Meuse, Simone spoke up. "Luke, I see several cars parked on both sides of the bridge and maybe a police car too."

"Are they blocking the road?" Luke asked.

"No, but there are people just sitting inside the cars."

"How can you tell? All I see is the reflection of the windows."

"I can see cigarette smoke puffing out of several of the windows. Also, I can see movement inside," Simone replied.

"Damn. You've got sharp eyes." Luke turned right onto Rue des Gaux and wound through the neighborhood until they pulled back onto N915.

Next, Luke took a left back onto N989 and headed northeast toward Falmignoul where they could get to the N95, which would open up several more escape routes. Like the bridge across the Meuse, it was monitored.

"That's the brewery where my caretaker gets the beer for the bar," Luke said, turning onto Rue Paquette to circle back around.

Luke grew more frustrated with each route blocked. Jan had found every choke point and blocked it. So far, he'd seen dozens of cars with multiple people in each. With binoculars, Pieter, Simone, and Henri even spotted a few people they recognized from their various packs. The numbers arrayed against them were staggering. As they wound through the hills trying to find any exit out, the sun moved ever closer to the western horizon, to darkness and the arrival of Jan's vampires.

Luke's frustration and anger spread through the SUV, seeding silence in its wake. As orange tipped into pinks and purples, they turned around and headed back to his manor to report and reevaluate. When they parked, Luke walked away from the SUV. He grabbed a chair from one of the patios, took it to the edge of the walkway leading to the water, and set it down. Once he sat, he collapsed in on himself, his head dropping into hands as he rubbed his eyes with the heel of his palms. He sighed and sat back.

"It's a lovely sunset," Maggie said. "Do you mind if I join you? I brought beer, if that'll entice you."

Luke turned his head and smiled sadly up at her. "You're the enticement; the beer is just a bonus."

Maggie handed Luke the 750ml bottle of Boon Mariage Parfait Oude Kriek and two glasses, then grabbed a chair. Luke uncorked the bottle and filled a glass, handing it to Maggie after she sat down. Filling his own glass, he set the bottle between them, then leaned back in the chair. Maggie reached out and took his hand.

"Too bad we only caught the tail end of the sunset," Luke said. He sighed. "I wish we could share more sunsets together."

"Working the night shift kind of interferes with normal evening activities," Maggie said.

"Working the night shift. That's a good euphemism." He took a drink of the sour cherry beer, sighing happily as he let the flavor wash down the bitter taste of their situation. "Why'd you pick this beer?"

"I like cherries, and it looked neat." She took a tentative sip. "Mmm, this is nice."

They sat watching the sunset fade to nothing. The feel of Maggie's hand warmed the growing cold at Luke's core. He wasn't ready to go into the house and face all the people relying on him to escape this trap. If it was just his well-trained team, they could take more aggressive risks and fight their way through, but they had nearly a dozen children and several non-combatants from the Portland pack. As a newer member of the pack's council, he was responsible for their safety, a responsibility he took seriously. His sense of concern was compounded by the lack of news from the people heading toward Cologne.

The crickets had turned out in force, filling the silence with their enthusiastic chirping. As the day's heat dissipated into night, Luke let the sound of the river and Maggie's proximity soothe him while he drank his beer. At some point, Maggie topped off their glasses with the remaining beer in the bottle. When he reached the end of his glass, he squeezed Maggie's hand and stood, pulling her into his arms for a tight hug.

"Thank you, Maggie." Luke kissed the top of her head.

"What for?" She rubbed her hand soothingly over his back.

"For being you. For being with me."

"That's sweet of you."

Luke sighed. "I suppose we should go inside and figure out what's next."

"Probably, but give me a kiss first." Maggie tipped her head up, puckering her lips.

Smiling down at Maggie, Luke lowered his face, sinking into her soft, warm lips. When he pulled back, he felt ready to face everyone. Maggie picked up the bottle, Luke the glasses, and together they walked back to the cottage to find the team. When they got closer, they saw people moving about in the solarium, so they dropped off the glasses and bottle in the kitchen and joined their friends.

"There they are," Pablo said. "There's food! Grab a plate and sit down."

"Your caretaker makes excellent stoofvlees," Pieter said around a mouthful of potatoes. "The mashed potatoes are good too, although I prefer fritje with my stoofvlees, but unless you can eat them fresh… Mashed potatoes are more practical."

Maggie and Luke changed directions toward the chaffing dishes set along the wall and loaded up their plates. They took the two seats people vacated so they could sit next to each other. The stew was tasty and filling and much needed after a disappointing afternoon. Comfort food probably translated in any language.

"Where are the kids?" Luke asked between mouthfuls of stew.

Sam took a drink to wash down her mouthful of food. "Fatima sent them to their rooms for the evening to watch TV so they'd be out of the way. Plus, they need to be rested in case we need to move fast."

When silverware scraped against ceramic, Luke pushed his plate aside. "Let's head to the sitting room so we can talk and plan what's next. Who needs some talking beers?"

When everyone nodded, Luke stood and led the way into the bar. Inside, they found Fatima and the other two Portlanders relaxing after getting the children situated. Since they'd be involved heavily with the evacuation, Luke decided to shut and lock the doors to the bar and hold the meeting there. Luke, standing behind the bar, poured beers for everyone as they relayed their drink orders.

Sam raised her hand to get Luke's attention. "Luke, I've got some good news for you. Looks like everyone is accounted for in Cologne. Jamaal said he thought they'd been followed but thinks they lost them on one of the train transfers."

Luke exhaled heavily, a bit of the tension draining from his shoulders with the breath. "That's good. Are they moving on or staying in Cologne for the night?"

"They've split up into a couple different hotels. He wants to know what they should do next." Sam took her beer and found a seat.

"Pieter, do they need to be officially welcomed by Heidi to be under her protection?" Luke asked.

"They should be good. I don't think Jan is dumb enough to violate the Rhein Pack's boundaries yet, and vampires leave all wolves alone in the city, even tourists, so they don't cross the Pack. It would be good to let her know, though, since the circumstances are what they are. I'll reach out to her," Pieter said as he waited for his beer.

"Give her Jamaal's number," Sam said. "He's in charge of that group and is a council member. That should keep things official. There, just sent you his number."

Pieter pulled the phone Luke had given him from his pocket and texted Heidi. Instead of dropping his sim card in the new phone, they decided a new number would be useful in case Jan had a way to track Pieter's old number.

"How are we going to get out of here?" Delilah asked once everyone sat down.

"I'm not sure. Their blockade is surprisingly well executed," Luke said. "We spotted mixed groups of werewolves from different packs so they could identify us in multiple ways. I imagine the same will be said of the vampires tonight. They've hijacked some police cars or maybe even police, so they can pretend they have legal authority to pull people over."

"Can we break up the group and sneak out in multiple different directions?" Fatima asked.

Luke shook his head. "It might work, but if one of us gets captured, we'll have to reverse and rescue them. It's too risky. We just don't have enough power to split it up; we need to stick together."

Simone, who rarely spoke up in planning meetings as the youngest and newest member of the group, sat up straighter and raised her hand diffidently. "Well, if we can't sneak out, how about we punch our way through? We pick a single spot and hit it hard and fast then make like bats out of hell for the border with Germany."

Delilah, a smile on her face, made eye contact with Simone. "Fury Road?"

Simone's answering smile lit up the room as heat sizzled between the women when their eyes met.

"What are they talking about?" Pieter asked.

"The latest Mad Max movie," Sam answered.

"Right," Delilah said, nodding at Sam. "It was one of the movies we watched while I was training Simone before we met up with you in Cambrai."

"Unfortunately we don't have a proper war rig." Pablo took a drink of his beer.

Simone looked around the room gauging the crowd. "Please don't take offense, but none of you seem to be very law-abiding citizens. So, take a truck. We didn't see anything besides cars or the occasional SUV. We find a truck, slam through their blockade, then make a run for it."

Pieter looked excited. "It's not the worst plan. If we stick to the smaller roads, a semi-truck would be able to command the road. If we hit them hard and fast and keep going, it'll take them time to organize their response. We can get a lead on them, and the truck can bring up the rear and keep them from overtaking us."

Luke, taking a sip of his beer, mulled over the idea. "The two rental vans have good engines in them. The BMW can move. Like Pieter said, this is not the worst plan."

"The only thing we need—well two," Simone said, "is a truck and someone to drive it. Can anyone here drive a semi-truck?"

Pieter, Sam, Delilah, and Pablo all looked at Luke.

"I can," Luke said.

Maggie raised an eyebrow at yet another new revelation about

Luke. They rarely talked about Luke's various operations around Portland, both wanting a clear delineation between the dark work Luke and the pack were involved in and their private lives together. That piece of Luke's past had never come up during their conversations. With nearly two-thousand years of history to pick from, a few years from the 1970s hadn't made it to the top of their list of conversation topics.

"So we just need a truck," Pablo said.

"And our point of attack and the route," Sam added.

Delilah looked around the room at her friends. "When do we want to go?"

Luke sat back and narrowed his eyes, thinking over the options. "If we're going to be committing wanton acts of vehicular violence, we should probably go in the middle of the night when there are fewer drivers on the roads. And frankly speaking, I'd rather deal with vampires than werewolves."

"So now that we have the outline of a plan, when do we go?" Pablo asked. "Do we go see if we can rustle up a truck tonight and make a run for it?"

"No, I want to scout out the vampire positions tonight and map out the blockades. We also need to see where we can snag a truck. I hope everyone is up for some running through the woods with their fur suits on. This seems like the perfect task for your four-legged forms. Delilah and I will drive you to a spot near our targets, then we'll pick you up later. I'd prefer to have you work in pairs. We've got some time, so no sense risking your safety by going alone. At this point, I'm taking volunteers."

Everyone raised their hands, including Maggie.

Maggie looked over at the other people who'd come to help her with the children. "Carlos, Brielle, I'd like you to remain here with the kids. Be sure you have Luke's and Delilah's contact information so you can get a hold of them if needed. That should still give you three pairs."

Maggie surprised Luke by not being one of the people staying with the kids. She'd always eschewed front-line action, preferring to come in after the operation was done to help with the medical needs.

This was a newer side to her, but he hadn't known her that long in the scheme of things.

"OK, Maggie, you'll pair with Sam. Pablo, you and Simone. Fatima, you can go with Pieter. Carlos and Brielle will stay here with the children. If no one has any more questions, thoughts, or ideas, I'm going to go work on the map for tonight."

CHAPTER
TWENTY-FIVE

Delilah drove one of the rental vans, taking Simon, Pablo, Fatima, and Pieter and dropped them off at their designated spots. She parked along one of the intersections where the wider roads met through the little area Jan had effectively blockaded to watch to the frequency of semi-trucks moving through the area. Luke, with Maggie and Sam, drove to their drop point so he could fall back to his designated intersection. As soon as he pulled over, Maggie and Sam stripped and shifted to their full wolf forms.

Luke had never seen any of Maggie's wolf forms. He wasn't even sure if she had a bipedal wolf form. He opened the back door of the BMW and let them out. Maggie's wolf—she was a few inches taller than Sam in human form—was a little bigger and bulkier than Sam's wolf. While Sam's wolf was tan and tawny, Maggie's fur was mostly blond with some tawny patches. Maggie surprised Luke by standing on her hind paws and placing her front paws on his chest, giving his cheek a wet lick of her tongue before disappearing into the woods, her fluffy pale yellow tail wagging as she disappeared into the darkness.

Chuckling, he wiped his cheek off with his sleeve and climbed into the SUV to go post up at his intersection. Maggie had always been a serious person since he'd met her, but the more he got to know her, and the more intimate their relationship became, the more her playful side emerged. It was a side of her he was coming to appreciate more and more the stronger their bond grew.

Pulling a U-turn, Luke drove back the way he'd come until he arrived at the intersection on his map. He found an out-of-the-way spot and pulled off the road. He had a couple hours before it was time to pick up Sam and Maggie. Since their location had two roads out, they were going to check one, then move onto the second before meeting him at their pickup spot.

While he waited, he put on one of his playlists to keep his mind awake and alert, turning the volume up for "Don't Wanna Fight" by the Alabama Shakes. He sighed. Stakeouts were a lot more fun when he had friends to goof around with while waiting. They were probably due for another round of *Luke versus*, although he couldn't quite remember if they'd finished the recent Luke versus Dean and Sam Winchester debate.

His boredom changed to excitement every time large, bright headlights blinded him—each passing truck, he tallied with direction and type. By the time his two hours ended, he'd tallied twelve potentially useful trucks. He'd have to compare with Delilah to see which road would be the best to set their trap.

After he parked at the pickup point, he only had to wait for a minute before they popped out of the brush. Luke stepped out and opened the back door for them so they could transform and dress. Once they were securely buckled, he returned them to the cottage.

"ARE you sure you're up for this?" Luke asked Maggie.

They sat at the bottom of the ramp out of Luke's property in Luke's VW bus, the engine idling. Maggie, looking straight ahead, nodded. At first, she was hesitant but grew more confident after a couple more nods.

Maggie turned to Luke, giving him a wan smile. "Between us, we speak more European languages than all the rest combined, and I speak several Slavic languages you don't. I'll be fine. I'm just nervous about everything, and we all need to pitch in however we can to make sure we make it out of here safely."

Reaching across the space between the two seats, Luke grabbed her hand and squeezed it. "Alright, let's go."

Luke put the manual transmission into gear and started up the ramp, then pulled out onto the road. When they got to the spot they'd investigated during the light of the day, they pulled over, leaving the bus on the edge of the road. He turned on the emergency blinkers, then turned the bus off. They slid out onto the dark road, taking their shotguns with them.

Luke pushed the talk button of the radio clipped to his belt. "This is Spartacus. We're in place."

"Roger. Out," Pablo replied.

Luke handed his shotgun to Maggie then opened the back hatch on the bus followed by the bonnet covering the engine compartment. "Let's prop these guns back here so no one can see them."

Maggie nodded and set them down on their butts. "So now we just wait?"

"Yup. This section had the best traffic, and it's harvest season, so there's a lot of heavy freight moving around the countryside." Luke pulled Maggie in for a hug. "That's the nature of operations—you spend a lot time hurrying up to wait."

Enjoying the pleasant late summer night, they chatted while they waited, periodically turning their heads if they heard distant sounds. They had people out spotting so they'd have an early warning when a truck was coming, but they still kept a tight watch to be on the safe side. Twenty minutes after they parked, a car passed by, stopped, then reversed, the driver rolling down their window.

"Hello. Do you need some help?" the driver called in French.

Luke gave them a friendly wave. "No, but thank you. We already called a tow truck. It should be here soon."

"Alright, good luck," the driver said.

"Thanks, drive safely," Luke replied.

The driver rolled their window up and continued on their way. Luke turned back and rejoined Maggie behind the bus along the shoulder of the road. She wore one of Luke's hoodies. He had plenty of spares since he consistently ruined them while fighting. She looked adorable in the extremely baggy hoodie.

Delilah's voice broke in over the radio. "Car incoming."

A minute later, a car flew by, not even slowing as it passed. Luke was starting to worry that the previous night's truck traffic might have been a fluke. He needed to get everyone out of Belgium before Jan and Le Mousquetaire tightened the noose further.

Pablo's voice sounded in Luke's earpiece. "This might be it, buddy. Truck coming your way."

Luke pushed the radio's button. "Understood."

He squeezed Maggie then stepped away from her, grabbing two flashlights sitting on the seat of the bus. He handed one to her. They had a good straightaway between the curve where Pablo was situated and where they were parked. They stepped out into the road and started waving the flashlights as soon as they saw the bright headlights of the truck. The driver gave them a toot on his truck's horn, then the brake lights flashed on. The unmistakable sound of the truck engine dumping speed drifted down the road as the driver moved onto the narrow shoulder.

They grabbed the shotguns and set them in the back of the bus, the angle of the bonnet effectively blocking them from view, and pulled up their hoodies and the head scarfs Maggie had provided for face masks. When the mask was over his face, he inhaled, taking in Maggie's scent from the scarf. He smiled underneath his mask.

As soon as the truck stopped, the driver opened the door, climbed down, rocking the cab of the truck, and stepped in front of the headlight of the still running truck. It was hard to see much in the way of details beyond a man of medium height and a stocky build.

"Hello, having some trouble?" the driver called in Polish.

"Yeah," Maggie replied in her native tongue. "It just stopped. We can't figure out what's going on, and our mobile phone is dead."

The man walked forward. Maggie turned around and grabbed her shotgun, then spun toward him, pumping a shell into the chamber. Luke grabbed the other one and followed suit.

"What the…" the man said.

"Hands up." Maggie gestured with her gun.

The man shoved his hands into the air.

"Sorry about this, but we're going to need to borrow your truck," Maggie continued.

"What?"

"We promise we won't hurt you unless you try to stop us, but we're taking your truck," she said.

Luke reached into his pocket and pulled out an envelope with a thousand euros in it and stuck it out.

Maggie kept the shotgun pointed toward the man. "There's a thousand euros in that envelope for your trouble. Just wait an hour to call the authorities. And when you do, tell them a couple of drunk English lager louts stopped you and took the truck. Do you understand?"

"A thousand euros?" His voice seemed more calm after hearing about the deal.

Maggie nodded. "Yes. One thousand euros. I'm going to need your mobile, but I'll leave it here for you."

Luke pulled out a plastic sandwich storage box and set it on the ground near the man.

"Put your phone in the box. My friend will set it nearby." She gestured with the shotgun toward the box.

The driver looked warily at the box and the shotgun, but nodded. Luke kicked the box toward the man who squatted over it and set his phone inside, snapping the lid down tightly. He kicked the box back toward Luke. After it skittered to a halt, Luke picked it up, walked off the road, and set the box down behind a tree. Luke squatted down and opened the box. Reaching into his pocket, he pulled out a paper clip and popped it into the hole to release the sim card tray. Once it slid out, Luke pulled the sim card and dropped it into the box, closing the tray so it locked. That should buy them some extra time before he could call in. Luke snapped the lid shut then headed back toward Maggie and the driver. When he got back to the road, he took a stick and drew an arrow in the dirt pointing toward the tree.

"Now you see where your mobile is hidden and there's an arrow to guide you to it," Maggie said. "I'm going to need you to walk that way and keep going until you count one thousand, one for each euro we're giving you."

Luke was impressed with the calm force in Maggie's voice. It was almost like she'd been hijacking trucks all her life. He pushed the talk button on his radio and gave the code, signaling they had the truck. Now Pablo and Delilah could return to the manor, pick up the rest of their passengers, and form their caravan.

"Can…can I grab my bag please? It has my personal affects," the man asked.

Maggie looked to Luke. He nodded.

"Tell him to go to the passenger side to get in. I'll be in the driver's seat with my shotgun, so tell him to be calm and easy," Luke said. "Tell him I don't understand Polish very well, so no talking."

Maggie relayed the instructions. Luke quickly shut the engine bonnet and the rear hatch of the bus, then climbed into the driver's seat of the Volvo FH cab over truck. When Luke was in place, the man opened the passenger seat and climbed in. He reached into the back and grabbed his bag and threw in a couple items laying about the sleeper then zipped it, climbing back out.

Maggie met him at the side of the truck, her barrel still pointed at the man. "Now walk. Keep going. One thousand steps, then you can come back and get your mobile. Understand?"

"Yes. One thousand steps. Um…the euros?"

Luke chuckled. He was a bold man. Luke reached into his pocket and pulled out the envelope, tossing it out the open door. The man bent over slowly and picked it up, opening it. He seemed satisfied as he walked toward the back of the truck.

Maggie poked her head into the passenger side of the truck, her gun still pointing in the direction the man was walking. "We good?" she asked in French.

"Yes. Get in the bus and park it. Émile will put it away, so don't worry about where. Maggie, you did great," Luke replied in French.

She nodded.

"I'll be waiting at the meetup spot," he added.

Maggie nodded and shut the truck's door. Luke waited until she was in the VW and moving before he put the truck into gear and pulled back fully onto N989, heading west. When he got to the intersection with N915, he took a right while Maggie went straight. After he arrived at the narrow dirt and gravel farm road he'd driven down earlier, he pulled off and worked his way down. If it had been rainy, there'd been no way the truck would have made it. He took a right when he reached the end then another right a few moments later to pull back onto N915 heading the other way. He figured the detour would give the team time to get on the road while also hopefully throwing off the truck driver. He probably could see the truck turning down at the end of the road, but he wouldn't be able to tell what truck was coming the opposite way his had disappeared.

After he crossed the intersection with the N989, he kept his eye on the odometer until he reached a kilometer past the intersection. He slowed and stopped, throwing on the hazard lights. He checked his phone. Seeing the text from Maggie, he opened it. They were moving and should be along any minute now. Sure enough, a couple minutes later, he could see lights in his side mirrors, but instead of stopping behind him, one vehicle pulled into the other lane and passed him, stopping when they were level.

Maggie hopped out of the back of his BMW with her shotgun and walked in front of the truck. She knocked on the door when it didn't open. Luke pushed the unlock button. After the locks clicked, Maggie climbed in, propping the shotgun against the dash with the butt on the ground between her knees.

"What are you doing?" Luke asked.

"I'm riding with you. In case you need backup." She shut the door, then leaned across and kissed Luke briefly. "Now drive. No time to argue."

Luke opened his mouth to say something but decided against it, snapping his jaw shut again. Pablo pulled in front of Luke, moving slowly until the rest of the caravan was in place. Once they got to Mesnil-Saint-Blaise, they stopped to pick up Pieter who'd been observing the disposition of the cars blockading the way onto N95.

The ear piece in Luke's ear crackled to life. "Plan two. Road open."

"Understood. Give me the go ahead. I'll be rolling and ready," Luke replied.

"Moving out," Pieter replied.

The caravan started moving again; the cars going faster than Luke, opening a sizable gap between them. Turning the lights off, Luke rolled forward in first gear, then shifted up to second, waiting until the engine was in the high RPM range. In front of him, their two minivans and the BMW bringing up the rear flew through the intersection, running the stop sign the vamps were using to aid their blockade. That alone flipped on the hunter/chase brain of the vampires waiting to go into action. Lights flared to life as cars turned on and started moving.

Luke shifted into the next gear, coaxing as much speed from the truck as he could. Flipping the lights on, he grabbed another gear and pushed the accelerator down hard.

"Hold on, Maggie!" Luke yelled.

Maggie grabbed the shotgun with one hand and the door handle with the other as they plowed into the front of the first vamp car, sending it spinning into a second car. The truck slammed into the front of it, ripping the car's bumper off and sending up the sound of crunching plastic. Luke yanked the wheel to the left and sideswiped another car, sending it careening into the side of an SUV. His trailer followed behind him, whipping into another car and pulling it under the rear tires. As the trailer crunched over the car, it shook the truck, jolting the cab when the trailer's tires flopped back onto the road.

Luke steadied the truck, then yanked the wheel to the right, bringing the trailer swinging back to the other side of the road. He felt the impact through the steering wheel as it slammed into more cars. Once the truck cruised through the intersection, he pulled into the middle of N910, taking up as much space he could.

Since they had a moment of quiet, Luke pulled the ear piece from his ear and handed the radio to Maggie. "Would you mind handling communications?"

"Not at all." Her voice trembled as she took the radio, her hands shaking. "Can I take out the ear plug?"

"Sure. Ask them how they're doing and if any cars got through ahead of us." Luke took a couple calming breaths as he drove around gentle curves, heading northeast.

"Pablo says they've got one right on their tail," Maggie said.

"Have him slow them down and bring them back to us." Luke pushed the pedal down a little, picking up a bit more speed. The road curved ahead, but he had more road available to make up some distance. They needed to make sure there were no chasers between the semi-truck and the caravan.

"Luke." Maggie pointed ahead. "Do you see taillights?"

"Yeah. Tell them we're almost on them. Have the minivans speed up and open some space, but don't get too far ahead." Luke pressed the pedal a bit more.

"Pablo says he's going to slow down and bring them back to you," Maggie said.

Luke nodded. "Can you check the side mirrors and see if anyone's behind us?"

Maggie looked at the mirrors, moving around to get a better angle. "I don't know, it's hard to see since they're set for the driver. Wait… Maybe there's someone there. I think I saw lights, but I'm not sure."

"I can't spare a hand to adjust one for you." Luke focused on squeezing more speed from the truck while hogging as much road as he could.

"Brake lights!" Maggie pointed ahead.

They were closing quickly. Ahead, the car Luke chased swerved back and forth over the road, while Pablo, in the BMW, swerved to block the car. They'd worry about the car behind them after they dealt with the one in the middle of the caravan.

"Get ready," Luke warned.

He took aim and mashed the pedal down as Pablo hit the brakes. The vamp's car jammed their brakes, wobbling over the road as they struggled to keep control. Pablo, using the BMW's superior motor, flew forward to clear room for Luke as he slammed into the trunk of the car at an angle. The car went sideways, Luke t-boning it. He hit the brakes as the truck crunched into the side of the car. With the momentum of the truck, the wheels of the car gripped the road.

When Luke finally got the truck to slow, the car's tires bit into the road and flipped the car onto its side, sending it tumbling in a barrel roll of destruction, parts flying from the car as the road ripped it apart. Luke swerved to the left and caught the car along its front axle, sending it spinning off the road and into the trunk of a tree with a cataclysmic crash.

Breathing heavily, Luke decelerated while trying to drop his heart rate to a more reasonable speed. He had a bit of a straightaway before the upcoming series of curves, so he risked a look over at Maggie. Her knuckles were white on the plastic handle of the door and on the heat guard of the Winchester M12, and her eyes were wide. Her breathing sounded shaky and erratic. He felt for her. He was having trouble getting his breathing and heart back down to normal levels, and this wasn't the first violent car chase he'd been in.

He breathed a sigh of relief when he saw the nasty hairpin curves coming up, slowing the truck down to a near crawl. "We got rid of that car just in time."

"How can you be so calm? I'm about to have a heart attack or a brain aneurysm," Maggie said, her voice trembling.

"I'm not calm. I'm just better at keeping a façade. I'm just another duck on the pond. This has been pretty intense even by my standards."

Luke took the hairpins as best as he could. As soon as he was through them, he picked up speed as he crossed a bridge over the Lesse River. According to the map, they had a relatively gentle road ahead of them, at least as far as the highway conditions were concerned.

CHAPTER
TWENTY-SIX

Luke couldn't tell if they were being pursued anymore. Initially, he'd thought one of the vampires had escaped their destructive blockade run and fallen in behind them. Occasionally, he or Maggie would see the twinkle in the side mirrors, but the lights never grew closer. He didn't know if it was regular traffic or the vampires keeping their distance. Either way, the lack of close pursuit made him both cautiously optimistic and worried about other vampire devilry. When they passed through a tiny nameless village, more a cluster of buildings than a place worthy of name, Luke prepared for the next part of the plan.

"Maggie, we're about to make the next stop. I'll need you to cover me in case we get company," Luke said.

"OK. I can do that." She sounded unsure, but still managed to infuse a little confidence into her reply.

A couple minutes later, Luke found a likely candidate for his next bit of trickery, slowing the truck to a stop in the middle of the road. Putting the truck into reverse, he backed the trailer, turning the wheel to put the rear tires off the road as he turned the wheel sharply, practically jackknifing the truck and trailer so the nose of the trailer was off the other side of the road along with the rear axle of the truck, blocking both lanes.

Luke put the truck in park, grabbed the Steyr SSG 69, and jumped out, running to the middle of the truck and gently setting the sniper rifle down. He darted over to the landing gear of the trailer. Maggie lay down on the ground next to him, her shotgun pointed under the trailer back the way they'd just come. Luke unhooked the landing gear handle and cranked it for all his worth, using every bit of speed and strength. Soon, the gear made contact with the edge of the road. Luke kept cranking until he heard the truck's rear suspension groan as the weight transferred off the truck and onto the landing gear. Next, he jumped up between the back of the truck's cabin and the front of the trailer and unhooked the airlines, disconnecting the trailer from the truck's power. Hopping down, he pulled the pin locking the fifth wheel, releasing the truck from the trailer.

"Luke, they're coming!" Maggie whispered harshly.

Luke jumped over her and practically flopped to the ground behind the Steyr, folding out the gun's bipod and extending the lens hood on the scope. He pulled the bolt back and loaded a round. He peeked at Maggie as she lay with the shotgun not quite nestled into her shoulder. "Safety off, Maggie. And pull the butt into your shoulder, or it'll hurt on the recoil."

She flipped the safety off and pulled the butt of the shotgun tightly into her shoulder.

As the car slowed, rolling forward to see what was going on with the jackknifed tractor trailer, Luke squinted and turned his head to keep the lights from totally killing his night vision, closing his right eye to protect it. With the headlights blaring and the truck looming over them, whoever was in the car wouldn't see them as they lay in the shadow of the trailer. But he could sense the vampires now that they were only a few dozen feet away.

Taking aim at the driver's seat, Luke squeezed the trigger. The windshield spider webbed around the hole the .308 caliber bullet made. The horn blared to life as something thudded into it, holding it depressed. Luke adjusted to the left, anticipating the opening of the door. Sure enough, someone scrambled out. The moment they popped their head out, Luke fired, shooting them through the head. Luke pulled the bolt, reloaded, then waited. If there was anyone else in the car, they were holding still while deciding what to do. He'd taken out the driver and the passenger with two shots.

The car started wiggling as at least one passenger moved. Luke adjusted his aim for the driver's side rear passenger side. Luke picked correctly—or there were two passengers. The door he shot open, and someone dove out. Luke squeezed the trigger, missing any vitals but shooting them in the ass. He gave a juvenile chuckle.

"Luke, one got out the other side," Maggie said.

"Did they run away?" Luke asked. Sweeping the scope and barrel of his gun down the road.

"I don't think so."

Luke scrambled up. "Keep the gun pointed to the left. I'm going around our right."

Maggie nodded nervously.

Luke left the sniper rifle and pulled the gladius out. He snuck around the end of the trailer. Peeking around the corner, he didn't see any movement, so he crept out while he kept his eyes on the car, looking for any movement around the back where someone would likely be hiding. When his foot crunched on the gravel, he looked down for a split second, then up in time to see someone dart away from the car.

Maggie fired off a round, muzzle flash blasting from under the trailer. Along with the sound of a shot hitting the car, whoever had just tried to flee screeched as silver penetrated its skin. His stealth blown, he ran toward the screaming. The silver-loaded shotgun shell had clipped the vampire in the back of the calf. It tried to drag himself away or get up, but the hissing and smoking silver in its flesh was keeping it down. Luke stabbed down, ending the vampire's screaming and sending it puffing into dust.

"Luke!"

He whipped his head down the road. Headlights flared on as a car screeched to life, speeding toward Luke. With the vampire screaming, Luke hadn't noticed them rolling up. Seeing nowhere to go, he jumped up onto the trunk of the car just in time. The car trying to hit him slammed into the rear of the first car. Luke lost his footing and tumbled along the hood of the car, slamming into the windshield with his back. When he landed, he tried to tuck his head, but it still hit the windshield hard, stars flaring across his vision.

"Luke!"

The car under him shook as someone tried to get out. He attempted to move but couldn't quite get his mind going. A blond streak flew by, then a shotgun blasted near his head, sending his ears into a tinnitus-induced shrieking whine. The blond streak had to be Maggie. He forced his body into action and rolled off the hood, landing unsteadily on his feet. As the driver's door opened, Luke slammed it shut, rolling along the door until he was near the opening. He yanked the door open and stabbed into the cabin without looking. The gladius met the resistance of vampire flesh, a feeling he knew too well after over nineteen-hundred-years of it. He fell into the inside of the door, letting it prop his weight up.

He peered into the car. The fanger he'd just stabbed twitched and moved feebly. Luke wasn't sure where he'd stabbed, but at least it looked like he'd incapacitated it. Maggie stood behind the open door of the passenger side and pointed her gun inside, firing off a round into the backseat. The shot took the vampire on the passenger side in the face, caving its face in at that range. The vamp in the seat behind the driver shoved the door open. Maggie adjusted her aim.

Seeing the barrel sweep his way, Luke dove to the ground, grunting as he scraped his elbow. Maggie fired again. Glass shattered. The vampire screamed.

"Maggie, hold fire!" Luke yelled.

"Ok!" She sounded panicky, her voice rising a register.

He rolled onto his hands and knees and scrambled up, using the car door to pull himself up. The vampire Maggie had just shot writhed on the ground, trying to crawl away on one arm. Luke stabbed the fanger through the heart and pulled the gladius out with a grunt. The vampire dissolved into goo.

"Luke, this one back here's trying to get out," Maggie called.

Luke jogged around the back of the car, hobbling a bit as he went. When he cleared the trunk, he kicked out and caught the vampire in the teeth. He reached back and pulled the rudis from the scabbard on his back.

"Luke, someone's coming," Maggie said, stepping between him and whatever had drawn her attention.

Luke perked his ear up. Around the corner, headlights illuminated the road as a car crept forward. Luke's shoulders fell as he shook his head. The sound of motorcycle engines joined the sound of the car's engine.

"Back into the truck!" he called.

He took one last look at the vampire he'd not have time to drain, stabbed it so at least it wouldn't rise to chase them, then took off, running as fast as his banged-up body allowed. He managed to put his gladius back in his hip scabbard as he darted around the end of the trailer. While running by, he bent down and snagged the rifle off the ground. Tossing the rudis onto the driver's seat, he climbed into the cab, carefully handing Maggie the rifle. With his hands free, he moved his rudis onto the sleeper bed and pulled the door closed.

Putting the truck into gear, Luke pulled forward, the trailer grinding over the fifth wheel as he drove out from under it. When he was free from the trailer blocking the road and narrow shoulders, a hill on one side and a drop off on the other, he coaxed the truck faster. Without the weight of the trailer, the truck accelerated more quickly, though the added bulk of the trailer had been an effective weapon when bashing their way through the blockade earlier.

"That'll at least block the cars. There's not a road that'll get them around for a while. They'll have to backtrack quite a ways. Hopefully we can get some distance from them and lose ourselves," Luke said. Maggie nodded shakily. He laid his right hand on her thigh and gave it a gentle squeeze. "You're doing great."

He looked into the mirrors. A single headlight worked around the end of the trailer, and another one was trying to get around the nose of the trailer.

"Maggie, can you reload that shotgun, please? Those motorcycles are working around the trailer. I want to make sure we have options."

She nodded again, grabbing the shells from her ammo belt and feeding them into the bottom of the shotgun. Despite her trembling hands, she reloaded the shotgun quickly. After she set the weapon down, she grabbed the radio from the cubby. "I should check in with Pablo."

"Good to hear from you, buddy," Pablo said from the radio Maggie held toward Luke. "You get rid of that pesky wagon you were draggin'?"

Luke chuckled. "Yeah. We're bobtailin' our way to you as we speak, although we're about to have more company—motorcycles."

"Do you need us to come back and help?" Concern tinged Pablo's voice.

"Not for now. We'll let you know. Your main task is still to get those kids across the border."

Even though the truck was lighter without the trailer, the sport bikes were still faster and more maneuverable. Soon, the first two bikes were speeding after them. Luke swerved back and forth across the road as he tried to pick up more speed. The lazy side-to-side kept the motorbikes occupied on the narrow road. When Luke checked the mirrors, he saw a few more motorcycles. The trailer would block cars, but it would only slow down motorcycles briefly.

"Maggie, can you roll that window down?" Luke reached over and found the button to roll his window down. "Have your shotgun ready."

"Shoot out of the truck?" Maggie sounded uncertain.

"If we need to." Luke yanked the wheel hard, sending a bike swerving off the road. He chuckled as the bike disappeared into the darkness.

Maggie adjusted the shotgun, holding it in her left hand with her right hand on the pump so she could aim out the window. Luke swerved to the right. The biker, concentrating on getting around Luke, nearly ran into the truck but hit the brakes and skidded behind the truck. Settling in the middle of the narrow two-lane road, Luke looked back to see a cluster of single headlights moving about like a school of fish as they darted in and out and side to side.

"Maggie, they seem to be holding back for a second. I've got a bandolier of ammo under my hoodie. Can you unzip me and then unhook me? It won't do us much good hidden away and my hands are busy driving."

Maggie unbuckled her seatbelt and crawled onto her seat, then the center console. Reaching around Luke's arms, she unzipped his hoodie, then pulled it off his arms so he could continue swerving. She pulled back the shoulder of the hoodie, slipped her finger under the leather ammo bandolier, and worked it around until the buckle was within reach. Once she unbuckled it, she warned Luke she was about to pull it around. While she removed it, he kept the wheel still, but as soon as she was back in her seat, he returned to the back and forth.

"They doing anything?" Maggie asked.

Luke took quick peeks into his door mirrors. "I can't tell. I think they're just tailing us for now. Nope. A pair are moving up, one on each side."

"O-o-o-OK." Maggie took several steadying breaths.

"Maggie. You can do this. Keep the gun low, point it out and down, then pull the trigger. If they don't go down, fire again. Be sure to brace yourself, it's going to kick." Luke reached back and pulled his shotgun up, setting it on the dash in front of him where he could grab it easily.

Sweeping his eyes from the left mirror to the road in front of them then to the right mirror, Luke tried to keep everything in play. The two bikers were making their break toward the outsides of the road and as soon as they were lined up, they gunned the gas and shot forward.

"Luke, he's pulling out a gun!" Maggie said, bracing herself and standing as best as she could in the limited space. She took quick aim and fired.

Luke took a moment to enjoy the bike flipping and tumbling onto the side of the hill. Reaching onto the dash, he grabbed the shotgun and slipped the safety off. With his leg propped up against the bottom of the wheel to hold it steady, he took his other hand off the wheel and pumped a round into the chamber, putting the hand back onto the wheel. He nestled the heat shield covered barrel in the crook of his left elbow, peeping out of his peripherals to track the upcoming vampire. Judging the road straight enough for the next bit, he took aim and fired off a round. The motorcycle flopped over as the shot tore into the rider, pushing him away. The bike skidded along the pavement, sending up sparks as it bounced over the asphalt, dragging its rider along with it. He pumped another round into the firing chamber and returned the gun to the dash, the smell of gunpowder smoke wafting through the cab.

"There's a car blocking the road ahead," Maggie called, pointing forward.

He had no idea how the car had made it between them and their other vehicles, but better this than blocking the whole caravan. They must have guessed the route and zipped around to find a cross road. However they'd managed it, the feel of vampire grew steadily as they closed the distance between them and the car blocking the intersection.

Luke checked the mirrors—the motorcycles were pulling back but not stopping. "Gun down, safety on, and buckle up!"

Luke grabbed the Winchester on the dash and flicked the safety on, handing the gun to Maggie to secure. Everything in place, he pushed the pedal down, picking up speed. He didn't even bother reaching up to blow the air horn. He stared straight ahead, adjusting the aim of the truck slightly to the right.

They smashed into the front quarter panel, pushing the car forward as it spun, the rear slamming into the side of the truck. Every jolt shook them, bouncing them in the cab and drawing gasps and squeaks from Maggie. Once they blasted through the intersection, Luke focused on calming his breathing. He reached across the center console and squeezed Maggie's forearm.

"Luke, I'm scared," Maggie said, her voice small.

"Me too."

She turned her head and grabbed his hand in hers. "Are we going to make it?"

"I'm going to do everything I can to make sure we do," he replied.

When he checked the mirrors again, his tails were still there. After he dealt with the first few who'd tried making runs on them, they seemed content to merely follow and relay their position to their fanged comrades.

"Maggie?"

"Yes, Luke?

"Do you trust me?" Luke asked, squeezing her hand.

"Yes. Explicitly." She picked up his hand and kissed the back of it.

Luke drew in a breath and held it, releasing it slowly. "We're never going to outrun them in this beast. We need to draw them away from our people. If they think we're bringing up the rear, they'll keep following us. We're probably out of range of Pablo on the radio. Turn it off. Send them a message that they're on their own and should make for the border as fast as they can." He pulled his phone out of his pocket. "Can you turn my phone off? Let's save the battery on it."

"What's your plan?" Maggie asked.

"How would you like to visit Luxembourg?"

"If I'd known, I'd have packed fancier clothes. I hear it's pretty swanky," Maggie replied.

Luke chuckled, glad Maggie could make a joke under the circumstances. "I love you, Maggie."

"I love you, too."

"I'm hoping they won't mess with Luxembourg. The pack there is pretty wealthy. Pieter told me they're involved in a lot of high-end banking and loans for the various European packs. I'm guessing the local packs won't want to mess with their financiers and persuade their masters to not rock the boat." Luke checked the mirrors again. "Although, it won't do us any good unless we can shake these assholes."

With Maggie's help, he found a patch of road along their northeasterly trajectory that would work well for Luke's purposes. He went over his simple plan with Maggie, ensuring she knew her part and how to best help him. Maggie took the opportunity to reload the shotguns and slide a new magazine into the Steyr, though he doubted they'd need it.

Since they had a good straightaway, Luke depressed the pedal to get some distance on the bikers, but with their speed, he knew he wouldn't keep it long. But he didn't need to keep it long, just long enough.

"Ready?" Luke asked

"Yup." Maggie braced herself.

Luke locked up the brakes. The truck screeched to a slow halt, shuddering and shaking, on a stretch of dark road lined with trees. As soon as they stopped, Luke put the truck in park. They scrambled out of the cab and around to the front. Maggie looked at Luke, making eye contact.

"Go," Luke mouthed to Maggie. In French, he yelled, "Go, runaway, go wolf and run as fast as you can."

Maggie broke cover and ran off the road and into the trees. The high whine of a motorcycle engine revving to life contrasted with the low rumble of the semi's engine accompanied by the scream of a tire gripping. Luke pumped a shell into the firing chamber and brought the shotgun to his shoulder, raising the barrel. A moment later, a motorcycle ripped past the truck on Luke's left side.

Luke tracked the biker. As soon as the bike slid to a halt, its rear swerving wide, he fired, taking the biker in the chest and knocking biker and bike over. A second biker, using the first as a distraction, peeled by from the right side of the truck. Grunting, Luke staggered forward, the crack of a gun washing over him. Luke spun around and fired, most of the round sending up the din of metal on the plastic and metal of the motorcycle.

Something must have hit the biker; he staggered, dumping his bike. Luke chambered another round and took aim, firing. The vampire dusted, leaving empty bike gear. Through short gasps, he worked his way to the first biker, his head on a swivel, checking to ensure the vampire was still down and no new bikers were coming around.

The bike must have broken the vampire's leg when it fell on him. He tried to crawl away, but the motorcycle pinned him down. Luke ended him and spun around as another bike screamed to life. Yanking the bike up, Luke jumped over it, using it as a shield as he crouched behind it. When the fourth motorcycle emerged from behind the truck, it had a second rider on the back, holding an automatic weapon. The biker unleashed fire at Luke as the motorcycle looped around the truck.

A round or two penetrated the bike and slammed into Luke's armored chest. He fell backward, the bike flopping onto him. He groaned, trying to catch his breath. The smell of gasoline leaking onto the road inspired him to shove the bike off as he pulled himself up, his ribs throbbing under his armor. He ran back toward the front of the truck, ineffectually holding his ribs. With his back to the front of the truck, he grabbed some shells from his pocket and fed them into the magazine of his shotgun.

Creeping around the front, he leapt around the corner, leading with his gun. Instinctively, he ducked when he heard the loud blast of a shotgun. Looking behind the truck, a group of vampires on at least four motorcycles scrambled as another shot rang out. Luke smiled to himself and broke into a run. He started firing toward the cluster. More shots rang out from the trees lining the road. Two vampires went down, dissolving into goo. Luke wasn't sure if they were his shots of Maggie's. He only had a few more. When he'd emptied them, he dropped the shotgun and pulled his gladius, charging forward.

Maggie continued firing, only stopping to reload. One of the vampires realized Luke was running at them and turned, pulling a gun. Before it could fire, a shot hit it, blasting it into dust. Luke was on the group before anyone else could react.

He took the first vampire in the chest with this gladius, yanking it out then spinning to deliver a backhanded slash that separated a head from the next vampire. Maggie fired off another round. As several vampires ducked, one at the opposite end of the group fell backwards, writhing.

Luke kicked out, catching one of the ducking vampires in the face and sending it tumbling. Luke swung up with his sword, cutting into the vampire's side. His gladius caught a rib, so he yanked back and kicked out at the same time. His gladius dislodging, he ducked when Maggie fired another shot. Using his involuntary response, a vampire tackled him, pinning his hand with the gladius to the ground.

Luke tried to scramble back from the gnashing teeth of the vampire fighting to reach his neck. He attempted to punch the vampire in the side using his left hand but couldn't get any power into it. When he felt the weight shift off his right leg, he brought his knee up between the vampire's legs. The fanger recoiled, pulling back from Luke a short distance. Using the space, Luke bashed his forehead into the vampire's face. The impact sent sparks through his vision. The vampire fell back; Luke punched it in the face. The final hit dislodged the vampire's vise-like grip from Luke's sword hand.

He plunged the sword into the vampire's chest.

The weight on Luke disappeared as the vampire dusted. Clamping his mouth shut against inhaling the remains of the vampire, Luke scrambled away until his back bumped into one of the fallen motorcycles. Looking around for the last few vampires, he saw them working their way toward the line of trees where Maggie hid. The pair had left their friend to finish Luke, turning their backs on the dangerous predator in their midst.

Luke picked his way through the debris until he cleared the mess of tumbled bikes then sprinted at the vampires, a loud growl emerging from his throat. The sound halted the fangers' progress as they turned to see what was behind them, their eyes going wide once they realized it was him. A shotgun fired, and one vampire exploded into goo, spraying Luke. The last vampire tried to run away, but Luke tripped it. When the vampire went down, Luke finished it. He looked around, making sure it was indeed the last of the fangers.

"Luke? Did we get them all?" Maggie asked, still hidden in the line of trees.

"I think so." Luke reached inside the hoodie to investigate a burning sensation on his arm. He felt a thick slickness. When he pulled his fingers free, they had blood on them. He wished he could drain a vamp, but they'd been too thorough.

"Are you OK?" Maggie asked, drawing close.

"I think so. It's nothing serious. We can investigate it later. Are you OK?"

Maggie nodded. "I got some scratches, but that's it."

"Let's go." Luke turned and jogged toward the truck, stopping to pick up the shotgun.

Once they were buckled back in, a wicked grin spread across his face.

"What's that grin for?" Maggie asked.

He put the truck in reverse and hit the accelerator. As the truck's dual set of rear wheels crunched over the motorcycles, Luke's grin grew bigger. When he thought he'd hit them all, he put the truck into gear and aimed for the couple of bikes downed in front of the truck.

Maggie shook her head but had a grin on her face.

"What? You've got to take pleasure in the little things or this all gets very tedious," Luke said.

"Like taking a big thing and crunching little things?" Maggie replied.

Luke loved the twinkle in her eyes. "Exactly." He sighed, returning to his serious face. "We still have a ways to go though. I think we can change our course now that we shook our tails. By logic and evidence, we should be taking the fastest route out of Belgium into Germany, not winding through country roads toward Luxembourg."

"Do you think they'll fall for it?" Maggie asked.

"I hope so. Right now, our job is to buy more time to ensure the team gets the kids to safety. It's not a big country, so they should be close at this point. What time is it, anyway?"

Maggie pulled out her phone. "About three thirty."

"They've got to be close. Would you mind checking in with them?" Luke asked. "And when you're done with that, I could use some music to help me calm down, please."

Maggie sent a few texts, then hit play on her music app, playing Madeleine Peyroux's cover of "Between The Bars." A few minutes later when her phone buzzed, she checked it. "Sam says they just crossed the border. All three cars are safe."

Luke heaved a sigh of relief. "If you'd gone with them, you'd be safe now, too."

"Yeah, but you couldn't do this by yourself. You needed my help. And…I couldn't leave you to do this by yourself."

Luke reached over and squeezed her hand. "Thank you, Maggie."

They sat quietly while Luke navigated their way southeast, deeper into the Ardennes. Needing some music for the background, Luke started his playlist again, Kurt Cobain's raw voice setting the mood with Nirvana's cover of "Where Did You Sleep Last Night Last Night." When Luke checked his gauges out of nervous habit, he did a double take when he saw the fuel tank. They'd only driven about forty-five minutes since they'd had their fight with the motor- cycles following them, but the gauge was dangerously deep into the red. Five minutes later, the engine started sputtering.

"Shit, we're out of diesel," Luke said.

"What happened? Didn't we have enough?" Maggie asked.

"We did." Luke aimed the truck toward a shoulder, trying to find a place he could get the dying truck as far off the road as possible. When he found a likely place, he slowed and pulled off the road, until only the edge of the truck remained on the paved surface.

Luke unbuckled and climbed out of the truck. Pulling a flashlight out of his pocket, he flashed the beam over the panel covering the fuel tanks. Bullet holes riddled the panel. He walked to the other side of the truck and found the same. The second biker used the distraction of the first biker who'd attacked Luke to put bullets into the tanks on their way by.

He climbed back into the cab. "We're on foot now. They shot holes in the tanks. Let's put some distance between this truck and us before they find it. We've got a couple more hours before the vampires have to run and hide from the sun, but their pet werewolves will be out in force to sniff us out."

"Should we call Pablo and Sam?" Maggie asked.

"If we can, but I doubt we'll even have much reception out here. It's terrible through the hills. Let's get moving, and if we get some reception, we'll decide then." Luke grabbed the second ammo belt and strapped it around his armor, pulling the hoodie back in place over it.

Maggie looked around, her eyes landing on the radio stuck in the cubby in the console. She grabbed it and clipped it to her belt. Grabbing the Steyr, Luke took one last look around the cabin to make sure they had everything. They didn't need to wipe down prints since they'd been wearing gloves, but he pulled out the flashlight to make sure there wasn't anything else. Seeing some spent shotgun shells, he gathered them up. Maggie picked up all the ones she could see on her side. Satisfied, he climbed down, gave the floor a once over, and shut the door. He slung the Steyr over his shoulder so it hung across his back. He got the strap as tight as possible so it wouldn't bounce as much. His shotgun, he'd carry.

"Ready to go, Maggie?" Luke asked.

"One more thing." Maggie walked over to him and pulled him into a hug. "This feels weird to hug you in your armor when we're both carrying guns. It's very action movie."

Luke chuckled. "I'd prefer a rom-com right now. A nice sedate movie with no vampires or guns. Just kissing interrupted by hijinks."

Maggie sighed, gave him a last hard squeeze, and kissed him on the cheek. "Yeah. That would be pleasant. I think I'm ready now."

Luke groaned as he moved, his ribs aching.

"What's wrong?" Maggie ask, concern tinging her voice.

"Oh, I forgot about it in the heat of the moment, but now that the adrenaline has worn off… I took some shots on my armor. I think I might have some bruised ribs."

"Why didn't you tell me?" She looked slightly annoyed.

"You just reminded me with that squeeze. It doesn't feel as bad as that time I cracked those ribs. I'll be fine. Not like there's much we can do here, anyway."

Maggie pursed her lips, shaking her head. "Let me know if things get worse. No being Mr. Tough Guy."

"I promise." Luke turned and walked off the road and into the trees; Maggie followed him.

LUKE SAT BY A STREAM, dangling his feet in the cool water as it trickled by, the occasional sound of civilization drifting around from the other side of the hill. For the hundredth time, he nervously checked to see if Maggie was approaching before returning to his enjoyment of the stream. She should be back soon from the village that lay on the other side of the hill with some much needed sustenance.

They still had at least six or seven hours of hard hiking through hills and forests before they crossed into Luxembourg. The fact that they were heavily armed necessitated the cross-country, off-the-beaten-path hike. So far, they'd avoided any pursuit. Who knew if the vampires—or werewolves working with them—had even found their truck, yet.

Luke had tried to take them through streams, walking upstream or down to confuse any trails. Although he'd spent most of the twentieth century in cities, he hadn't forgotten two thousand years' worth of woodcraft, particularly in these hills. He'd spent a good deal of his time during the second World War moving through the forests of western Europe attacking Nazi targets then melting back into the countryside. He knew how to avoid being tailed, but rarely was he being tracked by supernaturals.

Fortunately, Luke and Maggie were supernaturals, using every bit of their strength and stamina to eat up as many kilometers as possible until they needed to make a stop. Maggie left her weapons and headed into the nearby village to pick up some food. While they could keep running on empty, they agreed it would be best to get some food, so they'd have the energy when they needed it.

When a twig snapped, Luke whipped his head around, the muscles in his torso seizing up. He groaned but didn't get up when he saw it was Maggie. He unclenched and tried to release his muscles, grunting as he gently twisted his torso. Pulling his feet out of the stream, he set them on a rock so they'd have a chance to dry out while he ate.

"Ribs tightening up?" Maggie asked.

"Yeah."

"I picked up some ibuprofen." She pulled a bottle from a bag and handed Luke four tablets, then a bottle of water to take them with.

Luke popped them into his mouth and took a deep swallow of water. "You're the best." He chugged the rest of the bottle.

"I brought us a couple sandwiches and some fries. I hope they're still warm enough. The friterie smelled so good when I walked by I couldn't resist." She handed Luke a cardboard box of fries.

The bottom of the box was still warm. He opened it and grabbed a fry, dragging it through some mayo before popping it into his mouth. He groaned happily, grabbing more fries. Soon, his box was empty. Smiling, Maggie handed him a sandwich. When he finished that, he drained another bottle of water and gathered up their debris, shoving it back into the bag Maggie'd carried everything in.

"I wish they'd had a store where I could pick up a backpack," Maggie said, looking at the bag of refuse. "I can go back through town and meet you on the other side. I hate to litter."

"That'll work." He squeezed her hand. "See you in a bit."

Maggie took the bag from Luke and headed back into town. Luke pulled his socks and boots on, sighing unhappily about having to put on damp socks and boots. While crossing streams might be a good way to throw off their trail, it decidedly had its disadvantages.

When he stood, his ribs felt better, though still noticeably sore. It would take more than a few ibuprofen to fix his ribcage. He'd need a vampire or two for that. Unfortunately, the sunny day rendered them hard to find. He slung on the sniper rifle and Maggie's shotgun, picked up his own, then made for the southerly route around town. An hour later, he met up with Maggie and together, they continued their trek through the Ardennes to Luxembourg.

Maggie halted. "Luke…"

"Yeah, I hear it too. They're not being very careful," Luke whispered.

They still had a couple hours until sunset, then maybe another hour until they crossed into Luxembourg.

"Do we run?" Maggie asked.

"Not yet, but it wouldn't hurt to pick up our jog a bit. Were you able to get a message to Sam when we passed near that town?" Luke asked.

"I sent it, but I lost reception before I saw if Sam replied," Maggie said, her voice worried.

Luke nodded tightly, reaching out to give her arm a reassuring squeeze. "Let's get going."

Maggie nodded and picked up her pace. Luke followed, grunting at the dull pain in his ribcage. Another round of ibuprofen had taken the edge off, but less so than before. Sighing, he caught up with Maggie. There was nothing he could do about it now except soldier on, something he'd been doing forever.

Maggie's footfalls were nearly silent as they picked her way through the forest. Luke wished he could move as silently, but he did the best he could with a tight and sore body. At this point, he chose the fastest path they could. It was too late to shake their tail. Now it would come down to speed and probably a fight.

Once they made it up the shallow hill, Luke picked up their pace. Off to his right, he heard new sounds.

"Luke, to the right," Maggie whispered between gasps of air.

"Yeah, I hear. Let's stop for one second." Luke took in their surroundings. "There, that'll have to do."

He changed their path and ran up a wash. Once he got far enough, he called a halt, then checked out where he wanted to set up. The wash opened up into a wider, shallower section. On one side, a large boulder jutted out of the earth, tall trees surrounding it. On the other side, several trees clustered together at the top, further back than the boulder on the other side. He waved for Maggie to follow as he ran down the wash until he felt they'd gone far enough.

"Maggie, up to the ridge, then work back behind that boulder. I'm going up behind those trees. I'll see if I can take out a few with the rifle. If they draw within range, open fire." He looked back down at where they'd just come from. "See that sapling in the middle of the gully? Once they pass that sapling, that should be about the max effective range. Go easy on the ammo; we're a bit thin. We've never really had a real chance to test its efficacy against werewolves, so it might just piss them off."

Maggie nodded once, leaned in and kissed him quickly, then ran up the hill to get situated. Once she was behind her boulder, he worked his way up the edge of the wash until he was concealed in the small grove. He set his shotgun nearby where he could easily reach it and then pulled the sniper rifle off his back. With the bipod extended, he laid down and took aim down the narrow wash.

He wished he had more time to lay a better trap, but this would have to do. If they could survive and take out a few werewolves, it would hopefully slow them down and make them more cautious. They didn't need all the time in the world, just enough to get to the border.

He took a moment to look over at Maggie. He smiled tightly. He had not wanted to expose her to this level of violence and the world he lived in, but she'd been a real trooper. Pulling his eyes away from the pretty woman who'd captivated him since she'd placed herself firmly in his path, he pulled the sniper rifle into his shoulder and looked down the scope and prepared.

The wolves trailing them had slowed down, cautious after their quarry made a course change. Luke knew the wash looked like a good place to lay an ambush, but he was hoping their overconfidence and superior numbers would force them down the gully and through the narrow gap. Squinting, Luke thought he saw movement just at the edge of the rise into the wash. He was thankful the vampires hadn't scrimped on the scope. It was a fine piece of precision optics that allowed Luke to shoot above his weight class. When they returned home, he'd have to book some time with Jung-sook so she could help him up his shooting skills. It had certainly come in handy, but it would be a lot more useful if he didn't miss so frequently.

A figure in full wolf form popped their head up, surveying the wash. Keeping low, they returned their nose to the ground and crawled forward. He didn't know if Maggie could sense the wolf through any of magic werewolf senses, but he was pretty sure she could hear it making its way down the gully. He peeked up from his scope. Maggie looked toward him. He signaled for her to wait, pointing at himself. When she nodded, he hoped she understood. So far, they'd only sent one wolf down the wash. He wanted a few more, so he and Maggie would have a better chance of taking out several of them. If the werewolves stayed too cautious, they'd be able to keep up their harassment. Luke needed them to commit.

The rustle of leaves above Luke sent a spike of anxiety through his veins, and he feared the breeze would carry their scent back toward their enemies. He didn't want fresh scents making it down the wash and alerting the wolves to their position. He wanted them to follow the trail on the ground until it was too late for them to break out of the trap.

Luke followed the first wolf with his scope for a few seconds, then set his aim back to the entrance of his trap. A second and third head popped up and committed to the advance. He didn't know how many were following them, but three was a good start. He took aim at the second wolf, waiting until they'd both fully entered their trap. Luke peeked to the side of the scope, seeing the lead wolf still inching along, its nose snuffling the ground. When he put eye back to scope, he smiled. The two wolves had drawn close to each other.

He took a calming breath and adjusted his aim, finally squeezing the trigger. The first wolf went down and the second yelped, falling over. The first one wasn't moving. He swung the rifle to the first one. It'd froze, flattening itself against the ground. He took aim at the immobile target and put one in its head. Luke didn't know if a were-wolf could heal from a direct shot to the head or not, but it would sure take them out of this fight for the duration.

Luke returned to the pair he'd shot first. The one was still down, but the other one was trying to awkwardly crawl out of the trap. Every once in a while, it would let out a yip, as if it was asking for help or support. Normally, Luke would never shoot a wolf. He considered them beautiful animals much maligned throughout history—especially in gun-happy, cattle-mad America. He had to remind himself they were people who'd sold their souls to serve the vilest of creatures—the vampire. It was kill or be killed, and he couldn't hesitate because he liked wolves or his best friends and his girlfriend could also turn into wolves.

He pulled his sights off the wounded wolf and returned to the entrance of the wash. He saw several heads poke up, then duck back down. While the wolves were indecisive, he checked on Maggie. She was still hunkered down, well hidden, checking back and forth on Luke and the progress of their enemies. He nodded, then returned his attention to his scope.

The wolves must have finally decided; they rose as one and sprinted into the wash as fast as they could. Luke took aim in the center of their mass and fired, cataloging the yelp in the back of his mind. He pulled the bolt and fired again, hitting another. The last shot in the magazine chambered. He missed. He yanked out the empty magazine and shoved in the next one he'd set beside the gun.

The first wolf had passed the sapling. A few moments later, the sound of an M12 shotgun barked out. The first wolf tumbled to the ground, yelping and screaming in an eerily human fashion. It was still moving, but the silver Maggie had peppered it with must be burning hot and nasty under its skin. The noisy and violent cries of their packmate caused them to halt their progress, unsure of what was happening except knowing their friend was in excruciating pain.

Luke aimed and fired, aimed and fired, aimed and fired, and struck three werewolves in the tight cluster. The last one, seeing its packmates felled, turned and sprinted out of there as fast as possible, its tail tucked between its legs.

Luke kept his eye to his scope, trying to close his ears to the sound of wounded wolves. After a couple minutes, no more wolves popped up their heads. Standing, Luke worked his way back down to the floor of the wash, still keeping the Steyr aimed down the gully. Still no hint of wolves.

Luke made a wide berth around the silver shot werewolf. It convulsed on the forest floor. The piteous noises it made filled his stomach with stabbing agony and nausea. He felt no shame for killing a vampire. A vampire was a creature devoid of a soul, the spark that made it human—its soul stolen when it was turned undead. A werewolf was still a human, capable of good or evil or turning away from an evil path. Wolves were his friends. This could be one of the Flanders Pack he'd broken bread with. When he passed the first wolf, he stood still.

"Stop your movement, all of you. Do not try to escape," he called in French, then repeated it in Flemish Dutch.

The few trying to crawl away stopped moving. Keeping the rifle tucked to his shoulder, he let go with his left hand and awkwardly pulled the gladius from the scabbard on his left hip. He rarely pulled the sword from that location with his left hand.

"Change back to your human form if you can," he ordered, again in both languages. When no one did, he walked up to the nearest, pointing the gladius at it. The wolf growled. Luke, still holding the gladius, put his hand back on the rifle and aimed at the wolf. "Change."

One by the one, the wolves changed, save for a few who hadn't moved since Luke shot them. When the last had changed, Luke lowered the gun slightly.

"What language do you prefer?" Luke asked, keeping his voice hard and full of steel.

"Vlaams," replied the one nearest him.

"Can you speak for everyone here?" Luke asked in Flemish.

The man nodded, peering toward the wolf convulsing on the ground. "Since he can't, I will."

"I'm granting you mercy. I'm sparing all your lives, if you stop following me." Luke cast his voice so all could hear, though he doubted that would be a problem with their wolfish abilities.

"Why?"

"Werewolves aren't my enemies unless they choose to make themselves my enemies. If you choose that path, I will show you no mercy. And to show you I have the tools to do it…" Luke aimed the gun at the man he was speaking to and moved the gladius toward his leg. "Don't move."

Laying the gladius on the skin of the wolf he'd been talking to, he held it there for a second. The man shrieked but couldn't pull his leg away. After a couple seconds, Luke removed the sword from his skin.

"I have the knowledge and the tools to kill more than just vampires. I will grant one final mercy." Luke backed away from the man until he drew near the weakly convulsing wolf. He sighed, then plunged the gladius down into its chest and through its heart.

The wolf gave a final yelp and twitch when the blade entered, but then went still, a thin stream of smoke wafting up from where the blade met flesh. When Luke pulled the gladius free, the creature made its final transformation back into a human. The man's body was riddled with ghastly wounds and burns around where the silver shot had entered its body.

"He's now free from his agony. Take your wounded and get out of here and don't come back. Tell your pack what will happen if they follow me. After this, there will be no mercy. Tell it to the Nord pas de Calais and Bordeaux Packs. Make me an enemy at your own peril. Come against me and die. Stay away and live and let live." He looked up at Maggie and gestured with his head for her to get moving away from the carnage and further up the wash.

He wanted to get her away from the scene of violence. They could figure out a new course when they cleared the gully. This little diversion had burned more of their daylight. If they didn't hurry, they might have too many kilometers and too many vampires in their way. Luke kept moving backward, carefully feeling his way with his feet so he didn't trip.

Those werewolves who could rose and helped their packmates back the way they'd come. Luke didn't know how far out they needed to move, but dealing with their wounded would keep them busy for a while, and hopefully, his threats would keep them off their back. Once the gully took a turn, Luke darted in the new direction until he could no longer see or be seen.

Maggie was waiting for him, sitting on a downed tree, her head in her hands. He stowed his gladius and squatted down in front of her.

"Maggie?" he said softly. "Maggie?"

"I did that to that man..." she said between her hands. "I shot him and...and the sounds he made..."

"I know, Maggie. They didn't give us a choice. If we didn't defend ourselves, they'd have killed us or dragged us back to their masters for worse. But we need to keep moving, or this is all for naught. When we get to safety, we can talk about it." Luke tried to be as gentle as he could. He would have given everything in his world for her not to have to feel these feelings, but that ship had sailed. Why hadn't she just stayed with everyone else? She'd be safe now if she had.

Maggie nodded weakly. "I know." She took a deep breath and stood up, tears streaking down her face.

Luke, setting down the rifle, pulled her in for a hug, stroking her hair. She clung to him tightly, resting her head against his chest. When she pulled back, Luke kissed her forehead.

"Are you ready to move, Maggie?" Luke asked.

"Let's go so we can get away from here," Maggie replied.

Luke picked up the rifle and took her hand. Picking up her shotgun, Maggie squeezed Luke's hand. They walked in silence for a few minutes before breaking into a jog, dropping each other's hands. Maggie seemed more determined than ever, picking up her pace until they were moving through the woods and hills, once more running towards Luxembourg.

CHAPTER
TWENTY-NINE

The sun dipped into the west, the last rays fading into deep blues and purples. Sweat streamed down Luke's face and back, soaking his shirt. Maggie had remained silent since leaving behind the valley and the fight. They knew, with the sun's protection gone, vampires would soon be a factor again. They may have bought some time from the werewolves with their mercy, but Luke had few delusions he'd bought their silence.

They'd drifted even further from any signs of civilization in trying to avoid any place that would provide access to their pursuers, although that wasn't easy even in the lesser populated southern forests of Belgium. They were forced to cross roads of various sizes, having to wait until there was no traffic. Two people with multiple guns was not a sight many in Belgium were used to, even in the country. They didn't need the police becoming involved, especially if they'd been infiltrated by the vampires like Portland's police.

At least with the dark, they could avoid people by avoiding the light. Maggie's superior wolf eyesight guided them through the landscape, although Luke guessed his was probably almost as good. Under the dimming light of twilight, they'd crossed a large highway with two lanes going north and south. Luke assumed it was the E25.

Since then, they'd cut across a couple smaller roads, cutting paths between clusters of lights in the distance that might be villages.

When they approached a road splitting the fields they'd been working through, they ducked and waited for a car to pass before crossing it, then climbed over a fence into a field. If Luke was correct, they'd just run over the N838, leaving maybe a couple miles until the border.

"It's not long now," Luke said. "We should arrive at the border soon."

"Good," Maggie said, finally breaking her silence.

Behind them, a car screeched to a halt, doors opening and slamming. He didn't have to turn and look; he knew what was behind them.

"Maggie, we've got to run. Vampires." He pumped a shell into the shotgun's firing chamber.

Maggie followed suit, picking up her pace and readying her gun. In the distance, Luke saw lumps moving about. They were in a cow pasture.

"Go," Luke hissed.

They took off running. Luke let Maggie open a lead on him.

"Fence," Maggie called behind her, leaping over it.

When Luke reached it, he vaulted over it. He risked a quick look. A half dozen vampires sprinted across the field. He chuckled when one of them slipped and fell.

"Cow pattie," he mumbled to himself, taking off in a run.

Ahead of him, Maggie leapt over another fence. As she neared a small grove of trees, a new set of shadows burst out of them, making for Maggie. Luke was about to yell to let her know, but she spotted them and changed directions, angling away from the grove. The flair of a muzzle flash shattered the darkness, its bark following almost instantly. It looked like one of the shadows disappeared, either dead or knocked down.

Jumping over the fence, he made for Maggie. Another blast rent the night. Behind him, Luke heard at least one vampire clear the fence, grunting as it landed. Luke spun around and took aim, firing. The vampire exploded into dust. Luke chambered another round and fired again. His next target didn't disappear but was knocked to the ground, tripping up one of his companions. The rest dove to the ground.

He was about to finish them when he heard Maggie fire another round. Turning, he sprinted toward the muzzle flash. He heard Maggie scream as she went down. His heart, beating like a drum, leapt into his throat. Throwing caution to the wind, he sprinted as fast he could. When he found them, Maggie and a vampire wrestled on the ground.

Growling, Maggie tossed the vampire aside, rolling away. Luke took the opportunity and shot the vampire as Maggie scrambled up, reaching for her shotgun. She scooped it up and continued running. Luke ran after her.

"Maggie, keep right," Luke called.

Maggie adjusted her course, getting back on an easterly course. Slowing, Luke tried to see if any new clusters of vampires might be trying to join them. The vampires who'd fallen to the ground were back on their feet, chasing after them. Luke and Maggie splashed through a stream. A handful of seconds later, the vampires waded through the same stream.

Luke spun, fired three shots, then turned and ran after Maggie. He wasn't sure if he'd hit anything, but it bought them a few more seconds. He fumbled desperately, groping for a shell to shove in the shotgun's magazine, but he only felt empty leather loops. When he found one, he managed to reload without dropping it. He tried to locate another one but couldn't. After another minute of running, they trudged through another stream.

Luke's lungs and legs burned as he struggled to keep moving and pull in air. He knew Maggie must be laboring as well, but she kept going, determinedly putting one foot in front of the other. Any time now, they'd be crossing the border. Although, he wasn't sure the vampires hurtling through the night after them would respect the border without someone to enforce it. And they weren't close enough to the nearest road even if the Luxembourg pack kept watches on the crossings in and out of their small country.

"Maggie," Luke huffed out between gasps of breath, "we're going to need to find a place to fight. We can't keep up at this pace, and they're fresher."

"I know…" she gasped out.

Squinting into the darkness, Luke spied the dark shaggy outlines of trees but in too orderly of a fashion to be a natural grove. "Let's head toward that tree farm."

By way of answering, Maggie changed course toward the farm with its neat rows of pines. Hearing footsteps too close, Luke skidded to a halt and turned, taking what aim he could, and fired several rounds. He thought he caught one vampire but wasn't sure if he'd hit anything else. The rest of the fangers dove to the ground. Taking advantage of the dive, he turned and ran after Maggie, his legs feeling like lead. The stop, while sending the vampires to the ground, hadn't helped his legs by taking them out of motion; he was having trouble getting them going again.

Growling at himself, he forced them to move, but he knew he only had so much left in him. Every part of his body ached, and he could no longer ignore the throbbing around his ribcage. He worried he was worsening the damage caused by the earlier gunshots, but he'd keep going until his heart exploded and his limbs refused to respond if it meant getting Maggie to safety.

Ahead, she disappeared down a row of trees. He aimed for that row. The vampires he'd sent tumbling were nearly on him again; it was a race to the trees, and Luke looked in danger of losing it. When he saw the trees rustling ahead of him in too many places for it to be Maggie, his heart dropped into his stomach. They'd gotten around him. He only had maybe two shells left in his shotgun. The fight would come down to his swords, and he didn't know for how long he could keep his arms going. *"Once more unto the breach…"* he thought, steeling himself for what looked to be his last fight. *"Although, a bevy of English longbow would be nice about now…"*

A series of deep, low growls washed over him from the depths of the tree farm. The werewolves belonging to the vamps had flanked them and had them surrounded. His anger grew, speeding his legs through their deadness. He would take the fight to them, hoping to surprise them with the ferocity of his assault.

"Luke! Hit the deck!" a male voice yelled.

It took him a few seconds to process Pablo's voice. Once it clicked, he slid to the ground feet first, grunting at the impact on his abused body. The growling grew closer as several wolves jumped over him and sprinted toward the pursuing vampires. Struggling to get up, he saw several wolves transform from their four-legged form to their bipedal form to really take it to the vampires.

He wanted to turn toward the fighting, but Maggie, emerging from the trees, grabbed his arm and tugged him toward the neat rows of pines.

"No, our fight is done for now. Let your friends handle it." She pulled him around so she could make eye contact with him. "Luke, please."

Seeing the pleading and weariness in her eyes and after all she'd done over the last day, he couldn't deny her. He nodded and let her guide him into the trees. She let go of his sleeve and took his hand. Her hand trembled. She hadn't reached her breaking point, but she probably didn't have much left to give. He barely had anything left himself.

Once they cleared the trees, Maggie led him to a tall elm, then collapsed onto the ground, leaning weakly with her back against its trunk. Luke sank down next her. She let her head fall on his shoulder. Luke could feel her body heaving. Soon, it was joined by tears and her soft sobs. He wrapped an arm around her as best as he could at the angle. Wanting more, Maggie crawled between his legs so she sat between them, her legs over the top of his right leg. He pulled her in tightly, hiding a wince of pain, as she buried her face in his shoulder, crying. Luke blinked, his tired eyes burning as his own tears fell onto his cheeks. He tried to block out the sounds of growling and screaming coming from the fight.

"I'm so sorry, Maggie." He felt terrible for subjecting her to everything. He knew how much she must be hurting after being forced to shoot a werewolf. If he could, he'd do anything to make it all go away, but since that was impossible, he held her and resolved to treat her with extra tenderness.

She didn't reply, just gripping him tighter as she sobbed. He stroked her hair gently, the motion as soothing for him as he intended it to be for her. He wasn't sure how long they sat there. He'd lost all ability to tell the passage of time in his bone deep weariness and sadness. For all the world, he wished she hadn't gone through everything she had that day, but he couldn't unwish time. He'd do whatever was in his power to make it up to her—to help her through it.

After a while, Maggie's tears dried up though her body still shook in his arms. She nuzzled her face into his ruined hoodie over steel armor. It wasn't the softest shoulder in the world, but she needed it right now. He needed her too. Off in the distance, they could still hear growls and howls of wolves punctuated by the occasional scream of a vampire.

In their place of relative silence, the sweet sound of Maggie's voice rose to his ear, singing a sad melody. As her quiet voice soared to hit the notes, he thought his heart might break at the poignant heartache saturating her voice. He recognized a few of the Yiddish words, but he couldn't put meaning to the song.

Kissing the top of her head, he stroked her hair. "That was beautiful."

"It was a lullaby my mother sang to me as a child," she replied.

"What's it about?" he asked.

"It's a very sad song." Maggie paused for a while. "It's about death and tragedy. I'll translate it for you sometime when I'm not feeling so down."

"Of course. What inspired you to sing it, Maggie?" Luke asked.

"I'm exhausted and my heart aches, Luke. I...I killed a man. I can still hear his screams."

"I know. I can still hear them too." Luke sighed.

"Luke? Maggie?" a voice called from the trees. "Where are you?"

"I think Sam is looking for us," Luke said.

Maggie nodded and moved her legs so she could get up. Luke hoisted himself up. Still needing contact, Maggie grabbed his hand, holding it tightly.

"Sam, we're over here," Luke called.

A few moments later, Sam walked out of the trees, still naked after the fight. "Looks like the last few are on the run. We've called in everyone so we can go as soon as they're back."

"Will they respect the border?" Luke asked.

Sam folded her arms across her chest, shivering in the cool night air without her fur on. "There's not enough to do anything about it, but we'll be going to Luxembourg, the city, since we're already in the country."

"I'd offer you my hoodie, but there's not much of it left." Luke lifted the rags of his hoodie with his free hand to demonstrate.

"That's OK, our clothes are just back there a ways. If you'll follow me, I can get dressed and you can sit in the cars." Sam turned and beckoned over her shoulder.

"Are we welcome here in Luxembourg?" Luke asked. "I'd figure the local pack wouldn't want our trouble knocking on their door."

"For now. Pieter called in some personal favors," Sam replied. When they arrived at the cluster of vehicles, Sam pulled her clothes on hastily. "It's too chilly for walking around in my birthday suit."

"Are the kids safe?" Maggie asked.

"Yeah. They're with Fatima, Carlos, and Brielle in Cologne, getting their paperwork so we can get them to Portland." Sam took a minute to look them both over from head to foot. "You two look like you went through the ringer."

"We did." Luke didn't elaborate.

"Once everyone is back, we'll get you into the city so you can rest. We're free for the next few days, then we have a meeting with the packleader." Sam led them to Luke's BMW. "If you don't mind me driving, you two can relax in the back seat."

Luke opened the door for Maggie. She climbed in and scooted to the middle. Since she'd moved to the middle, Luke sat next to her. Once they were buckled in, she snuggled into Luke, resting her head on his shoulder. Luke slid his hand under her hers, winding his fingers through hers. Resting his head against the window, he fell asleep to the slightly discordant strains of "Cry Wolf" by Soap&Skin as Sam pulled onto the road leading them away from the border. When next his eyes opened, the BMW was pulling into the parking garage of a luxury hotel. Sam led them to their suite, turning over the key to them.

Seeing the large jacuzzi tub, Luke turned the water on hot and went into the bedroom to undress. His bag had already been unpacked by his friends and his armor stand set up. Maggie sat on the end of the bed, staring into nothing.

"I turned on the water for a bath. I need a good soak to get the grime out of my pores before getting into bed. The tub is more than big enough for both of us." Luke unzipped the shreds of his hoodie, hissing and wincing as he took it off.

At the sound of his pain, Maggie shook herself to alertness and stood up. "Is it getting bad, Luke?"

Luke shrugged, cringing at the movement. Sitting and sleeping in the car had further stiffened his muscles. "Yeah. It's been getting steadily worse. The ibuprofen helped at first, but it's been less effective with every go. Mostly I just ignored it until it reminded me when I moved the wrong way." He pulled the leather thong from the front of his armor.

"Here, let me help you." Maggie took the shoulders of Luke's armor and helped him slide it over his shoulders.

She set it on the armor stand, then helped him peel off the sweaty padding and shirt. Once he was undressed, Maggie sent him into the bath, telling him she'd join him in a moment. Before he slipped into the bathtub, he hit play on Blur's "Tender," then sank up to his neck in the giant tub with a sigh of relief. Maggie dropped the pile of ruined and filthy clothing into an out-of-the-way corner. She stripped and added her clothes to the pile, then joined Luke, sliding into the hot soapy water. After he situated himself, Maggie snuggled in between his legs—her back to his chest—and pulled his arms around her like a comforting blanket.

When the water had cooled to tepid, they climbed out of the bath and dried off before slipping into the plush bed to find their sleep.

EPILOGUE

When Luke woke, Maggie was still asleep next to him. Checking his phone, he saw it was near noon. Careful not to wake her, he slid out of bed, shut the door to the bedroom behind him, and called in an order for room service. While he waited for his order to arrive, he sank into the armchair and opened his phone to find out what was going on. Mostly, it was simple messages from his friends telling him to check in once he was up. He held off on sending any kind of message, planning on waiting until Maggie was up. He didn't want to rouse her earlier than she wanted to be out of bed.

Thirty minutes later, a knock on the door alerted him to the arrival of his room service. He let the server in so he could arrange their breakfast on the table. When the server rolled out the cart and Luke closed the door, he turned to see a nude Maggie standing in the doorway.

"You ordered room service? That was sweet of you." Maggie strode forward.

Luke had trouble keeping his eyes up, enjoying the sway of her hips.

"Eyes up here, mister."

He felt butterflies flutter about inside him at her soft smile and teasing eyes. When she stepped into him, he wrapped his arms around her and pulled her in for a good morning kiss.

Maggie pulled back, patting Luke's cheek softly. "I'm going to grab a robe out of the bathroom, then we can have breakfast."

When she returned, they set about breaking their fast. Luke, still groggy when he ordered, had only ordered a normal breakfast's worth of food, forgetting they'd had nothing besides fries and a sandwich at lunch time about twenty-four hours earlier. When his plate was empty, he looked at it forlornly, wishing he'd ordered more.

"That'll hold for a bit, but I think I'm going to tap into my inner hobbit and have a second breakfast," Maggie said, picking up her coffee for a sip. She stared into her coffee cup for a while before she raised her eyes to Luke, sadness coloring her blue eyes. "Do we have to go out today? Can we just not? Can we exempt ourselves from the world? I want to spend the rest of the day in bed with you, just being. I don't want to face everything. I just want to make love to you and disappear from the world for half a day."

"That sounds wonderful." He picked up his phone and texted Sam and Pablo. *Is there anything that needs to happen today that can't wait until tomorrow?*

No, I don't think so. Not that we can't handle, Sam replied.

Go wild, we'll see you tomorrow, Pablo texted back.

"We're all clear," Luke said, turning his phone to do not disturb.

Maggie smiled at him, her eyes still terribly sad. He wished he could take the pain away, but he knew she felt guilty about shooting the werewolf. They'd survived for now, but they still had a long way to go to get home. Right now, she needed to disappear and hide from the world. He needed that as well. For a few hours, they'd disappear physically and pretend the only world that existed was the two of them and their bed. They could face the world tomorrow; today, they had each other.

**Luke Irontree will return in Blood Empire Avenged
Available Now!
Keep reading for a short preview.**

LUKE IRONTREE WILL RETURN IN

BLOOD EMPIRE AVENGED

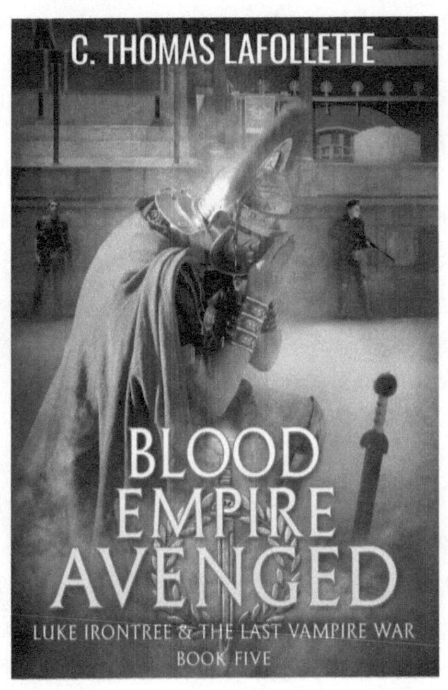

BLOOD EMPIRE AVENGED: BOOK FIVE

CHAPTER ONE

Luke stared out over Luxembourg City, the small city's lights eclipsing the stars above on the clear night. He stood in the eye of a hurricane after their tumultuous exit from Belgium and before their next leap into action to get back home to Portland. At the sound of the balcony door, Luke turned and smiled at the curvy blond woman opening it. She wore a shawl against the cool, fall air.

"Mind if I join you?" Maggie asked, a light Polish accent coloring her voice.

"Of course not." He swept his hand toward the chair next to him. "Can't see the stars, but the city's quite nice at night, especially from here."

Maggie scooted the chair closer to Luke's and sat, taking his hand in hers. "What's got you so troubled?"

Luke took a deep breath and let it out as a sigh. "I'm not sure what to do next, Maggie. My friend was killed by his son. His other son is buried in grief. He's lost his home, and I've been denied the land of my birth and the ability to travel to my sanctuary. The pack I'd been helping is now my enemy, and they have several of my properties under their control and the income that goes with them."

He rubbed a hand over his eyes. "We're in the territory of a pack with dubious loyalties, and we have to travel through another pack's territory to get to an airport when we have no assurances of their loyalty." He looked into Maggie's eyes, his brow furrowed as his anxiety opened a pit in his stomach. "I feel trapped, Maggie. Trapped with no safe escape for the people I'm responsible for."

Maggie leaned her head on his shoulder, bringing his hand up to her lips for a kiss against his knuckles. "I know, Luke. We're in a tough place. We'll figure this out together. We'll get the children to their new homes safely. We'll get back to Portland. Then we can figure out what to do as a pack and as a family."

Luke kissed the top of her head. "Thank you for listening to me complain."

"I wouldn't call it complaining. It's a stark recitation of facts." Lifting her head, she looked into his eyes and caressed his cheek. "Besides, you should be able to complain to someone you care about and who cares about you. You can complain to your…" She hesitated for a moment. "Your girlfriend."

A surge of warmth filled him, bringing a smile to his face. "Are you asking me to be your boyfriend?"

Maggie nodded, her eyes twinkling. "I love you, Luke."

"I love you too, Maggie. I want to have an official status with you." Luke leaned into Maggie and kissed her, running his hand through her silky hair. When he pulled back, mischief sparkled in Luke's eyes. "Although, I'm not sure a nineteen-hundred-year-old man qualifies as a boy."

Maggie laughed, patting Luke on the cheek. "I left my girlhood a long time ago in another century and another country, but I'll still be your girlfriend."

"And I'll be your very old boyfriend," Luke replied. "We feel very modern and contemporary."

They settled back into their chairs and enjoyed the sounds of the city below. When it grew too chilly, they retired to their bed to continue enjoying each other's company and an early night's sleep. Despite his best efforts, sleep didn't come easily, nor was it restful when he found it. Nightmares he couldn't remember plagued his dreams, leaving him fuzzy-headed and bleary-eyed in the morning.

At one point, he rolled over and found an empty spot where Maggie should have been. Jolting up in the bed, he tried to clear his head enough to figure out where she was. Once he heard her voice in the other room and the jingle of plates, he relaxed and slumped into his pillow. Maggie peeked into the bedroom after the hotel suite's door clicked shut, probably behind the person bringing room service.

Maggie moved around the bed to Luke's side and bent over to kiss his forehead. "Breakfast is here, as well as fresh coffee."

Rubbing his eyes, he sat back up and swung his legs out of bed. Maggie handed him a robe and left to set up their breakfast. When he sat next to her, he pulled the filled coffee cup over and raised it to his nose, inhaling deeply of the steamy dark aromas. He was nearly finished with his breakfast and halfway through a second cup when someone knocked at the door.

Laying her hand on his forearm, Maggie smiled and stood up. "I'll see who it is." After peeking through the peephole, she turned back to him. "It's Pablo and Sam."

"Well, if they're both here, I doubt it's entirely a social call," Luke said.

Maggie nodded and opened the door, stepping out of the way for them.

"Morning, Luke! We come bearing gifts," Pablo said.

"Good morning, Maggie. I trust you had a pleasant evening." Sam winked at Maggie. "We have another pot of coffee."

Luke raised his coffee cup to salute his friends. "Morning, you two. I just killed this pot, so your timing is excellent. I'm afraid we don't have much left in the way of food."

"No worries, buddy. We already ate. Heidi's been showing us around a bit." Seeing the puzzled look on Luke's face, Pablo elaborated. "She knows the city since she comes here regularly on pack business."

"Ah. That explains it. What brings you two here this morning?" Luke asked.

Sam grabbed an unused cup, filled it with coffee, and added some cream to it. "Heidi says the local alpha wants to meet with us."

"I guess we should, though I'd rather get everyone moving toward Portland. Every day's delay is another opportunity for something else to go wrong, and we're quickly running out of resources and allies. Speaking of allies, how is Pieter doing?" Luke blew over his coffee before taking a sip.

"No one has seen him. As far as I can tell, he hasn't left his room since we arrived two days ago," Pablo replied.

"Are you sure he's still in his room?" Luke asked, his eyebrows furrowing.

Pablo frowned. "He's told me to go away a few times, so he was there when I checked, but beyond that, he's said nothing."

"I think he was only holding it together until we got everyone to safety," Sam said. "The need to get our non-combatants and children evacuated superseded his need to grieve. Now that we're all reasonably safe, his pain has taken over."

Luke nodded. "Yeah. He's effectively lost both his father and his brother in the most brutal way possible. I suppose I should go check in on him. When does... I guess I don't know the packleader's name."

"Mathis Heinen," Sam supplied. "As far as time, he's invited us to dinner and cocktails. Heidi says we should dress up. I think she was a little concerned our American informality might inform our choice of dress."

"Hmm, I should make sure my shirt and sport coat are not too wrinkly. I don't have anything besides my best jeans to go with them, though." Luke pursed his lips and as his eyes narrowed.

"Good thing you didn't put your luggage in the truck," Sam said.

Luke snorted. "Yeah. Carrying all that across the forests and hills of the Ardennes would not have been fun."

Pablo laughed. "Don't worry about what you wear, dude. You can get away with whatever. You are who you are. You could probably show up in your birthday suit, and it would be fine. Apparently, you're a bit of a celebrity among the European packs."

"I have nothing appropriate to wear," Maggie said, looking worried.

Sam leaned toward Maggie, patting the back of her hand. "Heidi offered to take us shopping. We'll find you something, then get you all dolled up."

"I just want to look nice if I'm going to represent the pack and be Luke's date." Maggie reached over and squeezed Luke's hand.

He squeezed back, smiling fondly. "You always look lovely, Maggie."

"He's such a nice man," Sam said, smiling at Luke. "He's come a long way since he washed up in Portland at the pack's doorstep."

"Ha ha." Luke shook his head. "I'd better get dressed so I can go see Pieter."

Maggie followed him in to grab some things before heading to take a shower. Before she left the bedroom, she pulled Luke into a hug and gave him a kiss on the cheek. "Good luck with Pieter."

"Good luck with finding something to wear," Luke replied.

Maggie disappeared and left him to finish dressing. When he was done, he gave Sam a quick hug, then waved Pablo after him.

"Let's go see Pieter. He could use some friends," Luke said.

"Later, Sam," Pablo said, before raising his voice to speak toward the bathroom door. "See you, Maggie!"

Pablo and Luke headed to the elevator and waited for it to reach their floor.

"So, you and Maggie are going as an official couple?" Pablo asked.

"Hmm?"

"She said she would be your date," Pablo said.

"We are dating. Why wouldn't I want to go with my girlfriend?" Luke replied, slyly slipping in his status change.

"Wait… I've never heard either of you say boyfriend or girlfriend. Are you two official now?" Pablo waggled his eyebrows at Luke, stepping into the elevator.

"Yeah. We made it official last night."

Pablo grinned. "Congratulations, buddy! You finally asked her."

Luke's cheeks flushed as he looked down at the elevator floor.

Pablo reached out and pushed the button for Pieter's floor. "She asked you, didn't she?"

"Yeah."

Chuckling, he patted Luke's shoulders. "Good for her. You two make a good couple. I'm glad I told her to make her pass at you hard and to just be obvious."

"Me too," Luke said. "I love her, Pablo."

"Wow. The big 'L' word? Have you told her that?"

Luke chuckled. "Yeah. I did."

"After she said it first?" Pablo teased.

"No. I said it first. I couldn't not tell her anymore. It's been so intense. I needed to let her know my feelings in case something happens." Luke shuffled nervously.

Pablo pulled him in for a one-armed hug as the elevator dinged and opened. "I'm proud of you, buddy. Sam was right. You really have come a long way."

"Yeah. It's been one hell of a year, that's for sure." Luke knocked on Pieter's door. "Pieter, it's Luke. Let us in."

"Go away," Pieter called back.

"Come on, dude. We're your friends, and we care about you. Let us in, please?" Pablo added.

Pieter sighed heavily. "Fine."

A few moments later, Pieter let them in. He looked terrible—dark stubble on his face, eyes red, and disheveled hair. He wore a pair of boxers and had pulled a robe over his shoulders, though he hadn't closed it. He flopped onto the edge of the bed, letting his head sink into his hands.

Luke sat next to Pieter and put his arm around Pieter's shoulders. "We all care about you. We'll be here for you. You don't have to go through this alone."

Something in Luke's words broke a dam inside Pieter. He leaned into Luke's shoulder, tears falling from his eyes—first slowly but heavier as he let go of the emotions he'd been trying to hold at bay and failing. As Pieter cried like a broken-hearted child, Pablo sat on his other side and held his hand. They let Pieter cry as he wept for his murdered father and the brother who'd pulled the trigger. When he finally calmed, Pablo fetched him some tissue and water.

Taking a deep breath, Pieter sighed. "I miss my papa."

Luke squeezed Pieter's shoulder. "He was a good man. Have I ever told you about the first time I met him?"

"No," Pieter replied.

"You probably don't remember. You were a squalling little toddler at the time..." Luke regaled Pieter with the story of how Luke commissioned a painting from Pieter's father, Pieter Bruegel the Elder, back when the artists were all in their original life spans.

Pablo, using his ability to meld with people, coaxed stories about Pieter's father from him until they were laughing at some of the stories he told. Luke and Pablo worked to bring Pieter back into the world of the living. They couldn't make his grief disappear—it was too fresh and raw—but they helped him back into the light a little bit. After a while, they ordered room service, then went back to their respective rooms to get ready for tonight's dinner.

LUKE JOINED PIETER, Pablo, and Jamaal in the hotel bar for drinks while they waited for Maggie, Sam, Delilah, and Simone to come down for their ride to dinner with the Luxembourg packleader. Delilah and Simone were the first down the stairs. Delilah wore a simple black suit with a white shirt.

Simone, who'd shown up with virtually nothing when she joined their band of misfits, had gone with Sam and Maggie to get a dress for herself. The young woman with onyx black skin looked stunning in an egg yolk yellow dress accented with a rich blue that dropped to just below mid-thigh. Luke stood and hugged both of them.

A few minutes later, Sam stepped out of the elevator. Luke caught a flash of blond hair behind her. When Sam stepped aside, Luke gasped. She wore a silvery sapphire blue dress with a sweetheart neckline, midnight blue velvet accenting the waist and hem. Five-petaled flowers in the same midnight blue velvet covered the sheer outer layer, with the same material forming three-quarter length sleeves and a wide bateau neckline, teasing her collar bones. Strappy heels and a silver shawl accompanied the dress.

Maggie stopped in front of him, her hands clasped in front of her. "What do you think?"

"You look stunning," Luke said, taking her hands and leaning in to kiss her cheek.

"You're looking very handsome yourself," Maggie replied.

Luke smiled, giving her his flirty eyes. "When we get back to Portland, I think I owe you some fancy date nights."

"You don't owe me expensive dates," Maggie replied, smiling softly.

"I know, but I still want to take you on some. We can afford to treat ourselves. Besides, you'll need an excuse to wear that dress again. You're absolutely lovely."

Maggie blushed, her pale cheeks taking a pink hue

Luke wore dark wash designer jeans with a black shirt and a sport jacket. Jamaal and Pablo were similarly dressed, going for Portland sharp. Pieter wore a suit, as did Heidi. Everyone gathered near Luke and Maggie, talking among themselves and complimenting each other on how nice they looked.

"This is a good-looking crew," Pablo said.

"Yeah. We scrub up pretty good." Sam slipped her arm through Pablo's. Nodding toward the exit and a couple men walking in dressed as drivers, Sam cleared her throat to get everyone's attention. "I think our rides are here."

Luke's chest tightened slightly. Without his weapons and armor, he felt naked. They were putting a lot of faith in a man they'd never met, but they had little choice. It's not like they could arrive packing their usual heavy arsenal.

Heidi strode toward the drivers to check, then waved Luke and his friends after her and the drivers. Together, they headed toward the exit.

"Do you need to take care of the drinks?" Maggie asked.

"No. We put them on the rooms, so we're good." Luke held out his arm for Maggie to take, then led her after their friends.

The drivers held the doors open on the high-end SUVs, taking three to a vehicle. After Maggie slid in, Luke walked around to the other side, while Pieter took the front passenger seat. Once the three SUVs were loaded, they took off into Luxembourg's capital. He tried to relax but couldn't get his body to untense, not as they drove into the unknown, a small group without their weapons. A few minutes later, the drivers pulled up in front of an elegant-looking bistro, parked in front, and let everyone out.

Blood Empire Avenged is Available Now!

NEWSLETTER

The Centurion Immortal is a Luke Irontree prequel novella and is exclusive to the Dispatches from C. Thomas Lafollette newsletter. Please sign up for your free copy and you'll also receive a twice-monthly newsletter with news, book updates, recipes, drinks tips, and other fun stuff. Your email will never be given out, rented, or sold.

CThomasLafollette.com/newsletter/

ACKNOWLEDGMENTS

I'd like to thank all the people who made this book possible.

Suzanne, your editorial eye has made this book and series infinitely better. Your belief in my vision for these characters has made this a kick ass team effort.

Ravven, your covers are amazing and really capture the essence of Luke and his world.

Amy, you're my alpha reader and my proofreader. These books wouldn't be possible without you.

C.D. Tavenor, you stepped up when I needed to change my copy editor and did a fantastic job.

Doochie, you've been my earliest reader and a great hype man as well as a wonderful friend.

To my critique group, thank you for all your hard work. Your eyes and efforts have made my writing better.

ABOUT THE AUTHOR

C. Thomas Lafollette is a writer of Urban Fantasy and Historical Fantasy and is the author of the forthcoming Luke Irontree novels. He earned a degree in Ancient History with a specialization in Classics at The College of Idaho. He's read poetry on stage with Yevgeny Yevtushenko and dined with the Belgian Prime Minister. C. Thomas has lived in Portland, Oregon for over Twenty years. He lives with his wife, fellow author Amy Cissell, his stepdaughter, and his three jerkface cats. He and Amy also run their own freelance editing business - Cissell Ink

twitter.com/CTLafollette

facebook.com/CThomasLafollette

tiktok.com/@cthomaslafollette

instagram.com/CThomasLafollette

bookbub.com/authors/c-thomas-lafollette

amazon.com/C-Thomas-Lafollette/e/B09JMTR7W7

goodreads.com/cthomaslafollette

ALSO BY C. THOMAS LAFOLLETTE

Luke Irontree & The Last Vampire War

Book 0 - The Centurion Immortal

Book 1 - Dark Fangs Rising - March 22, 2022

Book 2 - Dark Fangs Raging - April 19, 2022

Book 3 - Dark Fangs Descending - May 17, 2022

Book 4 - Blood Empire Reborn - August 23, 2022

Book 5 - Blood Empire Avenged - September 20, 2022

Book 6 - Blood Empire Infiltrated - October 18, 2022

Book 7 - Blood Empire Burning - November 15, 2022

Book 8 - Ancient Sword Falling - March 21, 2023

Book 9 - Ancient Sword Unyielding - August 22, 2023

Book 10 - Ancient Sword Shattering*

The Luke Irontree Historical Adventures

Rise of the Centurio Immortalis - April 5, 2022

Fall of the Centurio Immortalis - May 31, 2022

The Moonlight Centurion*

The Highway Centurion*

Red City Reaper - A Dark Urban Fantasy Adventure

Book 1 - A Shot For Death* - Winter 2024

Book 2 - Death Orders a Double* - Winter 2024

Book 3 - Death on the Rocks* - Sprint 2024

*Forthcoming

Titles and release dates may be subject to change.

www.ingramcontent.com/pod-product-compliance
Lightning Source LLC
Chambersburg PA
CBHW031313210726
48287CB00005B/1536